S. Me. H. S.
March 5, 2016

Jeremiah's Hunger

Canadä

Borealis Press gratefully acknowledges the support of the Government of Canada through the Canada Book Fund (CBF).

Library and Archives Canada Cataloguing in Publication

Osta, Elizabeth A., 1945-
    Jeremiah's hunger / Elizabeth A. Osta.

ISBN 978-0-88887-433-7

    I. Title.

PS3615.S82J47 2011   813'.6   C2011-906385-9

Also available as an ebook (ISBN 978-0-88887-447-4)

Cover design: David Tierney

Printed and bound in Canada on recycled acid free paper.

Jeremiah's Hunger

Elizabeth A. Osta

Borealis Press
Ottawa, Canada
2011

To my husband, Dave Van Arsdale,

whose wisdom, love and

Celtic spirit encourage me,

throughout all.

Author's Notes

The major events portrayed in this book are based on actual facts. The details around them are fictionalized.

Jeremiah Buckley was my great-grandfather, his daughter Maggie my grandmother. Births, deaths and emigrations are all based on historical documents, as are the political events that are portrayed.

The central characters are composites based on stories handed down over the last century.

Acknowledgments

This book was written because of Finvola Drury who encouraged me to begin the journey, Sonja Livingston who has helped me complete it, and the five women of my writing group who over the past twenty years have listened, encouraged and inspired: Jennifer Lloyd, Pamela Pepper, Jane Shosten, Maxine Simon and Kathleen Van Schaik. Special thanks to Timothy Wright of Rochester, New York, and John O'Connell of Donoughmore, Ireland, for their interest, counsel and encouragement. And a special acknowledgment to Janet Shorten for her sharp editing skills.

Michael Riordan Family

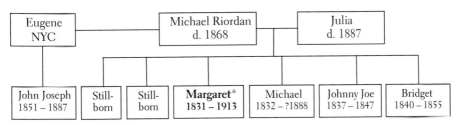

Eugene NYC		Michael Riordan d. 1868		Julia d. 1887	

| John Joseph 1851 – 1887 | Still-born | Still-born | **Margaret*** 1831 – 1913 | Michael 1832 – ?1888 | Johnny Joe 1837 – 1847 | Bridget 1840 – 1855 |

Timothy Buckley Family

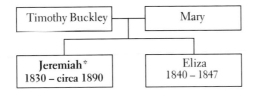

Timothy Buckley	Mary
Jeremiah* 1830 – circa 1890	Eliza 1840 – 1847

Jeremiah Buckley Family

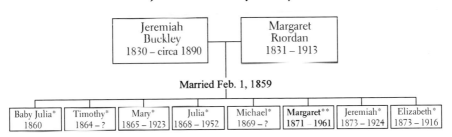

Jeremiah Buckley 1830 – circa 1890	Margaret Riordan 1831 – 1913

Married Feb. 1, 1859

Baby Julia* 1860	Timothy* 1864 – ?	Mary* 1865 – 1923	Julia* 1868 – 1952	Michael* 1869 – ?	**Margaret**** 1871 – 1961	Jeremiah* 1873 – 1924	Elizabeth* 1873 – 1916

* Actual person and dates   **author's grandmother

Map of Cork and Surrounding Area

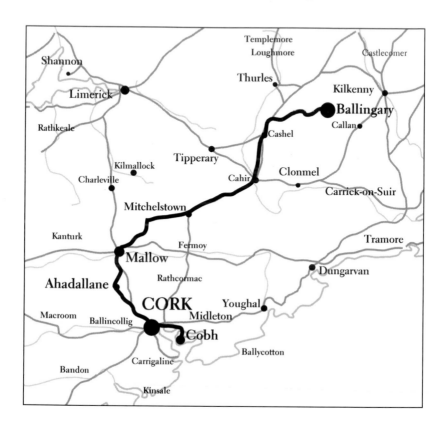

Chapter One

An Gorta Mor

May 1847

Had there been more food, they still would have perished. That's what the da had said, not to anyone in particular, but he had said it aloud. The priest had come at the end but to no avail. It had been Mary's way to help those she could. They couldn't know she'd get the fever, her face red as fire. That her young one would be caught in the same web of torment, fever bringing cries of pain that rang out into the night, reminding them all of the death grip that held the two like a vice, squeezing their life from them. And for all his strength and love, the da couldn't fix it. Oh, how he had tried. He boiled water, fixed broths, washed clothes and kept up with his work in the fields, coming in four and sometimes five times a day, to look in on them, to pray, to hope.

Jeremiah knew that nothing could be done. He bit his lip to keep from crying at the sight of his da, big as he was, his red hair falling over his forehead, bent over his child, tears running down his cheeks. He kissed her and lifted her from her mother's arms, her cries finally stopped, her body gone limp. The soft weeping that came from his ma filled the silence with a respectful air—it wasn't a moan, for she was too sick to give rise to much sound. Rather it was a quiet, rhythmic sighing, that had the cadence of prayer, the tones rising and falling in a regular pattern. Jeremiah found it oddly consoling, if only for the fact that he knew his mother to be alive.

September 1837

Jeremiah sat swinging his feet, hazel eyes darting around the smoke-filled pub, stomach churning. His mother sat across from him, chestnut brown hair pinned back neatly, hands folded atop the polished surface of the dark brown table. Even at age seven, he knew Mary Buckley to be a proper woman.

His da, Timothy Buckley, stood in the center of the room with his back to the mahogany bar, thick red hair combed back, liquid blue eyes scanning the room. His black suspenders sat squarely on his gray flannel shirt. The early evening's light spilled into the room and shone through the glass of dark foamy liquid that he held on high:

"I raise me glass in memory of twelve-year-old Catherine Foley. Is there a man here to join me?"

In the far corner, the fiddler stopped playing. Silence filled the room. Jeremiah ran his fingers back and forth along the table, and kept his eyes down, listening for and praying for someone to stand.

Finally one man did.

"I'll join ye, Timothy," Sean Murphy said, "and any man who knows the evil that needs to be driven from this land will join ye as well."

Jeremiah recognized the man from church, his short, solid frame and straight black hair familiar. He heard the sound of chairs scraping the wooden floor; three more men in farmer's clothing stood.

One table of men eyed Timothy and Sean and turned back to their card game.

"I don't know if ye heard the man," Sean said loudly. "He's raising his glass to Catherine Foley, the child from Rathkeeran killed as she led the peasants in face of the police six years ago."

A dark-eyed, burly man said, "Ah,'tis that Catherine Foley. Why didn't ye say so?" as he stood and motioned to the other three men to stand. "Why sure 'tis been a long while ago but we'll not forget now, will we men?"

A few others in another corner got to their feet. Jeremiah's breathing was tight as he watched his da raise his glass higher: "To the memory of a courageous girl shot in the face by a policeman yet to be punished for his deed. To Catherine Foley."

"*Sláinte*," Sean said, the others joining in. The men drank slowly.

His voice steady and jaw set, Timothy continued: "And to the twelve killed in the Rathcormack Massacre protecting the poor widow and her few belongings before they were taken as pay for the pittance of a forty shilling tithe." He slowly glanced around the room, his stout moving in the glass as he looked at each man and said evenly: "None will be forgotten in this town."

"*Sláinte*," the men said again in unison, the Irish word for "health."

The fiddler struck a chord and together the men remained standing and sang "Eileen Aroon," an old air about a gentle maid.

"*Do shiúlfainn féin i gcónái leat, Eibhlín a Rún. . .*"

Jeremiah and his mother remained seated. He listened to her sing along and wished once again that there wasn't a ban on the Irish language at his school. When he complained, his mother counseled, "Ye need to be with the times. 'Tis a sign of education to be speaking the English now. The language of the old ways is for old times. Ye need to be of the new times." She saw to it that English was the language spoken in their home as often as possible.

As the song ended, the card players returned to their table while the others moved to the far corner. Timothy came to sit with Jeremiah and Mary. His face was flush, his eyes satisfied, like when he was telling the stories of the Tithe Wars which were fought when Jeremiah was an infant, farmers resisting payment of tithes to the Anglican Church whose numbers were sparse compared to Catholic parishes.

Jeremiah remembered the story of the five thousand who marched in protest, like soldiers in formation, behind the red, green, blue, orange and yellow banners of their baronies. "Our people were no longer willing to pay for the upkeep of the Protestant churches," the da had told him.

Jeremiah's stomach felt better now that his father was seated with them. He watched his da's soft, round face and blue eyes that shone as he looked about the room. Jeremiah was spellbound by his father, whether they were mending a fence post or looking after their few cattle. He hungered for the feel of his da's strong arms around him when he'd hoist him upon his shoulders to go off to the fields. Or when he'd toss him in the air and ask: "Are ye my favorite boy?" to which Jeremiah would answer, "Amn't I yer only boy?" His da would chuckle, a deep resonant sound that Jeremiah relished. He rubbed his fingers over his da's red-blonde whiskers, the same ones that scratched when they played tug of war or when Da nuzzled his ears pretending to be a charging bull.

The da's stories of his own youthful days fed Jeremiah, who listened hungrily, enthralled by Ireland's history and heartaches.

"These tales I'm telling ye, boy-o, ye'll not learn in that National School of yers," his da said. "Mind ye, study yer lessons there, but don't forget there are two sides to every story and sometimes three."

At his mother's insistence, Jeremiah attended Rathcoola East, the recently opened school up the road. "Ye'll learn to read and write and do yer sums. It's an educated man ye'll grow up to be," she had said in her soft, determined way.

In the evenings, clay pipe in hand, Jeremiah's da told tales of Ireland's past. "From the evil days of Cromwell almost two hundred years ago, we've come a long way thanks to great men like Patrick Sarsfield, Wolfe Tone and Father Murphy himself. Now we have the brilliance of Daniel O'Connell to lead us. The sun is finally shining in Ireland."

Jeremiah's head swam with the stories: the bloody rising of 1798, the hated 1800 Act of Union, the 1830s Tithes War, but his favorite was the 1829 emancipation for Catholics under Daniel O'Connell's leadership.

As bedtime drew near, Jeremiah often begged for the story, both to delay sleep and because he loved to hear the da tell it and see his eyes smiling.

"We were at Barry's pub the night the word came round. All of us held hands in a circle and did a mighty jig and Sean Murphy sang us our favorite, "Boolavogue," about Father Murphy from ol'

Kilcormack. The emancipation was won for us the very same week we learned that ye were to be born to us. We rejoiced for we could finally be fully released from the ancient tyranny of the Penal Laws."

Often after his da finished a story, Jeremiah's mother would croon a tune, sometimes the Connemara lullaby, a tune so slow and soft that Jeremiah would fall asleep. "Hear the wind blow, love, hear the wind blow. Lean your head over and hear the wind blow." He'd wake as his da carried him to his cot by the inside wall and covered him with the gray wool blanket that itched his chin.

* * *

Eliza was born when Jeremiah was ten years old after his mother had taken a cure at the holy well for her barrenness. His delight mirrored his parents' in this fair-haired child's birth, and Jeremiah gathered her up in his arms as often as his mother would allow to take her with him across the fields and streams, eager for the day when she would ride with him out on the ridge.

Their home in the hills of Ahadallane was closer to Mallow than to Cork; the main road bypassed this tiny hamlet. No one passed by on the way to somewhere else. There was nowhere else.

Jeremiah lived the whole of his days amidst green rolling hills, lush with thickets of gorse and deep purples, the dense underbrush forming a vast network of growth that covered stones and stream banks. Up on the ridge, he could see the rugged Boggeragh Mountains that reached down to the dark waters of the Blackwater River and to the River Lee.

On school days, Jeremiah would walk up the boreen, the same path the cows traveled, dodging their leavings as he watched the hedgerow for foxes and rabbits. He'd hear the caw of the crows as they swooped across the fields and listen for his favorite, the black and white magpie, and wait for its dramatic dive as it captured a field mouse. The great chestnut and oak trees shimmered in the soft winds that shook the barley below and set the soft green of the spring oats into a slow dance.

When he wasn't in school, Jeremiah's days were filled with the land, whether helping his da clear a field of stone or bringing the cows home after the evening meal. He'd imagine himself landlord, looking at the freshly plowed rows of newly planted potato with a swell of pride in his chest. Jeremiah and his family were good tenants of the land, each doing their part. His mother fed the chickens, churned butter, spun yarn and fixed all their meals; his da repaired their thatched roof, shod the horses, milked the cows, sowed the seed and reaped the harvest.

Jeremiah's chores included feeding their dinner scraps to the pigs, his favorite the black and white runt of the most recent litter whom he named "Magpie" after the black and white bird he admired.

Once he turned twelve years old, Jeremiah would accompany his da to the Friday Mallow market day. Knowing it to be important to be in place at first light, he'd hitch up Toby, the brown speckled pony he groomed daily, eager for the adventure to begin.

The market square was in a great flurry as carts pulled up around the edges to display their wares for sale. The auctioneer, a stout red-faced man with a waistcoat and watch fob, stood on a great platform at the far end and shouted out facts about the animals to hasten their sale.

"What am I bid for this fine Irish greyhound pig? This 'gentleman in the corner' will bring ye security and prosperity for many years to come. Do I hear two punts? Is it three?"

Jeremiah relished the conversation and commerce that took place as customers bargained for their oats, barley, potato and butter, proud their own hands brought this bounty for sale. Folks in their finery bantered back and forth, socializing as they enjoyed the customary drink once payment was received.

"'Tis grand to see ye and yer son, Mr. Buckley. And 'tis some fine oats ye've brought for sale this day," one petite young woman offered as she began the negotiation. "I can always be certain yers is the best price."

Another older woman with a sour face surprised Jeremiah as

she said, "Sure an' yers is the finest butter in all the county. Tell yer ma she has a magic touch."

At they wearily set off for home, the da would often hand the reins over to Jeremiah, silently acknowledging the day when Jeremiah would be a man.

***

May 1847

He was seventeen and wasn't sure he could do it. He stepped up to his da and reached out for his baby sister. In his grief, his da looked up, nodded and gave over the tiny melted body. Son and father looked at one another for a moment, and as Jeremiah stepped away with the child, they both knew he'd become a man.

Jeremiah carried his little sister, her blonde hair matted and stringy, her blue eyes still open, out beyond the fence in the yard, out past the first field. She was light in his arms and he hugged her to him, his own heart opening up as he moved.

Out in the fields where no one could see, the tears began to flow. This little girl, whose birth had been such a surprise after so many years of his parents' trying. This little girl whose arms he could still feel around his neck when he'd carried her on his back for their berry hunts. He cried into the heart of his little sister and then, with a sob, laid her in the soft down of the wheat field and closed her eyes.

As he began to dig the dirt and pile it opposite little Eliza, Jeremiah felt someone watching. He looked up to see the black-robed presence of Father Lane.

"Sure we can make her a fine pine box, there, Jeremiah. Ye needn't do this, son."

Jeremiah looked up and lifted another spade full of soil. A pine box indeed. "There'll be no need, Father. No need at all."

He dug deeper and faster, groaning under the weight of the next shovelful. Jeremiah had been just fifteen at the start of *An Gorta Mor*, the Great Hunger. During the worst of it, he helped bury neighbors in numbers too great to imagine. The hinged

coffins they used with the bottoms that released at the burial service freed the corpse to slide into the opened earth. Then the coffin
would be taken to the next burial, coffin makers unable to keep
up with the demand in these harsh times.

And now, out on the hillside, the priest, his black cassock
spread out in the wheat, knelt opposite the mounded dirt, laid a
hand on the tiny child, blessed himself and prayed the prayers of
the dead he'd said too many times to count in these last years.

Requiem aeternam dona eis, Domine. Et lux perpetua luceat eis.

Jeremiah raised his eyes toward heaven and felt a sob come
from his stomach. Father Lane finished the prayers and stepped
back to survey the scene. The fields beyond were plowed under,
the rotted potatoes gone now, rows upon rows cleared of the poison
that permeated the air with its pungent odor. In their place were
rows of dark soil mounded on each side, their uniformity and sym-
metry a contrast to the calamity and chaos they represented. This
small victim of the blight was but one of hundreds of thousands
wasting away for want of nourishment, for want of survival.

Father Lane had seen many of the dead go unburied for over
a fortnight, others buried in ditches by their homes. Eliza's burial
rite had its own dignity. He bit his lip as he watched this boy, now
a man, bend to lay his sister's body into the opened earth.

It was in this parish of Donoughmore, with a population of
eight thousand, that Father Lane would write in the church
records:

"This was the famine year. There died of famine and fever
from November 1846 to February 1847 over fourteen hundred of the people and one priest Reverend Dan Horgan,
Requiescat in Pace . . . Many without coffins, though there
were four men employed to bury the dead, and make
graves and two and sometimes four carpenters to make
coffins. On this day also we were visited by the cholera.
Five only died of it in this parish."

Chapter Two

The Days After

Fall 1847

The stench was still in the air. His da didn't speak of it but it was there. He stood looking over the hillside, the luscious green rolling terrain interrupted by two tiny white crosses on the near ridge.

At seventeen, Jeremiah had already learned the lesson of loss as his red-haired ma and his baby sister slipped from his grasp, slipped through his da's embrace, and any attempts to save them. The anger hadn't ripened yet, but it would someday. For now, the sadness overshadowed his days, each moment like a pendulum tolling its painful passage of time. He could feel it no matter what he was doing, no matter where he was.

He looked beyond the crosses at his da walking up to the back acreage to continue his work, tilling the very soil that held the rotted potatoes and his wife and daughter.

Jeremiah hoped that one day this soil, which had been the center of their lives, would be his. It was this earth, and its owner Joseph Bennett, they'd had to thank for their survival. It was Mr. Bennett's decency and his faith in them that allowed them to stay.

They'd heard about other landlords whose callousness and greed were beyond reason. Those who stripped the land of tenants, tumbling their small cabins, preparing the land for cattle and for profit at the cost of human life. They'd cleansed it of the Irish, whose very name often brought revulsion to their faces.

The hatred between men was everywhere. The dying was everywhere. No one was untouched by it. Hatred grew in bellies of the townland men whose spirits wouldn't be crushed. Hatred that was planted over the centuries, sown carefully and rooted deeply.

Each time another editorial was read at the pub, men gathered round, listening with hearts that hardened daily as the famine grew worse, roaring their resistance and roaring their pledge to Ireland.

> . . . there are vast accumulations of misery in certain parts, owing partly to the immigration of outcasts and partly to the secluded nature of the region, and the consequent extraordinary ignorance and inaction of the people . . . The people there have always been listless, improvident, and wretched, under whatever rulers . . . In Canada we have Indians in our borders, many of whom we yearly subsidize and maintain. In Ireland, we have Celts equally helpless and equally the objects of national compassion. Such cases are only to be met by some form of public alms.
>
> *The Times*: London

"Public alms is it?" the da roared. "Public alms. Is that what the filthy, disease-ridden workhouses are intended to be, public alms?"

The da stepped toward the bar and took a deep breath. He spoke in a low growl, as if to the London journalist himself.

"The very workhouses that create more death with their filth and overcrowding, their soup if ye denounced yer religion? *Listless, improvident and wretched under whatever rulers?*"

His breathing became short as he continued, his face a deepening red.

"Dear God, man, do ye not know of the great ones, the giants who strained against the tide, who struggled to secure God-given freedoms entitled to human beings: Hugh O'Neill, the Great Earl of Tyrone, Red Hugh O'Donnell and Wolfe Tone? Have ye no memory of Jonathan Swift and the great writers whose words have decried the very presence of the likes of those who offer national compassion? Is it national compassion that keeps the Irish landless? Is it national compassion that imposed the Penal Laws? Have ye not paid mind to Daniel O'Connell who aroused hundreds of thousands with an eye for freedom, an eye for justice?"

He placed his glass on the bar, signaling, with a turn of his wrist, his request for a refill.

Young Jeremiah watched and listened as the men joined in with his da, roaring back in protest. Age-old hatreds were alive and well; the written words of *The Times* carried venom that tried to drain the life from the people of Ireland.

The da's own anger vented, he turned to Jeremiah and spoke gently. He warned him not to believe for a minute the words written in *The Times* or to get caught up in the self-poisoning hatred and anger that would only do more harm. He counseled him to be proud of who he was—a Buckley from Donoughmore.

"Be steady in yer work and show yer respect and ye'll prosper. Don't be yielding to the wild words of others. 'To thine own self be true,' lad. Mark me words."

Jeremiah listened, aware of the losses his father had suffered, aware that despite his da's mighty temper, calmness prevailed in this counsel.

* * *

In the end it was steadiness, respect and diligence that helped Jeremiah survive. The emigrations to Canada and America forced by landlords who had their tenants sign away any right to land or payments in exchange for ship passage hadn't reached into the hills of Donoughmore. Few of his parish were among the half-million evicted from their cottages. None were jailed for their inability to pay, their wives and children forced out onto the streets. None had been lured to the overcrowded British sailing ships—coffin ships as they came to be called—headed for Grosse Isle in Quebec, Canada, to join the line of waiting ships that extended two miles down the St. Lawrence, ships that dumped hundreds of the dead into the river's waters.

Rather, many of the people of Donoughmore benefited from a compassionate and decent landlord, Joseph Bennett, who like a handful of others of kind spirit, became a part of the history of survival for those like Jeremiah and the Buckleys. Their forty-six acres of leased land gave them status as one of the strong-farms, and they were able to offer help to others without interference.

But because they heard stories of landlords evicting already starving families, who with grass-stained teeth gave testimony to their desperate scraping for nourishment, children who grew facial hair, their hormonal imbalance so great, workhouse horrors, soup kitchens and poorhouses where disease and filth made survival even more difficult, Jeremiah and his da knew daily what they had escaped. Word had come to them from Mr. Bennett after Jeremiah's mother and sister had died, expressing his sorrow.

"I've been blessed with fortune beyond my own understanding," the agent read from the letter. "I find no reason now not to share some of that fortune."

His letter acknowledged the good people of the townland who labored for him. His sympathy seemed genuine and Jeremiah, his da nor any of the families who worked his land could find fault with it.

The sorrow that ran so deep and the anger so near the surface were kept at bay by such acts of decency. These tales of kindness told and retold kept a spark of faith alive at a time when all else seemed lost.

Chapter Three

Carrick-on-Suir

July 1848

"Up here," Jeremiah called to Michael Riordan from atop his horse, high on the hillside of Carrick-on-Suir It had been a long but exhilarating ride east from Ahadallane.

The vast skyline on this July day was cloudless and endlessly blue. Jeremiah marveled at the lush hillsides of green that surrounded the River Suir as it coursed through the heart of the town with the Slievenamon Mountains to the north and the Comeragh foothills to the south.

"We've made good time, now, haven't we?" he said as Michael rode up to join him. "And ye were right to urge me to come. It's a grand spot, Michael, grand indeed."

Michael was the oldest son of the Riordans, their land adjacent to the Buckleys. The two had been friends since childhood, raised amidst the beauty and burden of the Irish hillsides where the land meant life or death. In these days of the famine, the losses were so great and hope so sparse, that Jeremiah found Michael's fervor something to hold on to.

Michael had promised this trip to Carrick would be life-changing. Jeremiah had suppressed his skepticism and agreed to come, for he trusted Michael, whose own brother Johnny Joe had died the same year as Jeremiah's ma and sister Eliza. It was Michael and his family who had seen Jeremiah and his father through the worst of the hunger, helping in quiet ways. The extra oats and barley, the shared meals, the evening sing-songs, had all brought solace and healing.

Now as Jeremiah looked about the vast skyline, he saw the stately Ormond Castle, ornate architecture evident even from this distance. Two fortified towers offered a view of the river, complemented by several ivy-covered Tudor gables.

"This magnificent structure," Michael offered as he gestured toward the castle, "was originally built by the Butler family in 1328. Grand, isn't it?" Jeremiah nodded, shifted his weight on the horse below him and continued to gaze at the splendor.

"The story is told," Michael continued, "that Thomas Butler, the 10th Earl of Ormond, converted the castle into a mansion in 1560 to accommodate his cousin, Queen Elizabeth I." He paused for effect. "Rumor has it, she never visited."

Jeremiah breathed in the scene, satisfied to be here. A little more than a year had passed since the fever had ravaged his family. Ahadallane looked like a wasteland with so many cabins vacant, so much of the land untilled and unplanted. Food was still sparse. The bleak spirit of the people matched the landscape. It felt good to look into the lush valley, to be away from the heartache, to look beyond the borders of his own misery.

Jeremiah watched Michael, whose hazel eyes, the same color as Jeremiah's, surveyed the valley. Michael sat tall in his saddle, his sandy brown hair tousled from the ride, his worn gray jacket open at the collar, plaid flannel shirt poking out. They both scanned the crowd gathering at the bridge below that crossed the River Suir.

"Jer, let's ride down now to the speeches. It'll be worth the ride, I promise ye."

Side by side, they slowly wound their way toward the lowest part of the valley. The River Suir along which they rode was a rich source of excellent trout and salmon, Jeremiah imagined, for those who had the means and the right to fish, in these hard times; those who weren't stopped by landlords who owned the lands leading to the waters.

Michael spoke of the men who would be delivering the speeches. "They call themselves Young Ireland, Jer. They bring a spirit and energy we're all starving for."

With the worst of the famine over, Jeremiah realized that the more lasting hunger still had not been fed—the hunger for honor and a feeling of dignity and self-worth. The Church never taught, nor preached about such human emotions from the pulpit. Yet the longing was there, accompanied by a shame that spread throughout the land. An embarrassment that such a horror had been visited upon them, that they had been helpless to control the devastating loss of the potato. Some even believed the blight was a punishment from God, deserved because of the belief in the fairies and things supernatural that the Church had deemed sinful. It was this shame that kept many of the Irish from open rebellion.

Many, but not all.

"Over this way, Jer. We'll have a better view," Michael said as he rode down the southern part of the valley to the old wrought iron bridge that spanned the river in the center of town.

Throughout the years of their friendship, Jeremiah marveled at Michael's appetite for reading. He could often be found in the field, his work done, book in hand. It was Michael who read aloud from the popular weekly newspaper *The Nation*, at the pub as the men returned from the fields. The paper had been founded by two Catholics, Charles Gavan Duffy and John Blake Dillon, and a Protestant barrister, Thomas Davis, with the sole purpose of unifying the country into a nation.

Michael's fervor seemed bottomless. Ireland, Michael would caution, was dying all around them.

"Ye have only to listen to what they're saying, listen to what they're writing!"

There was abundant evidence that the English believed the Irish to be ignorant, indolent and not worth the land they lived on. Each time Michael read another of *The Times* articles degrading the Irish, he was ablaze in anger.

"Jer, every time I read such blather and hatred," he said, his face as red as lit coals, "I vow I'll not set foot in London, ever in me lifetime."

When Jeremiah heard Michael read aloud the frequently published poems of Speranza, the pen name for Dublin-born writer Jane Francesca Elgee, he found her defiance thrilling in its challenge of the status quo and argument for Ireland's freedom:

Abject tears,and prayers submissive—
Have they eyes, and cannot see?
Never country gained her freedom
When she sued on bended knee.

Yet while the readings stirred Jeremiah, Michael's intensity and talk of giving his life for Ireland sometimes frightened him. He'd seen too much life taken to be open to such talk. But Michael's passion was compelling, and despite himself, Jeremiah found himself listening and following.

* * *

Thomas Davis, one of the founders of *The Nation*, whose articles were stirring folks up with talk of Ireland's soul, had written several songs, one of which served as a national anthem of sorts. Jeremiah and Michael had first heard it at Josie's pub, the sentiment of its last four words often a popular chant:

". . . And Ireland long a province be a Nation once Again"

The music reached deep into Jeremiah, finding a place where sorrow began. His disdain had grown each day that he stood through his school years to sing "God Save the Queen." Hadn't his own sister and mother died in the midst of a famine that needn't have been so fierce had there been help from the very Queen they were asking God to save? Why didn't they sing God Save Ireland, God save the starving, dying Irish?

The anger, deep and entrenched, seethed.

Now, after a two-day ride, they were here in Carrick—on-Suir to hear something that would inspire and ignite them to action, to give them something to do with the anger. They'd seen enough of "outrages," as they were called, attacks on carts full of food that was being sent out of Ireland to pay landlords, while the Irish starved. A savagery had emerged. Something had to happen. Something had to get the attention of the British who weren't listening, that was certain.

The medieval town of Carrick-on-Suir, the Ormond Castle dominating its landscape, held shops, stores and buildings lined along its river. The beautiful parklands that led from the castle gave a pastoral flavor. A hush settled as the bells in the church steeples rang out over Gleann an Oir (the Golden Vale).

Jeremiah and Michael turned their attention to a point on the hillside where the leaders of Young Ireland—Smith-O'Brien, Meagher and Dillon—were silhouetted against the sky.

"These are the men who have parted ways from O'Connell," Michael leaned over and said to Jeremiah. "They've been open in their support of armed rebellion, if that's what it takes." Jeremiah winced at the thought. They stopped their horses on a slope just above the crowded bridge, with a clear view of the speakers on the hillside ahead.

The first to speak was William Smith O'Brien, a Member of Parliament from Ennis and a co-founder of the Irish Confederation. Jeremiah felt encouraged as he looked at the group assembled on the hillside, mostly men his age or a little older. Though this crowd of two hundred was far less than the thousands the da had told him had come out for O'Connell's infamous monster meetings, he knew that this was at least a beginning, and who could fault a beginning after so many endings.

O'Brien, clad in a gray striped suit coat and vest, attire befitting his position as MP, rose to a makeshift podium of crates and planks. As he stood on an upturned crate, his bearded face looked directly out over the assembly of farmers. He lifted his hands as the crowd roared acknowledgment.

"Thank ye all for coming, for leaving your homes and families, for making the journey," he said. "I know yer time is precious and this is the right time to stand up for Ireland."

The crowd roared its approval. His unbuttoned suit jacket flapped in the breeze as he raised his arms and challenged the notion that the famine had been a visitation of Providence:

"The Almighty, indeed, sent the potato blight, but the English created the Famine," he said, quoting another firebrand of Young

Ireland, John Mitchel, a Unitarian minister's son, who had been arrested this past May under a newly created Treason Felony Act.

O'Brien's voice rang out with a restrained anger:

"It is time to address those 'who have made the most beautiful island under the sun a land of skulls, or of ghastly specters.' Stand ready to rise up for Ireland."

The crowd responded with applause and shouts of "A Nation Once Again." Jeremiah felt his face flush and his breathing become shallow. Michael was right. The excitement of these men was contagious.

The two other speakers, fair-haired Thomas Francis Meagher, son of a Waterford businessman, and the diminutive John Blake Dillon, a lawyer and co-founder of *The Nation*, took turns speaking of the hope across Europe, telling of revolutions that had broken out like an epidemic from Paris to Berlin, Vienna to Budapest, all opening the way for freedom. They rallied the crowd, telling them, "The time for Ireland is now."

Jeremiah was spellbound.

With exquisite timing, O'Brien spoke again:

"'Tis to the married men I'm speaking now and telling ye the best thing ye can do to save Ireland is to stay home with yer families. Stay home and keep faith for Ireland, pray for Ireland and keep hope up in yer towns.

"For those of ye who are working men, remain at yer jobs. Now is no time to leave a chance at earning. These are times for surviving. Ye must provide the weight of yer worth with yer work. Yer toil is precious. Keep at it all for Ireland.

"It's to ye single, unemployed men I speak now. I'm asking ye to join this movement. Ye are the men who can be spared to fight for Ireland's freedom."

Jeremiah glanced at Michael whose face shone with excitement. With the crowd cheering, O'Brien told these laborers:

"Go home and say yer farewells and come back with just enough bread and biscuits for three days, for in these starvation times, we cannot take too much from those for whom we stand.

Now is the time that we must rise and stand for Ireland. Now is the time. Come back prepared to fight."

A wave of frenzy moved through the crowd as repeated shouts of "A Nation Once Again" were heard. Horses whinnied as their riders moved out from the crowd. Jeremiah and Michael watched as the Young Ireland leaders rode down the hillside and mounted their horses, riding off to yet another town to gather up more to join them.

Within minutes, the clergy who had been clustered quietly at the edge of the gathering moved among the crowd, begging the men not to follow, begging them to return to their homes. They warned of the lack of weapons available and of their ignorance of military tactics. Some men listened, others moved away quickly.

The crowd, small and bent from hunger, was careful about where its energy would be spent, careful not to squander food or toil for something that would have no return. Among them were those who were willing and even eager to risk an honorable death in action rather than one by starvation in a corner of a cabin.

With only a few words between them, Jeremiah and Michael made the decision to go. On their ride home they planned the details and within a few days, they were ready.

"I fear upsetting the da with our mission, Michael," Jeremiah confided. "I'm after telling him we're off to look fer some kind of work, if ye agree."

"It's good ye suggest that, Jer, for I'm of the same mind. We've no need to put any further burden forward. Besides, there's no telling what we might find."

They knew the travel would be arduous but their passion prevailed. Michael provided hand-held pikes; Jeremiah didn't ask where they'd come from. They both brought what little bread and biscuit they could spare, being certain that Michael's parents and brother and sisters as well as Jeremiah's da had enough to sustain them.

Chapter Four
Ballingary

July 1848

They started off at dawn on July 26 and rode 'til dusk, stopping often to water the horses and feed them what little they could. They met up with Smith O'Brien at Mullinhone two days later. He provided bread he'd paid for himself for the men who were helping to move toward the dream of independence.

Jeremiah looked about at the assorted men gathered round the orange-red glow of the embers, their young faces reflecting a mixture of fear and adventure, as did their music. Love songs, ballads and songs of rebellion were mixed with stories of fairies and kings. The evening ended with a rendition of "Slievenamon"—Woman of the Mountain—written by Charles J. Kickham, a trusted Young Irelander:

> By night, and by day, I ever, ever pray;
> While lonely my life flows on
> To see our flag unfurled and my true-love to enfold;
> In the Valley near Slievenamon.

The melody wafted through the silky mist with a somberness accompanying it. Then Smith O'Brien called the evening to an end, reminding them to rest up for what was to come. The ominous mood chilled Jeremiah as he joined Michael to find a spot to rest.

* * *

In the early morning light of July 29, two hundred strong, they rode together for Ballingary in County Tipperary. Their mission was to win self-government, this small town a beginning. They joined a small rebel band of coal miners who were setting up a barricade just outside the town to block the constabulary from overtaking them.

Jeremiah noted the familiar gray skies, the town quiet, shops, pubs and livery still closed. An eerie calm, he thought. No carts or wagons anywhere. A dog barked in the distance. The church bell tolled the hour. Jeremiah counted eight.

Then from around the bend in the road, they came, advancing in military formation—the police line—marching two by two and three by three, row upon row, too many to count, on foot, in perfect step, dressed in blue uniforms with gold buttons and elaborate gold cord epaulettes. The pageantry both intrigued and sickened Jeremiah as he wondered how this small band of ragtag men could overtake the likes of this organized and ornate constabulary.

His felt his neck tighten as he cautiously followed Michael's lead, joining the others as they shouted and jeered at the advancing line. When they were about a hundred yards from the barricade, without warning, the police line broke rank, turned to the left and ran off. The rebels began to race across adjacent fields to cut them off. As they followed up the low hill, they saw the police take possession of a small two-storied farmhouse that was surrounded by a stone wall.

From their position outside the wall, Jeremiah and Michael could hear Smith O'Brien at the window shouting: "Give up yer arms, we shall not hurt a man of ye, ye are Irishmen."

They moved through the gate and could see several hands thrust through the windows. Jeremiah saw a gun being handed over. Then, from somewhere behind them, a stone came crashing forward. They heard glass shatter and shots ring out from the house. Men scattered away from all sides of the hillside and charged down the hill. Two men near O'Brien fell from their horses. Several men rushed to help them. Then there was silence.

From their spot on the rise, Jeremiah and Michael waited. There was no sound, no shouts or noise of any kind. A quiet murmur spread throughout the assembled men.

They watched as two priests, likely called upon by men who

had gone for them at sound of the shots, came up the hill to give last rites, an act familiar to all in these times. Finally, word came to disband. Jeremiah and Michael watched as Smith O'Brien and a man called Mac Manus withdrew. The remaining men rode off in all directions. Jeremiah felt light-headed. He rode closer to Michael and called out, "Is there to be no retaliation? Men have been killed!"

Anger forced its way into his fists. Michael said nothing but pulled his horse's reins in the direction of the departing men.

Within a few hours, they reached Fethard, half a day's ride from home. As the dozen or more men poured into P.J. Lonergan's pub, a solidly built man from Mallow named Maloney with beet-red cheeks declared, "It's a mighty thirst I have." He tipped the pint, drained it and asked for another. After he quenched his thirst, he answered questions before they'd been asked, his bushy eye-brows moving up and down as he told the tale.

"The farmhouse belongs to a widow named McCormack who'd been away when all the commotion began. She was mighty in her fury when she returned and rushed up to Smith O'Brien after those first shots were fired. She begged him not to retaliate, putting on him the blame for police taking over her farmhouse in the first place. And it was then she told him of her five children within.

"'Glory be to God, sir,' she said to him as she went down on her knees, 'Ye can't risk the lives of those innocent little children for the sake of a couple of constabulary men!'

"And men, if ye didn't know the heart of William Smith O'Brien before, ye know it now."

With this, Maloney hoisted his pint and declared, "A salute to William Smith O'Brien."

The men raised their glasses, nodding one to the other. Michael and Jeremiah listened, the meaning of it all too clear.

***

It had been a folly, this revolution, this first attempt at freedom.

The dead men were honored with a a song or two and within the hour, Jeremiah and Michael rode into the night, returning to Donoughmore, not saying a word of their adventure to anyone.

While the hunger that led Jeremiah and Michael to join this fight was still unsatisfied, the desire for freedom was more firmly rooted. And though it would take two decades, it would be fed.

Chapter Five

The Petition

October 1848

The light from the opened pub door served as a beacon for Jeremiah as he rode through the unbroken blackness that covered the balmy October night sky.

As he dismounted, he glanced in and saw a dozen or more men standing at the bar. Two dogs slept under a huckleberry bush at the right of the door.

Though no sign indicated the name of this public house, Jeremiah knew it well. His da had brought him here since his youth. The small whitewashed building with a warm welcome within, its bar central to the small room in the front, was owned by the FitzGerald family, whose children had gone to school with Jeremiah.

It was here that Jeremiah first sang songs about Ireland as a nation, and listened to the readings from newspapers and journals. More than once he had watched the assembled men call out in response to the vitriolic *Times* articles. The stories and songs he'd heard here were part of his family folklore. It was from this place he learned about the world inside and outside Ahadallane.

Jeremiah lifted the latch to open the lower portion of the half-door and entered into the subdued light. Three men stood at the far end of the mahogany bar talking with the barkeep. Another looked at Jeremiah as he entered. The toffee sweetness of the stout and a strong tobacco fragrance filled his nostrils. Several men gathered in a small alcove toward the back where the musicians often sat. The area known as the snug, the small partitioned space reserved for women and small groups of men, was empty.

Jeremiah stepped up to the bar and noted Michael emerging from the back room, closing the door marked "Private" behind him. He nodded to Jeremiah and took a place at the far end of the bar. An air of expectation swept the room. Conversations quieted, chairs scraping along the floor the loudest sound to be heard.

Michael, his eyes focused, cleared his throat and began:

"To His Excellency George William Frederick Earl of Clarendon, the Lord Lieutenant General and General Governor of Ireland.
May it Please Your Excellency,
We the Undersigned, the Mayor, Clergymen, Magistrates and other inhabitants of this town of Ahadallane in the County of Cork approach your Excellency humbly to solicit the interposition of the Royal Prerogative, in behalf of M. William Smith O'Brien and the other state Prisoners, now under sentence of Death for High Treason."

Silence, save for the occasional squeaking chair or floor board, filled the room. This petition, fashioned after the one written in the city of Cork, was among many being signed throughout the county. The sentence imposed on O'Brien had been harsh, as had all the legal responses to the recent violence plaguing Ireland.

Michael continued:

"It would be unbecoming of us to make any appeal to your Excellency's humane feelings. We are satisfied mercy unsolicited would prevail, if these feelings were allowed alone to sway your Excellency's decision."

After he finished, Michael placed the parchment on the shiny surface of the bar and anchored it with two small glasses. With a gentleman's poise, he signed it and stepped away, leaving the pen and ink.

Throughout the pub, men eyed one another warily. Jeremiah watched for the da's reaction. There was none. The da stared straight ahead and took another swallow of his drink.

Jeremiah admired Michael's boldness, his ability to stand up pub-

licly in support of the men known as Young Ireland with whom they
had ridden little more than three months ago. It was common knowledge that there was a price on Smith O'Brien's head. His August 6th
arrest after what had become known as "the Battle of Widow
McCormack's Cabbage Patch" was no surprise. The trial started on
October 3rd and lasted five days, ending with a verdict of death.

The Nation reported the proceeding in excruciating detail,
including O'Brien's words before hearing the sentence:

> "I have done only that which, in my opinion, it was the
> duty of every Irishman to have done, and I am now pre-
> pared to abide the consequences of having performed my
> duty to my native land. Proceed with your sentence."

The sentence was then read:

> To be drawn on a hurdle to the place of execution on the
> 13th Nov, and there hanged until he be dead, his head
> then to be cut off and his body to be cut into four quarters
> then disposed of as her Majesty shall think fit . . .

It was this that Jeremiah pondered as he stood alone in the
shadows, listening to the crowd of men and the few women react
to the words, watching those that stepped up to sign the petition.
The da, his favorite tweed cap in hand, moved toward him, his
gray hair more silver, his shoulders more rounded than Jeremiah
remembered. He spoke in a whisper.

"Ye're better off on yer own, lad!" his da said to him, touching
Jeremiah's arm. "Ye're better off not thinking about all the wrongs
done to Ireland or ye'll end up angry and bitter like ol' McMike
and his ilk who haven't spent a happy day since before O'Connell."
Jeremiah looked at him and saw the determination in his eyes as
he continued. "It's no good that bitterness, no good at all. What's
done is done. The good Lord'll see to ye. That's all ye need."

Jeremiah listened and looked past the da's pale blue eyes, only able to picture the two men falling from their horses in Ballingary, their bodies crumbling to the ground. Where was the good Lord for them? He felt his body tighten and a burning sensation rise from within. The da had taught him of Ireland's past. Now did he think he could just forget it all? Jeremiah looked down at the da, whose pleading moved him, whose advanced signs of aging distressed him. He seemed smaller, less robust and more fragile, his fierceness gone into the hillside with his wife and child.

He respected the da for so much of what he'd endured. Yet Jeremiah couldn't reconcile the realities of these days with saying "what's done is done," or "the good Lord'll see to ye." There had been too much to bear to let it go at that.

He nodded to the da and moved toward the petition. In what felt like a single movement, he took pen in hand and signed his name, nodded again to the da, and swiftly went out the door.

* * *

The petition was not mentioned after that night. One day followed another as Jeremiah and his father settled into their pattern of work that followed the worst of the famine. At times, they worked side by side, planting oats, barley and wheat, the very crops that had been shipped from the land during the early days of the hunger. They plowed, planted, and continued to work the land. They kept up with the rent, selling what they could on Mallow market days. They fed their livestock and themselves sparingly, thankful for the bits and pieces.

Through all his years, the da had taught Jeremiah to be proud, had taught him things that would keep him in good stead. His most recent counsel had disturbed Jeremiah.

"Ye should have no mind with their kind. Lads like them have let the troubles of this country poison them until they've become a poison themselves. Steer clear, lad, I'm telling ye now, and mind me words, ye'll rue the day if ye defy me on this."

The words echoed in his ears as Jeremiah rode through the hills atop the chestnut mare that had been like his own since he was ten. With all the death and disease around him, he felt quietly grateful for this steed that he privately called Macushla, the Gaelic term for "darling." He'd kept her fed with what little he could scrounge and she had somehow survived. Jeremiah stroked her before he loosened the reins and let her take the lead. She ran free now and he felt the breeze through his worn gray shirt; the soothing air entered at the holes in the elbows.

As he crouched over in the saddle watching the hillside go past him in a blur, he focused on the far ridge, the land of the Riordans. The township of West Pluckanes touched their land in the north and as he rode to the edge, he saw Michael on the ridge.

Jeremiah called out and rode toward him, signaling the mare to a slower gait. As he crested the hill, looking forward to a chat, he saw Michael's horse dart down the hill and was surprised to see Michael's back as he rode away.

He mustn't have seen me, Jeremiah thought, or he wouldn't have gone like that, without even a salute.

He sauntered to the spot on the ridge where he'd first seen Michael and stopped. He watched after him now, wondering what had made him leave in such a hurry. When he saw the mound on the side of the hill, he pulled on Macushla's reins and moved through the sparse brush of this November season. He found a spot where the earth had been disturbed, the soil freshly turned. He couldn't imagine why. It was on Michael's land and he knew it was none of his concern. Yet curiosity seized him. He dismounted and knelt at the spot, wondering.

Chapter Six

Michael Riordan

December 1858

As winter temporarily yielded its grip and the rains softened the land, Michael knew he had to go. He mounted the horse and rode onto the ridge without a trace of sunlight beyond the brown fields of harvested oats. Nightfall would be upon him soon.

He rode the black stallion deliberately until he saw the opening in the woods, then led the horse through a bramble and down a slope toward the stream that furnished water for the cattle. He was out of sight of the fields, of the cottages and of Jeremiah, whose preoccupation with Margaret would keep him from knowing of this mission.

Michael, six feet tall and fair, had a soft, innocent face despite the losses he'd endured. He was a year younger than his sister who was the oldest of the three surviving children with little Bridget now the baby of the family. The first two children, a boy and a girl, had died in childbirth when he was an infant. His younger brother, Johnny Joe, was just ten when he died of the fever during the hunger, leaving cold in their home that was like the great gray stone at the edge of the field. They knew only how to go around it and that it could not be moved.

The only remaining son, Michael became a treasure, easygoing and helpful, always ready with a joke or story. He was well lauded in school, and his engaging manner added to his attractiveness. As keenly as he missed his own Johnny Joe, he couldn't fathom Jeremiah's double loss of his little sister Eliza and his mother.

Michael prayed often and counted his blessings; his da was able to remain a tenant on the land, and he still had his ma. Even a few cattle remained. As he grew older, he handled more and more of the chores, seeing to the cattle and tending the crops as the crippling pain in his da's left leg kept him from being much help.

His da had fallen during the muddy season five springs before when his mare had tumbled down the ridge and landed on top of him.

"The bone's been shattered," Doc Foley had said. "He's lucky to have what's left of it at all." Only the drink seemed to ease the pain, his da had said.

During the haying, spring planting or fall harvest, Michael and Margaret found time to help the Buckleys who had become the best of friends. Shared meals and evenings spent together around the hearth brought a relief and comfort for both families. He remembered how Bridget, too small to be of much physical help, had provided a cheerfulness and levity that seemed to come naturally.

"Show me again, Jeremiah," she'd beg when they were together, "how to whistle." Jeremiah would lift the ginger-haired girl to his lap and let her watch as he pursed his lips. With her blue eyes closed, she'd try with all her might, nothing but air coming out. She'd screw her face up in frustration, her freckled nose wrinkling as she'd try again and again. Her persistence was laudable. Finally her eyes opened wide as a barely audible whistle was heard, applause waiting as she tried once again and this time gave a full whistle.

"Aren't ye the smart one little, Bridgie. Sure Michael's trained ye well," Jeremiah would say, giving credit to his friend.

In turn, Michael gave another kind of support to his friend this past fall, when Jeremiah asked for his sister Margaret's hand in marriage.

"Ye think ye hadn't known us for all yer years. Why, yer eyes were darting around like ye'd seen one of the fairies," Michael teased with a gleam in his eye. "If I didn't know ye better, I'd think ye were scared. But ye're a stronger man than that now. Sure don't I know that."

The evening Jeremiah and his da came to supper, Michael

recalled Jer, dressed in his cleanest shirt and trousers, his hair combed back from his forehead. Even his fingernails were cleaned. Michael had been privy to the affection between Jeremiah and Margaret, each of them having confided their feelings to him.

The celebration meal—a bit of bacon and potato—was meager, but far more than Jeremiah and his da had lately. At the end of the meal, a "drop" of the poteen, a homemade whiskey known to be stronger than the legal limit, was shared among the men as the talk turned to the dowry.

Jeremiah's da had been his spokesman, offering the merger to Margaret's da. Michael hadn't worried about the arrangements or the dowry, the friendship between the families strong.

The final arrangement had been simple. The two families had leased neighboring plots from the same landlord, Joseph Bennett, for over thirty years. Now they would merge the two leases and Jeremiah would hold it. Michael gladly consented to the agreement, freed to pursue his own dream. As much as he loved the land, his passion for serving in the Church was far deeper and soon he would begin his studies for the priesthood.

Money from the parish along with a scholarship he was awarded from Maynooth Seminary—£50 a year, a mighty sum in sparse times—had helped him get started. The pride on his mother's weary face and his father's lack of comment told him they approved. His passion for Ireland's freedom had sustained him during these last ten years of waiting to begin his studies. His involvement with the cause had grown steadily since he and Jeremiah had ridden to Ballingary though thus far he had never let Jeremiah know of it.

Now Michael pushed aside thoughts of family, priesthood and marriage and dismounted the dark stallion. He'd called him "Your Grace" for, like a Bishop, the steed had an ecclesiastical bearing. Your Grace had been a true companion during the darkest of times, carrying Michael faithfully in the night when his own fear might have told him to turn back. It was the horse's soulful eyes and the white patch on his forehead that beguiled Michael to this day.

He patted Your Grace, his black coat aglow, and lashed his reins to a bush, signaling he'd be here a while. He pulled the metal shovel from his pack and began to move the damp brown earth, digging not more than a foot deep. It was here. This was the spot he remembered. He heard the clink of the shovel against metal, as it sounded through the tan burlap. He knelt down, pushed away the remaining soil with his hands and lifted out the carefully wrapped bundle. He was at the far boundary of the land that was to be Jeremiah's. He felt relief not to be destined for a farmer's life. He was bound for something more, something away from this land.

He stood with the bundle and stroked Your Grace to steady him.

"This is for Ireland," he said aloud. "God save her, and ye and me with it." He hoisted the bundle and balanced it as best he could across the length of his horse's ebony back. None would be the wiser when he'd delivered it to its destination.

As he mounted Your Grace, a fog enveloped the landscape. He touched the bundle once again then rode with purpose through the mist.

Chapter Seven

The Marriage

Fall 1859

Jeremiah stooped as he entered the sparse cabin, vowing silently to make a doorway a man could walk through without having to bend. He smelled cabbage and potato as he entered and looked about to see if there was a bit of ham to go with it. He'd fancied having the means to have meat a few times a week and was proud that Margaret didn't hesitate or worry about using it. After all, she'd come from people with means and Jeremiah wasn't about to have her go with less. Despite his losses, he'd been able to hold onto this small cabin with its fieldstone hearth, pine table and small bedroom. One day he'd add on to it. One day he'd make a fine entryway, a vestibule he'd call it.

Margaret looked up as he came in, her blue eyes lighting up the room.

"It's just on time, ye are," she proclaimed, her hair pulled gently back from her cheeks, her print dress clean. "The supper'll be ready by the time ye've washed yourself. And then ye can tell me the news of the day. It's half-daft I am here alone. Mind ye I'm not complaining, but it's different not having all the commotion going on."

Ach, she's missing them indeed, Jeremiah thought, as he hung his earth brown jacket on the peg by the doorway, placing his gray wool cap on top of it. He pushed his chestnut hair into place as he moved over to the white ceramic basin, wet his hands with the water from the matching pitcher, and lathered them with the soap Margaret had brought with her. 'Tis quiet for her here without all the comings and goings of her own home, what with Michael gone to seminary and the da and ma on their own. And the loss of little Bridgie was still close, pneumonia taking her as quickly as a thief just after the new year. They'd added her to their prayers, along with Ma and Pa Riordan who seemed to age ten years overnight. Margaret was relieved in one sense to be on her own, he knew, but still it could be lonely for her. She used to do it all for them and now she's only got me.

He was tired but he'd had a good day and he couldn't be more pleased with this season's oats. Their sage green color waving across the hillside like a green ocean was something to behold. They would harvest well.

Lavender, an honest scent, he thought as he moved the soap between his hands. Clean and not too sweet.

He wiped his hands on the white linen towel and turned back to Margaret. Her eyes danced as strands of her red hair fell from the ribbon that held it back. A lovely color, he thought, a rich dark red. Indeed, she's a handsome woman.

How strange it seemed to be married, and to someone he'd known for most of his life. He remembered her as Michael's little sister and now she was his bride. He smiled each time he recalled the years he hardly noticed her trailing after them when he and Michael were out in the fields. And then one day she was wholly different. Her face had lost its fullness and the eyes that had been full of wonder were deeper and more serene. A soft blue dress shaped gently by her modest young breasts had replaced her brown overalls. She was something to look at, and look he did. It didn't take long for him to court her, for after that first glimpse, she was all he could think about. And for her part, she seemed happy enough to return looks to the one who had been at her brother's side for years.

Now, as he watched her across the table of their own home, he could hardly believe his fortune. Her feminine touches dotted the two-room cabin: bits of embroidered cloth, curtains on the two windows in the main room, everything swept neat as a pin. On the shelf above the hearth, a statue of Our Lady sat next to a book of poetry by Jonathan Swift, a small candle beside it. His mother's dishware lined the shelves, Margaret's favorites, she said. A little glass of water with wild roses sat on the table.

He watched as she carried the iron pot to the table. Two bowls, two spoons and two cups were already set out. She nodded to him, and as she did, another wisp of hair fell across her eye. After she pulled out her chair, and pushed her hair up, she reached for his hand and together they bowed their heads in prayer, as Jeremiah remembered his own ma doing.

"We thank you, Almighty God, for this food we receive, for this love that we share. Amen." She filled his bowl with the watery potato and cabbage broth sprinkled with chunks of ham. He breathed in the aroma as she put the bowl in front of him and waited until she filled her own bowl before he started to eat.

"Denis is ailing," he said as he began to eat the broth. "Young Mary is looking after him for a time. He's taken to wandering with no telling where he's going. It's a trial for them."

Margaret returned to the hearth, took the teakettle from the hook and brought it to the table and filled the teapot. "He hasn't been right since his own poor Mary's gone," she said. "'Tis no wonder. She was everything to him and more. It's not right, him being left alone like that."

Jeremiah touched her hand as she poured and looked up at flushed cheeks. He knew now how much care she must take, for just the evening before last she'd told him there was to be a child.

* * *

Their wedding had been simple. They followed the tradition of marrying on Shrove Tuesday, the last Tuesday before Lent, since marriage wasn't performed during Lent. The festivities of their February 1st wedding on St. Brigid's Day made for a memorable event, with special thoughts of little Bridgie who had been gone from them less than a month. Margaret was bedecked in a fine new blue dress, sewn for just such an occasion by her mother. Jeremiah had worn his only suit, dark blue with the thinnest of stripes through it.

Friends and family crowded into their little cottage as Father Lane asked all the church questions and Margaret and Jeremiah each pledged aloud their love:

As the sun follows its course, mayst thou follow me. As light to the eye, as bread to the hungry, as joy to the heart, may thy presence be with me, O one that I love, till death comes to part us asunder.

The ancient ritual with all its tradition evoked tears from the women. As Father Lane offered the wedding blessing, stifled sobs spread throughout the cottage.

May God be with you and bless you;
May you see your children's children.
May you be poor in misfortune,
Rich in blessings,
May you know nothing but happiness.
From this day forward.

As the bride and groom exchanged a tender kiss, applause filled the room followed by an expectant silence as the da came forward. He gazed about the room filled with family and friends, looking older and frailer than many had remembered him. He raised his voice in song, singing his own wishes to his son and new bride—freedom from hunger and freedom from fear, his message to Jeremiah all of his years. He raised a glass and called out the traditional toast, *Sláinte*, his hope for their health as his own continued to fail. His eyes were moist as he made his way to the door, tonight giving over his bed to the couple along with a handmade wedding quilt sewn by his niece Julia.

A grand party followed, filled with jigs, reels, songs and stories, along with what for these times could be considered a bountiful feast, with fowl, bacon, brown bread and cake.

Jeremiah and Margaret were surrounded as they danced their first time as a married couple. Those assembled watched as the two moved slowly and smoothly, the harmony between them evident in the small circle cleared for dancing, their eyes intent on one another.

Then the traditional highlight—a visit from the Strawboys

whom Jeremiah eagerly welcomed when he discovered them at the threshold. While called Strawboys, often women were among them, all of them dressed head to toe in straw with straw masks. The leader, following custom, went over to the bride, wished her great joy and courteously asked for a dance. Then Jeremiah and Margaret held hands as these six young people surrounded them in an exhilarating eight-hand reel. Afterwards everyone was treated to a step dance by a lean young man whose agility astounded them, legs kicking high. The Strawboys' visit was a cherished tradition and just as the ladies began to guess their identities, the Strawboys departed for another home, the season for weddings upon them.

Tall, elegant, black-haired Eileen Murphy, whose voice commanded silence, gave a light-hearted song, about a fellow on a wedding night. Jeremiah gave a wink to his bride who returned it, both of their eyes sparkling. The laughter subsided as Margaret's brother Michael gave them a song. Her throat tightened and she fought back tears as his sweet tenor voice sang out "Boulavogue," telling the story of the 1798 rising and of the slain Father Murphy from old Kilcormack.

God grant you glory, brave Father Murphy
And open heaven to all your men;
For the cause that called you may call tomorrow
In another fight for the green again.

She knew her brother's heart and his passion around Ireland's fight for freedom; his intensity scared her and while she had little influence on him, she had hope that Jeremiah would be a sensible force.

More songs and dances filled the night along with more speeches and stories. The whole town was there, all of them glittering with hope that had been absent for far too long.

Dawn broke before the house was once again quiet. Jeremiah and Margaret walked out into the early morning light as the sun was just coming up over the near hill. A hare ran across the dewy field, as they stood silently, hand in hand, memories recent and ancient filling them. After a time, Jeremiah looked into Margaret's eyes and saw tears glistening, his own eyes moist. They held each other, arms reaching out in silent embrace. Trusting in the tomorrows about to unfold, they walked slowly back to their cottage.

* * *

He was glad the da had lived to see him married. Three months after the wedding, Jeremiah buried him up on the hillside with Mary and little Eliza. The da had been ailing less than a month with a pain that ran down his arm. The doctor ordered bed rest and the da roared back, "Are you daft, man? There's work to be done."

During their few months together, the da had taken to Margaret, allowing her to cajole him to rest as she sang a song or read his favorite verse. But rest wasn't enough.

Jeremiah knew the da was at his best on the land, astride his horse, his face as contented as a just milked cow. The da had seen to it that just seven years after the worst of the hunger, they started again to pay the eleven pounds rental that Mr. Bennett had forgiven for the time. Though it was never spoken of, Jeremiah knew that the da had earned every hectare of the land that he tilled. He'd sowed and harvested it for most of his fifty-two years and he was proud to have a son who would follow him, tilling the land and paying the rent.

So it was natural, when his da breathed his last, that Jeremiah arranged a third white cross on the hillside and laid him to rest in this very same land.

Chapter Eight

Baby Julia

January 24, 1860

"I hear her, I hear her! Oh, dear God. It's the banshee. Oh dear God!"

Jeremiah woke to see his wife sitting straight up in bed, her white dressing gown damp and clinging to her chilled body. The light of the full moon illuminated the rich red hair that fell over her shoulder. Her blue eyes stared straight ahead, her body, full with the weight of their first child, perched as if ready for flight.

"What is it, Mairéad?" he asked, lapsing into the Irish name for Margaret that he'd first heard her called as a child. "What's frightening ye so?"

"Didn't ye hear her? Was I the only one? Did you not hear the banshee?" Margaret looked to her husband in disbelief. "She was calling, calling. I heard her, plain as day. The low moaning sound It was awful! Did ye not hear her?"

Margaret reached out to Jeremiah who wrapped her in his arms and rocked her and soothed her, saying he had heard no such thing, no such thing at all.

"Sure, your mind's playing tricks on ye with the baby due anytime now and all ye've been taking care of, what with the New Year and all the doings. Hush now, hush. It'll be fine. Just ye wait and see."

He wouldn't go so far as to say there was no such thing as a banshee for he himself had heard the wailing when little Eliza died. The dreaded banshee, the fairy who foreshadowed death.

He was as certain then as Margaret was now that he'd heard her. It was real and it was just as she said. Awful. He'd never said a word of it to anyone and now wished he'd never heard it so he could tell Margaret there was no such spirit. He laid her back down and brushed her hair from her brow. Then he lay down close beside her. After her breathing returned to a deeper rhythm, he said again, "Sure it's only yer mind playing tricks on ye. Sure, there was nothing. Aren't ye as fit as a fiddle and ready for this wee one? Isn't this child an answer to prayer?"

***

Jeremiah had called on his cousin Julia for help. It was January 24th and Julia stayed with Margaret throughout the long afternoon and into the evening as she writhed from the pain of the impending birth. Julia noted the fleeting smiles on Margaret's lips and was glad of them. Before her pregnancy even, Margaret had shared with Julia her desperate desire for a child, her thrill that she would be bringing life to this earth and their town of Ahadallane where little more than ten years ago there had been so much death.

Jeremiah watched as her pains came in a regular rhythm now. He stayed by her as she struggled, loving her more than he thought possible. He kissed her and wiped her brow, overwhelmed by awe. Cousin Julia received the child as it was delivered to them, wrapping it in a blanket, and shot a glance of alarm to Jeremiah that left him alert. Finally, Margaret's efforts and moaning ceased, her body bathed in perspiration, her damp hair clinging to the pillow, her weak smile a sign of release and hope. Her beauty stunned Jeremiah, as had this experience. He'd never before witnessed the birth of a child. And this was his child. His heart pounded and tears filled his eyes. He reached for Margaret's soft hand and gently held it in his own rough ones. He could find no words, no words at all.

***

It had been cold that January; the frosty days brought a biting wind that chilled the bone. Jeremiah reviewed again the night of the birth. Cousin Julia was there helping, hearing the first cry and then, the awful slow struggle for air. Followed by the veil of quiet.

Margaret heard it and saw it too. The look that crossed her face was like none Jeremiah had ever seen. He'd moved to her, but she'd pushed him away, instead asking for her baby, her little Julia, whom she'd name after her own mother, in the custom of the day. Without hesitation, Cousin Julia wrapped the baby in the white cotton blanket and placed her in Margaret's arms. Julia and Jeremiah exchanged glances as Margaret held her and sang a low, sweet lullaby. Their grief turned to fear as they watched Margaret; her hair matted and tangled, an unsettling look on her face, as though something in her had somehow gone with the baby.

It was only after the hour struck that Jeremiah reached to take the tiny baby from her. Margaret laughed out, "Ye'll disturb her sleep now. Away with ye. She's fine in her mother's arms. She's fine here with me where no harm will befall her. Away with ye now." Even her voice had an otherworldly quality.

So it went for forty-eight hours. Julia had left them and he sat with Margaret throughout the first night. She sat rocking the infant and singing to her the same song over and over again.

"On the winds of the wind oe'r the dark rolling deep
Angels are coming to watch o'er thy sleep
Angels are coming to watch over thee
So list to the wind coming over the sea."

The next day, he'd convinced her to sip a little soup by holding the cup to her lips, so she wouldn't have to let go of the child. He was certain that somewhere within her she knew the baby was gone and that somewhere within her she couldn't summon the reserve to face it.

Margaret hadn't felt the cold for she'd not left the cottage, or the bedroom for that matter. She had done all she could to keep her precious new one warm against the howling wind, holding her close and feeling her softness against her breast. "Have ye ever seen such perfection, Jer?" she said, touching the tip of the child's nose and stroking her small lips. She told of being old enough to remember her little brother Johnny Joe's birth, but not old enough to appreciate how fragile, tiny and perfect this miracle of a child could be. Jeremiah came in and out of the room, cajoling Margaret and looking after her with broth and warm towels for the baby. He sat next to her and ran his hands through his hair again and again, not knowing what else to do. It was his cousins, Julia and her brother, who suggested they call Father Lane. Margaret agreed to have the priest come for a baptism soon.

* * *

As Margaret continued to rock the baby in her arms, she talked of the great midsummer bonfire on the eve of the feast of St. John the Baptist, just six months earlier.

"Jer, do ye remember when I told ye about the baby coming? I remember how ye took me hand with such tenderness. I can still feel it."

Jeremiah did remember the intimate feel of holding her hand as they said the prayers that started off the summer festival. They were only a few months into their marriage, hoping they were well on their way to the start of their own family. As the festivities wound down and the singing and dancing ended, they joined the others in the long held tradition of scooping up the ash from the "big fire" to bring to their own hearth, a symbol of good luck. He looked at the woman before him, who had seemed as brilliant as the bonfire six months before, and could not believe how much had changed.

* * *

The baptism was their only hope. Michael and Julia Buckley, Jeremiah's cousins, were the godparents, a brother and sister—big, burly Michael with his ruddy complexion, eyes as black as his hair, and petite Julia, with fair features and ash blonde hair. They were the children of the da's brother Cornelius and had been there for Jeremiah and Margaret throughout their brief marriage, this time no exception.

Father Lane paused to ask Jeremiah about Margaret when he arrived in the yard, Michael and Julia just behind him. He'd heard enough about her strange behavior to recognize that the Church in its mercy might bring a bit of healing through some sort of ritual. He knew this wasn't the time to talk of limbo, not when sorrow was so deep.

"It's the same, Father," Jeremiah told the man who'd been in the parish for almost twenty years, witness to so many trials.

"She's crooning almost constantly with a far-away look," Jeremiah said, his eyes ringed with red. "The child's been dead now almost two days and she hasn't let go for a moment." His worry was evident in his furrowed brow and anxious tone.

"It's the baptism I'm hoping she'll believe in, the sacrament that will let her loose her grasp so we can take the infant. There'll be no consoling her, I'm afraid. We're praying ye can help her."

As they went into the cottage, Jeremiah took the unlit candle from the ledge above the hearth and led the priest into the bedroom. He also brought the tiny white dress Margaret had made and placed it on the bed. The priest waited as Jeremiah kissed Margaret on the forehead. "It's high time we have a baptism for this wee one," he said, forcing his voice into reassurance he did not feel.

Michael came in and stood near the window in the nearly empty room. Julia followed, and moved past him to be closer to Margaret and the baby. At the sight of them, Margaret startled for a moment, then looked down at the baby and resumed the lullaby.

"On wings of a wind o'er the dark rolling sea.
Angels are coming to watch o'er thy sleep."

Father Lane stood next to Jeremiah on the right of the bed, closest to the doorway, and leaned down. "Ah, she's a fine-looking girl now, Margaret. And what name will we be giving her today as we baptize her?"

"It'll be Julia, Father, after me own mother, who'd be here but for her terrible rheumatism. She'll be so proud to know it's a girl." Margaret beamed with pride at the child in her arms. "She is grand, isn't she now, Father? She's a good baby, a good baby."

Father Lane noticed the air, thick with the scent of death, then put the clerical stole around his neck, took the candle from Jeremiah and handed it to Michael. "Will we be dressing her in the baptismal gown, now? Cousin Julia, will you help us? Here we go."

A fear came over Margaret's face as he moved to take the child. "And sure, we'll dress her as God intended as she takes her place among his saints. For it's a saint she is, a true saint."

The priest continued talking as he eased the infant from her grasp, saying what a fine lass she was, watching Margaret as he handed the wrapped bundle over to Cousin Julia.

Jeremiah and Michael looked on as the priest took a vial of holy water from his pocket. "I'll ask you to hold this now for me, Margaret, so we can assure this child enters the celestial beauty meant for her. I'll ask the godparents to hold the child close as we light the candle and bless this newest saint, Julia. In the name of the Father and of the Son and of the Holy Ghost."

Margaret blessed herself, and seeing his wife resume such an ordinary habit made Jeremiah sigh with relief.

When the prayers were said and the candle extinguished, Father Lane nodded to Julia and Michael, a signal for them to leave the room with the child. Margaret's eyes were wide, but she was silent.

"Sure the Lord loved this little one so much he's taken her to himself," he said directly to Margaret. "What a gift you've offered. What a beautiful child," he said gently.

He moved closer to the bed. "You're a good woman and sure she's up there now with yer own great grandmothers and with all the saints. Blessed Julia we'll call her." He patted her hand and said, "Ye rest now and when ye're well enough, ye get some food and I'll be back to check on ye. Ye're a grand woman, ye are."

Margaret's frightened eyes followed the priest as he went out the door, her lip quivering, and though she did not speak, Jeremiah somehow knew the worst was yet to come.

***

For six days Margaret did not leave the bed, crooning to the infant as if she still held her, as if she was just sleeping. She'd hush Jeremiah and tell him not to wake the infant, a gift to God, the Father had said. The priest had been back to see her and she repeated that she'd given a gift to God, hadn't she now. He'd blessed her and prayed with her and left with a nod of concern to Jeremiah. Margaret ate sparsely and washed only if Jeremiah brought the basin and water to her. With no infant to nurse, she moaned under the weight of her laden breasts. The sage tea would dry up the milk, Jeremiah had learned from the townswomen, if only she would drink it.

* * *

He was never clear what it was she had seen or heard, but it was the last day of January in 1860, St. Brigid's Eve, when he came in from the fields, that he found her standing, still in her dressing gown, looking out at the lambs. She turned to him and said, "Are you satisfied now, there'll be no other mouth to feed? She's gone, ye know, our first child, our baby girl. She's gone."

Jeremiah stood motionless. She didn't look wild. He couldn't tell what it was she saw or heard. He moved hesitantly, never losing her gaze. She spoke again as he put his cap on the hook. "That's right, go ahead, as if I haven't just told ye our world has come crashing down, torn now to smithereens. Just act as if ye didn't hear me say it, our baby is gone. She's gone."

He stood transfixed. After a moment, he gingerly reached out a hand, afraid he might startle her. She slowly moved in his direction and finally reached out to him. As he enfolded her, she whimpered and mumbled words he could barely make out. ". . . not here. I looked everywhere. She's gone, gone to God."

He held her for a good several minutes and then led her to the table, where she sat watching him as he warmed their supper, tending the fire and hanging the kettle for tea. He put the fork and spoon in place as she would, and then served the colcannon the neighbors had brought to them. He was pleased to see that she was eating, the potato and cabbage a familiar and comforting food. Her eyes looked distant and a little frightened when the knock came at the door.

It was the annual St. Brigid's procession that had come to them, bringing a special cross and blessing. None other than Cousin Julia had been chosen to be *An Brideog*, the virtuous virgin. As those in the doorway recited the litany, Margaret slowly stood and moved toward them. One of the group, a tall, dark-haired woman, presented the Brigid's cross to her as those in the procession recited:

> "Take the sword with which the great St. Brigid fought against her enemies and remember to bear the crosses of this life with true Christian fortitude after the example of St. Brigid."

Jeremiah joined Margaret at the doorway, knowing it would be too much to invite any of the procession members in. Cousin Julia briefly embraced Margaret and then the procession was on its way. Jeremiah put his arm around Margaret and after they watched the procession move down the lane, he said, "'Tis the cross of St. Brigid that will help us now." Silently they thought of little Bridgie, who was so proud of her feast day. They never spoke of their own first wedding anniversary.

Together they placed the handmade straw cross on the nail above the doorway, their first cross to bear witness to their faith and their suffering.

* * *

As the days grew longer, the weather milder, Margaret resumed her chores, never speaking of the baby. Sorrow overwhelmed Jeremiah as he watched her, wishing she could have what she had so desired. The time was coming when he would take her to the burial spot, up on a hillside overlooking the valley, opposite where his people were buried. But not yet.

The day of the baptism, Cousin Julia had removed the baptismal gown and wrapped the baby in a muslin cloth before the burial. There would be other children, she had assured Jeremiah. As she'd laundered the tiny white dress she told him she'd prayed for Margaret's recovery. There had been sorrow like this before, she reminded him; her own mother had lost twins in the same heart-rending manner. Julia had only been nine but she remembered the sounds of the grief, not unlike the unearthly moans that had emerged from Margaret. Depth of sorrow like this, she had said, could only be met in prayer.

Jeremiah had heard Julia's attempts at comfort, the words not able to relieve his heart's heaviness at the loss of these little girls, Eliza, Bridgie, and now his own baby, Julia. Would the heartache ever stop, he wondered as he watched Margaret staring out the window.

Chapter Nine

The Priest

April 1860

The sound resonated in Margaret's head as she went about her chores, sweeping, sewing, washing, cleaning and tending their few chickens. No matter what she did, the sound followed. Even as she drew water from the well, the echo down the cavernous opening frightened her. She told Jeremiah some of it but she could see that he had troubles of his own and had grown weary of her fears and complaints about the banshee's moaning.

She'd thought about the priest, Father Lane. Maybe he could reassure her; maybe he could help her know how much longer the dangers would continue.

At breakfast in late April, she told Jeremiah her plan. "I'll be going to see the Father today. He's told me to come whenever I'd like, and today I would."

Jeremiah felt a restrained relief. It had been more than three months since the death of Baby Julia, and though Margaret had physically regained her vigor, he knew she was not right, becoming frightened and weeping at the least thing. It was just within the last fortnight that she'd come in from the field, trembling and wrapped in her shawl, tears streaming down her cheeks, a look of terror in her eyes.

"What is it, Margaret?" he asked. "Whatever has given ye such a fright?"

She hadn't answered. She moved to the hearth and stared into the embers, pulling away from the arms he offered, and tugging her shawl tighter around her. He stood helpless as she sniffled and shook. He fought back feelings of anger, praying that time would help and that she'd return to him from whatever place she had gone.

He steadied himself when he remembered her as Michael's little sister, a fun-loving young girl skipping in the fields, darting in the bracken, her red hair flying in the breeze. He recalled her voice as she sang, light and clear and gay. Throughout their courtship and marriage, she was always bustling about, concerned about others, not thinking much about herself.

He knew that the very act of having a baby brought a mix of confused feelings and notions. He remembered his own mother when she was pregnant with Eliza, fine one minute and vexed the very next, with no telling what had prompted it. It was something he'd learned to skirt around, taking cues from his father. But now with Margaret, though she'd lost the baby, it was something more, something he didn't trust. He felt uneasy and couldn't say why, and was glad she was her off to visit the priest.

* * *

She wore a pale blue cotton dress with buttons up the back and pleats along the bodice. Next to her wedding dress, it was her best. Her shoes were well worn but clean. She wore her black shawl in a fashion she'd seen her own mother wear while mourning, off the shoulders a bit and pulled around the back; today's mild breeze didn't call for much more.

Jeremiah held the cart as Margaret lifted her skirt and stepped in. For many years, the old pony had taken this cart to town and to church. It would deliver Margaret the mile and a half to St. Joseph's at Donoughmore and Father Lane. Jeremiah watched after her, hoping that the priest could lift whatever burden was so present in his wife.

* * *

Father Lane was surprised and delighted to welcome Margaret Buckley into the rectory parlor. A handsome woman, it was good to see that the pink in her cheeks had returned and the gauntness of her face had receded. He'd visited weekly after Baby Julia's death, but when Margaret returned to Sunday Mass, he'd turned to more needy parishioners.

Though it had been ten years since the end of the famine, things were far from stable. The relentless rain threatened to run the crop amok. The economy held no promise, with prices for grain plummeting across Europe. Difficult times indeed.

Father Michael Lane was well familiar with the people in his parish at Donoughmore. He'd been born in Stuake, a small town just up the road from Fornaught and for a time had farmed with his father. There had never been a question that he would become a priest. His studies at St. Patrick's in Maynooth, the seminary in Dublin where Michael was going, had been an opportunity and blessing, his tuition paid in part by assistance he'd won through the Church. He'd been supported by his family, their monetary sacrifice but one part of their dedication to the Church. His father had long been an admirer of Daniel O'Connell, the patriot who captivated the country with political savvy and a commitment to non-violent resistance. As a young boy, Father Lane had learned about the penny rent that helped win the brilliant victory of the Catholic Association. He'd been raised to remember that he was Catholic first, Irish second. "Ye can leave Ireland," his father would say, "but ye can never leave yer religion."

He wondered what brought Margaret to his door. He gave her tea, a bit of cream and a scone, and listened as she began.

"'Tis the banshee, Father, I can't think for the memory of it," she said, twisting her fingers around a handkerchief. 'Tis as if she's taken up in my eardrum. No matter what I'm doing, I hear the distant sound of her and it causes me a terrible fright."

He watched her fidget with her handkerchief, her eyes darting about the room, her occasional gestures of smoothing her blue dress upon her lap.

"Sometimes it's louder than others. I've tired poor Jeremiah with the worryin' of it and I'm doubtin' at times that he even hears my fear anymore. I've come to ye for some blessing, some help to rid me of this terrible scourge." She paused and, blinking away tears, said, "I'm no good for it, if it doesn't stop now. No good at all."

Michael Lane, his faith firm, had served the St. Joseph's parish of Donoughmore during its most dreadful season—when the sacraments for the dying far outweighed those of the living. He drew hope from the people, who still believed, in the face of evidence to the contrary, people who found a spirit within to help them continue amidst devastating losses. He remembered the cabins he'd visited where dead children lay in their mothers' arms, where husbands held wives long dead, where animal carcasses lay strewn about the yard. He fought to keep the images from invading his memory; he fought to keep from crying aloud in horror when they made their way into his dreams.

Belief in fairies, or the "sidhe," and other things supernatural were still common among the parishioners. Stories of cures and curses abounded. Newer church teachings left little room for such beliefs, but their history went back further than the church in Ireland, and Father Lane understood their powers.

He looked at Margaret and saw the tired lines from lack of sleep and the fear in her eyes. He'd known her since she'd been a tiny girl in the parish school. He remembered her as a joyful child, dancing about with the other girls and throwing her head back in gales of laughter. She often led the children playing mumbly-pegs, her voice of authority resonating throughout the schoolyard. "We'll play right here in the shade and everyone will have a turn. Let's start with you, William Graney." He smiled to recall her confidence.

He felt the heaviness that accompanied his priestly role, as he watched the fears, similar to Margaret's, that had erupted since the famine, overcoming many of the best and brightest of the parish. It was as if the malevolence of the hunger had taken root and had yet to be driven out.

"I've not said a word of this to anyone else, Father, it's so frightened I am." She sat forward, her speech rapid. "I've tried everything I know to stop it, but none of the cures I know—holding onto the stone from the hearth, turning my head away when I hear it, walking a circle before bed—none of them seem to help."

He remembered a healing ritual for warts from his own childhood, a stone thrown into the hedgerow after his mother rubbed it on his hand, the offending wart gone. He had no trouble at all dealing with "the other world" for, despite his education, he himself saw little proof to dispel it.

"Ah, now, Margaret," he said in a hushed tone, "it's good ye've come to see me. It's good indeed." The controversy that was brewing within the Church about this persisting pagan belief in fairies and ghosts gave him pause. But having been raised on the belief as well, he knew it wouldn't do to just whisk it under the door.

As a parish priest, he had done what he was bidden, sharing the pastoral letters from the Bishop when they came and holding special collections when asked. The generosity of his own parish was far greater than he could have hoped. Whether the cause was for St. Vincent de Paul or raising money and troops for the Papal army—a call from Pope Pius IX to the Catholic countries of Europe to send troops and money to defend the remaining Papal States against the aggression of Piedmont—he was inspired by the level of giving. Many still struggled in these post-famine days, yet they continued to give—even the unemployed. Their generosity touched him. They were faithful and obedient and they trusted the clergy. Sometimes too much, he thought.

"Ye say ye're hearing the echo, is it, of the banshee?" He sighed heavily. "Would it be the same one ye heard before, or is it different? Can ye tell me that now?"

"It's faint, Father, like a low moaning, and I daren't listen too close. It's there whether I'm at my chores or trying to go to sleep." Her breathing became shallow as she tried to continue. "I'm put to fright by it. I'm fearful of being taken away. I'm . . ." her voice only a whisper.

The parlor in which they were sitting was modestly appointed: an oak sideboard along the far wall with a few scattered linens and a candle upon it; in the center was a pine table and two chairs where they sat, the table bare except for the priest's breviary: a well-worn black leather-bound book. A crucifix hung above the side-board and a holy water font was affixed to the wall by the doorway.

The priest stood and went to the window, his back to Margaret. He was not a tall man, but he had a noble bearing. Although his fair hair was speckled with gray, his vigor belied his expanding girth. Silence filled the room as he looked over the hillside.

Then he turned back to Margaret and said, "There's no point in me telling ye to ignore the noises now, for I know ye to be clever enough and ye would have tried that. So here's what I propose."

He came back to the table, placed his hands upon it and looked into Margaret's hopeful eyes.

"I'll tell ye what I can do now, Margaret. And I'll ask ye not to be letting Jeremiah know or worry for it. There's much afoot these days about the fairies and the like that we won't bother ourselves with. So, now. Are ye all right with that?"

"I am, Father," Margaret replied, intent on having the noises in her head cease.

Father Lane moved behind her chair. A bronze image of the crucified Christ, nailed to a small pine cross, faced them both.

Margaret waited.

Father Lane blessed himself and raised his eyes upward. He then placed his hands on Margaret's head, traced the sign of the cross in the crown of her thick red hair, and said, "In the name of the Father and of the Son and of the Holy Ghost. May the fairies be gone from within and without. May ye rest unattended and may ye go forth with thanksgiving and faith in their kindnesses and belief now in our Lord Jesus Christ, Amen."

He dipped his hand into the holy water font behind him and let some fall onto Margaret's hair as he again blessed her. "In the name of the Father and of the Son and of the Holy Ghost, Amen."

Margaret sat, transfixed, afraid to move her head, afraid to look front or back. The silence in the room was unbroken by any sound, within or without.

Chapter Ten

Beltane

May 1860

On the first of May, the beginning of Beltane, the beginning of the pastoral summer season, Margaret led Jeremiah out into the early dawn. She was already barefoot and encouraged him to take off his shoes.

"'Tis good luck, ye know, to walk in the dew on the first of May," she said. "It'll cure yer calluses from wearing those brogues that are too tight. And 'tis healthy feet we'll both have now with the dew healing us. We'll have not a corn or bunion to trouble us."

As a child, she remembered her own mother had gathered the magical May Day dew. She would shake the sheaves of wheat to capture it. There was enough for a small bottle, which her mother had kept on the windowsill sitting in the sun. It was a medicine of sorts that could heal and beautify.

And today, Jeremiah noted, Margaret was taking in the medicine and breathing in new life.

They were in the meadow just beyond their farmyard and the coolness of the dew brought them both a bit of joy. Jeremiah looked at his wife and smiled at the playfulness in Margaret that he had thought might never return. And she smiled, knowing he was no longer troubled.

After they returned home, Margaret put on her shoes, went off to pick yellow primroses and buttercups, and carefully placed them on the butter churn.

"Another hope of good luck for a season of plenty," she said to Jeremiah. And plenty there would be, she thought, for she was able to save enough flour to make hasty pudding, the stirabout of flour and milk that signaled abundance for the season to come.

"There'll be more milk and cheese coming along now as the days warm. Praise be to God, there will be enough," she said aloud.

Jeremiah enjoyed the lilt in her voice and was pleased to realize that at long last the summer seemed upon them.

By tradition, May Eve was the night that the fairies changed residence, a night when mischief was bound to be at hand. It would not surprise either of them to hear that there'd been a sighting of a traveling band of fairies, or of a mermaid, or a puca—the sleek horse with sulphurous yellow eyes and a long wild mane. Jeremiah had placed a piece of iron in his pocket for protection and gave Margaret a spent cinder from the hearth for her apron, both known antidotes to the fairies and their mischief. Cautions and blessings were in abundance.

Since Father Lane had helped free her of the sound of the banshee, Margaret was able to follow the time-honored traditions that accompanied May Day. She went to the garden and gathered medicinal herbs, boiled nettles and whitethorn blossoms to provide what was known as a powerful protective potion. It would be good for her mother, who seemed more and more to mind the ever present dampness, her rheumatism becoming more of a scourge. And it could certainly help her da. His leg was getting worse each year.

She also gathered the first milk of May Day to make the All-May butter, the best base for all ointments or salves. She was glad to be able to carry on the rituals that her mother and the other women of the parish had taught her, rituals that provided comfort and solace. This was a fine May Day, and it felt like a new beginning.

She went inside and after putting the milk on the sideboard, went to the sewing basket and picked out Jeremiah's work trousers. She pulled the little pine rocker closer to the window—the light made her task easier—and began stitching Jeremiah's britches, the gray work overalls that had snagged on the fence post just yesterday as he was coming in with the cows.

She felt peace come over her as she stitched. She smiled as she remembered May Day two years ago, which in one sense felt like a hundred years ago and in another, seemed only a fortnight.

"Do ye remember me telling ye of waking on that May Day two year ago now, and slipping out to the garden to gather in a snail?" she called to Jeremiah.

Jeremiah turned from the hearth after stoking the fire into flame.

"Indeed, how can I forget the story for ye've told it time and again," he replied. "I haven't wearied of it yet. But someday I might, ye know," he said smiling. "Go on now and tell it, for I can see that ye're aiming to and it's a good thing to rehearse'and remember it."

"Then ye do remember what happened?" Margaret asked. "Me bringing the snail in and putting it on the plate? It's really grand when you think of it. Sprinkling it with flour and covering it with the cabbage-leaf. Can ye just see it, now, Jer? It's really something."

"What's something is all ye women, and what ye'll do to catch a man." Jeremiah came up beside her and laughed. "Mind ye, caught I have been."

"Ah but now, Jer," Margaret said while pulling the needle through the gray fabric, "'twas the snail that told the tale, plain as day. For after sunrise, don't ye suppose that little bit of a creature traced your letters in the flour, just as he was said to do: J. B."

"A spelling snail, ye found," Jeremiah cajoled and let his hand rest on her shoulder.

"Ah, Jer, quit with yer teasing. It's ye I found and I'm glad of it, at least most of the time."

With that, Jeremiah knelt beside her.

"Also ye found that little snail within its shell. Wasn't that to mean your lover would be rich? And isn't it rich I am for finding the likes of ye, right in me own backyard."

With this, he touched her chin and she turned her face away from the stitching, her eyes meeting his. As he leaned forward and kissed her, he recalled the tomfoolery of the snail legend, for rich he was not. Yet he didn't dash hope of it, for this Riordan land that adjoined his own was now his to manage—land that he hoped would make a fine farm for his family in the years to come.

Chapter Eleven
The Land

September 1863

Looking east over the valley, Jeremiah saw the far ridge where he would soon harvest the wheat that had grown rich and plentiful. To the west, fields of green dotted with the black and white cattle grazing gave him a deep satisfaction, yet with it, a longing. With a total of forty-six hectares to manage he missed the da more than he had thought he might, and with each passing year, more greatly appreciated the stories and wisdom the da had passed on.

One of his last conversations with Da had been about the land agitations that for so many years plagued the townland, most recently in their own parish.

"But, Da," he had protested, "they threatened the parish priest? How did they dare? Threatening the landlords I understand, but the priest?"

Jeremiah was reacting to a yet another spate of threats and agitations, their familiar patterns of sending threatening letters, maiming livestock and torching fields all too familiar. What was not so common to Jeremiah was that this time a threat had been leveled at the priest in a neighboring parish.

"Ah, Jer," the da had consoled him, "that priest isn't the first to be threatened, nor will he be the last. The times have been queer in my day and it looks to me like there'll be more like them coming in yer day."

The da recalled stories of his own parish priest who, from the altar, laid a personal curse on the land agitators.

"Jer," the da's robust voice rang out, "they say yer man the Right Reverend Father Scanlon, a short bit of a fella with a facial tic, was courageous beyond reason. He railed from the pulpit, 'Ye should know, ye men who wreak havoc on landlords and agents, the divil is in yer deeds. May God smite ye fer yer sins.'"

The da told him that soon after the Reverend Scanlon received a letter so threatening that he barricaded himself in the rectory, not attending to any church functions until a new priest was assigned to take over. "'Twas a Reverend Cornelius Buckley, a relative of ours who ultimately would baptize you," the da said with some pride.

The image of his da drawing on his pipe as he told him this tale not too many days before his death flooded Jeremiah's mind.

* * *

Jeremiah rode up to Josie's alone. The evening was clear, his mind muddled. He dismounted Macushla and moved into the pub wearily. The land question was as ancient as Ireland itself. Jeremiah had learned as much from the da and from Michael, whose book knowledge seemed to have no end. He recalled Michael's words about the land agitations.

"Outrages," Michael had called them. Tales of the disturbances grew like folklore, becoming grander and greater with each retelling.

"Horrific crimes have been committed in the name of Ireland, Jer," Michael had once told him. "Cows maimed, crops destroyed, threatening letters telling of horrible things to come if rents weren't lowered. Still the landlords don't listen and the injustices roll on."

Jeremiah sat alone in the alcove by the front door at the corner table, suddenly aware that he missed Michael as much as he missed the da. He longed to be nourished by their stories and strength. The current land agitations deeply troubled him—stories that he couldn't reconcile with his own way of viewing the world.

"After a while," he remembered Michael saying, "ye can listen no more. After a while, ye have to act." Perhaps his friend had been right.

But how? he thought, as he sipped his pint.

Word had spread throughout the parishes of the Bishop of Meath who told of seven hundred of his flock evicted in one day, cabin after cabin, decimated by the gombeen men, who acted for the landlords to do the dirty work. Winnowing sheets were placed over the sick and unconscious people as they lay in their beds while the roof was pulled down over their heads.

Michael had counseled Jeremiah to know his history, but he wondered now what good would it do. He could hear the catch in Michael's voice as he told of the Earl of Tyrone, Hugh O'Neill and Red Hugh O'Donnell who led the 1601 Battle of Kinsale.

"'Twas brave men they were, Jer, fighting, as they said in their own words, to 'free the country from the rod of tyrannical evil.'" Yet here they were, two hundred years later, with that same tyrannical evil, as the da would say, a bloody reality.

Jeremiah gazed out at the land through the open door. The sun cast a sheen on the hillside that made its green seem endless. From this doorway, he could see the land he and Michael had grown up on, land that he was now responsible for—his legacy.

He ordered another pint and continued to stare at the landscape, lands taken from Catholics by Oliver Cromwell, lands that had been stolen in a blood bath that targeted Catholic priests.

The words of the songs being sung filled him and after he finished his pint, he nodded to the fiddler and the young singer. ". . . The cause that called ye may call tomorrow." Indeed, he thought, indeed.

As he saluted the others and pushed through the door for home that Sunday evening, he let Macushla lead the way to the turn at the fork in the road, lost in thought about moving forward, and how, despite so many setbacks, as a people, the Irish indeed were going on. As he neared home, his thoughts turned to Margaret and the news they were hoping to share.

She was sitting in her rocker when he arrived, a book of poetry in her hands. The Riordan children had been well schooled.

"Well, yer just in time for a bit of verse to fill yer soul now that ye've filled your head with all the nonsense up at Fornaught. Listen to this, Jer, and tell me if we aren't blessed.

"The dew-drops sparkle, like diamonds on the corn,
Fair Hills of Eiré, O!"

Jeremiah joined Margaret by the hearth as he listened to her read the verse. The glow of the oil lamp lit her page, though it seemed she'd recited it from memory, so effortlessly it flowed from her tongue.

When she finished, he told her about his thoughts about going on despite all the trials, the history, the losses. "Isn't that what we're doing now, going on? Living each day in hope of the next," Jeremiah asked pensively.

Margaret stood, took the iron kettle from the hook over the hearth and filled it with water from the blue stenciled pitcher that stood on the sideboard.

"We had a visit tonight from Tim Healy up the way. His da has passed on this very evening. The funeral will be on Tuesday. He's asked for ye to be there."

"Ah, the suffering is ended for 'ol Brian," he said, as he watched Margaret return the pitcher to the sideboard and move the kettle over the flame.

"'Twas a long siege for poor Tim and Ellen, mind ye. It's glad I am to know it's over." He paused and then asked, "Will ye come with me on Tuesday, Margaret, or shall I go on me own?"

"Indeed, I'll come with ye. It was just this night I was thinking about what we do for one another. I suppose it's just being there. That's the whole of it. I'll be mending your dark pants for the occasion. And I'll wear me tried and true lavender dress. It's respectful for the situation and one of the few that I fancy will see me through the spring."

***

The funeral procession wound its way down the road from the church. The stately coffin, draped in a black cloth, was carried aboard the family hay wagon as the mourners walked along behind. The sun shone through the clouds briefly, a sign, many would say, of the Almighty's favor for this gentleman.

Jeremiah was one of the pallbearers and walked with other men of the parish who'd been called into service. Once they arrived at St. Joseph's Church, the men lifted the coffin, a simple pine box, and carried it down the center aisle for its final blessings. Father Lane, dressed in his black vestments, stood as the bells rang out. He elevated the Eucharist and spoke the words of the consecration: *"Hoc est enim Corpus meum"* — For this is my body.

Listening to the words of consecration, the essence of the Catholic doctrine, Jeremiah remembered that ol' Brian Healy, the man he'd known so long, had told him that during the time of the Penal Laws, he had refused to denounce the transubstantiation — the belief in the changing of the bread and wine into the body of blood of Christ — as Catholics were being required to do. Another image flooded Jeremiah's mind now as he sat with Margaret.

"Mass rocks," great flat stones out in the fields where the faithful gathered for Mass since there were no Catholic chapels to be had, outlawed as they were. He imagined the scene his ma had described of the people gathering close around the priest as he read the prayers of the holy office, while sentinels watched on every ridge, guarding the flock from the priest-hunter and the redcoat.

Old Brian, the man whose body he'd helped carry into the church, had lived through those fear-filled times. It was good now that they could openly pay tribute to him and reflect on the meaning of life itself without the old fears. Somehow, the faith had survived. Men like Brian and his da had helped preserve it. Jeremiah had been baptized into that once outlawed faith. The faith of his fathers, he thought, this Catholicism, a hard-fought faith, indeed.

As the priest intoned the closing blessing, *Ite, Missa est,* Jeremiah's mind drifted. Tomorrow he would see to the land. He would start with the wheat on the west ridge.

Chapter Twelve
The Oath

October 1863

"I, Michael Riordan, in the presence of Almighty God, do solemnly swear allegiance to the Irish Republic, now virtually established; and that I will do my very utmost, at every risk, while life lasts, to defend its independence and integrity; and finally, that I will yield implicit obedience in all things, not contrary to the law of God (or "the laws of morality"), to the commands of my superior officers. So help me God. Amen."

Michael blessed himself, touching his forehead, his chest, his left shoulder and then his right. He bowed his head and added his own silent amen.

He had said each word clearly and with deliberation, fully aware that this oath was fueling no small passion. He felt so deeply about Ireland, her potential and her right to independence that he sometimes found himself having difficulty breathing.

He looked around at comrades on every side: Billy Graney, Dennis Carroll, Tim Healy, Hugh Cogan and Paddy Murphy. Men he respected. Men who had earlier taken the oath. From this small oak-paneled room in the back of the Fornaught Pub, Michael was glad to be home for this holiday week, proud to join ranks with these men, aware that life, as he knew it, was about to change.

He emerged from the room without notice and slipped out the back door to relieve himself. He returned to a place in front along the familiar mahogany bar, signaling that he'd have a drink now.

Gerard FitzGerald, the proprietor of Josie's, served him the neat whiskey alongside the pint, a drink he ordered to celebrate this milestone. He sipped the whiskey and realized that though he had stepped across the line into a world he knew could lead him to danger, he would always be able to raise his glass in pride when they sang for Ireland.

"Ah, Michael, there ye are now," Jeremiah said as he moved beside him. "I was hoping to find ye here. I've some good news at last."

Michael forced a grin as he felt his facial muscles tighten. He couldn't tell this man of the oath, even though he was like a brother to him. After their run in Ballingary, they'd parted ways on how the freedom could best be won. Jeremiah would not risk his home and his hopes for a family for Ireland. All that he held holy, all that he held dear could be lost to him. He loved Ireland all right, but what good would come of Ireland, he argued, if there was no one left to live in Ireland?

Though Michael wished he could share the importance of this evening with Jeremiah, he respected his friend enough to allow their differences to remain unspoken.

He remembered that it was at the rising in Ballingary, when he and Jeremiah had ridden into the night, that Michael first saw men willing to die for Ireland. The battle at Mrs. McCormack's cabbage patch, that some called a failure, had ignited him. He had listened and learned from the men of Young Ireland about ways to secure freedom. He saw action as part of the hope and promise.

Now, fifteen years later, as Michael studied to take priestly vows, he had taken his own action by assenting to a vow that put him in company with a renewed rebellion, this time led by men called Fenians, whose belief was finally translating itself into action. He believed this most recent vow was as holy as those he was studying to take, for they were saving Ireland as a country. The last time they had discussed the Fenians—rebels who Michael believed were Ireland's only hope—Jeremiah had been vehement.

"Leave the fight for the single men, Michael. Leave it for the young ones who have no hope other than in the fight. Ye've your own dreams. Yer on yer way to being a priest, yer dream since boyhood. And I have mine. I have responsibility now. I've a wife and I hope to have a family of little ones running about my feet, bothering me like we bothered our own parents. A fight for Ireland?" Jeremiah asked, his breathing shallow, his face reddening, as his father's had. "I'll let me da lead me on this one. He warned me again and again of the poison found in the fight. God rest him now, I've finally begun to listen." He paused and took a swallow of stout. "Mind ye, it'd be grand for ye to listen as well. There's no good in it. No good at all."

Michael knew that there was no talking to Jeremiah on this topic. There was no persuading him. As they grew older, Jeremiah had become more certain that the political route would make the change and that violence would wreck it, and Michael, for his part, had no faith in politics, believing that action needed to be taken now, the time for talk over.

Michael had known enough two years earlier not to invite Jeremiah to go with him to the Mac Manus funeral. Jeremiah's concern for Margaret was too great and Michael knew that the outrage accompanying the ceremony would only find them divided again. The refusal of the Bishop of Cork to allow Mac Manus' body to lie in state in the cathedral of Cork had angered hundreds.

Terence Bellew Mac Manus had been at Ballingary. Michael and Jeremiah had seen him. He was one of the heroes who had been arrested, convicted and sent to Australia until he escaped and fled to San Francisco, where he lived in poverty until his death in January 1861. The American Fenians arranged to have Mac Manus' body returned to Ireland for a proper farewell after an American funeral was held. Accounts in *The Nation* told of Mac Manus' body being transported by trains across America to New York City, where Archbishop John Hughes, a proud Irish immigrant, gave a eulogy in old St. Patrick's Cathedral:

"Some of the most learned and holy men of the Church have laid it down . . . that there are cases in which it is lawful to resist and overthrow a tyrannical government. The young man . . . to whose memory and remains you pay your respects . . . was willing to sacrifice—and I may say did sacrifice—his prospects in life, and even his life itself, for the freedom of the country he loved so well, and which he knew had been oppressed for centuries."

Hundreds filled the old Cathedral, *The Nation* reported, organ music adding power to the moment. The Irish in America lauded Mac Manus and bid him a hero's farewell as they returned his body to Ireland. Fenians in both America and Ireland hoped that the pilgrimage of Mac Manus' remains would breathe much-needed life into the cause of Ireland's freedom.

Disappointment awaited them.

At the Bishop of Cork's refusal to have Mac Manus in his cathedral, talk became threatening. Michael heard of the violence that smoldered not far beneath the surface. It was only the sympathetic gesture of the neighboring Bishop of Cloyne, who allowed both a funeral and a procession, that had averted the trouble.

Michael had joined the hordes of people who lined the roadways and railways to glimpse a bit of the casket, to be a part of the movement, to feel the energy. Michael was proud to stand shoulder to shoulder with farmers and merchants, businessmen and laborers, aware that the moment was a rebirth for the cause as Mac Manus' coffin passed before his eyes, never more proud to be Irish.

* * *

While his friend seemed lost in thought, Jeremiah waited, standing tall and open, bursting to tell Michael his good news. He ordered a pint for them both, not taking note that Michael had a shot of whiskey already in place alongside his stout.

"Ah, 'tis fit to be tied I am." Jeremiah's eyes sparkled even in the dark of the pub. "I'm after telling ye what I hope will be good news for once and for all."

He hoisted his pint and beamed, "Here's to ye!"

His smile was wider than Michael had ever seen it.

"For God's sake, Jer, will ye tell me what it is ye're so wrought up about?" Michael stared into the face he knew almost as well as his own. "Why, I know I've been away a bit. But I haven't seen ye

this agitated since the mare had her foal! Jer, ye don't mean . . .?"
He thought he saw the smile on his friend's face grow even wider,
and despite himself, his voice grew louder. "Is there to be a child?
Glory be to God, man, is that it?" Michael asked as he brought his
hand down on Jeremiah's shoulder. "Is it a baby, man?"

Michael watched Jeremiah as he turned to face him, noting
that he hadn't seen his hazel eyes so lit with hope since Baby Julia's
death more than three years ago.

"There is to be a child, indeed. A child at last," Jeremiah
replied. His voice sounded full, and Michael was glad to think of
such joy coming to his friend and his sister's husband. Michael
hoisted his pint and the two men drank to the health of the yet-to-
be-born child. Each of them, as friends and brothers, on this
evening of celebration, lifted and drank from their glasses, knowing
what they each held back from the other.

Jeremiah said nothing of the "brat"—the ribboned cloth that
had been blessed on St. Brigid's day and brought to Margaret by
Cousin Julia, Ellen Cogan and Ellen Healy. It had been these
women who had hoped to heal the barrenness.

And as for Michael, he said nothing of the oath, witnessed by
the husbands of those same women—an oath that the men hoped
would heal Ireland.

Chapter Thirteen

The Family

April 1864

"He's the image of the da, wouldn't ye say so, Margaret?" said Jeremiah as he studied the boy in Margaret's arms, "He's got the da's chin with that dimple in it and when he's bawling he sounds just like 'im."

"I wouldn't know that, now, Jer. I never heard your da bawl. It's only yerself I'm listening to, carrying on."

Their eyes met and they laughed as they shared the magic of this child. Jeremiah knelt in front of them and stroked the infant.

Though it had been four years since the loss of Julia, the pain of her death took its place in the background of their days, and like the air, was ever present. They had hoped and prayed for another child and been bolstered by friends who counseled them about the Lord's mysterious ways, confident He would bless them with a child.

They had endured a spate of harrowing times with harvest after harvest failing and relentless rains that dampened everything from the clothing on their backs to the hope in their souls. They called again and again on the strength of their history which had helped them to survive the famine. They grew in their understanding of one another and as the days turned into years, they celebrated the seasons, capturing what little joy they could around the hearth. Their music and stories, shared with neighbors and family, brought them comfort and a cheering element within to counteract the dampness without.

The hope to which they clung was finally rewarded as Margaret's belly swelled with the child. As the days drew closer to the baby's birth, Jeremiah whistled about the house and Margaret sang tunes that she hadn't sung in years. Jeremiah crafted a golden

pine crib for the infant and Margaret crocheted a new blanket.
Jeremiah danced Margaret about the small cottage, hugging her
to him with tenderness. Margaret would sometimes come up
behind him as he sat at the table and kiss him on the back of the
neck. While both had endured enough to allow room for caution,
hope prevailed.

Once born, the baby's robust spirit sent a squalling throughout
the cabin that Margaret and Jeremiah thought they would never tire
of. They held hands as they watched him, his pink skin wrinkling
up as he bawled. As they comforted him, they too were comforted.

Jeremiah held the infant close to his heart, his big hands
cradling him easily. As he handed him to Margaret, he saw in her
face a peace that had been absent for so long. Her eyes glowed as
she nursed the baby as contentedly as if she'd done it all her life.

He was as handsome as babies could be, his feathery red hair
and smooth pink skin set off by brilliant blue eyes full of light. It
was the light of the tiny child that Margaret and Jeremiah lived in
now.

They celebrated lavishly when the neighbors and friends came
round for the christening, the table set with Margaret's best linens.
Ham, beef and lamb, potato, corn and oatcakes were all a part of
the feast. Poteen, the favored Irish drink, was in plenty, along with
the music. Even the clay pipes were filled.

There were tears of joy from several of the women as they
crowded round the hand-wrought wooden crib, with its special
carved dove adorning the headboard, to see the child that had
graced all their lives, for this was how they lived, together in joy as
well as sorrow.

Father Lane's smile lit the room as he called for the sponsors
of the child. William Graney, a tall, dark-haired man with bushy
eyebrows and a long-time friend and neighbor, stepped forward,
as did the recently widowed Ellen Cogan, whose chestnut hair and
trim figure belied her age.

The assembled guests joined in a circle as the priest began: "*In
nomine Patri et Filii et Spiritu Sancti. Amen.*

"And what name will you call this child?" he asked the parents.

"Timothy," they answered in unison.

The da's name, the custom for the firstborn male.

Father Lane's eyes were focused as he poured water over the infant's scalp and intoned the name. With that, the baby let out a grand squawk and the assembled crowd giggled. As the sign of the cross was traced in oil on his forehead, Timothy squirmed, further testimony, his father proclaimed, of his independent spirit.

"He'll be one to keep yer eye on, that's certain," Jeremiah said proudly.

As the ceremony ended, Cousin Julia and her brother Michael exchanged a glance, each happy to have a new memory to replace the sorrowful one of the last "baptism" in this house.

A fiddle broke into the murmuring that followed the baptism, and after a few reels, Godmother Ellen gave "The Rose of Tralee," sweet and soothing. She reached out for William as she sang, and the two danced around the tiny cradle.

It was time for celebration, time indeed.

Chapter Fourteen

The Rising

February 1867

"It's for Ireland." Michael's face glowed as he spoke. "Ye know it's what we've dreamed of since we were boys, Jer. It's finally here."

Jeremiah stilled his horse and eyed the man before him. Michael's earth-brown hair, darkening as he grew older, was brushed back off his forehead, hazel eyes alive and shining. His cap was tilted at the same angle he'd worn it since he was a boy. Jeremiah listened and looked into the face, but could barely believe what he was hearing. Michael, now a priest, a servant of Christ, was talking about revolution as naturally as if it were blessed by God.

"Ye're a priest now, Michael. Jaysus, man, ye're ordained," Jeremiah said, aware of how much he sounded like his father. "Ye don't mean to tell me ye've signed on. Ye can't mean this, man! Ye're half daft."

Jeremiah shook Macushla's reins and rode ahead to a rise and gazed out over the hillside. His arms were tense as he slowed the mare. His eyes locked onto the hedgerow. The jumble of deep green vines and the brown branches mirrored his confused feelings. There was a danger in Michael that Jeremiah couldn't fathom. What led his closest friend to this madness, this insanity? What led him to believe that a small group of men, armed with pikes and a few rifles, could stand against the constabulary any better now than they did almost twenty years ago in '48?

Michael rode up alongside Jeremiah. He spoke gently, his hands fiddling with the reins.

"I'm not daft enough to ask ye to join me. I know better," Michael said as he looked sideways at Jeremiah. "I know ye've children, like my own they are. And my very sister, whom I love with my life, is in yer care. I'm not asking ye to risk anything of yerself. I wouldn't be wanting that for a hundred thousand pounds."

Michael paused as he sat back in his saddle. He drew in a deep breath and then searched Jeremiah's face. "What I'm asking is that ye understand; understand that until I've seen this through, there'll be no peace within me. I've made a pledge, man, and I'll not go back on it. Priest or no priest, I'll not go back on me word. Can ye hear that, now? Can ye?"

Jeremiah swallowed hard. This man had held him like a captive since their childhood with his words, his logic and his passion. Understand him, he did. He understood him from the time they were school chums and Michael had told him of his dream to be a priest, his dream to serve in the church. He watched him as they served as altar boys together, his eyes aglow in the early morning hour, when Jeremiah still felt the sleep in his own.

Jeremiah had watched Michael as he took over the work when his da's crippled leg kept him from offering any substantial help. Michael never complained. He simply shrugged and smiled when Jeremiah asked if it was too much.

"Ah Jer, the Lord fits the back to the burden. I'm young and strong and able, not like ye, ye slender runt."

Michael was a big man, and though Jeremiah stood almost six feet, Michael was broader. He didn't look at all like his sister with her rich red hair. Rather, he favored his mother's coloring, and not unlike Jeremiah at one time, had rich chestnut highlights in his dark hair. They'd been mistaken for brothers more than once. And after he'd married Margaret, Michael had been a brother and an uncle to his own children.

Jeremiah knew Michael to be a hard worker, swinging from his stallion like he'd been born to ride, threshing the wheat with the agility of ten men, often staying at it well into the twilight.

It had been twenty years since they had ridden together to Ballingary and twenty years since Michael had led the men to sign the petition that saved Smith O'Brien's head. And after that, they'd both watched Ireland settle down, the intense hope of independence for the time being muted. Somehow, they'd gotten on. Michael had finally received his tuition money and went off to Maynooth to pursue his dream of priesthood. It wasn't too much after that Jeremiah's dream of a family became a reality, first with Tims and nineteen months later, Mary, this second girl named after Jeremiah's mother, as custom called for.

Michael shared in the joys of these children, each of his visits lasting longer. The cabin filled with squeals of delight when the children saw him. Tims would run to him and Michael would scoop him up into his arms, proclaiming how much he'd grown and then sit him high upon his head. He was gentler by far with two-year-old Mary, waltzing her about the room and whistling tunes as he did. He was their delight, and they his. They'd both achieved their dreams, so why would Michael risk it all now?

Jeremiah turned to Michael, his jaw firm. "I hear ye man, I hear ye. And do ye know what I hear? I hear a man whose half daft with a vision for Ireland that's not coming into focus. A picture that's for dreamers alone. I hear a man who's throwing away his lifelong dream, as if his priesthood isn't enough, a man whose passion hasn't found release."

The two horses, Michael's taller by a hand than Jeremiah's, their riders looking straight ahead, stood side by side overlooking the hillside, the hues of browns and greens quietly subdued. Michael stroked the mane of Your Grace and continued to stare off into the distance. After a long silence, he spoke.

"There's something else I haven't told ye, Jer. I haven't told anyone. And I'll ask ye to mind this, 'til I do." Michael held Jeremiah's gaze, his eyes moist, his voice strong. "I'm off for America. Just after this, I'm sailing for a new parish. I'm being assigned to go. I had a choice and I said yes. I sail the first of May."

Jeremiah felt a wrenching in his chest. He could barely take in the words. He could argue with Michael about his politics, about his intensity. But Michael to America? Michael away from Ahadallane, Michael gone from home? He had no words. He gave a tug to Macushla's reins, turned around and looked at Michael.

He saw the same eager, comic, intelligent friend he'd known more than thirty years.

"All's I can say for now is yer secrets are safe with me," his eyes looking away, his heart pounding, his fist clenched. With that, he rode toward home.

***

Michael stood a long moment watching Jeremiah ride through the hills. He'd seen fear in Jeremiah's eyes and felt it himself sometimes. He knew that Jeremiah's attempts to get him to retreat from this rebellion came from love. But he'd made up his mind, and wouldn't be dissuaded. Just a year after he'd taken the oath, he had read the outspoken and powerful Archbishop Cullen's words, calling Fenians "the worst enemies of Ireland and its ancient faith."

That was it, Michael thought. Ancient faith was one of the problems. Living, breathing people needed a modern faith that made sense to them, a faith that allowed them to think. One of the troubles with Ireland was this love of the past. There was a future for Ireland, a free Ireland, and he would do what he could to help make it so.

Michael remembered Archbishop Cullen, with his austere bearing and red robes, who had described Fenians as "sordid" people whose goal was to "preach up" socialism, to seize on the property of those who had any, and to exterminate both the country gentry and the Catholic clergy. His directive within his pastoral letter was issued to remind the flocks that anyone joining such a society would incur instant ex-communication.

Strong words, but Michael didn't worry. The Archbishop was not the Almighty. He knew that the God he worshiped would have no end of mercy for those who won the freedom for Ireland and he hoped this mission would prove that.

But even with his certainty, a heavy feeling, like wet sod, overcame Michael as Jeremiah rode off. He thought of Jeremiah's da saying that the anger was poison. Michael could see others in whom the anger had taken over even as they marched weekly in precise formations, part of the secret circle he drilled with at night when he was able to sneak away, their rigorous rehearsals building bonds, some boots pounding harder onto the ground than needed. He'd also listened to penitents who in his short time of hearing confessions had broken the seventh commandment time and again, stealing weapons and materials to prepare for this rising. Their tone was far from remorseful. Michael was determined not to let the anger devour his spirit. He would act only enough to help the cause. He would act only enough to honor his word.

* * *

March 5, 1867

Michael arrived at the hillside above Donoughmore Cross at ten-thirty at night, the appointed time. Snow had been falling steadily for several hours.

"It's grand to see ye here, Father Michael," Dennis Carroll said. "Not that we doubted ye, but just the same. Ye never know these days."

Trust was the key to the work of these men who had pledged an oath in a secret society. Michael knew there was nary a black-guard among them, though some might not show up if there was trouble getting away or any danger of being followed. They were farmers' sons, men of the land, shopkeepers and merchants, men who worked hard, went to church and wanted only freedom for their homeland.

"We're all here indeed with a better turnout than we thought," Dennis said as he pulled his wool jacket closer around himself. "This weather is doing us no favors. Have ye no special influence from above to shape the clouds, now, Father Michael?" Dennis asked playfully. This late blizzard was unusual and one of the worst in memory.

"It's just another test of our courage and belief," Michael replied with a wink. "And sure, we're up to it!"

Fits and starts over the past several years as to when the risings would take place had been frustrating and demoralizing. James

Stephens, the founder of the Irish Republican Brotherhood in Ireland, and known by his detractors as "Little Baldy," had finally been deposed by the organization, for his endless delays, his leadership no longer respected despite the fact he had once been a well-regarded veteran of the Young Ireland Ballingary Rising of '48. His long relationship with John O'Mahoney, founder of the Fenian Brotherhood, the companion organization in America named in honor of a mythical band of Gaelic warriors, the Fianna, did little now to help his status.

Thomas Kelly, a recently returned former Union colonel in the American Civil War, replaced Stephens in Ireland and ultimately made the decision to launch the Irish rebellion on March 5. The military tactic was to capture police barracks and their weapons throughout the country, disrupt rail transportation and cut telegraph lines, and have a general harassing effect on government movement so that the army of the republic would be recognized. The excitement and release that came with the decision to finally act was palpable.

While Stephens had lost credibility for his leadership, his organizational skills were brilliant, the system to maintain secrecy intricately designed. Yet despite such caution, spies were everywhere and had served to weaken the resolve of the men. No one knew whom to trust. There were even informers among the priests. The British Secret Service had bought their way into the Fenian movement both in Ireland and in America.

Dennis reminded Michael that it had only been a little more than a year since the organization had first been compromised.

"Sure, 'twas that wart of a man Nagle who helped give over Stephens for arrest. Wasn't he one and the same that caused the seizure of the *Irish People* newspaper? May he burn in hell."

"That's for God to judge, now, Dennis."

"Ah yes, Father Michael, and also we're to remember whatever ye say, say nothing, when ye talk about ye know what. Ye never know who's to be trusted. That's what's certain," Dennis said furtively. The fear and rumors were as rampant as the discontent.

Despite these setbacks, plans for the rising went forward, and finally, after seven long years of waiting and praying, Michael stood among his countrymen, who despite any blizzard, were all eager to act.

* * *

Dennis called the men to order and within seconds they stood at attention, in organized rows, their pikes and rifles glistening in proper position. They were a ragtag bunch, in dark wool coats and caps, some with dark hand-knit scarves. The young men, many of them boys with whiskers barely starting, stood shoulder to shoulder with men as old as their fathers. Some came with their fathers' blessings; others, their spirit of patriotism burning for expression, had stolen away in the night.

"Men, the night isn't one we'd have chosen, but as our own Father Michael says, 'We're up to it.'" Dennis's tenor voice cut through the rows of men, before he turned to Michael: "Would ye lead us now in a prayer, Father?"

Michael stepped forward and blessed himself. And as he moved his fingers first to his forehead, then chest, the seventy assembled men joined him in word and action. "In the name of the Father, and of the Son and of the Holy Ghost."

As the men responded with "Amen," Michael felt a shiver and pulled his black wool coat tighter around him. "We come before the Almighty and beseech yer blessing as we stand in unity and faith, begging that ye look with mercy on the work we know we must do for Ireland's freedom. We ask the intercession of the Blessed Virgin Mary, and the communion of Saints. Amen."

He stepped back and listened as Dennis shared the plan.

"Men, ye're about to put our much discussed plan into action and disrupt the communications of Ireland. We've comrades all across this nation depending on us to stop the Dublin-Cork train from arriving on time. We'll stop it just after it leaves Mallow. I trust ye men, and I trust that ye'll follow orders and watch out for one another." Dennis paused and cleared his throat. He looked

over at Michael, whose eyes were fixed on him, and then continued. "Disperse to yer homes as soon as yer task is done. We've
made an oath. Now let's put it into action. God save Ireland."

* * *

"The rails are gone," the conductor shouted to his assistant as he
felt the first crunch of the engine against the gravel and saw the
evidence of tampering as far as he could see up the tracks.

"Brakes! Brakes!" the usually quiet engineer cried out. The terror in his voice rang throughout the engine and cars as brakemen
worked feverishly to force the metal rods into position. Within
minutes, cars were bounced and tossed as the Dublin-Cork train
ground to a stop. The engineer and conductor stepped from the
engine to see what had caused the break in the rails. Passengers,
confused and jostled, emerged behind them into the numbing
cold.

Upon inspection, it was evident to the trainmen that this was
a deliberate derailment. The rails had been pulled out and lay
askew for as far as the men could see.

"It's them that's done this," the conductor muttered to the engi
neer, his voice a growl, his cheeks red with fury. Several passengers
who overheard looked at him, fear in their eyes. "Mark me words,"
he continued. "It's them Fenians. They said it was coming and now
here we are." His deep-set eyes were filled with rage. The engineer,
a small man with wire-framed glasses and thin lips, surveyed the
damage of torn tracks, and returned to the engine, leaving the conductor to deal with the passengers.

People murmured and cursed. The fierce and blinding snow
made it difficult to see. The conductor, a short, stocky man with a
stubby mustache, urged them to get back on the train.

A young mother, wrapped in a dark green cape with an infant
held securely in one arm and another child whose hand she held
firmly, burst into tears. "I'll not risk the lives of me children for this
nonsense. Ye must do something, ye must! We'll all freeze to death
if we're not killed first." The unusual blizzard happening this late

in the season added to the fear and frenzy. The conductor tried to quiet her with a hand to her shoulder and a more soothing voice. Others huddled around to hear what he was saying. A silver-haired gentleman in a black overcoat and a woman with a fur bonnet and matching fur collar on her coat approached the conductor.

"If you'll pardon the intrusion, sir, we're due in to the next station where we're to be picked up and taken to hospital." His face was furrowed with concern. "My wife isn't well, ye see. Isn't there something ye can do, please?"

The conductor looked at the shivering woman, who appeared ghostlike in her pallor.

"We'll do the best we can, sir, I assure ye, the best we can. Now all of ye, will ye help out now by going back into the train? Keep the doors shut and do all ye can to keep warm." He didn't voice his own fear of running out of fuel if they were to keep the engine fired up too long.

"We'll need some able-bodied men to help fix the rails. And a few others to go back to Mallow."

The passengers shuffled back to the train. Curses and prayers could be heard as they re-boarded the stilled cars.

"Them that's done this don't know nothing about Ireland. They'll pay for this, they will," the conductor heard one of the passengers say.

From the hedgerow, a handful of the Fenians listened, Michael among them. There were dozens of them scattered along either side of the pulled-up tracks, listening to the mayhem. A young lad, no more than eighteen, grinned and whispered to Michael, "Just what we had hoped for. The train won't make it. Them police in Cork won't be the wiser 'til morning."

A band of nine newly volunteered passengers armed with picks and sledgehammers walked in front of the engine, the conductor in the lead. Two of the men hiked down the track to retrieve some of the rails from snow that had piled on top of them. Another four men, bundled in borrowed hats and scarves, stood ready to begin the ten-mile trek to Mallow.

"Mind ye, tell them we've been caught by them that thinks they're saving Ireland," the conductor called after them. "If we don't freeze to death, we'll show 'em what they're saving. God be with ye."

As the conductor turned back, six men emerged from the hedgerow across from Michael, two with rifles pointing, another with a pike who stood behind the man who spoke.

"We wouldn't advise ye to do any fixing or go off anywhere jest yet. If ye'd kindly get back in the warmth of the train, ye'll find things to be fine by morning. Be good lads, now, so there's nobody hurt. It's all fer Ireland, ye know."

Michael's group remained within the hedgerow. He was unfamiliar with the speaker but he liked his manner.

With a streak of movement, a sledgehammer careened its way toward the six men, barely missing them. One of the young Fenian lads rushed forward toward the "engine" men, pistol pointed. The Fenian speaker pulled him back.

"Now, boy-o, that's jest what we're talking about. These folks have been inconvenienced by our tactics and they've every right to be angry. Back up now and we'll see that no one gets hurt." The young one retreated into the hedgerow.

The speaker picked up the sledgehammer, walked toward the conductor, and handed it to him.

"I suspect ye'll be needing this for later on. We'll ask ye again to move back onto the train cars. We'll stand watch for ye so nothing more happens."

The conductor eyed the six men and then turned to his own small band. "Do what he says, boys, or we'll have no peace ever in Ireland."

The men grumbled and cursed but disbanded. The small group of Fenian men receded into the hedgerow.

Michael knelt in his hiding place and blessed himself with a silent *Deo Gratias*.

Chapter Fifteen

Erin's Hope

Spring 1867

Jeremiah stood up straight as he stepped into the cabin. Last season he had finally re-framed the doorway to accommodate his height. As he moved into the newly added hallway, he saw evidence of his little ones: Mary's dolly lying on the bench and Timothy's favorite ball peeking out from underneath. He felt a swelling of love in his chest as he thought of them. Even their squabbling didn't turn him from his delight. "If ye were blind and deaf," Margaret had said often, "ye couldn't be any more oblivious to their shenanigans," her pleasure evident at his open affection for them. "But if ye leave it to me to be the only one to scold them," she cautioned, "one day they'll not mind ye at all. Mark me words."

As he watched Mary dance about or play in the garden with not a care in the world, his sister Eliza often came to mind. Mary's dainty gestures—a wave of her hand and her delicate features— petite nose and rose-tinged lips—all reminded him of her. His memory of taking her lifeless body from his da and burying it on the hillside was with him still. In delighting in his daughter, Jeremiah felt he was delighting in Eliza, and doing honor to her memory. Even Mary's hair had the same strawberry cast when the sunlight caught it.

Jeremiah stepped inside to see Margaret fussing over Tims, as he was called now. It seemed he had made yet another mess of himself, his shirt covered in mud.

"Shall I put ye out with the pigs, is that it? Would ye like to play in their mud all the day?" she said as she pulled his shirt over his head and hugged him to her. He was still favoring the Buckleys in his looks, his red hair becoming thicker as he grew. He was walking and talking up a storm, with a comment on most everything.

As he spotted Jeremiah, he broke loose from Margaret and ran to him. "It's a little piggy Ma says I'm to be. Am I a little piggy, Da?"

Jeremiah bent down to meet him.

"I'd say yer a little boy who's one day going to be a grand farmer, never fearing the dirt," he said, kneeling to embrace him. "That's what I'd say ye are."

He picked him up and tossed him in the air and the sound of Tims' delight filled the cabin. As he handed him back to Margaret, Jeremiah kissed her on the cheek. Then he spotted Mary sitting on the floor in the corner with a picture book. She looked up at him and pointed to her picture book. "Horty, Horty," she exclaimed, and Jeremiah picked her up and pulled her onto his lap. His legs tapped out the rhythm of the "horty" as she bounced on his knee, giggling in childlike joy.

"This is the way the ladies ride, bumpety, bumpety, bump," he sang as he gently jostled her. He found himself laughing aloud at Mary's joy.

"Was there any word from him?" Margaret asked as she continued to clean the mud from Tims, scrubbing his hands with a wash rag. "It's six weeks without a word."

"I talked to Paddy Murphy and he says the mails are even slower now, what with everything being watched. He doesn't think Michael can risk a letter home, not yet at least," Jeremiah replied as he put Mary back on the floor.

Margaret finished washing Tims, put a clean red striped shirt and blue trousers on him, stood him up, gave him a pat and sent him on his way.

She moved to the sideboard and started shelling the peas while Jeremiah stoked the embers to keep the turf sizzling. It had been a damp day and the warmth was comforting.

"There's more news from the *Times*," Jeremiah said as he began to fuss with the kettle. "They're saying that the Yanks' ship *Erin's Hope* arrived in Waterford Harbor filled with weapons and supplies. The police greeted it and took all on board into custody, ordering all the supplies to be impounded."

"Whatever were they thinking, sailing into the harbor like that?" Margaret asked as she filled a pot with the small green peas.

"It gets worse, I'm afraid," Jeremiah said as he paced around the room. "A mob of eight thousand was on hand and attacked the police. One man was killed and thirty-eight police wounded."

Margaret sighed. "Glory be to God, I hate hearing of these awful goings-on."

"What's more," Jeremiah continued as stood at the hearth, "Paddy told me that Corydon, the informer, who with Nagle saw that Stephens and the lot of them were arrested last year, was stoned in the streets. Word is that the police blackmailed him into service for they knew him to be homosexual."

Margaret shot him a glance and then looked at the children.

"Ah," she said aloud, "they may as well know the truth about this country of ours. They have to grow up in it, now don't they?" She put the filled pot of peas aside and turned to the potatoes.

"But I suppose they needn't grow up too fast. God willing, maybe we'll have sorted things out for their generation."

Jeremiah picked up his pipe from the mantel. "Yer hopefulness is indeed something to hold onto," he said as he glanced at her and pulled the small bag of tobacco from the shelf, dipped the pipe in and filled the bowl of it.

"I'm sorry to say there's more to the story," he continued as he tamped the tobacco down with his thumb. "All the while they were stoning the police, the crowd was calling out 'Hurrah for the Fenians, hurrah for the Fenians.'"

He gave an audible sigh, picked up a twig and lit it from an ember, held it to the pipe and sucked until the tobacco was lit. "What troubles me so, Margaret, what shakes me soul, is that not one good thing has come of any of this."

He put down his pipe, picked up the poker and jabbed at the fire. "And on top of it, Michael has gone from us to America. It vexes me so."

Margaret didn't respond for she knew Jeremiah was inconsolable about this issue. Essentially, the rising appeared to be a failure. Torn-up railways, telegraph lines that needed repair, and a further insistence from the English press that the Irish were worthless was all there was to show for it. She understood Jeremiah's distress.

When he came to her in bed later that evening, she comforted him as best she could, knowing there was part of him that wished he could have gone to the rising with Michael, a part of him that wished he could let go of all reason and become an active part of the fight for Ireland. Despite knowing his desire, she had no fear of his ever going off for the fight, for she knew that reason was more forceful within him than any violent means to an end. She knew he would never risk his family, not even for Ireland.

***

Hand-to-hand combat was never the intention of the recent Fenian rising. The goal had been to get the attention of the government by destroying rail and telegraph communications and attacking police barracks to secure more weapons. While there was much to admire about the Fenian organization, there was also much to worry about; it was fraught with disputes among the members (O'Mahoney and Stephens being a fine example), false starts, leadership issues and betrayals from within. Yet, despite all this factiousness, Jeremiah and many others with whom he spoke couldn't help but admire the dedication and persistence that drove the men who were risking so much. These were the men who would be known in books and ballads, for generations to come, as "the Bold Fenian Men."

Jeremiah had never mentioned to Michael his discovery of the weapons buried in the hillside, nor had he said a word to anyone but Margaret about Michael's involvement in the rising. Her distress matched his, as did her love of Michael. Once the rising was over, it had been two days before they were certain that Michael was all right and then within two months he was gone, headed for America, to a parish in New York City, with apparently no one the wiser about his participation.

Jeremiah remained ambivalent about the Fenian tactics. While the list of injustices that needed to be addressed grew daily

—outrageous rents and evictions topping the list—he couldn't accept that armed rebellion was the way. Over the years he'd learned not to look to Queen Victoria for any hope. Her first visit in '49, just a little more than a year after the Ballingary rising, did little to quell hostility.

The Queen's visit that August had been arranged by Lord Clarendon, the Lieutenant of Ireland, just after the worst of the famine. Word came to the people that the Queen had renamed the port of Cobh, Queenstown, "in honour of it being the first spot on which I set foot upon Irish ground."

Despite her long absence, Irish warmth and loyalty greeted her, with thousands lined from Dublin Square to Phoenix Park, cheering and waving handkerchiefs and hats of reds, blues, greens and golds jubilantly on high. The disappointment was that the Queen did little to acknowledge such loyalty. While her personal donation of two thousand pounds sterling had seemed generous to some, others faulted her repeated refusals to establish a royal residence in Ireland, some suspecting, with just cause, she feared the Fenians.

Unsure as he was these days of the current militant approach, Jeremiah was glad that someone was doing something. While freeing Ireland from the Act of Union and achieving Home Rule were both important political goals, Jeremiah found himself with less and less energy to give to them.

The struggle to keep the farm prosperous, provide enough for Margaret and the children, and pay the rent kept the litany of Ireland's grievances removed from his day-to-day affairs. For now, he thought, rebellions and risings were better left to those who had notions of grandeur and freedom in their heads. His growing family was far more compelling and satisfying.

* * *

Spring 1868

"She's a beauty, Margaret, a beauty. She looks like ye already, her face wrinkled up in a whimper," Jeremiah teased.

"Ah, go on with ye. She's the image of ye with a gab wide open and making no sense," Margaret retorted as she looked down at this newest child, born just a day after the feast of St. Patrick. Such a blessing.

They would call her Julia, a chance again to honor Margaret's mother. Eight years had passed since the birth of their first Julia, this newborn child well on her way to a healthy beginning.

She was a beautiful child with eyes like the sage of the fields. She had the same wispy hair that Tims had at birth but hers was a new-potato blonde.

Margaret and Jeremiah spoke very little of their firstborn Baby Julia. The sorrow that had held them for so long had at last abated, healed by Tims and Mary who had been born within twenty months of each other. Faith, traditions and rituals also encouraged healing. Margaret saw to it that prayers were said regularly, that the "old ways" were respected and that celebrations were held. This fourth child, born twenty-eight months after Mary, was hale and hearty. The time for rejoicing had surely arrived.

**

Jeremiah sat in Macushla's saddle and gazed out at land that stretched over the horizon and seemed to meet the sky. He worried, as he looked across the hectares, about how he could keep up with it all. Da Riordan was ailing more and more, most likely wouldn't last the winter. The children were far too young to be of any assistance.

Though they couldn't afford much, Jeremiah had come to Margaret with a plan to hire Eugene Cronin to help with at least the haying and the harvest. Jeremiah could keep up with the cattle and Margaret had kept the chickens and pigs all right, especially now that he had built a hen house and sturdy pen. She'd agreed with him.

He turned Macushla toward the high hill and rode toward the Cronins. He hoped his offer would be seen as the plea for help that it was and nothing more. Eugene's bad turn of fortune after the famine hadn't reversed itself. A neighboring farmer had squeezed Eugene out of what little land he rented as a cottier. Eugene had confided in Jeremiah that he was just barely able to pay the rent. Jeremiah hoped that Eugene would be willing to lend a hand, for the pittance he could offer.

As he crested the hill and looked down the valley, the scene below gave him a physical jolt. He felt his stomach turn and his fists clench. On the hillside that had once been dotted with cabins and neat rows of potato, he saw now only a broad expanse of pastureland. Hundreds of evictions had cleared the land of tenants no longer able to pay the exorbitant rents demanded. Many had gone to poorhouses, or if they were lucky enough to get passage, to Liverpool or America. Large numbers of speculating British farmers bought up huge tracts of land, drained them, often inhumanely clearing them of tenants, and readied them for pastureland. Dairying was the wave of the future.

Jeremiah had gone along with the wave, and with Mr. Bennett's approval, he'd made a partial switch from tillage farming to grazing and dairying. Fortunately, it proved to be more prosperous lately since there was an upward swing in the prices of cattle and butter. He had also taken care to maintain his barley: the price actually increased, despite the success of Father Matthew's temperance movement and the dramatic population decline, with the recent merger of several city distilleries including Murphy's of Midleton that formed the new Cork Distilleries Company.

He rode through the small gate that marked the Cronins' boundary. In their early years of marriage, Margaret and Jeremiah has spent many a pleasant evening with Ellen and Eugene playing cards, talking and singing a song or two. The Cronins had three small children and Ellen was pregnant, due next month. Despite the promise of new life, there was sadness about this family. It seemed to Jeremiah they were always just one step ahead of disaster, this time being no different. As he approached, he was hoping that this was the right thing to do.

"There ye are, Eugene," Jeremiah offered as he dismounted Macushla and lashed her reins to the fence post.

Eugene stepped into the yard, pipe set in his teeth, hands in his pockets. His gray overalls were in need of mending and he seemed to stoop a bit more than Jeremiah remembered. He hadn't seen the Cronins since Julia's birth in March and here it was already July.

Eugene took the pipe from his mouth and slipped it in his pocket. "What brings ye this way, Jeremiah? It's been a long while since we've seen ye. Is everything all right with Margaret and the children?"

"Ah, things are fine with them. I'll tell ye, I'm half daft with the goings-on. But ye know I wouldn't trade it," Jeremiah replied, as he took off his tweed cap and held it.

"I've come to ask ye something and I'll be pleased if ye say aye but want nothing but an honest reply, now. Will ye give me that, Eugene?"

Eugene eyed him. He was a bit taller than Jeremiah, his gentle face now curious. "Was there ever a time I wasn't straight with ye? And why would it be any different now? What are ye up to there, Jeremiah?"

Jeremiah saw the kindness in Eugene's face and remembered why he'd decided to ask this man for help. There wasn't an ounce of malice in him.

"I'm after asking if ye can give me a hand on the land. I'm lost now with so much to work; even after turning almost half of it to grazing, I'm still working long days and finding little or no time for anything else."

He twisted the cap in his hand as he continued. "I can pay ye nine shillings a week if ye'll say yes. It'll be a grand help if ye can do it. A grand help."

Jeremiah waited, taking a step to the side, considering what he would do if Eugene rejected his offer.

Eugene moved toward him, his gray eyes shining and open. "Ye've got me, Jeremiah, ye've got me. I can see yer need what with Michael gone and his da lame. And I don't mind saying, nine shillings is a fair offer. Until something else comes along, 'tis an offer I'll be all right with. When do ye want me to start?"

"Ah, Eugene," Jeremiah said as he moved toward his fair-haired friend and clasped his shoulder. "'Tis grand indeed. Ye've brought great relief to me. If ye can start right away, I'd be the happier for it."

He released his grasp on Eugene's shoulder and continued, "If ye can meet up with me first thing tomorrow, I'll be showing ye what I'm hoping to do. It's a rare find to have one with yer strength and good sense coming on board," Jeremiah added.

"Ah, now don't go laying it on too thick for I might have to change me mind. I thought we'd be dealing in the barnyard with all that stuff," Eugene said playfully.

The two men shook hands and Jeremiah unlashed Macushla's reins and mounted her. He saluted Eugene and as he rode from the yard, felt a great weight lifted from his shoulders.

Chapter Sixteen

Michael's Letter

July–December 1868

As Margaret nursed little Julia and felt the warmth in her arms, she thought of Michael, whose letter was on the table, awaiting Jeremiah. She missed her brother greatly, his playful spirit especially. He'd always been the one who could lighten her heart, seeing the humor in life, and finding the good in most things.

"Do ye remember auld Mrs. Sheehy?" he'd once asked her when they were kids. "Did ye know she's got two cats in her house that can talk? She swears to it. I've heard them meself. If ye listen carefully, ye can hear them. One says 'me' and the other 'ow,'" he'd end with a chortle.

Margaret felt a smile come to her as she thought of Michael's crazy "goings-on." He could make fun out of anything, that one.

She found in the days since he'd gone, already a year now, that she cared so much more for him than for his cause. It wasn't that she didn't care for Ireland. It was that she cared little for the politics or the things men did to create troubles. She knew well enough that the English held the power, but she wondered what was wrong with that. Surely, the English weren't all out to kill the Irish. Surely, some of the troubles could be averted if there were someone in office with a bit of sense and reason. From what Jeremiah told her of the new Prime Minister Gladstone, it seemed there was finally some turn in the politics of the day. And wasn't the church right in the thick of it, reading letters from the pulpit telling the faithful which party to support?

She was glad to see Jeremiah come through the door. He wore the newly mended green plaid shirt and his new pair of black suspenders. He'd be delighted with the letter from Michael. The missives that came about once a month were a bright spot for him.

Michael's wit and intelligence shone through in his "epistles," as he called them. Jeremiah nodded as he entered and went to the sideboard. He put the basin and pitcher in place and washed himself, a habit she'd grown to appreciate.

She looked down at this littlest child at her breast, the feel of whom brought a swelling to her heart. While she was worried for the health of the children, these days finally seemed far enough removed from the starvation she'd known as a child. The difficult harvests in the early sixties before Tims was born had put her in mind again of the Hunger, but even those days seemed over at last.

Margaret prayed the rosary each evening after the children were asleep, thanking the Almighty for the blessings bestowed upon her. She knew some might describe her as devout beyond reason, but she didn't mind. Her gratitude for the release from a fear beyond reason by the simple blessing Father Lane offered from the church was something she'd carry with her always.

She kept her place in the rocker, waiting for Jeremiah to spot the letter. With Tims and Mary down for their naps, Jeremiah quietly went about finding himself some noontime tea and a bit of biscuit.

"'Tis a fine day we're having today, wouldn't ye say?" she offered in hope of bringing his glance round to the table. The day was one that held no threat of rain, a sky dotted with puffy white clouds pushed about by a soft breeze. She'd been out earlier to hang the sheets and linens in the wonderful clear air.

He grunted something and then turned to her. "I've just put Macushla down." His voice was soft and he stood still as he spoke, his hand on the teapot, his eyes looking out the window toward the pasture. Margaret gasped and held her breath. For as long as she could recall, Macushla had been Jer's faithful companion. "She lost her footing out on the back acreage and couldn't get up. Her leg broke right out from under her. I had to leave her there to come get the gun. I found Eugene and we went to her together. We'll be carrying her back this afternoon as soon as we can hitch up the wagon."

He brought his tea and biscuit to the table and sat, still gazing out the window as if looking out to see Macushla in the yard. His silence filled the room. Margaret pulled the dozing child from her breast and laid her in the cradle under the window. She went to Jeremiah, stood behind him and stroked his hair.

* * *

It wasn't until after dinner that Jeremiah discovered the letter. Margaret had put it up on the shelf over the hearth, knowing that when the time was right, he would find it.

"Ah, Margaret, ye've read this, have ye?" he asked, as he opened the pages. She'd been in school for more years than he had and with Michael's help, was one of few women of her town who had learned to read remarkably well.

Jeremiah took the letter to the table and poured them both a cup of tea.

"I was after worrying a bit; there'd been such a long time since his last letter. What with the news of yer da's death and word that we'd be bringing yer ma home to be with us, I had a notion he might come home. I wonder if he has any thought of what should become of the house."

Michael Riordan Senior had died a year after Michael left for America. There'd been no fast way to notify Michael, the letter carrying the news of his father's death actually crossing in the mail with one Michael had sent that told of a special ointment for the da's leg, which he'd learned of from a doctor who was one of his parishioners. He had promised to send it soon, certain it would bring some relief.

Da Riordan's death wasn't unexpected. His pain had intensified as his stamina declined. Michael had been visibly agitated as he prepared to leave for Queenstown, where he would take the ship to Liverpool and on to America. It was Margaret who sensed what was troubling him.

"Is it Ma yer worrying after? After the da passes? Ye needn't be minding. Sure Jer and I will have her with us when the time is right. She'll be a help with the little ones. Ye needn't bother yer head now. Just remember to be about the Lord's work and offer yer Masses for her intentions. That'll please her more than anything else."

Margaret knew her brother well. The two of them had shouldered the weight of the family since their youth. The deaths of Johnny Joe and Bridget had given them a sensitivity to each other, aware of their importance as the remaining children.

"Will ye listen to this now?" Jeremiah called to Margaret, who had left the table and begun to wash the dishes. "Michael's still worrying for Ireland and says that there's been agitation from Yanks against the Brits in Canada. Imagine it. All that way across the sea, they're still after worrying for poor ol' Ireland.

"Sure, he's taking the death of the da like I might have expected, offering Masses each day this month for the repose of his soul. And he's sent word to young Father John to remember him, too."

Margaret smiled to hear their cousin Johnny Joe referred to as Father John, though his seminary days were just beginning. John Joseph Riordan was the only son of Uncle Eugene, who had emigrated just after the first of the famine. The da seldom spoke of Eugene and there had been very little contact. They did however receive word of Johnny Joe's birth, happy that he'd been named for their deceased brother.

"It's grand, so, that young Johnny Joe is attending the Troy seminary, isn't it Margaret?" Jeremiah asked. "And he'll have Michael to watch out for him as he can. Yer Uncle Eugene would have been mighty pleased about that if he were still alive."

Jeremiah folded the letter, placed it back on the stone ledge above the hearth, pulled his pipe from the shelf and lit it, drawing in the taste of the tobacco with great satisfaction.

Margaret watched him, wondering how much of the longing to be a part of the fight still lingered. Even though he spoke against it, since Michael had left he seemed obsessed by it. He went daily to the pub to hear the reports from his favorite newspapers, the *Cork Examiner* and *The Nation*. He eagerly followed the detailed accounts of the rising and any other disturbances that occurred.

He learned all he could about the '67 risings, how they'd been set across Ireland in Dublin, Drogheda, Cork, Tipperary, Clare and Limerick, and in the small towns like Stepaside near Dublin as well as their own town of Donoughmore.

He told Margaret of the various police barracks that were attacked and the numbers of arms seized. The date, he told her as he stood at the hearth, had been deliberate.

"They planned it for March 5th, Shrove Tuesday, when all the marriages would be held with so many preoccupied."

Margaret interjected, "I'm glad there were no such shenanigans February 1st, nine years ago, for our own Shrove Tuesday wedding."

Jeremiah smiled at her and went on, eyes shining, as he told of the American-trained soldiers who commanded and organized the tailors, shoemakers and tradesmen who had been armed with guns, revolvers or pikes.

"The weather alone that night might have killed a man. One of our fiercest blizzards ever," he said, as moved to the window. "Yet most of the men stayed the course."

He drew from the pipe and continued. "Despite what ye hear, there were some successful risings all right, Margaret. Lest we forget, some were right here in our own County Cork."

Margaret put down her tatting, her eyes tired from the intricate lacework. The children in bed, the dishes washed and put away, she moved to the table and continued to watch Jeremiah and listen. She worried about him as he retold stories which she had heard time and again.

"The three men here in Cork were J.F.X. O'Brien, William Mackey Lomasney and Michael O'Brien who led over two thousand men in Ballyknockane and captured the police barracks. And for my money, the best part was that they derailed the Dublin express without a single injury to any passengers."

Beneath the tales of rebellion, Margaret heard a longing she couldn't identify. He wanted something, she was sure of it, but didn't know what it was.

*＊＊

With the arrest of Fenian leaders Colonel Thomas Kelly and Captain Timothy Deasy on September 11th, Jeremiah had started on a string of rantings. He'd become more agitated than she could ever remember.

"It was pure murder, Margaret," he shouted as he paced the cabin, "pure unadulterated murder. They hung them in sight for all to see, to teach a lesson."

As he carried on, Margaret did her best to keep the children out from underfoot.

"Well, it's a lesson they'll learn now for the people won't stand for it anymore," he said as he sat down at the table. "It's enough, now. It's enough."

Jeremiah's face grew red as he spoke of the public execution of men who became known as the Manchester Martyrs. As he pounded the table, the sugar and creamer jumped and the lid flew off the teapot, which Margaret caught before it fell to the floor.

No doubt, she thought, he felt the weight of responsibility for their growing family. With Mrs. Riordan about to move in with them and all the work despite Eugene's help. Their plan to have Eugene's family live in the Riordan home was looking less possible, Mrs. Riordan being the realist in that matter.

"Ye can go off and give away the store, but what of yer own growing family? Ye'll need something for their futures. Have ye no mind for them?"

She was right, yet all the same, it troubled him to let the cottage go for sale and not be able to help out Eugene who, despite the small amount Jeremiah was paying him, was in arrears.

Margaret consoled him as much as she could. "Ye'd think it was the house ye grew up in for all yer goings-on. Didn't Michael and me ma both give ye their blessing to sell it? Give it over, Jer, give it over."

But for all her comforts, Jeremiah's agitation continued to grow. He talked day and night of the event that led to the executions.

"What galls me the most, Margaret, is the wholesale disregard of the facts. The men were only after rescuing Kelly and Deasy, not killing someone."

He put the kettle on the hook over the open flame. "With the prison van surrounded by thirty Fenians, some armed with revolvers, all Sergeant Brett had to do was open the door. If he had, he'd never have been shot."

He stood at the end of the table and ran his hand through his hair over and over. He fidgeted and brushed at the dried mud on the knees of his overalls.

"The five arrests that followed the escape included a man named Maguire who had never even been near the scene of the rescue. Can ye imagine it?"

It was one of the women criminals in the van who took the keys out of the dying sergeant's pocket and passed them out through the ventilator. Kelly and Deasy, still in handcuffs, made their escape, never to be recaptured.

"They kept saying that William Allen fired the fatal shot but the truth was it was Rice who they say escaped to America with Kelly and Deasy."

He looked at her, his eyes dull with sadness.

"At least they finally granted a free pardon to Maguire." He sighed. "But what they did to the others . . ." His voice drifted off.

The whole of the parish had been up in arms. They knew that according to English law, William Allen, Philip Larkin, Michael O'Brien and Edward Condon were guilty of murder by mere association. The newspapers carried accounts of their speeches from the dock that told of their deep regret over Brett's death, idealistic speeches that helped raise the level of their action above that of common murder.

Condon, one of the two Americans, was saved by the insistence of Secretary of State William Seward, the American legation unable to intervene for the other American, William O'Brien, who had already been released from British justice once before, in 1866.

"Michael would love Condon's speech the best: 'I have nothing to regret, to retract or take back. I can only say, God save Ireland!' I can hear him right now shouting right along with the others, God save Ireland."

He ranted for months, unable, it seemed, to focus for very long on any other subject, until, on a foggy day on the 24th of November, Allen, Larkin and O'Brien were executed. Larkin and O'Brien suffered greatly because of a botched job by the hangman.

And as they hung, and Ireland took great notice, Jeremiah's passion turned to resolve. Margaret knew he would never participate in violence, but it was clear that he was as intolerant of injustice as ever. He was primed to act, and for that she was actually glad.

* * *

With a special visit to Father Lane, Jeremiah took the lead and on December 8th, the Manchester Martyr Mass at Donoughmore drew a great crowd, with a collection taken for the support of the dead men's families. The parish came out in grand numbers, contributing more than parishes twice their size. High masses held throughout Ireland became a rage. Crowds across the country exceeded even those in attendance six years earlier for Mac Manus.

Jeremiah's leadership and involvement brought with it a new focus for his energy. He'd never been as vocal as he was now. It had always been Michael who had spoken out. Jeremiah, it seemed, had suddenly become a force within their parish church of Donoughmore.

Margaret watched as he moved down the aisle at Sunday Mass. Many tipped their hats and afterwards made small talk with him. She saw that this recognition seemed to satisfy him somehow. He was doing his part for Ireland.

Chapter Seventeen
The Church

July 1869

"Sure now his name will be Michael, don't ye think?" Margaret said to Jeremiah with satisfaction as she rocked the infant swaddled in a blue flannel blanket back and forth. "And wouldn't Father Michael be proud to have such a strapping baby boy named after him? 'Tis sure he's as loud as Michael with his bawling."

The day was dreary but there was light within. "'Tis the eyes that are so like Michael's, looking right through ye. Michael it is," she said to Jeremiah.

This newest child, born in mid-summer, brought their young family to four, with Tims just five years old. Margaret was weary, but pleased with the children's health and vigor. She hadn't thought they'd be blessed with another child so soon. Julia was just a year old in March. But she remembered the loss of her first child and was nothing but thankful for the children they'd been given.

Jeremiah seemed pleased as well, cooing at the tiny boy and gladly rocking him when he could, though his time was more and more taken with the land, not only the tilling, cultivating and harvesting, but the liberation of it.

He had seen that the methods Michael had subscribed to were not bringing much success. Jeremiah was becoming more certain that a constitutional approach could work. He was dedicated to seeing it through and had written as much to Michael, their correspondence occurring now almost weekly.

Jeremiah, with pen and ink bottle at the table, looked to see Margaret nursing Michael. He smiled from a place within.

"I'll be writing to Michael about his namesake. I imagine he'll be pleased as if he were the father." He stroked his chin as he continued. "It's odd that a priest is called Father, yet has no children of his own." Margaret looked up, laughed at the thought, and then went back to nursing while Jeremiah paused and read a few lines silently from Michael's last letter. Then he spoke again.

"Ah, listen to this will ye, Margaret, from Michael's last letter?

"The Irish in America are not forgetting their homeland. I've recently learned that some three thousand Fenians live in the city of Buffalo and eight hundred of them crossed the Niagara River to occupy the village of Fort Erie on the Canadian shore, in hopes of taking the city and declaring a free and independent government.'

Jeremiah paused and twisted the pen in his hand.

"Can ye imagine that the fight in them is so deep, Margaret, that they've carried it across the sea? I wonder what the da would think of it all."

He put the pen down.

"Michael goes on to say here there's some speculation that the Yanks turned a blind eye to the Fenian preparations. They were still angered at British actions that assisted the Confederacy during their recent Civil War."

As Jeremiah read the description of the battle and of the seven in the Queen's Own Rifles of Toronto who were killed and the thirty-seven wounded along with the loss of half a dozen Fenians, he felt a familiar overwhelming sadness. He resolved to tell Michael in his reply once again of his belief in the futility of this approach. But first he would tell him of the birth of Michael, and would also report that William Gladstone was now Prime Minister with a stated mission "to pacify Ireland." Any movement toward rectifying the injustices done to Ireland was of great significance.

He dipped his pen and continued:

"On Sunday last, we heard the pastoral letter sent by Cardinal Paul Cullen. It's official now that the Anglican Church of Ireland is no longer the state church. The Royal Assent had been granted for the disestablishment on the 26th of July. It is something to watch the once powerfully positioned Church find itself poised to fade into the background."

Michael would be pleased with the disestablishment, Jeremiah mused as he stood from the table and put the kettle to boil. He recalled Michael telling of the embarrassing statistics of the 1861 Census that Archbishop Cullen had once quoted: there were more Catholics in a single parish in Dublin—St. Peter's—than there were Protestants in eleven of the Protestant dioceses.

Jeremiah wrote about the glebe house which would now be vacant, a place where as boys, he and Michael had once thrown stones over the fence. The end of so many injustices was wrapped within this disestablishment but not the end to them all.

Jeremiah knew that Michael hadn't much use for Archbishop Paul Cullen, now elevated to a Cardinal, whose pastoral letter Jeremiah had referred to, nor would he be pleased that Cullen had been the first Irishman to be honored with the high-ranking office in the Catholic Church. Cullen and his bishops had outlawed the Fenians and continued to lobby Rome for their ex-communication. Cullen had refused to sign the Amnesty Committee's petition as well.

Jeremiah stood, lifted the black kettle from the hearth and filled the teapot. Once he'd returned the kettle to the hook, he pulled up on his suspenders, stretched and looked about to find that Margaret had put Michael down to nap and had gone off with the three other children into the yard. She often arranged time alone for him like this. He wondered how he could ever reciprocate.

He finished his letter to Michael, remembering hearing of Father Patrick Lavelle who stood with the Fenians, relieved that Michael wasn't the only priest who had such an allegiance.

He covered the ink bottle just in time to hear the door open and the scamper of little feet bounding inside. Margaret had Julia in tow, with Tims and Mary trailing behind. Michael had yet to meet Julia and now his own namesake, Michael. Jeremiah thought of his old friend, and longed for a day when they might all be together.

Chapter Eighteen

Lughnasa

August 1, 1869

"Mind ye," Margaret called to Jeremiah as he started for the door, "bring enough for the lot of us. We'll have our own festival right here at home, with every new food ye can gather. There should be a bit of potato, some corn, beets and cabbage. It'll be a grand feast."

As he reached for the door handle, he asked, "Do ye think we should have some fowl? Let me know what suits ye once I come back."

She watched him stride out with purpose and continued to nurse Michael while Julia played at her feet, tipping Mary's dolly back and forth. Tims and Mary were in the yard on this gray but dry Sunday, building a grand castle, so they said, with sticks they'd gathered up. Jeremiah moved past without disturbing their play, anxious to meet up with Eugene.

Margaret's mother, Mrs. Riordan, had gone off for the special feast day with her friend Agnes Naughton, who had been a godsend. Weekly, she took Mrs. Riordan for an outing that began with the Rosary at half–nine, sometimes a noonday meal, and a shopping foray of some sort. Because today was Sunday, there'd be no shopping, the celebration of the Mass being the more important focus. And custom still held with some community celebration of Lughnasa later in the day.

Lughnasa, the special Celtic harvest celebration, named after the Irish god Lugh, one of the chief Celtic gods of the mythical race *Tuatha De Danann*, had been a special day since childhood. Margaret had helped her mother prepare the special harvest foods like colcannon, a dish made from the first digging of potatoes which were seasoned with onion, garlic and cabbage. Today she hoped her mother would help her.

It had been good for the children to have their grandmother with them. Mrs. Riordan was fine enough with them, often reading a story or tying a stray shoelace or bow. After supper, she sometimes gave the two older children a giggle when she pulled them to her and tickled them. They would each wait their turn but never very patiently. "Me next. It's my turn." The children would cling to her and muss her hair, the brown strands threaded with silver slipping out from her bun. But her gray eyes didn't show dismay. There was a playfulness that was great fun while it lasted. It was good for the children to know the pleasant side of her.

But there was another side, too, and that was the one she showed to Jeremiah. She rarely said a kind word to him. It was as if he existed only to be criticized, ever since Michael had gone to America.

"The fields never look as good as when my Michael was here. He had a way with the land, ye know."

"Ye might talk to the men at the market. They might lend ye some advice about growing the corn. Yer rows don't seem as productive as when me Michael grew it."

"Ye shouldn't talk with food in yer mouth. Little eyes are watching."

She never relented. Margaret was afraid to say anything to her for fear she'd turn on her as well. And though he seemed patient with her, Jeremiah spent less and less time at home, finding relief at the pub or off with the business of the land.

* * *

Today as Jeremiah continued on his way to meet Eugene, he recalled that Lughnasa was known as the time to forecast the weather. The blue hue that covered the distant hills was a signal, some would say, of a fine harvest. It was time, he thought, to believe in one.

He saw Eugene, his wide-brimmed hat covering his fair-skinned face, across the field, exactly as they had arranged. While Jeremiah and Eugene would have welcomed more hands to help with the work, they went about their tasks with a steadiness and determination that spoke of discipline and peace. Something in the spirit of working side by side calmed them both, as they took turns pressing the spade in under the tubers and pulling them from the soil to fill their burlap sacks, relieved that "Hungry July" with its threat of crop failure or delayed ripening was past.

They passed the time talking of the politics of the day, how the church in America was as involved in them as the church in Ireland. "It may have started with the Penal Laws, when you think of it, Jer," Eugene offered as he tossed a potato to the sack. "From the Mass Rocks that took the place of chapels to the outlawing of priests, we've come a long way." Both men knew of the "devotional revolution" since both their wives were faithful attendants to bene-dictions, rosaries and whatever other devotion was offered, a chance to socialize as well as to gain much-needed spiritual suste-nance.

By the time they reached the end of the field, they'd shared more conversation than they had since they'd started working together. As they parted ways, their sacks over their shoulders, they saluted one another with a deliberateness that acknowledged this new camaraderie.

The harvest had indeed been plentiful.

* * *

A little before noon, Jeremiah returned to the yard. He still won-dered whether they should have a chicken for the feast or not. Margaret would know. He also thought about harvesting the grain this coming week. There was more than enough to do to prepare it, with first the reaping, then the threshing, winnowing, drying, grinding and sieving.

The older ones, Jeremiah had been told by his da, used to "burn in the straw," combining the results of threshing, winnowing and drying in one swift operation. The whole sheaf or the ear end of the sheaf was set on fire. The grain would separate from the straw, burning the chaff and hardening the kernel all at once. The final act was to shake or wipe the grain clean of the ashes. It seemed economical enough, except that it burned the straw which could be used for cattle, or for thatching. The custom eventually became outlawed because of the waste. As he headed toward the house, Jeremiah thought of how much had changed since the da's time. And how much had stayed the same.

For today's feast, the rest of the preparation, cooking the corn, beets, potato and cabbage, would be simple. There was sure to be a big bonfire up on the high ridge which they'd look forward to seeing from their yard. He could just imagine the children's delight at the sight of the huge fire.

Before he went in, Jeremiah picked a small bucket of gooseberries to add to the festiveness of the day.

He noticed Tims and Mary in the yard, still busy at their castle. "Right here, Mary, is where the horses prance in the courtyard, see?" he could hear Tims saying. "You can put your horse right next to mine up here."

Had they been there since he'd gone off more than an hour before? They were still playing nicely, so he left them. He didn't hear a sound as he stepped inside the cabin. Michael was in his crib by the hearth, fast asleep. It was naptime for little Julia as well, he imagined. He paused at the table, put down his sack and placed his bucket of berries next to it. He tiptoed to the bedroom, wondering if maybe Margaret was rocking little Julia. He reached the doorway with warm thoughts, but what he saw froze him in place.

A pool of blood led to Margaret's body, which was crumpled, and curled up on the floor in the corner of the room near the foot of the bed. Little Julia lay beside her, whimpering, her eyes wild with fear.

Though Jeremiah's heart was pounding, he forced himself to kneel cautiously and stroke his daughter's hair. "Hush now, little lady, hush now." He picked her up as gently as he could, pulling her out from under Margaret's arm. The child clung tightly, her small arms around him, and started to bawl. He held her close, soothing her as he leaned over Margaret, whose eyes were closed, wondering what to do next. With his free hand, he tipped Margaret's head up and called to her. "Margaret, Margaret, me love. What is it? What is it?" Julia quieted as he spoke as if she, too, wanted to know.

Margaret felt warm to his touch yet her ghostly pallor alarmed him. Her unpinned hair was tangled, apron and housedress askew, feet twisted under her. He carried Julia to the other room as her cries stopped, hugged her to him, kissed her and set her down with her dolly. "There's me darlin' Julia. And here's her own sweet dolly."

He went next to the basin, poured water on a cloth, returned to Margaret and placed the damp cloth on her forehead and then her neck, praying that would rouse her.

The blood, he noticed as he looked closer, had come from between her legs and was almost black now. He alternated the cloth between her forehead and the back of her neck and then moved it to her wrists. He put his head on her breast and listened for a heartbeat. He hoped it was her heart he was hearing, but it was so hard to tell with the sound of his own heart racing. He held her hand as he continued to call to her.

"Margaret, me lass, come back now. It's all right, I'm here. Come back now. Come back." He lifted her head and squeezed the water from the cloth onto her lips. What should he do next? Dear Lord, what could he do?

He decided to lift her to the bed. As he reached under her shoulders and buttocks, he felt the dampness. He carefully laid her down, mindful of the blood on her pink floral dress. She moaned as he moved to get a cloth. He looked back and saw her eyes flutter. She was still unconscious. He went back to her and held her and whispered, "Hang on Mairéad, hang on, me darling."

She moved slightly. He pulled the blood-stained coverlet out from under her and covered her with it. The bleeding seemed to have stopped, thank the Lord. He prayed that Michael wouldn't wake up. He scooped Julia into his arms and went to the yard with a candy for Tims and Mary.

"Aren't ye the good children, playing out here while Mammy has a rest? The da will be back in a flash with some more chocolate. It's grand ye are now, grand indeed."

With that, he dashed out of the yard, Julia still looking alarmed, but silent now, and holding him tightly around the neck. He loosened the chestnut mare's reins, sat Julia in the saddle, as he had done only last week for the first time, and climbed up behind her.

"Another horty ride for little Julia! Aren't you the good girl?"

He snapped the reins and the mare quickly went to a gallop. Every bump and rock seemed like a boulder as Jeremiah hugged Julia close and they bounced along the three miles to the church.

As he came round to the rectory, Mrs. Ryan, the priest's housekeeper, who was hanging the wash, rushed out to them, before they dismounted.

"Whatever is it, Jeremiah? Ye look a fright. Is it the baby?"

"It's Margaret. She's fainted and I haven't been able to rouse her. She's still breathing, but she's fading fast. She's lost blood, hemorrhaging, I'd say. It's a doctor I need. The three little ones are there alone. I didn't know what else to do."

"Ye've done the right thing, indeed," she said, her attention now totally with Jeremiah, the last piece of wash, an apron, half hanging on the line.

"Now give me this little one, and go off now to fetch the doctor. He's up in Firmount," she said, her voice in command, her black and white hair mostly pushed back, her blue eyes moving to the child. "I'll take Julia home in the pony and trap and stay with the others. Father Lane is due back any minute. I'll leave him a note and I'll be off."

With that, she held out her arms for Julia and held her tightly. Julia went easily to the woman, and settled into her embrace.

"Go off with ye now," she directed. "He's up in Firmount. Father Lane was with him at the O'Farrells'. Go on with ye."

Jeremiah turned the mare, moved up the hill and took the first left to the parish of Firmount. His mind raced faster than he could go, his fists clenching the reins, hoping against hope that he would find him in time. As he rounded the last bend, he spotted the doctor's black carriage in front of O'Farrell's and saw Doctor Foley come out of the house.

"Doc Foley," Jeremiah called. "It's Margaret. She's fainted and she's bleeding. I need ye to come with me straight away. I couldn't rouse her. I'm praying not to lose her. We've no time to lose."

The small, square-framed man, his dark suit well tailored, his wire-rimmed eyeglasses in place, listened carefully to Jeremiah and nodded. "I'm on me way, Jeremiah. Don't ye worry. It's just two weeks after the birth all right. She'll be fine. She's a strong woman."

With that, Doctor Foley climbed into a carriage with its shiny black leather seat and well-polished trim and placed his black bag next to him. He followed Jeremiah at a quick pace, slowing at the turns to keep his balance and speeding up on the straight-aways.

By the time they arrived, Jeremiah found Mrs. Ryan in with Margaret, standing at the foot of the bed, the baby Michael in the older woman's arms. Julia, Mary and Tims were in the front room, a bit of biscuit and milk at the table for them. Margaret was still lying with her eyes closed, not responding to words. Jeremiah went to her side straight away, and held her right hand as if he could pray her to health.

"Do ye think she fell, Jeremiah?" Mrs. Ryan asked, her voice calm, her eyes watching Margaret. "Would there be a lump from her fall?"

Before he could answer, Doctor Foley came into the room, bag in hand. He took his hat off, placed it at the foot of the bed, went to far side of the bed and took Margaret's left hand and leaned down to listen to her breathing and her heartbeat. His simple nod brought a great sigh of relief from Jeremiah.

"She's steady in her breathing. Do ye have a basin with some warm water, please?"

With that, Mrs. Ryan left the room while Jeremiah stood, transfixed.

"I'll ask ye, Jeremiah, to go out now and be with the children," Doctor Foley said. "It's a fright they've had and they need their da. Mrs. Ryan will help me now."

Jeremiah nodded. He bent and kissed Margaret's forehead and reluctantly let go of her hand. He moved to the doorway and paused. Her color seemed to be returning. Dear God, let her be well, he prayed.

Chapter Nineteen

Isaac Butt

Later August 1869

"It's no wonder she's collapsed," Mrs. Riordan said to Jeremiah once she'd heard the news. "With all ye have piled on her, it's a wonder ye haven't killed her. Me Michael was far more of a help to me than ye ever are to me Margaret. I don't know what's to become of her."

In the week since Margaret had fallen, Mrs. Riordan had become harsher in her words and manner toward Jeremiah. Her deep sighs whenever he was about, her scowl when he spoke, and her impatient manner with him were taking their toll. He didn't know the cause and tried to be patient, but wasn't sure he could endure much more.

As she spoke, he bit his tongue and rose from his chair, turning his back to Mrs. Riordan and tending the fire. With Margaret requiring bed rest, much of the work of the household fell to Mrs. Riordan. Her fear of losing Margaret might have the better of her, Jeremiah thought, trying his hardest to give her the benefit of such thoughts.

He tried his best to help out when he could, especially with the children. They seemed more whiney than usual and, to make matters worse, Julia and Tims had come down with the sniffles. The doctor had been encouraging, explaining that Michael's birth, especially with Julia still so young and recently weaned, had taken a huge toll on Margaret's body.

Father Lane's visits had been some help in soothing all their spirits. He was particularly helpful with Mrs. Riordan, reminding her of Margaret's strength and the good Lord's mercy.

"Don't waste yer time on worry now, Mrs. Riordan," he said in his gentle way. "Ye leave that to God. He's watching out for our Margaret like he's watching out for all of ye. He'll be hearing yer prayers more than yer worries. Mind ye, this family is counting on yer wisdom and yer strength. It's a time for coming together and keeping faith. Now let us pray together a Hail Mary, an Our Father, and a Glory Be."

The sound of the priest's voice, with the prayer cascading over them, brought some calm to Mrs. Riordan and to Jeremiah.

Now as Jeremiah stood in the open doorway to Margaret's room, he thought she looked peaceful and hoped she was improving. He couldn't imagine life without her. He breathed deeply and felt tears moisten his eyes.

Before too long, the sound of little Michael's yowling to be fed brought Jeremiah's attention back to the room. He picked him up before Mrs. Riordan reached him and presented him to Margaret.

"Here now, lad, is yer ma. She's gonna give ye jest what ye want." He sat at the bedside as Michael suckled eagerly at his mother's breast and Jeremiah smoothed Margaret's hair.

"How are ye feeling now, Mairéad?" he asked.

A tiny bit of pink colored her pale cheeks.

"Ah, Jer, it's hard to stay still here. If you must know, I'd like to get up and lend a hand. Is Ma being all right with ye, now?"

Her obvious concern brought a lump to Jeremiah's throat.

"Ah, she's fine. She's being herself and there's no more we can ask."

Margaret's smile warmed him as she said, "Mind ye, don't let her poison the children with her nastiness. It's hard enough to hear her talk against ye."

"I'm thinking she's right about one thing, Margaret. These children are wearing ye out. Ye seem to love it so but ye can't go on without some help and yer ma isn't able to do much with the rheumatism flaring up as it does."

He paused, stroked her shoulder and said, "I'm thinking of asking Paddy Murphy's oldest girl Eileen to give a hand. She's old enough now, would you think?"

Jeremiah waited for Margaret's reply, fearful she would object. I can do it myself, she would say. That her mother was more work than help had never been said aloud, but it was true. Her mother was not only difficult with Jeremiah, but she had begun to snipe at the children, then sulk alone in the curtained space in the front room they'd created for her. It was part of the "new house" that Jeremiah had added after the birth of Julia. It fit in neatly with the whole look of the house and it had allowed them to turn the back room into a bedroom for the girls.

"Ah, Jer, we can get by without anyone else, can't we? What good would Eileen do anyway?" she said, but he thought, despite her words, her tone was without its familiar resoluteness.

"She'll help with the children's meals, washing and bedtimes, and she can even help with yer ma each day. Maybe it'll help her disposition. It's worth a try, now wouldn't ye say?" He smiled, hoping to win her over.

"I suppose we can afford a bit of help and she'll be eager for the little we can pay, right enough." She stroked Michael's tiny nose and looked up at him. "Well, if ye think so, I'd say go ahead now. But only 'til I'm back on me feet, agreed?"

"Agreed," Jeremiah said and smiled again at his wife.

Margaret smiled and handed the sleeping Michael over to him. "Ye can rest a bit yerself now. I'll go straight off to Paddy's about Eileen."

He lifted the child from her and laid him in the cradle next to the bed, kissed Margaret's forehead and went out to Mrs. Riordan, who was sitting by the hearth.

"I'm thinking yer right about more help for the children and the house. We'll be asking Paddy Murphy's Eileen to give a hand. It's a good idea ye had," he said generously.

"It's about time ye used yer noggin. Eileen's a good one and I won't mind having her around. Her grandmother Nora's a friend of mine, ye know." She smirked, her slate-gray eyes following him as he moved to the door.

"Ah, then I've hit the mark for once, have I?" he jested as he went out, closing the door behind him.

* * *

The day had turned gray, a threat of rain suspended over the hills. By the time Jeremiah reached Paddy Murphy's place, a soft rain had begun. As he rode into the yard, he saw Paddy riding in from the south hill where his cattle grazed.

"Ah, Jeremiah, to what do I owe the pleasure?" Paddy shouted as he rode toward him. He hadn't seen Jeremiah since baby Michael's baptism. Paddy had been the godfather and Julia Sweeney, from up the road, the godmother. Both families had been friends of the Buckleys and the Riordans, and it honored their friendship to be called upon.

"Paddy, I see yer hard at work, as we all are these days," Jeremiah said as he watched his friend dismount from his horse. He had a pleasant face, dark hair with slight slivers of gray at the temples, deep-set brown eyes and a solid, lean frame and a soft smile which he gave now to Jeremiah, who dismounted and hitched his horse next to Paddy's at the fence by the barn.

"I've come in search of some help," Jeremiah said, watching Paddy's face in hopes that he'd be open to the idea. "Have ye heard that Margaret's been poorly this last week?"

"I did miss seeing ye this past Sunday at Mass," Paddy said as he stroked the horse's mane. "What seems to be ailing her?"

"Well, Doc Foley's word is bed rest," Jeremiah responded as he took off his felt hat and smoothed his auburn hair. "It's been too much, what with Julia and Michael so close together."

The two men walked toward the barn, Paddy a head taller than Jeremiah.

"Our Tims is not even five and little Mary just rounding up to four." He paused and scratched his neck, surprised at his own agitation.

"They're good children, mind ye, in all senses of it. We wouldn't trade a one of them. Maybe it's the added burden of Mrs. Riordan with us. I can't say for sure, but Margaret collapsed under the weight of it all and lost a lot of blood."

Paddy stopped and turned to him as they stood in the doorway.

"The doctor's giving her a potion to build her up again but he's ordered her to stay in bed." His brow furrowed, as he continued.

"Ye can imagine the strain of keeping her down and keeping her mother out of the thick of things is more than I can handle on my own," he admitted, his voice weary.

Once inside the barn, Paddy signaled to Jeremiah to wait just a minute. He hoisted himself up the ladder on the left, pulled a harness down from the nail on the lowest beam, handed it to Jeremiah and climbed down.

"Shall we set up the pony and cart for today?" he asked.

Jeremiah said nothing, his confusion evident in his expression.

"Isn't it my Eileen ye're after to give ye a hand, now? Yer Mrs. Riordan was over here only yesterday saying we should send her." Paddy grinned.

"Ye don't say," Jeremiah said quietly. "Ye don't say."

* * *

Paddy and Jeremiah waited in the kitchen while Eileen finished her own chores and went off to change her dress and fix her hair. Paddy put the kettle to boil, and he turned to Jeremiah, who had taken a seat at the table. "Well, what do you think of yer man Gladstone these days? Do ye think he can do as he says and pacify ol' Ireland?"

Jeremiah looked up at Eugene and smiled for the first time since he'd arrived. "'Tis yer man Isaac Butt I've me eye on these days. He's the one that's had the good sense to turn from the Union." He pulled the chair in to the table and continued. "From what I hear, while Butt served in Parliament, he saw first-hand its foolishness during the worst of the famine, thousands starving while laws and philosophies were debated to no satisfaction. It outraged him."

Paddy set two cups, cream and sugar on the table. He pulled at his suspenders.

"Jer, is he the one that served as defense counsel for Smith O'Brien and Meagher of Young Ireland and almost went broke?" He placed the teapot in the center of the plain wooden table.

"If I'm right about this," Paddy said with a flush in his cheek, "there's word he's a bit too fond of the drink."

"Drunk or sober, Paddy, he's the man for the job." Jeremiah tipped back in his chair and pushed his hair back. "He not only defended the men you mention, he's grown to admire them so much, he's after working for their amnesty."

Paddy poured the boiling water from the kettle into the teapot, put the kettle back on the hearth and joined Jeremiah at the table. His brown eyes were lively as he continued.

"Yer man Mr Butt is now President of the Amnesty Association that the wives and sympathizers of the Fenian leaders have organized. They say it's brought floods of memorials and pledges in from all classes of our people. Almost a million are expected to have attended Association meetings before this month is out."

Jeremiah spooned sugar into his cup, and noted the attractive circular pattern on the mug, the matching pottery in the hutch, remembering that Paddy's wife Mary was known among the women as having quite the decorator's eye.

Paddy leaned forward. "Have ye heard of reports in the *Freeman's Journal* about the torturous conditions and treatment of the Fenian prisoners? That alone is swelling the call for Amnesty, I'd say, Jer."

Jeremiah took a swallow of the tea. He heard the sounds of Eileen gathering her things and looked about the small cottage with its compact stone hearth, windows covered with hand-sewn curtains, a small table and chairs, and saw for the first time how much it was like his own home. Though Paddy's cabin was a bit smaller, evidence of caring filled it—a small glass of violets on the table, a bed with a purple coverlet by the front wall, a small wooden chair by the window with a newspaper and several books stacked on a table next to it. It was a home he felt comfortable in. He turned his attention back to his friend.

"Yer right, Paddy," Jeremiah said as he sipped his tea, "something's bound to happen. Last I heard Mr. Butt will be soon in England presenting the Queen with a national petition for Amnesty with 250,000 signatures. He's calling the question and for these times, that's something."

Jeremiah turned as Eileen emerged from the back part of the house, a worn satchel in hand, her dark hair pulled back with a pink ribbon. A beige shawl about her shoulders covered her pale pink blouse and matching skirt. She had brogues that were in need of repair, but the smile and sparkling blue eyes that shone from her face took away from any shabbiness in her dress.

"'Tis not a long ride there now, Eileen," Paddy said as he stood. "I've harnessed the Princess and the cart up for ye."

Turning to Jeremiah, he asked, "Do ye expect she'd be back by twilight now, Jeremiah?"

"Aye, I do," Jeremiah said as he smiled at Eileen. "We'll just have a look about and see what ol' Mrs. Riordan has in store for ye, Eileen. And don't be minding her ways. She will not say so perhaps, but she's glad for yer coming to us."

With that, Jeremiah finished the tea in his cup and stood from the table, and the three went out into the yard to find the rain had let up. Paddy stood back and watched as Eileen and Jeremiah set off, none of them knowing exactly what to expect.

Chapter Twenty

The Yanks and Ireland

October 1870

Michael knelt on the priedieu, the small wooden kneeler in front of the statue of the Blessed Virgin Mary, and repeated the *Memorare*, a prayer from his youth:

> "Remember O Most Gracious Virgin Mary, that never was it known that anyone who fled to thy protection, implored thy help or sought thy intercession was left unaided . . ."

He felt comfort in the words that united him with his past and his hope for the future.

He stood and straightened his black cassock, laughing to himself as he remembered his mother straightening her dress in just such a fashion. He was growing more accustomed to the long, flowing black robe that buttoned down the front past his knees and almost to the floor. He'd been taught in seminary that the honor of wearing clerical garb was reserved for men who consecrated their lives to the service of Christ and His Church. The Roman collar symbolized obedience and the color black signified poverty as well as a dying of oneself to serve the Lord. This service was his intention and his hope and he had learned to wear his robes proudly.

He inhaled the familiar fragrances of wax and incense that lingered from last evening's benediction, his thoughts drifting as he walked down the long aisle to the vestibule. Not for a minute had he forgotten Ireland or Margaret and Jeremiah. In the three years since he'd come to America, he'd spent a part of each day in prayer for them and the little ones. He savored the letters from Jeremiah and cherished the few that Margaret found time to send. He was happy to learn the stories of Tims and Mary at school along with the antics of Julia and his namesake, little Michael. The letters and his prayers connected him to those he'd left behind.

Though neither Jeremiah nor Margaret said it outright, he sensed his mother wasn't easy on Jeremiah. Michael remembered the old saying—"though there's no bone in the tongue, it often broke a man's head."   He knew that Jeremiah wasn't to be faulted in any way. By all accounts, he continued to build a fine life for his family, fixing his home to accommodate his growing brood of children as well as his mother-in-law. He managed the farm with the finesse of a landlord. He accomplished the sale of the Riordan home with honor, and though Mrs. Riordan fussed, he had placed the bulk of the money in her name and gave her a regular full accounting. Michael had declined even a penny.

Jeremiah's last letter addressed the land:

> In my last visit with Mr. Bennett, over tea mind ye, his servants fussing over us and making sure we had all the fineries, we discussed the current land issues. He's of a mind to keep things quiet even here and made reference to adding lands to our current holdings. He's not as bad a man as the da once made him out to be. But then, those were darker times.

From what Michael had been able to keep up with, he had come to understand that the level of agitation for freedom and reform had slowed in Ireland. William Gladstone, the new Prime Minister, had brought with him a bit of hope. Enough hope to have quieted many. Jeremiah himself had benefited from the 1870 Landlord and Tenant Act, which included the "Ulster Custom" allowing compensation when tenants made improvements to their land. Over the years Jeremiah had cleared away the relentless stones that emerged each season, creating healthy soil through tilling and harvesting of the crops. Such acts of loyalty and perseverance had finally been rewarded.

44

Yet as with much of Irish law, there were problems. Landlords often raised rents beyond the reach of farmers and then evicted them, despite the "Bright Clauses," named after their creator John Bright, designed to help tenants buy the land they worked. Irish land, Jeremiah continued to learn, was sacrosanct and British government policy directed no interference with private property.

"There are still the disturbances, Michael," Jeremiah had recently written. "Still the men agitating and plundering. The land question is with us even after Gladstone's great effort."

* * *

Michael stepped into the vestibule; the tiles gleamed under his feet. He pushed on the great oak door leading to the street and as it yielded, he stepped out into the daylight, blinking as his eyes adjusted to this mild autumn sunshine.

"It's a good day to you, Father," he heard from below.

He blinked again and saw Mrs. Doherty. Her twin altar boys served his Masses. The woman with bright blue eyes and hair the color of Margaret's stood at the bottom of the granite stairway that led to the massive doors.

"A good day to ye, Mrs. Doherty," he said as he walked down the steps toward her. "How are ye this fine day and how is your family?"

"Ah, Father, they're fine," Mrs. Doherty replied as her brown felt coat flapped in the breeze. She was dressed smartly, Michael thought, her matching hat held in place by a pin with an oyster-colored stone at the end.

"The boys are enjoying so serving your Mass. I'd never guessed it could be such an important thing for them." Then she chuckled, "Our little Eileen, just five years old now, is asking when she can have a turn."

"Well, ye tell her now," Michael said, smiling, "there's a special place for her in the church. The good sisters will see to that. And tell me now, how is your Liam? Is he managing all right?" The drink had captured Liam, as it had so many men who'd come from

Ireland in search of something more, men who'd used the last of their resources to cross an ocean, and had been rewarded only by disappointment time and again in their search for decent work.

"Ah, Father, we're managing," Mrs. Doherty said, eyes still blue, but the look in them darkening a bit. "He's going to try again for the docks. It's foul as can be down there, but the pay is decent. And the hours are right enough. He'll be glad to know you're asking after him. I'll be sure to tell him."

"Please do, Mrs. Doherty, please do. May the rest of your day be a blessed one as ye go on your way."

Michael waved as she moved down the walkway toward her home, an apartment in a row of tenement houses that lined the street.

He looked up at the church. Its brick was intact, the mortar between the stones firm. The stained glass windows in their majestic reds, blues and golds reflected the afternoon light, with the gold hues shining as if by sunlight. Even in the shadow of this beauty, Michael felt sometimes as though his three years were more like thirty. The heartaches of the parishioners brought a loneliness that sat like a physical weight in his chest. He stepped through the side gate to the little grotto, home to the tombstones of the late pastors. The coolness felt comforting. He breathed deeply and sent up a silent *Ave Maria* for Liam Doherty and the many like him whose families suffered from the drink.

He stood a long while in the shade of the church and felt the familiar longing for a woman, a family, and children to call his own boil up within him. An unbidden envy for Liam Doherty bubbled up inside him. Why couldn't Liam leave off with the bloody drink? Didn't he see what gift he had and how he was squandering it? He felt his anger, and prayed another Hail Mary for his own soul.

***

As he made his way back up the church steps, Michael's thoughts drifted, as they often did, to the Fenians. As he walked back through the church, passing the Stations of the Cross that depicted the death and crucifixion of Christ, he wondered how many of those fighting for Ireland were ready for such suffering?

The end of the American Civil War had helped swell the Fenians' ranks, veteran Irish immigrants who never lost love of their homeland, at the ready and now trained in military tactics, willing to fight for its freedom.

Jeremiah had honored his oath taken at the pub so many years before, to "yield implicit obedience . . . to his superior officers," and though no longer actively involved, his curiosity and loyalty led him to keep abreast of their activities. He learned that General F.F. Millen had been elected temporary head—Provisional Chief Organizer Irish Republic—only in office nine days, long enough to be recognized as a force within the organization. What kind of a force was yet to be revealed.

Once in the sacristy, Michael rinsed a chalice and tidied the table, glad to be heading back to the rectory. He would write to Michael and tell more of William Roberts, whose first attack on Canadian soil was discussed so openly that the New York Herald offered a prediction that there was some probability of success. Though the prediction wasn't realized, credibility was given to the belief that if the Irish flag, a tri-colored gift from France, could be raised upon Canadian soil, then certainly an independent Ireland would have to be recognized.

He closed the door to the sacristy and walked out into the afternoon light that softened the street with a golden cast. As he neared the rectory, he paused, his reflections interrupted by the song of sparrow. He breathed deeply as he listened, still believing in the moral rightness of the cause, but beginning to remind himself a bit of Jeremiah, as he questioned the methods. His own experience, in the folly of the '67 rising and the unsuccessful Canadian risings with their associated loss of life, led him to wonder how Ireland's freedom would ever be won. As he ascended the rectory stairs he renewed his resolve to pray for an answer to what was commonly being called "the Irish question."

Chapter Twenty-One

The Irish in America

January 1871

"My dearest brother,

I'm after telling ye some grand news. We're to be blessed with another child this spring. I'm feeling fine, thanks be to God. Tims and Mary are delighted with the prospect of a new little baby to spoil. They are forever taking Michael out for walks or carrying him about as if he were a dolly. He'll not put up with it much longer, I suspect . . ."

It was rare that Margaret herself had time to write so Michael savored her words. He often made a ceremony of his letters with a cup of tea and a biscuit. Now as he pored over the hand-written pages, he smiled, delighted to read of Jeremiah's bold steps as an emerging gentleman squire. Margaret wrote that his active role in getting a Mass said for the Manchester Martyrs and the time he spent hob-nobbing with the landlord seemed to bring him a renewed spirit.

Michael finished his tea, and as he returned his teacup to the sideboard in the well-appointed Manhattan rectory dining room, he thought about the most recent news of a new child, the growing family a joy more satisfying than he'd ever imagined. He was glad, too, for movement on the political scene. Isaac Butt's popularity and his start of the Home Government Association, even though controversial in some circles, at least provided action of some sort.

"The aim of the Association," Margaret had written, "is an Irish parliament elected from the Irish commons and gentry to control all but foreign policy." He was pleased that she was so astute in her literary and political skills.

Michael stood and looked out over the busy street and pondered the Irish in New York City, one of the largest concentrations anywhere in the entire world, including Dublin, a concentration he knew to be overwhelmingly Catholic and Democratic. His disappointment over the scandal surrounding Tammany Hall, the Democratic political machine and its leader William "Boss" Tweed, was great, but greater was his disillusionment when he learned of the Draft Riots of 1863.

The first national draft law enacted to shore up the Union forces in the Civil War required all able-bodied men ages twenty to forty-five to serve a three-year term in the army unless they found a substitute or paid the government three hundred dollars, a sum available only to a few It was this last clause that sparked tensions that erupted into flame.

An inflammatory press asserted that the fee protected the rich and targeted the immigrants and working class, many of whom were Irish or German.

Michael had never seen a Negro until he came to America and now learned that the great fear had been that Negroes, who were exempt from the draft since they were not considered citizens, would take Irish jobs, many of the very same jobs the Irish had taken from them upon their arrival.

Gangsters and criminals, many of whom in those days were Irish, poured out of Five Points, the infamous center of inter-racial social life in one of the poorest and most dangerous parts of New York. They began looting and burning, their two main targets the rich, who could buy their way out of the draft, and Negroes, whose existence threatened job security.

Mobs of between five and fifteen thousand stormed down Fifth Avenue, brandished sticks, clubs and pistols, and shouted defiance of the government and the police. The death toll was staggering, ranging into the thousands. One account told of the Second Avenue Armory that became a roaring torch, with rioters jumping from the second and third floor windows to their deaths. More than fifty baskets and barrels of human bones were collected from the ruins and ultimately buried in a potter's field.

Jewelry stores were looted, guns stolen from hardware stores, and private residences along Lexington Avenue near Forty-Sixth

Street pillaged and set on fire. Brooks Brothers on Catherine Street, a men's apparel store and symbol of the wealthy, was pillaged and set aflame, but not before the rioters attired themselves in suits and loaded up with shirts and neckties.

Michael understood something about the atrocities of war, but was appalled as he read now of rioters hanging three Negro men and burning them beyond recognition while dancing and singing obscene verses beneath them. This was followed by the burning of an orphanage for "colored" children on Fifth Avenue and Forty-Third Street, where through the grace of God and fast maneuvering two hundred twenty-seven children were removed to safety before the building was set into flame. When the senseless mob discovered a lone child who had hidden under a bed in fear—they killed him.

Michael searched the accounts to find a reason that such insanity was able to reign. Even *The Tribune* had come under attack, with editor Horace Greeley barely able to escape. Finally Republican Mayor Opdyke appealed to Major-General Sanford to send in the National Guard.

Where was the church in all this, Michael wondered? Governor Seymour had contacted the leader of New York's Catholic citizens for help. Archbishop John Hughes, a forceful figure in city politics, who had laid the cornerstone for St. Patrick's Cathedral and was at one time a personal agent of President Lincoln and a close ally of Governor William H. Seward, complied with the Governor's request by circulating a poster inviting his flock to a meeting: "Men, I am not able, owing to the rheumatism in my limbs, to visit you. . . . There is abundant space for the meeting around my house."

Five thousand attended the Friday, July 17th meeting and the Archbishop told the crowd: "Every man has a right to defend his home or his shanty at the risk of life. The cause, however, must be just. . . . I have been hurt by the report that you were rioters. Is there not some way by which you can stop these proceedings and support the laws . . .?"

His words came too late. The National Guard arrived and quelled the last of the rioters. It was the yet to be discovered corrupt Tammany Hall that saw to it that the Democrats in the city government appropriated two million dollars to buy draft exemptions for those who wouldn't or couldn't serve.

Anger filled Michael. He pulled at the stiff white collar that ringed his neck. The more he had read, the stronger his conviction that the Catholic Church had not only done nothing to prevent these atrocities, but had helped to fuel them. Archbishop Hughes, while favoring the Union, refused to support President Lincoln's Emancipation Proclamation and came into conflict repeatedly with Horace Greeley, whose editorial "The Prayer of Twenty Millions" demanded a more aggressive attack on the Confederacy and faster emancipation of slaves. Yet Hughes, while maintaining a pro-slavery stance, dared to fight over the *Tribune*'s negative portrayal of New York's Irish Catholic population.

The Church leadership as high up as the Pope, who made no secret of his sympathies for the Confederacy or his disdain for the growing liberalism infecting the north, disappointed Michael. Even New York's semi-official, high-brow Catholic newspaper the *Freeman's Journal* had to be shut down during the war, for its disdainful articles about "ugly black niggers" were too inflammatory in these times.

Such abuse of power of the Church in America angered Michael. As he stood wearing the robe of the Church he served, his jaw locked tight as he realized it was the same anger he felt about the Church in Ireland.

* * *

Michael left the window and retrieved his black wool overcoat. The time had come for his appointment, the reception for John Devoy and Jeremiah O'Donovan Rossa, two recently released Fenian prisoners who, he hoped, would bring new life to the American struggle for Ireland's freedom.

As Michael approached Sweeny's Hotel, a red brick building

that took up an entire city block, he saw crowds lined up on the street outside. He pulled his coat collar a bit tighter around his neck, ready for a long wait.

The two men being welcomed, along with their fellow ex-prisoners Charles O'Connell, John McClure and Henry Mulleda, had arrived, to much acclaim, aboard the USS *Cuba*._Each had chosen America as their exile destination, holding a belief that in America they could be guaranteed a secure base from which to continue the struggle for freedom.

Newspaper accounts closely followed the two weeks of celebrations which included a parade led by "Boss" Tweed. By this time, the *Russia* had arrived in port bringing nine more released prisoners, and hundreds congregated at Sweeny's Hotel to express support and solidarity with the Fenian heroes. Even President Grant scheduled a welcome for them on the steps of the White House.

A *New York Herald* reporter described John Devoy as having deep-set blue eyes that gave him an expression of shrewdness. Just what was needed, Michael thought, as he made his way into Sweeny's Hotel, where his now opened overcoat showed his Roman collar and granted him nods and a speedy entrance into the receiving line.

Michael knew that at age ten John Devoy had suffered a beating for refusing to sing "God Save the Queen," and eight years later had joined the Irish Republican Brotherhood. Five years ago, Devoy was arrested for recruiting British soldiers into the organization, was tried for treason, and sentenced to fifteen years penal servitude, which had been commuted to exile from Ireland. His release, more than the others', had been anticipated in the streets of New York with great enthusiasm.

Michael stood peering about the hotel lobby. Gold cords held back the rich ruby-red drapes that adorned the floor-to-ceiling windows. Light sparkles from the chandelier's glass danced on the pattern of the blue and red oriental carpet. He could smell the lamb stew that was being prepared, glad to see America treat these men like royalty.

When his moment came, Michael stepped forward and looked down at the much shorter John Devoy. His brown hair was close-cut, his face-clean shaven, his massive forehead furrowed as he shook Michael's hand.

"It's good of ye to come, Father. 'Tis blessed we are now to be in the land of the free and the brave," Devoy said, his small eyes gleaming.

"It's good of ye to come, yerself now, Mr. Devoy. We're in dire need of yer energy and yer passion. Mind ye, we've been at odds a bit without the likes of yer kind of leadership," Michael responded.

"Don't ye be worrying for lack of leadership, Father. We've plenty of energy left for just that. We'll be talking with the likes of ye."

With that, Devoy squeezed Michael's hand again and let go to greet the next in line.

Michael moved from the line, not waiting to see O'Donovan Rossa. Somehow he felt lighter. He slipped out a side door into the chill air and drew in a breath of deep satisfaction. He was certain of one thing: he had just touched greatness.

Chapter Twenty-Two
Mrs. Riordan

February 1871

"It's no good for ye now, Margaret, this Lenten diet. Think of the one you're carrying. Ye need to keep up yer strength," Margaret's mother advised as she stood stirring the porridge. She looked at her daughter, and saw the same flame-colored hair as always, but Margaret's face was still too thin. "I'll be asking Father Lane for a dispensation for ye. He'll be sympathetic to yer needs, of that we can be sure."

The Lenten fast for many of the parish meant abstinence from meat, eggs, butter and milk. Dry bread, porridge and black tea were the morning and evening meal, with a midday dinner of potatoes seasoned with fish or onions.

"In my day, the little ones under seven, once they were weaned, were given milk only sparingly; sometimes infants were allowed to cry three times before they were given any. Nowadays those rules are seen to be too harsh, yet ye must watch your own strength, even so. Ye're not quite strong yet, ye know."

Margaret shifted her weight in the rocker. "Ah, Ma, don't ye be worrying for me," she said as she cuddled Michael on her knee, her protruding belly making it difficult to hold him. "The good Lord is watching out for me and Father Lane's already told me to use me noggin and not endanger this little one. There's no need to bother him with any special permission. I'll be fine, Ma, just fine."

The two years since Michael's birth had been difficult, her energy decreased and the work increased. Thankfully Paddy Murphy's Eileen proved to be a blessing in ways that couldn't have been foreseen. Her manner with Mrs. Riordan especially had made all the difference in the household.

"Em, Mrs. Riordan," she would posit, her bright blue eyes clear, her black hair pulled back pertly with a ribbon, "could ye be showing me a better way to make the bread?" Or on another morning, "Me ma says yer brown bread is the best in all the parish. Me Nana says so too." Mrs. Riordan happily hummed as she mixed the flour and punched the rising dough. Eileen watched and learned as she kept Julia and Michael content, rocking and bouncing them like a little mother.

Margaret smiled as she did the few chores she was still able to manage. Today the wash, tomorrow churning butter to ready it for sale. As she hung the wash, she felt this newest child kick—already six months along. She secretly hoped for a girl who would carry her own name. Jeremiah had assured her that with two boys and two girls already, he'd be pleased with either gender. It was good to have the rough months past and finally feel a bit of vigor.

Not until the spring following Michael's birth did she feel herself, and then by fall she was expecting again. Funny to think that at one time she'd feared she'd always be barren. But at least now she was learning to pace herself and accept help, something she hadn't been schooled to do. Her own mother was learning a similar lesson.

Since Candlemas Day, February 2nd, the change in Mrs. Riordan had been for the better. Jeremiah's role in coming to her rescue with his quick thinking in fetching the doctor and his decision to hire Eileen had helped his status with his mother-in-law immeasurably, and relieved Margaret from the worry of her mother's harshness.

* * *

"Not a good omen, this weather," Jeremiah had remarked as he helped Mrs. Riordan into the cart, her tweed cloak wrapped about her. The morning had dawned clear and sunny with a nip in the air, supporting those who believed good weather on this day to be a sign of more winter to come. Mrs. Riordan didn't respond to Jeremiah's comment, and instead arranged herself on the seat.

Ever faithful to church rituals, she was off to church for the blessing of the candles.

"With all our sickness of late and all these small children to care for, it's God's blessing of light we need to be asking," she said, clutching the candles she had made to donate for the church's use as well as those she would get blessed for home use.

She insisted they leave by "half-eight," to be in time for a "good" seat, she had said. Church devotions were more popular than ever, thanks to Archbishop Cullen's "devotional revolution" which had spurred attendance at Mass, the Rosary, Stations of the Cross, and other feast day celebrations.

As they rode along, Mrs. Riordan, sitting tall in the seat next to Jeremiah, said, "I'll tell ye, there was a time, and me Michael and yer da would remember this, God rest them both, when we had what we called 'the stations' in our own homes." Her gray eyes were animated as she continued. "There was no need to go off to a church, indeed for a time it was even outlawed. A grand and privileged time in those days, scrubbing and polishing our humble abodes so's the priest and the neighboring folks could come to the Mass. There was an honor to it that young people will never know, a real honor," she said with a satisfied smile.

A bit of a frost covered the rolling drumlins as they clip-clopped by, the sunlight turning them into fields of sparkle, as if touched by fairy dust.

Once he helped her from the cart, Jeremiah watched his mother-in-law, her black wool scarf pulled around her graying hair, climb the few steps into the church; her cane had become more and more necessary. He had fashioned it out of an oak limb and given it to her for Christmas. "Ye think I'm an old woman, do ye?" was all she had said in thanks. But within the week, she'd started using it.

While the women within fingered their beads and prayed their devotions, Jeremiah waited outside with the other men, happy to have time to catch up on the local news and share talk of greater things than blessed candles.

As he walked up the incline where a few men stood, he looked down on the beauty of St. Joseph's Church at Donoughmore. Its spire was a testament to the devotion of the people, the Norman influence of the squared-off turret striking as it reached into the sky. Donoughmore meant "great church" and indeed, a great church it was, Jeremiah thought. As a child, he'd heard the tales of the patron saint Lachteen, whose "brazen hand," known for its miraculous healing powers, had been preserved in a bronze shrine at St Joseph's around 1120. Father Lane had once told him that church records revealed the British government purchased the hand sometime after 1740 and deposited it in the Royal Irish Academy in Dublin, where it remained a valued treasure. Jeremiah often wondered how the hand had come to be severed, thinking it a queer sort of relic.

Eugene Cronin, whose wife Ellen was in with Mrs. Riordan and the others, approached with his familiar brown tweed cap in place, interrupting Jeremiah's silent reverie.

"Margaret's continuing to do well, I trust," he heard, and turned to see his trusted co-worker approaching.

"She's fit as a fiddle and I thank ye for asking," Jeremiah replied. "Each day I'm glad to say she's carrying this newest child quite well, more peaceful than with the others." Jeremiah paused as he faced Eugene, with whom he often became philosophical. "I suppose she's more prepared for what to expect."

"Speaking of expecting, Jeremiah," Eugene said as he started down toward the walkway along the side of the church, "what do ye expect is going to happen with yer man Mr. Bennett? Have the outrages affected him at all, do ye suppose?"

Gladstone's Land Act of 1870 had given hope to some, but it was not bold enough for the revived secret societies who roamed the hills, destroying property and threatening landlords who had evicted tenants or raised rents. The most recent agitation had occurred at Lord Reynolds' estate, less than a dozen miles from Ballybawn, the Bennett Big House. Several cattle had been maimed and two outbuildings set to flame.

"With the eviction last week of the Donnelly family, Eugene, we're all concerned. I doubt it has escaped Mr. Bennett's attention," Jeremiah said as he followed Eugene toward the walkway.

Ned Donnelly was known among the parishioners as a hard worker and a decent man. The two oldest of his six children were in school with Tims and Mary. His pleas to Lord Reynolds for more time to pay had gone unheeded. The outrages were committed that night after word had come of the eviction.

"There's never been anyone who's openly admitted to causing the 'disturbance,'" Eugene said as they passed the stained glass windows of the church, "but I'd say there are some in the parish who know who's responsible."

Unruly scenes were not uncommon, the identity of the perpetrators usually safely guarded. Since all tenants had to vote the way the landlord dictated, or risk eviction, few dared to stray. There were others, freeholders—men who weren't owned by landlords—who agitated publicly in an effort to influence the vote. Fist fights often broke out, but usually to no avail. The power of the landlords prevailed.

As the women emerged from the church, Jeremiah watched for Mrs. Riordan. He would be glad to be on his way and see to his chores. He watched as women he knew, Margaret Healy, Mary Kildare, Ellen Cronin, Ellen Cogan and Julia Sweeney, all emerged. They chattered away in a fashion that reminded him of hens, their heads turning one to the other with an unmistakable clucking as they clutched their newly blessed candles. It wasn't unusual for Mrs. Riordan to stay behind to say an extra novena. Appearing pious was important to her.

Jeremiah ventured up the steps to look in after her, but she was nowhere to be seen. Had she gone out the front with the priest? He knew she enjoyed the special attention he gave her when he had the time. Jeremiah darted up the side aisle toward the east door, and that's when he saw her. She lay slumped over to the left in the pew, her mouth open, her eyes rolled back, the candles fallen to the floor.

"Mother Riordan, Mother Riordan," he called as he reached her. He forgave her meanness in a flash as she roused to her name.

"What's ailing you? Are ye all right, now?" he asked as he knelt down by her. He took off his canvas jacket, wishing now that the sturdy green fabric were cleaner. With concerned gentleness, he lifted her head off the pew and rested it on the folded jacket. When she faded away again he called her back and once more her eyes opened, this time with more focus.

"Can you sit up?" he said. "Shall we try it now? I'll hold on to ye. Ready now? One, two, three."

With that, he swung her torso up to face the altar. As he did, her legs moved under her. He pushed the kneeler back to make more room.

She was a handsome woman, one could say. Her chestnut hair, sprinkled with gray, was well styled and her face, though often pinched in a scowl, had a strong angular shape. Her well-defined jaw moved as she tried to speak.

Jeremiah moved closer. Her words were garbled.

Dear God, he thought, she's had a stroke.

"That's it now, don't ye worry. You'll be jest fine." He pulled the green coat over her shoulders and said, "Ye couldn't be in a better place to have a little rest now, could ye?"

He wished that Father Lane would come back so he wouldn't have to leave her, fearful she'd cause herself more injury if she tried to get up.

"Shall I go and get Father Lane for ye, would that be it?" he asked gently. "Ye can just say yer novena for a bit. How would that be? But mind ye, don't stir 'til I come back."

He hesitated to leave, hoping she wouldn't move from this spot. He looked at her and stroked her shoulder.

"Would that be all right now with ye? I'll go and get the Father."

She rested her body against him. He held her for a moment and then straightened her up and decided to make a dash for it before Father Lane left for the day. He pulled the jacket about her as if it would hold her straight, stroked her speckled hair and made for the door.

Chapter Twenty-Three

Eileen

February 1871

Eileen poked her head in the door at noon as the Angelus rang. Margaret knelt facing the window as she said, "I could be setting me clock by ye, young Eileen. Come in now. Come in."

Eileen joined her as they both intoned the noonday Angelus: "The Angel of the Lord declared unto Mary. And she conceived of the Holy Ghost. Hail Mary, full of grace . . ." As the bells ceased, so did their prayers, their familiar ritual ended.

"Our cranky little Miss Julia has gone down early for her nap," Margaret said as she stood up. "Nothing was quite right with her this morning. It was as if something was wrong and she couldn't tell me despite such a grand day. 'Tis a bit cold though, I'd say," Margaret said as she moved to put the kettle to boil.

"Would ye have the heat of some tea with me to take the chill from ye?" Margaret asked. "And I hope ye've some news ye've brought me now?" News and gossip were almost life to a woman, Jeremiah often said.

Eileen took off her beige shawl and hung it on the hook behind the door, noting that Jeremiah's coat and Mrs. Riordan's shawl were missing.

"There's nothing new since yesterday," Eileen replied. "I did see the cows at the McCarthys with their noses up over the fence like something was afoot. Me da says it could be an omen winter'll let up now."

Margaret set the table for tea, put plates, napkins and brown bread in place, the tea cozy ready once the pot had been filled.

"I'd say, in all me years, they've never been quite right with their predictions," Margaret said as she put the tea in place. "The cows could predict one thing, and they say the sunny day means we've six more weeks. Judging from this brilliant day, it's hard to believe it'll go on. But other years have proved me wrong and this one might well again."

Eileen picked up Michael from the corner where he'd been playing with blocks, ready to feed him and get him settled for his nap. His chubby pink cheeks and dark hair were attractive and Eileen held him to her, kissing his forehead.

"Mr. Buckley and Mrs. Riordan are out and about, are they?" she asked as she rocked Michael in her erms.

"Mr. Buckley took herself to the Candlemas service and though I expected them a while ago, I imagine me mother has hornswoggled him into some errand or another. I hope she's not giving him a time of it. She's been known to be rough on him. I imagine ye've noticed," Margaret said.

"Me Nana sometimes says, 'Two persons never lit a fire without disagreeing,'" Eileen replied as she sat Michael up at the table and pulled the high chair in tight.

"Yer Nana's a wise woman and well she knows me ma. They've been friends since yer da and me brother, Father Michael, were wee ones. Speaking of Father Michael, has yer da heard from him since the holiday card? Those two have been thick as thieves for years. We've no word lately," Margaret continued.

"I don't know, now, Mrs. Buckley, if there's been any word, but I can be sure to ask, if you'd like," Eileen replied.

"That'd be grand, Eileen. I'm always anxious for word of him. And while yer about that, do remind yer ma how grateful we are for yer help, Eileen."

Eileen smiled as she put the last bit of porridge on the spoon for Michael. He had a good appetite and wasn't fussy at all. Today he reached for her as she came round the table.

"Shall I put him in for his nap, now, Missus," Eileen asked as she lifted him, "or will he go with ye now so ye can both rest?"

Margaret smiled at the wisdom of this young girl. She was all of fourteen, yet she knew how to turn a phrase to make ye think it was yer own idea. She certainly had a charm with Mrs. Riordan.

"I think I will go in now, Eileen. I was too much at it this morning and I'm feeling the back pain again. A little rest will be just the cure for it."

Margaret bent to pick little Michael up and he cried for Eileen.

"Ah, there now, Eileen's got some jobs to do for yer ma. Leave her to them and ye come with me. We'll have a story and a little shut-eye for us."

Margaret and Michael went into the bedroom, Margaret cooing as he sputtered. Eileen picked up the dishes, stoked the fire, and went out for water and potato to begin the supper. Tims and Mary would be home from school by half-one.

* * *

The knock on the door startled Eileen. Who could it be, she wondered, not sure if she should wait for Margaret to rouse. After a moment, she set her knife on the table along with the potato she was peeling, opened it and gasped. It was Jeremiah cradling Mrs. Riordan in his arms like a baby, his work jacket draped over her. Her eyes were closed and her head rested on his chest.

She pulled the door open wide and stepped back to make room. No one said a word. Jeremiah went straightaway to Mrs. Riordan's quarters in the front parlor. Eileen followed them in and pulled the bed covers down. After Jeremiah had laid Mrs. Riordan down, they took off her coat and shoes and positioned her in the bed. Jeremiah covered her with the blue blanket and pulled up the rose-patterned quilt that was folded at the foot of the bed. Jeremiah's movements were deliberate and tender. Eileen felt a lump in her throat to see such gentleness. Mrs. Riordan had been nothing but nasty to him since Eileen had first come to help almost two years ago.

Sometimes Mrs. Riordan berated Jeremiah using Eileen's behavior as a weapon. "Why even Eileen, young as she is, can see that the child is hungry. Why would you not give her a biscuit?" Mrs. Riordan would say after Jeremiah had picked up Julia when she was fussing. "Even our young helper Eileen knows better how to make the tea. Ye never put it to boil long enough. Whatever is the matter with ye?"

Jeremiah would often wink at Eileen in the midst of these tirades, never once talking back to Mrs. Riordan. She wondered how he kept his tongue.

She looked at Mrs. Riordan as her eyes flickered now and again, and then closed. Jeremiah lit the little stove that heated the room. Eileen went out to put the kettle on and saw Margaret standing in her bare feet in the bedroom doorway. Had she heard Jeremiah come in? Michael must be asleep, she thought.

Before Eileen could think what to say, Jeremiah came out and went over to Margaret.

"Mairéad, me love, come sit for a minute."

Eileen kept her back to them, knowing they needed to talk alone, but she couldn't help overhearing bits and pieces.

"Father Lane was wonderful and so was Mrs. Ryan. The doctor says . . ." Eileen clinked the kettle on the hook, stoked the fire and noted that she should leave to gather more turf soon. A part of her wanted to stay to hear what had happened but she knew better than to intrude.

Eileen had grown fond of the couple, who had been friends of her parents since she was young. The children had a warmth about them that seemed a direct result of the loving way they were treated. In her home, there was a physical distance that allowed for no embrace. She envied the hugs these children received.

Not that there wasn't discipline. Tims could be a bugger, no doubt about it. But Margaret had a way with him that kept him in line without even shouting. Eileen sometimes had to threaten Tims to get him to comply and wished she knew how Margaret, with just a look, seemed to manage him so easily.

Eileen went out into the yard for more water, wondering what had happened. As she lifted the bucket full of water from the well, she saw Tims and Mary on the far ridge coming from school. She took the bucket and put it beside the door, then reached inside for her shawl. She saw Margaret's head resting on Jeremiah's shoulder and knew whatever had happened had been serious.

As she walked out the lane and started up the hill toward the approaching children, Biddy McDowell came by. To Eileen, even Biddy's stride seemed nosy.

"Well good day to ye, Eileen. Isn't it a shame that yer Mrs. Riordan is doing so poorly? Hasn't it been a burdensome time for the Buckleys? A burdensome time indeed."

Eileen agreed and quickly went on her way, saying she was off to see to the children. She wasn't about to give satisfaction to that ol' gossip Mrs. McDowell by asking her anything, though she longed to know. Mrs. McDowell had a way of twisting events into something further from the truth than one could imagine. Eileen didn't want to hear her version of anything.

Doing so poorly? Eileen thought. Well, she'd know soon enough.

She heard the squeals of delight from both children as she climbed to the crest of the hill. She felt her heart lighten as they drew near. She was pleased to see that Tims' pants had held her most recent mending as he raced down the hill.

Mary grasped her hand and looked up at her. "Ye've come after us today?" she said. "Is there to be a party?" With this, Tims came back up to them, eager to hear the reply.

Eileen marveled at Mary's association. She was right, of course, for the last time she'd come up to greet them, it was for a party to celebrate Mary's sixth birthday. Soon enough Mary would choose a feast day for her special day, but for now her November sixteenth birthday was celebrated.

"No, there's not to be a party today. But there is something I want to tell ye." She paused and knelt down and brought them both into her arms. She loved the warm, soft feel of them as they curled into her.

"Yer da brought home yer Gran from church and she's feeling poorly. So ye'll have to behave yerselves, especially ye, Master Timothy," she said as she mussed his red hair.

"Is she gonna die?" Mary asked, her serious blue eyes searching Eileen's face. "Jesus and Mary can take her to heaven. They took me grandda away when I was just a little girl," Mary said soberly as she pulled on her bonnet tie. "And they took me other gran and grandda before I was even born," she finished up, stuffing the string in her mouth.

"Ah, ye needn't be worrying about such things. No one's being taken away. We just have to be quiet," Eileen said as she pulled the string from Mary's mouth. "Yer gran will need her rest. Everything will be fine. Now, tell me about yer day. Did ye hear the end of yer story, like ye hoped?"

Both Tims and Mary loved stories. They remembered the smallest detail.

"'Leen, ye didn't say about her dog with the red ribbon on his neck to keep him safe? Remember?" they'd responded to one of her stories.

Eileen was glad that the few shillings she earned helped out at home. But she often thought she'd do this work without pay, for the children were so fulfilling to her. She also enjoyed being off on her own. Her ma was so often cross. Her aunt Eileen said it was just her change of life. Eileen knew that her little sister Meggie took the brunt of her mother's wrath. Eileen felt bad and, whenever she could, brought Meggie a treat upon her return from a day at the Buckleys.

As the three of them came down the lane, Eileen saw Jeremiah hard at work on the new outbuilding. The farm was growing steadily. Just like for her da, the switch to pasture from tillage meant more storage was needed for hay.

The children ran ahead of Eileen but waited at the door, as she had instructed. When they went in, Eileen was relieved to see that Mrs. Buckley was busy in the kitchen.

"Ah, there ye are, me little scholars. Are yer heads stuffed full of stories and letters and numbers to tell yer ma?" Margaret said as she hugged each of them.

"Ma, is Gran going to die?" Mary asked before Eileen could offer a word.

Margaret glanced up at Eileen, then looked back at the children. "She is, one day, but not today or for a long time, we hope. She's had a bit of a spell today, a stroke they call it. Do ye know what that is?"

"It's when yer head goes weird and ye can't make yer body do what it should. It's what happened to the school master, Mr. Mahan's da. He told us his da had trouble making his hands work. Can Gran's hands work?" Tims asked.

Mary started to tiptoe to Gran's room.

"Oh, me darling," Margaret bent to hug her, "it's best not to disturb her jest yet. The doctor will be here straightaway and then we'll see. Now off to a quiet time with ye and yer brother."

With that, Julia awoke and toddled out to Margaret. Eileen peeked in on Michael who was still asleep. She went to the sideboard and continued peeling the potato where Margaret had left off. They would know soon enough. And soon enough it would be dinnertime.

Chapter Twenty-Four
Rome

May 1871

"Ma, what's a bloody papist?" Tims asked at breakfast. Margaret had just sat down to her tea when his question came, and she saw from his eyes that Tims was troubled. "Billy Cooke says I'm a bloody papist. I told him I was no such thing and he said, 'Ye are too. Me da says so's yer whole family.' Is it true, Ma, are we bloody papists?"

Margaret sighed and wished Jeremiah were here to give the answer and not off in the fields. The weather was holding fine. She sometimes resented his devotion to the fields. He had children that needed his devotion as well.

It pained her to realize that the long-standing tension between Protestants and Catholics, whose roots went back beyond four centuries, had seeped into the life of her seven-year-old son. National schools, promising a sectarian education, had a mix of Protestant and Catholic children, yet the promise was far from fulfilled. Stories of name-calling and punishment for speaking Irish, along with demands to pledge loyalty to the Queen, were common.

Margaret sipped some tea, and tried to hide her distress.

"Well first off, Tims, ye needn't be saying bloody for anything. It's not polite talk. Remember that Gran always reminds us to speak the King's English to be proper and it's a proper boy I want ye to be."

Margaret lifted Michael down from his chair and felt the familiar twinge in her back. It would only be another month, she thought, and silently reiterated her prayer for a little girl.

"Ye know yer a Catholic little boy, is that right?" Margaret watched as Tims nodded his head and bit into the brown bread slathered with butter.

"Well, Catholics believe that the Pope is the leader of our church. The Cookes, they're the ones up the lane are they? People like them and other Protestant families don't agree about that. They use that term papist to mean belief in the Pope."

Margaret knew from Jeremiah's talk that the First Vatican Council had defined papal infallibility just last year. While Pope Pius IX was declared to be infallible in matters of faith, there were critics from France, Germany and Hungary who didn't agree. There were many in Ireland who had reservations about this move as well. Father Lane had been vocal in his opposition to it. "They'll stir up the ol' hatreds with that doctrine, mark me words," he had told Jeremiah after church one Sunday.

The fact that Gladstone himself raised an old anti-Catholic specter, questioning the ability of English Catholics to be good English citizens, didn't help matters.

"Home Rule means Rome Rule" had already been heard in the Parliament in opposition to Butt's movement toward Home rule. Margaret put politics out of her head, and looked back to her son, nibbling on brown bread, looking like he wanted to know more. Once again, she wished that Jeremiah were here to provide counsel.

If it weren't for Henry VIII, Margaret thought, we mighn't be in this fix, his break from papal authority changing the history of Irish Catholicism forever.

"Where did ye see this Billy Cooke, now? Is he playing in the lane with ye?"

"Naw, he brings his little sister in the pram up and down the lane. She's driving his ma daffy for her crying, so he takes her out in the pram when it's not raining."

"Well, ye might tell young William that yer proud to be 'papal,' if he brings it up again. Can ye remember that word? Papal. It's yer generation that's our hope to stop all the name-calling.

"And mind ye, tell him to tell his ma I'll be bringing up some herbs to help calm the baby."

Chapter Twenty-Five

The Christening

June 1871

"Gran, can ye give us a story now?" Mary asked, her blue eyes pleading. Father Lane had gone now, the baby was sleeping, and the music and feasting of the christening activities had subsided.

Margaret's namesake was born at the full moon in June. She'd started howling just before midnight. Despite her fatigue of the last year, Margaret seemed to be in her element, as if she could deliver six more children. She had smiled between pains throughout the birth and her high spirits had continued. It took only a few weeks for her to regain her stamina. She hummed and sang as the days warmed to the sun. She even hummed on the rainiest of days. At the age of forty, she didn't know if the Lord would bless her with more children after this, and reveled in this latest child, little Maggie.

The christening had been splendid; the children were all aglow with their new little sister. "Margaret Agnes is her name," Mary declared to any who would listen. "She's named after me ma and St. Agnes, who's a special musical saint." Michael clung to "Leen," Eileen Murphy, who stood with him at his new sister's baptism and played an important role in his early years. As Father Lane poured water on Maggie's head, Julia asked, "Is he bathing her with her dress on?" Tims and Mary looked like little parents, watching every move of their new "dolly."

"There's something special to this one," Jeremiah declared. "Her blue eyes are determined when ye look into them." Maggie had the softest of blue in eyes that were actually more gray when the light was right.

The godparents, cousin Eugene Riordan, who carried along his fiddle, and Ellen Cremin, a long-time friend, brought a festive spirit to the day. Billy Graney's accordion, Paddy Murphy's tin whistle and Julia Sweeney's Jew's harp, the tiny metal instrument played with teeth, provided grand music. Ellen Cogan's batch of potatoes colcannon along with a loaf of brown bread from Paddy and Margaret Riordan, cousins from the neighboring town of Grenagh, added just the right touch.

The music had been grand, the children joining in the jigs and reels. Eileen had given them the song "A Spinning Wheel," which she sang with more feeling than she intended.

"Merrily, cheerily, noisily whirring." Her foot tapped with the beat as she sang of the blind grandmother sitting by the fire knitting while Eileen spins and longs to go with her true love as he taps at the window.

Paddy Riordan's version of "The Rose of Tralee" followed and he sang the words right to little Mary, whose bright blue eyes sparkled with the attention.

"She was lovely and fair as the rose of the summer . . ." He finished by sweeping Mary up into his arms and dancing about with her. And then, as if on cue, she repeated her earlier plea.

"Gran, 'tis a tale we need from ye, please, now?"

Mrs. Riordan's recovery had been remarkable. She began to regain her speech a few days after her stroke. The more surprising part of her recovery was her peaceful disposition. She was reminiscent and thoughtful, often deferring to Jeremiah. She turned to him now. "Shall I tell of the swans upon this day?"

His hazel eyes smiled as he nodded, the graying hair at his temples becoming. "Ye tell the tale better than any I have known."

"All right then. Here we are now," Ma Riordan said as she straightened herself in her chair. Her hair, a rich silver now, was drawn back in a bun, her face lined and weary but her blue-gray eyes alive. "Ye may know that in the old kingdom of Ireland, before all this Union talk, there was a king whose name was Lir. Do ye know about him, children?" The littlest ones from the assembled families came forward to sit by Mrs. Riordan's rocking chair, which had been drawn into the center next to the hearth.

She watched for their attention until she saw some head nods. "The king and his beautiful wife had four children, all splendid creatures like yerselves. But a very sad thing, I have to tell ye, for the king's wife died in the midst of a cold, cold winter. So it was he set out to get another wife, not for himself mind ye, but to be a mother to his children. But there was trouble." She paused and gave a frown that made the children giggle. "It seems the woman the king had found to marry was a very unhappy one. She was downright miserable ye might say and jealous of the children, if ye can believe it, for the king loved them so very much. Can ye imagine, jealous of children? She longed to be rid of them for she thought she'd have the king all to herself."

Margaret stood, after nursing the baby, and joined Jeremiah by the doorway. "Isn't she grand, Jer?" she whispered into her husband's ear as she looked down at the sleeping infant in her arms. "She's like a miracle." Jeremiah smiled and put his arm around her. "And would ye listen to yer ma? Holding court, would ye say? Now there's another miracle as well."

They stood together listening as Mrs. Riordan continued. "And so the wicked woman, thinking only of herself, cast a spell on the four lovely children as they swam in the lake near the castle. 'Ye'll be swans for all yer days, now.' And indeed the little children were turned into handsome, white-feathered, long-necked, regal swans. But they could talk, and talk they did. And do you know what happened next? When their father learned what had happened he turned the wicked stepmother into a moth."

The children giggled and Mrs. Riordan leaned forward. "If ye be seeing any moths, it might be the ol' wicked stepmother. Ye can never tell."

"But did the children ever come back to being children, Gran?" Tims, who sat closest to Gran, wanted to know.

"They did Tims, me lad, they did," she answered as she rumpled his hair, "but not 'til many years after their da had passed on. Before his death, their da visited them every day that he could while they swam in the lake by the castle. When he died, the children still had hundreds of years of the spell to live out." Gran pulled little Mary to her side as she ended. "And finally, nine hundred years later, right there in Inish Glora where they'd been swans, they heard a church bell ringing more beautifully than any they'd ever heard." She looked around at the children's wide-eyed attention, the adults in polite silence as well. "The swans saw a monk who came close enough so they could tell him their story and luckily he was so moved by their tale that he reached out to stroke each one of them. It was then they became children again, their feathers gone." The children oohed and aahed as Gran continued.

"And so they returned to the castle where they once again played in the forest, swam in the lake and lived out their own days as the children of Lir."

Gran sat back satisfied, surveyed the children and said, "So, ye fine young ones, each time now ye see a swan in Ireland, ye might wonder what spell it could be under. For ye never know who's been up to mischief."

"Gran, can children really be turned into swans?" Mary looked up and asked, her eyes wide. "I mean really, or is this a fairy tale that's for make-believe fun?"

Mrs. Riordan looked to Jeremiah. "Yer da will have to tell ye about that, me little lass. His is the task of straightening out fact from fiction. I'm just the story teller. And a tired one at that, so now I'll take me leave."

With that, Mrs. Riordan made her way from the appreciative crowd to her room, planting a kiss on her newest grandchild's head as she went. Paddy Riordan picked up the fiddle and resumed his playing, this time with a lullaby.

Chapter Twenty-Six

The Vote

July 1872

Jeremiah hefted another forkful of new hay up into the loft, happy to have it inside before the clouds burst again. This new barn had been worth the effort. He'd set it on the rise above the house, just beyond Margaret's beloved garden. The stone exterior provided coolness within and allowed what little sunlight there was to send shafts through the inevitable gaps, enough light to see the height of the mound he and Eugene had raked. The cattle wouldn't go hungry this season.

Tims called to Jeremiah as he pitched the last of it. "Da, is there some help ye need? Ma said I should be asking ye."

As the red-haired eight-year-old ran toward him, Jeremiah knew enough to suspect Margaret's effort was to get Tims out from underfoot.

"Ah, there is something ye can do for me this very minute if ye'll meet me on the upper pasture."

Jeremiah planted the pitchfork deep into the pile of hay and moved to the pasture bordering the farmyard.

"Whatever is it I can do, Da? Now that I'm eight, I can be a bigger help, wouldn't ye say?"

"Ah, I would that, Tims. Now that ye're eight, ye can learn to bring the cattle on home," Jeremiah said, and he whistled for Tess, the mare he'd chosen after he'd lost Macushla. "They're not so difficult to move along, if ye keep yerself in front of them." Tims put his foot onto Jeremiah's knee as he'd done so many times before and boosted himself into the saddle. Jeremiah settled in behind him.

"Once ye get 'em started, they pretty much know their way. Take care, for ye'll see there's always a stray one here and there to look out for."

"We'll be bringing all the cows home, Da? Is that our work today?"

"We will, Tims, we will. And then we'll be off to see Mr. Cronin. We've some business to discuss."

* * *

Eugene Cronin brought Tims a biscuit and showed him round to the barnyard where nine-year-old Theresa was feeding the chickens. Tims joined her, careful to eat the biscuit quickly, to avoid having to share

Eugene and Jeremiah watched the children from the railing where Tess was tethered. "They're good little ones we've been blessed with, Jer. Your Tims is a handsome fella. Ye can be proud, indeed. Theresa tells me he's quite the one with the mathematics."

"He is that, Eugene." Jeremiah smiled as he received the compliment. "He knew his sums when he was just a little fella. There's no telling but that he will go on heads and shoulders beyond us all." With that, he inflated his chest and pulled on his suspenders.

"On another topic now, Eugene," Jeremiah said and looked at his friend, his eyes more serious. "I've come to see if ye'll be joining us at Josie's tonight? It's not every day we get one step closer to freedom for Ireland."

The gathering scheduled for Josie's in Fornaught was to celebrate the passage of the Secret Ballot Act, a breakthrough that brought an end to the days of public voting, preventing landlords from intimidation and holding sway.

Paddy Murphy had brought an article to Jeremiah from a Dundalk newspaper that summarized it best.

"At length the Ballot Bill has been passed. . . . The great argument against it was that it was . . . un-English. That is, that the English people were so stout and manly that they liked to vote in the faces of their neighbours . . ."

Jeremiah looked up at the sounds of laughter coming from the barn, then continued. "Why, Eugene, now that we've the secret ballot in place, we no longer need to fear expulsion from our farms for an honest vote, no longer have to go to the polls like 'a flock of sheep to a fair . . .'"

As Jeremiah continued, Eugene turned his eyes away and, staring out at the field, interrupted, "I won't be there tonight, Jer, though it's not what you think."

Eugene turned to face the man who had been a friend to him for so many years. "I'm happy enough for the vote and more safety to me own farm, but me Ellen is more poorly than usual. She's set about to be suspicious of every move I make, more to be pitied than censored, I'd say, still 'tis hard to go out."

Jeremiah had known Eugene to be wary of anything political but he also knew from other comments Eugene had shared that Ellen was a hard woman. That combination was enough to keep him away, although the outbreaks of violence from those on opposite sides of the issue might keep others from venturing out.

"Eugene," Jeremiah said as he gave Eugene a pat on the back, "'tis a mighty burden you're carrying." He then turned away and looked toward the two children, Theresa looking free as she chased Tims about the field. "Shall I leave Tims here for a while? Would it be good for yer Theresa?"

"Ye know, it just might be. I'll tell Ellen 'tis to give him a break from home. Our Liam will be glad of his company as well."

Jeremiah bid Eugene farewell and called over to Tims, "I'll be back after ye by half-seven. Mind yer manners, now." Tims waved, smiling, and Jeremiah mounted Tess. The change would be good for them all.

* * *

As he rode toward home, Jeremiah thought of the newly won right to vote in private, a milestone in the long struggle for freedom. His thoughts returned once again to how many Irish had come to be without the very land they once had owned, the Battle of Kinsale being a major turning point when the Flight of the Earls, O'Neill and O'Donnell, changed the climate forever—the last great Gaelic

chieftains going into exile, English domination at the end of
Queen Elizabeth's reign complete.

He slowed the horse's gait, and as he looked out over the land,
memories of Da and Michael filled him. They'd both cared so
much, both taught him so much. In the space of only two hundred
years, from 1601 to 1801, the Act of Union took Ireland further
from the Irish. There would be no peace for Ireland, Jeremiah
knew, until the issue of the land was settled. His personal quest
to finally own the land that his father and grandfather before him
had toiled upon was the next part of the evolving history of the
nation.

* * *

Father Lane hailed Jeremiah as he saw him turn down from the
Cronin place. Jeremiah slowed, and as he got nearer noted again
the changes in the man of late. The priest wore the same friendly
smile and cassock, but his posture was more rounded, his height
diminished, and his hair, what remained of it, was pure white. He
was a good priest, Jeremiah thought, one of the best. His even-tem-
pered spirit never seemed to waver. He had served the parish well
for close to thirty years, with Jeremiah and so many others benefit-
ing from his patience and care.

"It's a good day to ye, Father Lane," Jeremiah called as he dismounted. "I've just been up to Eugene's for a bit. How are ye this
day?"

"I'm grand for an old man, Jeremiah, and glad I am to see ye
riding by," Father Lane said, as he walked to Jeremiah who was
tethering Tess's reins to the wooden rail in front of the church.
"I've been aiming to have a talk with ye."

The two men moved from the church yard to the walkway next
to the church.

"I'm after asking if ye know anything about this gathering
tonight at Josie's. I've heard word of it and I'm wondering if ye
know of it at all." The old priest stared into Jeremiah's face, and
he could see by his manner that the matter was important to him.

Jeremiah eyed Father Lane with hesitancy. He saw the lines in the older man's brow and decided he must speak the truth. "Well, I do, Father. I've just come from talking about Eugene coming to it. It's an important marker in our history, Father, wouldn't ye agree?"

"I would, Jeremiah, I would. But I'll tell ye, there's caution from the Archbishop. He's particularly concerned about the spate of violence that accompanies some of these events. He's sent out a cautionary epistle to be read at all the Masses. He's advising all priests to discourage any such gatherings. Is there a leader for tonight's event, Jeremiah, would ye know now?"

"Ah, yer looking at him, Father," Jeremiah said as he turned to face Father Lane. "And as far as violence, I think ye needn't worry. It's only the remnants of the Knights of St. Patrick who are planning to attend. The group isn't so active these days, ye know, but they're grand for a celebration."

The lines in his brow receded, and Father Lane looked a bit relieved, trusting Jeremiah as he might a son. Still, he continued his questions, the Archbishop's letter clearly plaguing him. "Ye know nothing of the other element who've been agitating after the evictions? They wouldn't be involved, now would they, Jeremiah?"

Jeremiah kicked a stone from the walkway. "I couldn't say for certain they wouldn't be coming, Father, but I won't stand for any shenanigans, of that ye can be certain." Jeremiah looked up again into the old priest's face, his own face determined. "The occasion of this new voting victory is no time for violence, and it won't be if I have me way."

"I know I can trust ye to do what's right, Jeremiah. Yer da must be smiling down on ye as we stand here now," Father Lane said as he reached up and put his hand on Jeremiah's shoulder. "I'm glad to have had these words with ye. God be with ye."

Father Lane moved back toward the little cemetery that held gravestones of former pastors, the familiar string of black beads moving through his fingers.

Jeremiah watched for a moment, letting their conversation seep in. He thought of his da and Michael again and as he mounted

Tess, he wondered what tonight would bring. Enough daydreaming, he thought, and rode with deliberateness toward home. There was plenty to do before the evening.

Chapter Twenty-Seven

Josie's

July 1872

As Margaret and Jeremiah rode up the hill to Fornaught, Margaret remarked on the whitewashed building. "They're keeping it up well, I'd say. The windows are all looking fine, indeed. And the pots of flowers make ye feel welcome, wouldn't ye say, Jer?"

Jeremiah agreed as they moved up the small walkway to this unmarked building.

No marker indicated this place as a public house, yet everyone in the neighboring towns and villages knew it well. As they entered, Jeremiah noted the patchwork quilt, hung within the small vestibule, the black letters, *Josie's*, placed in the center. The main room was handsomely appointed with framed portraits and photographs, all familiar to him after so many years—Daniel O'Connell, the hillside of Tara, and a portrait of Jonathan Swift. One day Jeremiah would ask more about its origin, since Swift held a special meaning to him, his "Modest Proposal" being a favorite of Jeremiah's.

The pub was full, and Jeremiah nodded in greeting to many as he ushered Margaret to a table in the corner, near the other women. Jeremiah noted several men from the parish at the bar. Billy Graney, his wide-toothed grin hard to miss; Paddy Riordan, his square jaw set firmly round his pipe; Johnny Connor, his blonde hair cut short; Dennis Carroll, his dark eyebrows hiding his eyes; and Paddy Murphy, fair-haired, his brown eyes scanning the room. Even Doc Foley had joined them, his dark mustache tinged with white. There were others as well, men that Jeremiah counted on, men whose families had shared baptisms, burials and, God willing, one fine day would share some weddings. Once Margaret began to chat with the other women, Jeremiah joined the men at the bar to get their drinks.

As he looked about, he realized he wasn't acquainted with the several dozen more gathered in the other room; some he knew might be from as far away as Kilcullen and Kilmartin at the far reaches of the parish. He re-joined Margaret, glad the music was starting. Mary Carroll, Dennis's wife, was singing "Eileen Aroon." It was a sad, lonesome tune that didn't reflect the optimism Jeremiah hoped for to celebrate the victory of the vote; a movement toward some freedom, any freedom, was worth a celebration.

Soon Billy Graney gave them a crisp jig on his accordion and then tapping and clapping filled the room with a gaiety that spoke of celebration.

Jeremiah looked at the woman at his side, her hair, though beginning to fade, still the color of sunset. He was glad that Margaret had come along tonight, glad that Mrs. Riordan was now able to watch after the children once they'd been settled for the night.

"It'll do ye good to get out, now," she had said. "Go on with ye. If there's any fussing from little Maggie, I know just the tune that'll calm her."

Maggie had been a joy to Mrs. Riordan, who rocked and crooned to her any chance she had. She was born at the right time for Mrs. Riordan, who had finally discovered a peace within that allowed her to be a pleasant part of her daughter's growing family.

Word from Michael seemed to come regularly enough to satisfy them all. He told of an America they might never have learned about, for many glamorized it beyond reality, but Michael didn't sugar-coat the hardships, nor the hard hearts he had encountered. His vivid descriptions brimmed with an intense love for Ireland, whose flame seemed to burn brighter in him than the hillside celebration bonfires from their shared childhood.

"Sure wouldn't I be content to walk the luscious hills of Donoughmore and look down on our verdant farmland and feast me eyes on the rich soil that feeds those I love? No matter where I go, nothing can compare with me memories of home."

The sound of the jig stirred Jeremiah back to the room. As he watched Margaret dance, noting the freedom in her step, he felt a thrill run through him. He thought of the difficult times they'd weathered yet here they were, thanks be to God, dancing and singing as if they hadn't a care in the world. The children were healthy and brought joys they could never have dreamt of in their own childhood days. Red-haired Tims, a crackerjack of a boy who took easily to his chores, reminded Jeremiah of himself at times. His eagerness and ability were reassuring, a promising combination for this life.

Mary, with her fair brown hair and sea-blue eyes, was proving to be a good student and a good help at home. She adored little red-haired Maggie, she and Mrs. Riordan holding to an unspoken pact that the child should never cry. The most they heard from her were giggles and coos. Dark-haired Julia was a grand one for organizing, and a good thing too, for fair-haired Michael hadn't a practical bone in his being. Indeed, there was much to celebrate, and at Josie's tonight, a reminder of how much they'd gained was present, the time for celebration right.

After a few more jigs and reels, Paddy Murphy sang the haunting ballad "Kathleen Mavourneen," popular in America during their recent Civil War. A hush blanketed the room as he sang.

"Mavourneen, mavourneen, my sad tears are falling,
To think that from Erin and thee I must part!
It may be for years, and it may be forever . . ."

A crisp tenor, he sang the closing notes with a chilling clarity. A thunderous applause greeted his finish, and in the midst of it there came a sharp bang, sounding like a gunshot, from outside. A startled silence settled over the room. Jeremiah left Margaret at the table and signaled the others to go on with the music. He moved swiftly out the door and around back in time to see a horse and rider go off into the blackness of the night, with no evidence of any other disturbance.

"Did ye see anything, Jer? Was anyone out here?" Jeremiah turned to see his cousin, Michael Buckley, who'd come from the pub as well.

"I'd say there was, Michael, but they've gone for now with no trace." Jeremiah sighed. "These are troubled times, are they not? We're not sure even among our own."

"Do ye know any of the lads that are afoot from Kilcullen and Kilmartin, Jer?" Michael asked as he scanned the darkening hillside.

"I can't say that I do. Do ye think there's something queer about them? I knew a McMike Egan from Kilmartin but I haven't laid eyes on him in more than a year."

The strains of another popular ballad, "The Ministrel Boy," began as they moved back around the front of the building to the door.

Something moved as they came to the doorway. They both stepped beyond the door and found a fair-haired young lad, wearing a brown work jacket and cap, crouched against the building, holding his side.

"Are ye all right there, son?" Jeremiah asked.

The lad curled up tighter as the men moved closer.

Michael knelt. "It's all right now, we won't harm ye. We've a doctor inside if ye need help. What is it that's ailing ye?"

The boy looked up at them. Jeremiah lit a match. "Not even eighteen," Jeremiah muttered to himself.

"I need a doctor," the boy said, gritting his teeth. "Can ye move at all so we can see ye 'round into the light?" Michael's voice was level.

The boy moaned as he tried to stand. Michael caught him as he moved under the window's light; they could see there was blood.

"What's yer name there, son?" Jeremiah asked as he knelt down to the boy.

"Michael Egan, from Kilmartin," the boy said between labored breaths. "Can ye see to the doctor?"

Michael stayed with the boy and Jeremiah stepped back in to fetch Doc Foley.

* * *

Jeremiah was able to slip Doc Foley out with little notice from the others. Doc Foley learned that the boy had been caught up in some of the agrarian "outrages" happening around the parish and had worked his way here hoping for some help.

As Doc shared the story, Jeremiah thought back to his conversation with the priest a few hours before. Might Father Lane's worries have come from some penitent's vow to "even the score"?

The bullet had only grazed the boy. Doc Foley offered to take young Egan to his home, patch him up and send him on his way. The boy agreed, and the three men decided there should be little said of the incident. Violence, regrettably, was still a part of their lives. Jeremiah kept the story from Margaret for the time in order to not spoil what had been a good celebration.

* * *

January 1874

Jeremiah was shocked that Gladstone had so suddenly dissolved Parliament. "There were only three weeks between dissolution and Election Day," he said to Paddy as they sat together with their pints at hand. "An impossible time frame to find candidates for over a hundred constituencies."

Paddy's fair hair was showing some silver but his brown eyes were as clear as ever. "Well, thanks be to God, the Home Rulers won seats in fifty-nine constituencies. That's saying something." He tipped his pint again.

Both men were aware that Gladstone had suffered the worst Whig-Liberal result since 1841. A Tory take-over of Parliament brought Isaac Butt, who had served as legal counsel for the arrested John Devoy and his Fenian colleagues, to popularity.

Jeremiah was dismayed as he spoke. "Paddy, Butt's blathering about, making little speeches of appreciation for Disraeli, isn't what we need. It's clear that he's trying to avoid rancor but he's bound to placate himself right out of office." As they exchanged stories at the pub, Jeremiah thought of the recent prosperity of the harvests as something far more satisfying than anything political. His enthusiasm for Home Rule was tepid at best, and he held little hope that Butt would be a force for the most needed change, land reform.

Whenever he moved through the fields, riding at an easy trot, he would see from a distance the neat patches of property each with its own tenants. He could name most of the men who worked these fields, a majority of them for Joseph Bennett. Disturbing to him was the fact that less than eight hundred landlords owned half the country. Many of them, like Mr. Bennett, didn't even live on their own estates, leaving the management of the lands to gombeen men, who were out to make a profit for the landlord and themselves, often with no regard for the cost to the tenant.

He sighed now, as he pushed back his partially silver hair. "Paddy, I'd say the trouble isn't with Home Rule. Take a look at the evictions that are plaguing so many. That's the bigger problem."

Evictions of those who couldn't pay the rising rents were increasing and secret societies peppered the countryside with violence in an effort to even the score.

Paddy agreed. "Jer, yer man Disraeli can't hold a candle to Gladstone. He pays no mind to Ireland or what they're calling the Irish question." Paddy took another swallow before he continued. "And yer dead on about Mr. Butt. He's being ignored at every turn. As head of Ireland's delegation to Parliament, they say he's far too amiable and moderate. With the Tories as vehemently opposed to Home Rule as they are, we're stuck now with no movement of any kind."

A few minutes before Denis Murphy had joined the two men, listening quietly to their commiserating. His dark eyebrows fairly danced over his forehead as he spoke now.

"Have ye not heard of yer man yet? Charles Stewart Parnell, the Anglo-Protestant landlord from County Wicklow?" Denis ordered a stout and turned back for their reply.

"Now that ye mention it, Denis, I've heard a bit here and there," Jeremiah said as he stood to leave. "Some say he has the ability since he's British educated and Irish born."

Paddy turned now and asked, "Is he the one whose mother was American born, the grandfather an American naval hero in the War of 1812?"

Denis, like a cat who swallowed the canary, took another swallow, holding the men's attention.

"He's one and the same. And yer man Parnell is credible because of his parliamentary seat, and his fierce opposition to British rule. He's for us one hundred per cent."

Jeremiah recalled hearing that Parnell was known to be aloof yet highly disciplined.

"He might have just what it takes to work with the British parliament," Jeremiah said as he turned to leave. As he neared the door, he heard Paddy ask something Jeremiah wondered as well. "Can he deliver on land reform as well as home rule? Then we'd have some hope." While Jeremiah hadn't yet run short of hope, he wondered, along with Paddy, if this man might have what it would take to achieve the dream of land ownership.

He saluted his two comrades and headed for home.

For now, he would see to the fields and keep an eye on Parnell.

Chapter Twenty-Eight

Charles Stewart Parnell

Fall 1875

Margaret looked at the *Cork Examiner* that lay on the table. The sketch of Parnell, who'd been elected MP for Meath, intrigued her. His scruffy beard, somber brown eyes and receding dark hair weren't the stuff of a statesman, she didn't think. Even his steely look made him appear unfriendly.

In the past two years, the birth of the twins adding to the already burgeoning family, Margaret could scarcely find time to bless herself, let alone read the newspaper. The boy and girl had come along after Maggie had turned two; Eileen continued to be a great help and with Gran more peaceful and even a bit helpful, somehow she had managed. The twins were beautiful children in every way, both dark-haired and good-natured, with the Riordan hazel eyes.

Taking a chance to read a bit of news now and again helped her temper Jeremiah's rantings. As in the days after Tims' birth, Jeremiah's single-minded devotion to Ireland's future had flared once again. Gladstone's defeat in the 1874 election to Benjamin Disraeli had troubled her, not only because she didn't trust Disraeli but because she missed Gladstone, who had reminded her of her da. His gentle eyes were less intense than Parnell's; his clean-shaven face and thinning hair gave him paternal warmth. Over the years, she had clung to the hope that his mission to pacify Ireland would pacify her husband as well. For indeed, it seemed to her as she sat reading the newspaper, that the fate of her country and her husband had always been one and the same.

Jeremiah carried on relentlessly about the land. It was always the land, whether he was tending it, worrying about the weather or working out ways to own it. He repeated the stories they both knew by heart: that his family had tended the same fields since 1826, how the Riordan land was a fine addition. Though a good relationship with Mr. Bennett existed, Jeremiah was determined to own the land one day.

"I'll tell ye, Margaret," he'd said that very morning, as he walked about the cottage with Lizzie in his arms, "they can talk all they want of Home Rule, but it's the land that'll make the difference. I'm all for the Home Rulers and it's glad I am they've won the seats that they have." With his free hand, he brushed Lizzie's hair off her forehead and continued, "The real difference, though, is the land. It's where the heart and soul of Ireland rests." He bent to little Jeremiah, who'd been pulling on his pant leg, and lifted him into the other arm.

Margaret listened in silence, as she often did. She watched the children tucked into their father's arms, pleased when he paid attention to these two little ones. It seemed they scarcely knew him with all the time he spent doing the work of the land or the country. She knew there was no room for discussion when Jeremiah was fired up. They had talked in the weeks and months past of the Home Rule leader Isaac Butt who seemed to be taking them nowhere. Even Joseph Biggar, the Fenian pork butcher from Belfast, brought more hope with his antics of obstructing the Parliament.

"Do ye know what he did, that Biggar fella?" Jeremiah asked as he sat and bounced the two children upon his knees. "To prevent the passage of yet another coercion bill, he read extracts from newspapers and government blue books for four hours straight. That stopped 'em, it did."

Jeremiah laughed at the idea, stood again to march Lizzie and Jer around the room one more time, and put them down in their "castle corner," as he called it, by the window with their building blocks. The house was bursting at the seams, and Julia, Mary and Maggie now bunked together to make room for the twins.

Margaret and Jeremiah's discussion turned to Cambridge-educated Charles Stewart Parnell, a former high sheriff of County Wicklow, where he owned four thousand acres. Some said he had the potential to bring Ireland what she needed most—credibility and dignity.

"He's got possibility, I'd say, Margaret," Jeremiah said as he poured tea for them both. "And I learned recently that he's all for the cause of the Irish peasant, so there's hope that he could be our man." Jeremiah's voice was high as he spoke, the way it became whenever talk turned to politics and the land.

Margaret wondered if any one man could provide the salve needed to heal Ireland, the inner strength of the Irish people having been so badly bruised since the potato famine. She herself refused to believe that God had sent the hunger as a punishment. She had too deep a faith for that. But there were others who degraded themselves in an attempt to make sense of the suffering they'd endured, and felt no inner stamina. She couldn't fathom that the English were as insensitive to human need as it appeared they had been. Ah well, she thought, let other generations sort out their culpability.

At least, she thought as she sat in rare peace at her table, there are no derogatory pictures of the Irish in this newspaper. The dehumanizing depiction of the Irish in the British press often brought Jeremiah home in a rage. "Look at these pictures. For God sakes, we're not apes! Have they no idea what anger they're stirring up with this venomous journalism?"

The simianization of the Irish that appeared in *Punch and Judy*, as well as other publications of the day, was unmistakable. Jeremiah had gone red in the face after seeing one cartoon showing a gorilla labeled Hibernia with one fist clenched and the other hand open, begging. These and others like them only served to enrage the populace and perpetuate anger that no people could easily forgive.

Development of a nationalist press had finally come as the Nationalist Party grew. It funded newspapers in a few towns and counties that provided a balance to the papers that were often unionist in their perspective. Parnell owned *United Ireland* and used it freely to further promulgate the views of his party, which pleased the Irish peasants, farmers, Fenians and American Irish alike. "None of us," Parnell said, "whether we are in America or Ireland, or wherever we may be, will be satisfied until we have destroyed the last link which keeps Ireland bound to England."

The political reports and Jeremiah's distress could have worried Margaret, but for now, she found herself reveling in her growing brood of children and the fortune that was theirs on this land. Jeremiah's hard work and penurious ways had brought them to a new level of prosperity. He was well regarded in both the church community and their town of Ahadallane.

Growing into her respectable status, Margaret eagerly left behind her childhood tongue of Gaelic. She told her mother she'd like the children to speak the Queen's English and asked her help in teaching them the manners of the day, valuing as she did a refined decorum and polished demeanor. Education held an important place for both her and Jeremiah since neither of them had much formal training. Thanks to her own brother Michael's example and her great love of books, Margaret had tasted enough literature to make her long for more. "To thine own self be true," she would quote from her treasured volume of Shakespeare when the occasion warranted, "thou canst not then be false to any man." She hoped as much and more for her children.

If Parnell could help restore a bit of the spirit that belonged to the Irish, Margaret would be in full support, even though, as a woman, she didn't have a vote in the matter. She finished reading and had folded the newspaper when Maggie and Gran came back in, their tin bucket overflowing with blueberries and elderberries. Margaret would make a tart later in the day, one of the treats of the harvest.

"What do ye make of it, Ma? This new Irish-born MP for Meath and his American mother. Do ye think he could possibly have a heart for Ireland?" Earlier Margaret had read that Parnell's sisters were presented at Queen Victoria's court.

"Can ye tell me any of them at all who make a bit of difference in the long of it?" Gran replied as she peeked in on the napping twins. "I'll not put too much faith in any of them. They're all human, some of them far too human to make the difference we put on them."

She settled Maggie in the corner with her dolly and gave her an extra pat on the head.

"She's as bright as a shiny dollar, Mairéad," Gran said, looking at Maggie. "She reminds me of ye at that age," she said as she put her apron on. "Do ye know what she asked me just now while we were gathering the berries? Did I think that God could see the fairies? Can ye imagine a four-year-old with a question like that?"

Margaret smiled and as she rinsed the berries, turned to her. "Indeed, and I'm interested in yer answer now. Whatever did ye tell her? Mind ye, I have me own answer."

Gran joined her at the sink, smiling. "Sure, I told her that God sees everything and if there are fairies, sure he sees them." She turned and put the empty berry pails by the doorway, asking, "And what might ye have told her? Mind ye, I know about the church's dismissal of the fairies, giving us all the angels and the saints, but a good fairy won't harm the child. It never harmed ye, now did it?"

Margaret paused, remembering the struggle with the banshee that had gone on for so long within her. She was embracing the new traditions to replace the commonly held superstitions of her childhood. But she knew not to argue this point with her mother, who, devout as she was to her Catholicism, clung to the "old ways."

"Not much harm, Ma, and ye answered her jest fine," she said as she pulled the flour sack onto the counter. "Remember when Michael used to blame Archbishop Cullen for trying to cleanse the old ways from Ireland? I'd say there are plenty of the older families who still celebrate baptisms, marriages and funerals in their homes rather than even using the church building. Our own Father Lane says there's no need for disrupting what faith there is."

"There's a good man, Margaret, a good man," Mrs. Riordan said as she stole a berry from her daughter's bowl and stuck it into her mouth.

June 1876

"Ah, Margaret, he is indeed our man!" Jeremiah exclaimed as he walked into the cottage, newspaper in hand. "Wait 'til ye hear of Parnell's statement in the House of Commons this week!" He put his jacket and cap in place and, barely noticing the children and Mrs. Riordan, began to orate.

"Listen to this: 'I wish to say publicly and as directly as I can that I do not believe and I shall never believe that any murder was committed at Manchester.' He's brilliant, I'd say, absolutely brilliant."

Margaret listened as she put the potatoes to boil. The heat of the day tired her. She was grateful for Mary, now eleven, and Julia, eight, good helpers with all that had to be done to feed this family of ten. Mary was especially helpful since their long-time helper Eileen had gone off to America, like so many of the young people who were leaving in great numbers. The party held for Eileen's leaving had been grand. Margaret saw to it that the whole family was there to say good-bye. Eileen's presence in the Buckley household had seen them through some difficult times.

While they were sorry to see Eileen go, they knew her fortune would be far better in America. Her mother's physical and mental health had deteriorated significantly. Her sister, Meggie, was old enough now to help out and her brother Niall was on the farm full time with his da. Eileen's trip to America was meant to help seek a fortune for them all.

At the "American wake," as such celebrations were called, the uilleann pipe playing had been spectacular. Paddy Riordan was the master of them, effortlessly pumping the bellows under his arm and filling the air with haunting and high-spirited tunes. The children had taken easily to the dancing and Margaret thrilled to see them turning about in time to the music. She had brought along her most prized button accordion, a gift from Jeremiah for her fortieth birthday. She'd finally found time to practice now that the four older children were in school and Gran was still spending the mornings with Maggie and the twins.

It had been a grand send-off for Eileen. Each of the children made something for her to take to America. Mary gave her letter paper, asking that she promise to write. Julia and Maggie had woven straw dolls as reminders of them. Tims had helped Michael carve a small flute to carry music with her. Mrs. Riordan had sent along a handkerchief with special embroidery, saying it was from the twins. "To catch the tears that fall as ye leave dear ol' Erin." The keening—the grief-stricken wailing—had brought Margaret to tears, not just for Eileen but for the thought of her own girls, who might one day follow this same path.

The thought of losing any of her children took Margaret's breath away. As hard as the thought was of their leaving Ireland, she'd seen enough people go that she knew it to be inevitable. She'd rather see them prosper elsewhere than suffocate in a land unable to sustain them. In his letters, Michael told of the hordes of Irish that filled the New York parishes. He also sent a copy of Johnny Joe's ordination held two years ago in St. Joseph's Seminary in Troy, New York. It consoled Margaret to think if she did have to lose any of them to America, they would at least have family support, two priests at that.

With the prospect of owning the land more within reach, it still wasn't clear to Jeremiah or Margaret how it would be handed down; they were certain only that it would be a son who would inherit it. For girls born on farms without a dowry, there was little or no prospect. Marriage proposals were sparse and the lure of America was great. While nunneries were an option, they too required dowries. Margaret knew it would be her girls who'd leave. And though it tore at her heart, she knew there was no discussing it with Jeremiah. He displayed his passion for the topic with an angry silence reserved for anything that was non-negotiable.

She knew that when the time came, this would be a burden she would shoulder alone.

* * *

"If yer man is Parnell, now Jer, what will he do for the land?" Margaret said as she pulled the iron kettle off the hearth and began scooping out bowls of the meat stew. "Has he enough passion for it?"

The children had grown accustomed to these evening dialogues that often ended with their mother having the last word. However, the politics of the day were not allowed to be discussed when Gran was at the dinner table. But of late, Gran was taking her meals in her room. Though she'd had a good recovery from her stroke, her aging was evident, her gait less steady, her vigor diminished, and the fuss of all seven children at the table was more than she could handle. Mary and Maggie carried her plate and tea in to her. Julia had willingly turned her part of the chore over to Maggie, who begged to be of help.

"I'll walk ever so carefully with the tea, Julia," five-year-old Maggie promised. Julia didn't mind one less chore and one less reason to have to interact with Mary, who was so bossy. "All right Magpie, jes mind yer step and don't spill any on Gran. She mightn't like that."

Jeremiah continued to hold forth. "With less than eight hundred landlords owning one-half the country, sure Parnell sees that something needs to be done. There's something about him, Margaret. He says the right things and I'll tell ye," Jeremiah said, lowering his voice for fear Mrs. Riordan would hear him, "he understands something yer brother Michael never trusted. There's a way to change things in Ireland without force. Just keep an eye on Parnell and see if he isn't our man."

"Enough talk now of the political nature, would ye say, now Jer? Which scholar shall we hear from tonight?" Margaret looked at the children who sat round the table.

"Choose me, Ma, I'm bursting to be telling ye," Maggie exclaimed from her chair near Margaret.

"Well, what might it be that has ye bursting, little lady?" Jeremiah asked. "Ye've got yer scholarly brothers and sisters and yer ma and me waiting with wonder."

"I'm a scholar now, too. Gran told me so. She said I'd be the smartest of all of ye, for I can see things the others can't." Maggie's eyes widened as she spoke, as if she were imparting secret knowledge, "She says I have 'God's eye'!"

"Everyone knows that God doesn't have eyes," Mary said with great disgust, getting up to clear the dishes from the table.

"Well, Gran knows a clever girl when she sees one, that's for certain," Margaret said, as she stood. "Once ye start yer schooling next year, Maggie, we'll see about the rest."

"Ma, what's God's eye mean?" Julia asked as she carried the teapot to the hearth. "Does it mean Maggie's gonna be a nun? Our teacher says it's a special calling. Is that what Maggie hears calling her?"

Margaret paused and looked at the two older girls. "Help me with these dishes, now. We'll ask Gran about 'God's eye' in the morning. Now it's time for yer chores and mind ye, then yer studies."

As Jeremiah and the boys moved to the door, ready to bring the cows home from the pasture, Maggie went to the new window that Jeremiah had recently added to their main room. It overlooked the garden and the settling twilight. They all watched as Maggie smiled and waved.

Chapter Twenty-Nine

Michaelmas

September 1876

"Da, was this land always ours?" eleven-year-old Mary asked Jeremiah as they rode across the rolling green fields. She sat next to her father in the cart, as the pony pulled them along, looking up at him and then looking over the vast hillsides. "The teacher says that our lands were stolen from us. How do ye steal land, Da? Ye can't pack it up and just take it away now, can ye?"

Jeremiah slowed the pony's pace. How could he answer this most delicate question? And what was the teacher telling these children? Was there any good to be done by stirring up the harsh facts of English oppression? They heard enough of his diatribes at the dinner table, but at least he wanted them to have his perspective. Who knew what the teachers would represent, since many national schools carried out English bidding?

The children, he believed, were too young to understand anything of the sixteenth- and seventeenth-century plantations, Scottish people being moved into lands taken from the Irish. He was certain they needn't be burdened yet with the knowledge of the systematic slaughter and destruction of property, the confiscation of all Catholic estates in the country under Cromwell's bloody reign, the greatest atrocities in their own province of Munster. They would learn soon enough.

Gran had already told the children about the Penal Laws, how it had been illegal for her da to vote or hold office. "Why sure," she had said to them, "yer own grandda because he was Catholic couldn't serve in the militia, enter any honorable profession, nor purchase land."

It always gave Jeremiah pause when he thought about the severity of the laws and how indeed the Irish had survived them.

Gran spoke about Tess to the children to make her point. "Do ye know yer grand mare Tess out in the yard, there? Imagine if she was worth more than five pounds ye couldn't own her. That's right, they had the right to come right up to ye and take her away, pretty as she is."

She also made her point about schooling. "Ye know how important book learning is to yer ma and da. Wasn't me own Grandda a teacher and he couldn't use a schoolroom but had to teach in some of the very hedges around our land. And Mass couldn't be said in a church now but out on Mass rocks, they called them.

"Ye see your ol' Gran hobbling off to the Mass each day, don't ye? Yer da or one of the boys is kind enough to take me and ye know why I go? 'Tis a privilege I'll not miss, as long as me bones can get me there."

Jeremiah was glad for the children to learn of the old ways, yet conflicted, for he was growing in the belief that bemoaning the past would bring no good to any of them. They needed to remember above all that they were survivors and that was worth something.

He turned to Mary and saw her thoughtful look, as she sat primly in the front of the cart for this special visit. She was the first of the children to accompany the da to Mr. Bennett's, and knew the weight of this honor.

"No, Mary, ye sure couldn't pack up a land and sneak off in the night with it, could ye now?" Jeremiah replied as they neared the big house. "But there have been those in past days who have tried to do just that, and they've not succeeded. We're proof of that, ye and me and yer ma and yer gran and Tims, Julia, Michael, Maggie, little Jer and Lizzie. We're on land that will one day be ours, God willing. Our Mr. Bennett is a just man. One day we'll find a way to gather enough money to buy this very land upon which our noble mare dances us along." As he slowed Tess, he reached over, smoothed her soft brown hair from her forehead and smiled. "Yer a grand lass for wondering about such goings-on."

Mary's ocean-blue eyes widened as they turned down the lane to Mr. Bennett's estate where Jeremiah would pay the rent, a satisfying experience when times were good, as they were now. To Mary, it looked like a castle, its gray stone imposing and vast. The majestic color in the trees clustered on the hillside beyond almost defied nature, their golds, browns and reds brilliant in the morning sun.

Mr. Bennett's "big house" sat amidst a copse of woods looking as if it were a fairy land, its pillars announcing a welcoming front entrance, not the tall prison bars of other manses. It was fitting that this man, whom Jeremiah had grown to respect, had a house that was not as grand as some others. The opulence of shiny handles and manicured shrubbery was missing; only the treasured brass door knocker that had come from Mr. Bennett's own grandfather provided a hint at elegance. The foundation plantings flowed loosely in natural artistry; white framed windows softened the austerity of the gray stone building itself and added to its beauty. It was a respectable house for a respectable man.

"Look, Da, here's a rainy day place for umbrellas," Mary said as they entered the vestibule. "And look at the lights in the roof," she exclaimed as she gazed up at the chandelier. As always, Jeremiah was graciously received. Mr. Bennett was not here today, but the butler, Jonathan, extended the same welcome with special attention to Mary. They were invited into the drawing room where Mary's exclamations continued. "Da, look at the lady hanging above the hearth. She's beautiful."

"Your daughter is quite the lady herself," Jonathan offered. "And a good eye she has for beauty. That's Mr. Bennett's mother who recently passed on." The portrait revealed a handsome woman with clear blue eyes and rich silvery hair. She wore a black lace collar that stood high around her neck. Her hands were folded across the lap of a burgundy taffeta dress.

"She was one of the kindest women known to grace this earth. She visited us here often. She'll be sorely missed," Jonathan lamented.

Jeremiah and Mary sat across from the hearth. The maid, a dark-haired girl a few years older than Mary, moved soundlessly into the room, placed a silver service upon the mahogany sideboard, and then poured a cup of tea for Jeremiah and Mary. After presenting it to them, the pretty girl placed the silver sugar bowl and creamer on the small table in front of them, along with a plate of teacakes and cookies. Mary eyed the four small cookies expectantly. "May we eat these?" she asked politely.

Jonathan and the maid exchanged glances, and the maid was smiling as she left the room.

Jonathan turned to Mary. "You may indeed. The cookies are just for you, Miss Mary," he said with a gentle smile. "I see you have a harvest knot," he noted, referring to the small ornamental twist of plaited straw she wore in her hair. "Is there to be a festival this evening?"

Mary looked to Jeremiah, who nodded.

"Oh yes," Mary replied, "there is to be a festival at the church this very evening to celebrate Michaelmas. Me Gran says it's also our time to give a sheep to those without one." She glanced at the cookies and looked back to Jonathan, who nodded that she could indeed go ahead and have one as he said, "I remember those days with delight meself. I grew up quite close to here in Coachford. Michaelmas was one of the best of times, when the harvest was complete and the gloom of October hadn't yet set in."

Jonathan, an Irishman himself, in the service of an English landlord, smiled. He was only too glad to see the young ones celebrate the traditions.

The harvest celebrations varied from town to town, but most festivities included a celebration as the last of the harvest was brought in. Ceremony often attended the cutting of the last bit of corn where paid workers and volunteers gathered to witness some small creature, a hare, frog, corncrake or partridge, scurry out for safety from the last of the standing corn as the reapers advanced.

"Aye, Jonathan, we've put 'the hare out of the corn' for this season," Jeremiah said, quoting the popular phrase.

With that, he helped himself to a buttery teacake and stood.

"With yer help, Jonathan, I've some paperwork to attend to."

The two men stepped to the far side of the room and stood in the light of the tall ceiling-to-floor windows. The draperies were heavy rose-colored damask. The upholstered chairs on either side of the windows were covered in a matching fabric.

"I've this season's rent ready to give to Mr. Bennett," Jeremiah said proudly, "We've had a good harvest and a good turn at market. I'm grateful to ye if ye'll be telling him of our satisfaction and gratitude."

The man with whom he spoke was almost as tall as Jeremiah's six feet, his brown hair, not unlike Jeremiah's own auburn hair, graying at the temples. The softness around his mouth and eyes put Jeremiah at ease.

"I'll deliver your message as soon as Mr. Bennett returns, which I expect will be within the fortnight."

After Jonathan took the bundle of paper bills and left the room, Jeremiah returned to his tea and cakes and his delighted daughter.

"Da, is this the way a lot of other people live? In grand houses, with tea and cakes and cookies every day?" she asked as she reached for her second cookie.

"For some it is a way of life, though I wouldn't say it brings much more joy than the life we live," Jeremiah said as he lifted his teacup. "And doesn't yer ma make some fine teacakes for special occasions? I suppose ye'd tire of them if ye had them all the time, wouldn't ye now?" he said with a wink.

He saw her face screw up in disagreement.

"I'd never tire of cakes and cookies all the time, Da. I don't think any of us would."

Jeremiah smiled, took a last drink of his tea, and stood, indicating to Mary that it was time to go. As they wound their way back home, Jeremiah pondered his earlier statement to Mary of Mr. Bennett's goodness. Was he being too trusting of this man about whom he knew so little? Time would tell and, for now, there was a feast to be celebrated.

***

Michaelmas, the feast of St. Michael the archangel, was the traditional time for picking apples and pressing cider. Mary had helped Gran just before she left for Mr. Bennett's and Julia was next to help. Down plucked from live geese for the filling of mattresses and pillows was another time-treasured tradition at this season. The most popular custom, however, was eating the goose for dinner. And thanks to an abiding awareness of the poor, there was a ritualistic killing of a St. Michael's sheep, with the greatest part of it bestowed on the poor.

On the ride back from the "big house" Mary chattered non-stop and upon returning home, bounded into the house full of tales of grandeur. She spouted to any and all who gathered to listen. "Then a girl, not much older than meself, all dressed in a black dress and white pinafore with a sort of white bonnet set upon her head, came in with, ye'll never guess, a solid silver tea service, like the ones we've seen in the store windows on St. Patrick's Parade in Cork. Ye've never seen such elegance. And then as fancy as ye like, she puts a plate of teacakes and four cookies for me right on the table in front of us. The plate was fancy china like." Maggie and Julia oohed and aahed while Gran continued to rock by the hearth.

"When she said they were for me, I thought of ye, not there to share the sweetness with me. So, I did what any clever girl would do." And with that, Mary reached into her pocket and with a sense of great drama, pulled out two cookies and a teacake. Julia and Maggie shrieked with delight.

"Ye sound as if ye haven't had a sweet in yer life," Margaret said from her place at the sideboard where she was peeling the potatoes. "Wouldn't ye think they were starving for want of sweets and finery, Gran?"

"Ye've not spoiled them," Gran said as she looked up from her tatting, looking wearier, as she often did of late. "And for that ye're to be commended. Some of the young ones I see at church seem to have every fad of the day there is. Just this past week, I saw one with velvet ribbons in her hair and for no special occasion. 'Tis sinful and such a waste."

"Gran, velvet ribbons are all about now. Even Eileen's Meggie has some. They're for everyday dress now, not just for holy days," Julia responded, looking quite pleased to speak with such authority.

"What others are wearing should be no concern of yours, Miss Julia," Margaret intervened. "What kind of talk is this about what the others are doing or not? If they were to jump off St. Patrick's Bridge in Cork, would ye be jumping, too?"

Margaret hoisted the filled kettle to the fire. She turned and faced her daughters.

"On a different note now, it's time, me fine lasses, to prepare for the feast. I'll mind ye to be setting the table, for the goose is almost cooked for us. It's a grand feast we'll be having," she said with a soft smile.

"Julia, will ye fetch yer brothers and Da now and Maggie and Mary bring the utensils and plates to the table?"

She looked around the house, filled with sounds and scents of a feast in progress. Filled with years of good fortune, and children. But she never forgot the early days of hunger and want. She turned toward the mantel above the hearth and focused on the picture of the Sacred Heart of Jesus as she said, "On this day we'll thank God for our own plenty and share what we can with those who haven't as much. Amen."

Chapter Thirty

Joseph Bennett

June 1879

"Help me with this, now, Jer," Paddy Murphy said as he stood next to Jeremiah at the long mahogany bar. "How can himself in his grand 'big house' survive these awful days? Will ye tell me that?" Paddy took a long swallow and continued. "Ye know yerself the cost of things and ye've not any servants to pay, nor taxes. Yet here he is offering us an abatement. I'd say he's either daft or one of a kind. He'll have the wrath of the others, that's for certain."

His long-time friend Paddy, Eileen's father, from over in Pluckanes West, the land adjacent to Jeremiah's, was a tall, lean man with a treasured soft smile. They were at Pat Barry's, a familiar meeting place, just up the road from Josie's.

Jeremiah considered Paddy's question as he drank from his pint. It was a difficult one. Paddy was right. Landlords were losing ground yearly as Gladstone's Land Act took hold. Tenants weren't the only ones struggling in these days of unending rains, potato failure and disease.

And Paddy was right, too, that Mr. Bennett risked the wrath of other landlords who had no intention of reducing rents or offering abatements. Much as he longed for it, the quest for full Irish peasant proprietorship seemed almost utopian to Jeremiah and to other farmers as well.

Paddy looked to Jeremiah for an answer, as so many others did these past years. Jeremiah had continued to grow in stature in the tiny town of Ahadallane. Besides his easy manner, reputation for fairness and hard work, he was one of the oldest surviving sons of the hunger, and a member of this parish his entire life. His baptism, first communion, confirmation and ultimately his marriage on Shrove Tuesday had all been in this parish, all under the guidance of the recently deceased Fr. Michael Lane.

The good priest's death had been unexpected. The housekeeper, Mrs. Ryan, found him kneeling at his bedside, rosary beads wrapped around his fingers. Not an uncommon picture. He was a man whose holiness had a contagion to it. He honored the "devotional revolution" by making sure the people experienced what he called "the spirit of the ritual, encouraging attendance not out of obligation but rather one's own desire and satisfaction."

Father Lane's first year in the parish coincided with the start of *An Gorta Mor*, The Great Hunger in 1845, a time of great physical and spiritual need. Jeremiah knew that for Father Lane, it hadn't been a question of God allowing the deaths but rather of seeing God in the surviving people who buried their wives or husbands, young children and parents, and somehow found strength to go on. He remembered Father Lane's presence as he buried Eliza.

The entire Buckley family, including Gran, attended Father Lane's standing-room-only funeral, a testament to the love the parishioners of Donoughmore had for this man.

One particular sermon, emblematic to Jeremiah of the depth and heart of the man, stayed with Jeremiah. After reading Cardinal Cullen's words condemning the secret society outrages that were plaguing the countryside, Father Lane had gone on to speak of another kind of violence: the violence of spirit that would allow one man to take another's home without regard to his welfare and the well-being of his family.

Jeremiah would miss Father Lane's counsel. The issues of the day continued to be complex. The past two seasons had been disastrously wet throughout Ireland. The potato crop had failed two years straight.

When Paddy moved over to a vacant nearby table, Jeremiah followed.

"Jer, there's talk of a terrible outbreak of livestock disease. Throughout the barony, pig and poultry numbers have been decimated," Paddy said. He sat back and looked straight into the amber pint in front of him.

"'Tis this weather that's to be the ruin of us. Prices for butter have fallen and grain crops are flattened," he continued, making no effort to sugar-coat his comments.

The pages of the *Cork Examiner* were filled with reports of flooding: ". . . heaviest downpours of rain witnessed here for some time past . . . water fully some two feet high. It made its way into several houses and in some it was very high, being nearly three feet in a forge in the Glen."

Other reports told of delays in train service due to flooding as well as the fear being entertained by the failure of the potato crop, the principal support of the laboring class. Evictions were double what they had been less than a decade ago. Agrarian outrages and violence had escalated to epidemic proportions.

As he listened to Paddy, Jeremiah thought of his own fortune. His prosperity of just three years ago would be threatened except for the help of the children. Tims, now fifteen and with a strong back, had helped them manage an adequate harvest. Gran helped Mary to become quite adept at sewing. She'd even managed to sell some of her handkerchiefs and bonnets at market. Margaret taught Julia how to make fine butter and Maggie was in charge of gathering the eggs for sale. The twins were too small yet to make any significant contribution, but their joy gave them all a bit more light-heartedness.

Jeremiah and Lizzie had become inseparable, often speaking in their own language to one other. While they did squabble, the spats didn't last for long.

"Ye can't put it there, silly Jer," Lizzie, her blue eyes afire, would proclaim as they built villages in the yard, where Tims and Mary had once played. "Castles have to be in the center of the town." Little Jer would push at the village and wreck the progress they'd made, shouting, "Lizzie know it all, do it yerself." She'd pay no attention and stay at it. He would eventually join in again, with a grand new idea. "If we put it there, everyone can see it and they can see everyone." The older children enjoyed watching, the adults glad they could stay out from underfoot and be such company for one another.

It was the children's spirit and the strength of his family that assured him, despite downturns and despite politicians, they would survive.

His thought turned once again to Paddy as he continued to blather on, speaking of politics, of Isaac Butt's public criticism of

Parnell's tactic of obstructionism in July 1877 when the longest-ever House of Commons session was held, lasting over twenty-six hours.

"What good is any of it doing us, Jer, I ask ye?" Paddy said, sat back and took the last of his pint in a long swallow.

As tenant farmers, they were facing their gravest season since the famine. Corn-growing in the American West, along with the more efficient rail and steamship transportation, had flooded Europe with cheap grain. Prices fell, and many lost the ability to pay rent. The number of evictions doubled in 1878 to the highest figure in over a decade.

Jeremiah stood, moved back to the bar and turned to Paddy.

"If it were up to me now, Paddy, I'd make Parnell king, if we still had kings. He's not unlike O'Connell in his ability to avoid the violence. Me da was a man for that. He drilled it into me. 'An eye for an eye only gets us all blind,' he'd say. Parnell's 'new departure' seems like a good approach."

Paddy joined Jeremiah at the bar and slid his empty glass forward indicating he was finished. He then asked, "What of yer man Michael Davitt, Jer? I hear he's teaming up with John Devoy in America and it might be more trouble than anyone intends." Michael Davitt had recently formed a Land League in County Mayo, one of the poorest counties in Ireland, where starvation visited on a regular basis.

"Paddy, I'd say that Davitt's on the right path with this Land League of his. 'Tis the land these politicians should be worrying after. Give us our land and then we'll be free. Jaysus, man, how it galls me to watch them flounder about like fish."

Jeremiah walked out the back door to relieve himself. A cloud cover clung to the sky making the night black. He shook his head in annoyance; mention of Devoy had made him think of Michael's most recent letters, which had frustrated him so.

Michael had written in detail of his initial meeting with Devoy, over five years ago. Jeremiah had read into his words the same reckless fervor for freedom that had driven Michael when he left Ireland. The newspaper accounts, with their ugly details of informers and dynamitards, annoyed Jeremiah beyond words. Couldn't these men see that they were only blocking the way to freedom with such rash tactics? Couldn't they see that their violence wasn't reaching the hearts of men, but rather the basest part of them, their fear blinding them to reason? They'd never win anything with that. Did they really think that all their oaths to support violent revolution in Ireland would help the Irish gain land? And even if they made progress, at what price?

He went back inside and discovered that Paddy had gone home. The few men clustered in the far corner eyed him, since he wasn't a regular at Barry's. To assuage their suspicion, he raised his glass to them, drank the last of the pint and went back out into the night.

***

Though Parnell had won him over, Jeremiah was cautious in his wholesale support. While Parnell gathered the energy and support of the many dissident IRB men, he also formed an alliance with Devoy and his American resources. Such alliances could be dangerous.

After Isaac Butt's death in May, the way was cleared for Parnell to eventually take over leadership of the Home Rule party. To Jeremiah's delight, he turned the land problem into the most important political consideration of national life. But his collaboration with Michael Davitt worried Jeremiah. Davitt's recent release from Dartmoor Prison for his alleged part in an assassination plot led Jeremiah to believe that Parnell's association could prove pivotal in the direction of the day.

Jeremiah had looked into the background of Michael Davitt and learned that as a five-year-old, Davitt and his family had been evicted from their smallholding in County Mayo. At age eleven, Michael lost his arm in a factory accident. His intensity was understandable. After seven years in prison, he returned to County Mayo determined to change the course of history for those who would follow him. He organized a mass meeting and demanded reduced rents for the people. Within a few days, Canon Burke, the Catholic priest landholder, reduced the rents by twenty-five per cent.

Something important was beginning to happen.

Parnell's words at a recent meeting in Mayo at which Davitt had invited him to speak set the tone for the coming years.

"A fair rent," Parnell declared, "is a rent the tenant can reasonably afford to pay according to the times, but in bad times a tenant cannot be expected to pay as much as he did in good times. . . . Now, what must we do in order to induce landlords to see the position? You must show them that you intend to hold a firm grip of your homesteads and lands. You must not allow yourselves to be dispossessed as your fathers were dispossessed in 1847. . . . I hope . . . that those on properties where the rents are all out of proportion to the times, a reduction may be made and that immediately. If not, you must help yourselves, and the public opinion of the world will stand by you and support you in your struggle to defend your homesteads."

While he'd found hope in Parnell's words, the hope wilted when the news of the impending Cronin family eviction reached Jeremiah. Throughout the parish, there had been numerous evictions, but none this close to Jeremiah.

He rode with purpose, wondering what could be done. Eugene and Jeremiah had worked side by side these past dozen years; Eugene, accepting the meager wages Jeremiah could offer, had been struggling, as so many had. Jeremiah had helped when he could. There was no justice or logic in evicting this man and his family. Jeremiah's stomach turned when he reached the scene.

Two men, in waistcoats and polished shoes, carrying cudgels, stood in the doorway. Four children and their mother stood outside, none of them touching. The oldest, Theresa, was the same age as his Tims; they'd been playmates in years past. Not a word was spoken. A small table, a bed, two three-legged stools and a pile of clothing were stacked near them. Eugene, his small firm body tense, paced back and forth. Jeremiah had never seen him in such a state. Over the years they had shared conversations from potato growing to politics to the papacy and he had never seen Eugene even close to this level of agitation.

The crowd stood a respectful distance away.

The magistrate read the eviction notice:

"It is hereby declared that this dwelling is to be vacated by said tenants as of eleven o'clock on this day of June nineteenth in the year of our Lord, eighteen hundred and seventy-nine."

It was just a few minutes before eleven o'clock. A tall woman with dark hair stepped forward and said,
"Ye can leave our Lord out of this, ye bloody blackguards. There's no Lord that would have the heart to take a man's home. Ye can tell yer 'lord' that from me and all of us."

The men with the cudgels gripped them tighter. The magistrate spoke next.

"That'll be enough now. This is the law of the land. Ye all know that. Go on home with ye, while ye still have homes to go to."

A rock struck the magistrate, and within seconds, the two men with cudgels had to shield themselves from a barrage of stones. Eugene gathered his family and stepped back as the two men moved into the crowd, striking randomly. A shot rang out, a warning from one of the magistrate's men, and the crowd quickly dispersed. Jeremiah watched as Eugene made a dash at the magistrate. Eugene, no taller than five feet eight inches, was a powerhouse. Jeremiah had seen him lift beams of timber single-handedly instead of waiting to hitch them to a harnessed horse. He now saw that same strength channeled against the magistrate as he knocked him to the ground. Within seconds, the two suited men pulled Eugene from the magistrate and pummeled him on the legs and back with their cudgels, and shoved him toward his family. Eugene lay still, moaning.

Terror filled the children's faces, his wife frozen in place.

The same suited men now soaked tar-covered batons with oil and lit them. The smell of the ignited flame was pungent. Eugene rolled over and watched as each torch was thrust into the windows of what had been the Cronin home for more than thirty years. As the flames caught, the inside burned like a dry field.

Jeremiah struggled for breath, uncertain. Any movement he made could make things worse.

The smallest little girl, with her dark hair and big eyes, clung to her mother who was now bent over in grief. The oldest boy, Liam, Jeremiah recalled him to be, his head full of dark curls, went to his father and tried to help him up. Jeremiah dismounted and joined the child. Eugene wasn't bleeding, but his injuries were serious. Together with two other men from the parish, Dennis Carroll and Michael Buckley, they helped Eugene to a waiting cart. Several women clustered around Mrs. Cronin and the children, who stood frozen while everything they'd ever known to be home caught and became fire.

Nobody moved. Though their hearts beat in their chests, there was nothing to be done. As the flames shot higher, the silence deepened.

Chapter Thirty-One

Gran

June 1879

Jeremiah rode into the hills, away from home, from all that he knew, grasping Tess's reins in a tight fist. He rode faster and faster, the tears that fell on his cheeks pushed back by the wind. His heart held a familiar heaviness, sorrow mingled with the pain of helplessness. He rode hard, his gallop taxing. He rode past Bweeng and deeper into the hills. When he reached the foothills of the Boggeragh Mountains, he stopped to catch his breath and felt his clenched jaw and fists loosen. He watched a fox scramble out of his path. The fox understood a predator when he saw one coming. Had Eugene? Had Jeremiah?

He thought back to the declaration of eviction so recently read, and even worse than the sight of the children and mother put so cruelly out of their home was the realization of who had done such a thing: the evicting landlord had been Joseph H. Bennett, Esquire.

***

It was well past noon when he finally turned toward home. He'd been gone since mid-morning. Margaret would wonder, news of this latest atrocity not finding her so quickly. The pain he felt was not her fault and he had no intention of venting any of this to her. There had been more than enough trouble as evictions grew in number. Many in the parish received threatening letters; reports of maimed cattle grew. Others had been visited in the dead of night, threatened with physical harm if they dared to pay any rent that was excessive. None of these actions were "authorized" by the Land League. Jeremiah had been assured of the non-violent nature of this newest movement. Yet, word spread quickly. Fear abounded.

The relentless rains, the falling crop prices and the outrageous rents had wreaked havoc. Disraeli was doing nothing for Ireland. If it weren't for Parnell, there'd be nothing left to hope.

The new priest, Father Patrick Pope, seemed kind enough, but he was no Father Lane. With the death of Pope Pius IX and Paul Cardinal Cullen, the two conservative forces in the Church, there was a new strengthening of support for the emerging Land movement. But the movement had little chance without the priests. The scene of the eviction still heavy upon him, as were the questions of what might be done for the family, Jeremiah decided it was time to meet with Father Pope.

As he finally rode into the barnyard, Jeremiah saw ten-year-old Michael racing toward him. "Da, Da it's good yer here," Michael exclaimed breathlessly, his green eyes wide. "The priest has come now. It's Gran, Da. She's gone from us." Jeremiah dismounted swiftly, gave the reins to Michael and went into the house. The table in the small, quiet center room with its cloth and cup of roses seemed oddly serene. He went to his bedroom in search of Margaret and found no one. He listened and heard murmuring. He went toward Gran's room and as he looked in, found the source. Tims, Mary, Julia, Maggie, the six-year-old twins and Margaret were all kneeling around Gran's bedside saying the Rosary. He took off his cap, placed it behind him on the doorknob, knelt next to Margaret and took her hand in his.

He looked at the tears on his children's faces.

Was this how it was to be? A lost harvest that was devastating the countryside; rain that wouldn't let up; trusted people turning lifelong friends out from their home; rampant evictions; and Gran slipping away from them? He looked at his stalwart children. He could just imagine how Margaret had prepared them upon Gran's death. Was it Tims who had gone for Father Pope? Or Mary? Michael came in and knelt at the side of the bed with the children.

Jeremiah held Margaret's hand tighter and let his gaze fall upon Gran. His eyes filled with tears as he saw her hands entwined with a rosary and her thin silver hair combed as if it were time for church. Her eyes were closed and her tiny pale lips formed a serene smile. She wore her treasured blue housecoat with the embroidered collar. He dropped Margaret's hand, sank down, covered his face with both hands and listened as Mary intoned the final decade—the Glorious Mysteries.

Before the prayers began, he stood abruptly, took his cap from the doorknob and moved to leave. As he reached the front door, he heard the sounds of those he most loved in the beginning of their prayers: "Hail Mary full of grace. . ."

* * *

"Ma, there's still no sign of him. Shall I be bringing the cows in now? Won't Father Pope be here soon?" Tims asked. Margaret looked up from her chair at Gran's doorway.

"Ye should, Tims, and take Michael with ye. The girls will stay here for the time being. Yer father will be coming 'round in no time. Go on with ye, now."

Margaret had seen this behavior of Jeremiah's before. When her father had died, Jeremiah was gone for two days. She never learned where he'd gone and they never spoke of it once he'd returned. The same could hold true again.

Maggie sat near Margaret. "Ma, is Gran in heaven now? Do the angels take the souls that fast and go straight to heaven? Or do they float around and say their good-byes? Gran never said good-bye, Ma."

Margaret reached out for this little one, just eight years old but as wise as Solomon.

"I'd say that Gran is waiting to say her good-bye to ye. It mightn't be today or tomorrow, but ye'll know it when she does."

Ellen Healey and Ellen Cogan had come to wash Gran and prepare her for the wake. They dressed her in the traditional habit, placed the crucifix on her breast and the rosary beads around her fingers. Her devotion had been genuine, and therefore the rituals were so fitting. Sheets were suspended over the bed like a canopy and along the two sides. Lit candlesticks were placed on a small table near the head of her bed.

Father Pope would return at eight-thirty and say the prayers for the dead. Mary and Julia had readied the front room by pushing the table aside for the food that would be arriving from neighbors. Chairs and benches were put in rows. As tradition dictated, they'd already stopped the mantel clock as a sign of respect; covered the bedroom mirror with a cloth, giving the fleeing soul no chance to be trapped behind the glass; and opened a clear path to the window to allow the soul's release. It would be a quiet time, with stories and ballads. Gran was known for her devotion and her decorum. It would be an insult to honor her in any other way.

Margaret studied her mother's hands, bound in her Rosary beads, the long, thin fingers she held onto as a child and watched so closely as she learned to tat. Her eyes misted and she looked at her own girls, proud of the way they worked together to make things go smoothly. They'd forgone their ordinary bickering and digging comments. Julia, who at times adored Mary and at other times abhorred her, was compliant and almost compassionate toward her now. She listened and did what she was asked, gently offering ideas and suggestions. "Might we put the table going the other way now, Mary, to make more room for all the people who will be coming? Do ye suppose there will be a great number of them, being that Gran's friends were quite old, many of them dead themselves?"

Mary would miss Gran, as would Maggie. They both had a special connection with her that Julia did not have. Julia was her own kind of girl, mercurial, a loner. She was a good enough student and seemed to make friends easily, though she preferred more often to be home as to go off adventuring. She kept to herself, except when Mary encouraged her to join in some game or story. Her thoughts were her own, and she had the manner of looking cross even when she wasn't.

Maggie, on the other hand, was a winsome girl and when she twirled about, she'd win the hearts of those she encountered. Her innocence and idealism actually seemed to annoy Julia.

"She's always talking about God stuff. Shouldn't that just be for church?"

Margaret avoided the squabbles of these strong-willed daughters. Her own sister Bridget, God rest her soul, had been enough to contend with and she knew there would be no end to misery if one were to dwell on the complaints of one's sisters or daughters. Hadn't her ma seen to that?

Gran had been a force; that was the truth. The twins had been a new elixir for her, giving her joy each time she was with them, whether helping to bathe them or telling them stories. While she never apologized for any of the nasty things she'd said over the years, these last years had been a gift. She'd calmed so much and let go of things that would have caused a ruckus in her earlier days. Margaret would miss her. After the funeral, she'd write to Michael straightaway. He'd be pleased that she went so peacefully. And he'd be pleased to know that his namesake Michael had gone to fetch Father Pope all on his own. Tims had been off in the fields and the girls had taken the twins off to pick berries when Margaret had discovered Gran on the floor next to her bed. Michael had helped lift her, and Margaret knew right away that she was gone. A blessing to go like that, a gift to a righteous woman.

By seven-thirty a good number of the neighbors had gathered and the table was covered with sliced ham, smoked salmon, beef and pork, bowls of potatoes—some colcannon and some in their jackets—cabbage, turnips, baskets of brown bread and soda bread, plates of cheeses, tarts, cookies and cakes, all from the bounty of the countryside.

The keening began at eight o'clock, the sounds of grief low and respectful. Margaret joined in, her own voice resounding with the loss and sorrow both she and her mother had suffered in their lives. She longed to have Jeremiah at her side, and was suddenly angry that he had gone.

A few trusted women came in to lead the keeners from the bedroom. As they moved out, Father Pope and Jeremiah came in. The keening was such a part of the old ways, he thought, things

wouldn't be right without these women. Jeremiah, looking sheepish but calmed, came to Margaret as if he had just learned of
Gran's death. "Mairéad," he said as he embraced her.

Her eyes showed relief at his presence and she led him back
to Gran's bedside, where he knelt and offered his own sounds of
grief, his shoulders heaving with sobs. Father Pope stood in the
doorway so both rooms could hear the prayers. "*Requiem aeternam
dona eis, Domine.*" He then led those assembled in the Rosary.
Many of the mourners huddled around the hearth; others sat on
the settle, the low long bench on the far wall, as well as the chairs
that had been gathered from other parts of the small house to
accommodate visitors.

Maggie tugged at Margaret's sleeve as the last Glory Be was
intoned. Margaret hushed her and waited for Father Pope to give
the blessing. Then she knelt down to her.

"Whatever is it, Maggie? Are ye all right, now?"

"I am, Ma, I am. Gran said good-bye. Just now, from the garden window. She's fine and says heaven is lovely. She wanted me
to tell ye." Margaret looked into the wide clear eyes of the child
who had always been special to her mother. She embraced her
and wept new tears. Maggie broke free and went to Jeremiah.
"Gran says yer a fine Da and I'm to obey ye in all things. I told her
I would."

"Ye did now. I'm glad for that." He reached out for her but she
was gone again, as if on a mission. Jeremiah went to Margaret and
together they watched Maggie go back to her garden window. It
was just twilight.

"Do ye think she's all right, Jer? It's worried I am sometimes.
And frightened. She's young yet and so innocent."

"Weren't we both young once, too? She'll be fine. Gran will
see to that."

* * *

The evening wore on 'til midnight. The clay pipes of tobacco were
gone, the plate of snuff emptied. The porter was still in plenty, as

were the plates of food that never seemed to stop coming. All night, people sat with Gran, never leaving her soul to wander. A Rosary at midnight marked the end of the evening. Traditional prayers were offered by their friend Paddy Riordan, who was a cousin of Gran's. This was no place for talk of things political. This was a time to remember Gran and see to her safe passage.

The next day would be the funeral Mass and the procession to the graveyard. As he sat beside Margaret, Jeremiah thought of Gran, of Mr. Bennett, and of Eugene and his family once again, and longed for the comfort of sleep. He'd seen enough for one day

Chapter Thirty-Two

Devoy

Fall 1879

Michael lifted the host and said the words of the consecration, *"Hoc est enim corpus meum."* For this is my body. He offered this Mass for his mother, Julia Riordan, whose death had brought him a deeper sorrow than he was prepared for. She had irritated him so many times with her whining and critical tongue. Her continual boasting about having a son who was a priest annoyed him as well. Yet her true spirit—the one that survived the hunger, bore the loss of four children and the emigration of another, tolerated a husband whose love of the drink overshadowed his other loves, and still managed to instill a love of life and God into her surviving family—that was the woman he mourned. He held her silently in his heart as he lowered the host and genuflected. Her presence would always be with him, grateful to Jeremiah and Margaret that her last days were peaceful.

He looked out at the congregation, men, women and children, families together celebrating the holy sacrifice of the Mass. As he bowed and kissed the altar cloth and then raised the chalice, Father Lane's counsel before he left for America echoed in his ear. "Yer faith is yer own affair, Michael." He remembered the clear even voice. "The people ye serve will help strengthen it, if ye remember to let them. Mind ye, there's good in every one. It's just buried deeper in some than in others."

Michael had grown to love many of these people and respect their struggle. For more than ten years, he had served in America, in the heart of Manhattan in New York City. The suffering and loss paralleled any he'd experienced in Ireland. Mothers who lost babies at birth, husbands who drank up the little pay they made, children who craved attention from those who had so little to give, and old folks who clucked their tongues at what the world was coming to.

Michael had little worry of what the world was coming to either in America or in Ireland. He'd taken great hope after his initial meeting with Devoy in '71 and over the years read about him every chance he got. Devoy was now the leader of Clan na Gael, the secret organization in America linked to the Irish Republican Brotherhood that sought to unite the fractured remnants of the American Fenians. The successful arrival of the whaling ship *Catalpa* three years earlier that carried six rescued Fenian prisoners—James Derragh, Martin Hogan, Michael Harrington, Thomas Hasset, Robert Cranston and James Wilson—had been Devoy's brainstorm and had carried the new life and hope to those who struggled for freedom, a hope Michael and so many others he knew of sorely needed.

* * *

More hope came to Michael in the person of his cousin, Father John Joseph Riordan, who appeared to be thriving in his calling. Michael relished time spent with this man, almost twenty years his junior, his Uncle Eugene's son.

They had agreed to meet at Grand Central, where John Joseph was arriving from the upstate city of Troy, having attended a five-year reunion with his ordination class at St. Joseph's Seminary.

Today as the two priests walked toward St. Patrick's Cathedral and Central Park, they talked of Ireland, of Jeremiah and Margaret, their growing family, and of Johnny's Joe's mother, Uncle Eugene's widow. They walked down Vanderbilt Avenue and turned onto East Forty-Fifth Street. "I must get over to see her one day. She's still on the West side? Forty-Second, is she? Number three-o-one?"

"Aye, Father Michael, she's still there, and I'm glad to say she's finally slowing down a little bit. I'll be seeing her later today for supper," the younger man said.

They were strolling at a relaxed pace, the weather comfortable for just such a walk, the sun warming them as it peeked through the buildings and alleyways. Their pleasure at being together was evident in their occasional pauses to stop and look at one another.

Now Johnny Joe put a hand on Michael's sleeve as he said, "Ye know, she's always helping this one or that one besides keeping up with her work at Tammany Hall." His voice was full of concern. "It's hard to believe she's been cleaning there for nearly two decades."

His short auburn hair and green-hazel eyes reminded Michael of his own da. He noted the familiar cleft in his Riordan chin. His clean-shaven youthful face was handsome with a flush in his cheek showing vigor. He clucked his tongue as continued. "At last, she's taking a bit of time for herself. I've been after her and it may be that she's finally listening."

"'Tis many a story I imagine she has to tell," Michael said as they made their way onto Madison. "Did she know Boss Tweed himself?"

Johnny Joe glanced about him, noting the Roosevelt Hotel as he replied, "She did and she has kind things to say about him. He was good to her and that's how she judged him. She's equally pleased with the new fella, 'Honest' John Kelly, she says."

Their destination today was to see the recently dedicated St. Patrick's Cathedral, neither of them having been invited to the formal dedication ceremony held last May. The late Archbishop John Hughes, who hailed from County Tyrone, early on had been the cathedral's tireless promoter and had laid the cornerstone twenty years before in 1858, its completion delayed by the Civil War.

"Father Michael, I've wanted to ask ye something for a while now. About me da, would ye know very much?" The younger man faced him, his gaze steady and pleading. "Me ma doesn't say much about him and it's curious I am to know all I can about him. Ye mightn't know, I was only two years when he died."

Michael could only guess why Johnny Joe's mother said little of Uncle Eugene, who had left Ireland without his father's blessing. When Uncle Eugene came to say his farewell to Michael's parents, he told of his father's anger and disapproval of his notion of going to America.

Michael weighed his words carefully, watching the expression of eagerness on the younger man's face. He waited 'til a passing horse and carriage had clip-clopped by.

Michael learned that Eugene had been an angry youth and that while there was disapproval surrounding his departure, there had always been rancor between father and son. They fought bitterly, Michael's da had said, both of them headstrong and sensitive, more alike than either of them would admit.

"Well, Johnny Joe, from what I know, yer da never had an easy relationship with his father. Me da told of Uncle Eugene's last words as he left for Cobh. 'Ye can tell the da for me, I'm aiming to make something of meself, no thanks to him.'"

Michael paused and turned to start their walk again, trying to sound matter-of-fact. "Of course, Eugene had no idea of the devastating hunger that was to follow his departure."

John Joseph's eyes widened, holding his place still. "When he came to America, did he make something of himself, do ye think?"

Michael stalled for time, glancing up at the clouds pushing lazily above them. "Ah now, I wouldn't know for sure many details about yer da in America," Michael said cautiously, newly aware of how little this young man knew of his father and knowing little himself. The crossings he knew to be treacherous but Johnny Joe would have known that already.

Michael could feel a fatigue building within him despite his excitement about seeing this historic cathedral about which he had read so much, including the fact that James Renwick, Jr., the designer of the Gothic revival structure, had also designed the Smithsonian in Washington, D.C.

As they turned onto Fifth Avenue, their gaze was drawn to the ornate spires that towered above them, the sun casting a magical quality to the marble-covered brick.

"So this is what all the talk has been about," Michael murmured. "I'd say they haven't overdone it a bit."

After a few minutes, they ascended the wide steps into the cathedral, its cool interior and silence a relief. They each dipped their hand in the holy water font, genuflected and sat in one of the last pews, looking down the huge main aisle to the nave of the church, color from the stained glass windows dancing all around them. Michael was a bit breathless and glad for the rest.

Johnny Joe looked about like a small child, glad for this time with his cousin Michael, his looks not dissimilar to his father's, he suspected. It was relieving to have someone who could tell him anything about his da, hungry as he was for some connection with his past.

They sat silently for a time, and then walked up and down the grand center aisle, noting special altars for Saint Michael and St. Louis designed by Tiffany & Co. The beauty of the great rose window that faced Fifth Avenue, and designed by Charles Connick, was not easily overlooked. As they re-emerged into the day, they turned down the avenue toward Central Park to complete their time together.

"Do ye think this magnificence is a bit opulent, Father Michael, considering the poverty here?"

Michael sighed, glad for this young man's sensitivity, yet weary now and longing to sit. He made no reply but rather brought the conversation back to Eugene.

"Ye know there was no word about yer da for quite a time after he left Ireland, none knowing if he'd even survived the voyage."

Johnny Joe moved closer to Michael to avoid a woman and two children who were walking toward them.

"Gran saved an Easter card he sent that said he'd found work in America as a gardener. It was several years before he wrote again, this time to say he was to be married. To another Margaret, no less," Michael said as he steered them to the first bench he could find, eager for the rest.

John Joseph settled on the bench next to Michael and said, "Speaking of names, Father Michael, what was it about me being named? Me ma says there was something to do with a cousin."

Michael leaned back, the warmth of the sun upon him, and sighed as he recalled the scene.

"Yer ma is right. The cousin was me little brother, Johnny Joe. 'Twas on yer da's last visit to see us, when he'd come to say good-bye. He'd asked to hold the baby who'd been fussing and whimpering, racked with fever. It was coming on to the horrible time of the hunger. Little did any of us know what was to befall us."

Michael shifted on the bench and turned to Johnny Joe, smiling.

"Yer da had a grand tenor voice, I remember, and he sang the Connemara Lullaby to the baby. One of me ma's favorites. And didn't our little baby settle down in his arms!" Michael smiled at the memory. He told of the child's death later in the evening, and Eugene's departure for America the next morning.

"Things like that build up in a man. When we heard you'd been named John Joseph, we knew yer da had never forgotten."

Once Michael felt rested enough, they resumed their stroll through the park, talk now of Ireland and the apparition in August of our Lady at Knock, a "miracle" that reverberated throughout the Catholic world.

"Do ye think, Father Michael, that our Lady's silence at Knock meant there's to be an end to the fighting and the troubles that are tearing up Ireland?"

They stood at the edge of the graceful pond, part of the vision of Frederick Law Olmsted, another architect who captured Michael's interest.

"Ye needn't worry about an end to the fighting, Johnny Joe," Michael said. "'Til Ireland's free, there will always be fighting, I'd say."

They were strolling well below street level, the noises muffled, the feast of autumn colors reflected in the water.

Michael listened to the Irish cadence in this young American lad's speech as he continued to talk of the vision at Knock. The feeling of warmth he felt surprised him. Johnny Joe looked the way he'd remembered Uncle Eugene—straight brown hair, quick green eyes and fair skin.

"I'd say that there's caution to be found in over-depending on the visions and voices, Father John. Real men, like Davitt and Devoy, are where to keep your eyes planted," Michael said.

"Are you familiar with Clan na Gael, Father John?" Michael then asked evenly, not wanting to suggest too much, too soon.

"Is that the organization that Devoy heads up now? The American version of the IRB?" Johnny Joe asked as they came up from the park back onto the street.

"Yes, that's the group. I've met with John Devoy, who's teamed up with Davitt and Parnell to make progress a positive. The 'New Departure,' a phrase Parnell used once, is what they're calling it."

He smiled to think of how pleased Jeremiah would be that he and Johnny Joe were together, though he wasn't as confident that he'd be pleased that he was telling him of the Fenians.

"The ol' Fenians of my era have had a bit of trouble with this constitutional approach," Michael said as they turned onto Madison, now bustling with traffic of all kinds, minding their step as they walked back down toward Grand Central.

"I've saved a clipping from the *New York Herald* about his proposed alliance with Parnell," he said, pulling his wallet from his back pocket. "It gives me hope."

He stopped, carefully removed a worn and folded newspaper clipping and handed it to Johnny Joe, who read it and looked up, a skeptical look in his eyes.

"Am I right now, Father Michael that you're in favor of Devoy and this 'new departure'? The same one the Vatican has spoken out against?"

Michael motioned for them to cross to Fifty-First Street.

"Ah, Johnny Joe, the Vatican very often speaks out on things in which it should have no say. This is for Ireland's freedom we're talking. It's nothing to do with the Vatican."

Johnny Joe handed the clipping back and Michael said, "Think about it and we'll talk again. There's much work to be done and I think young people need to be a part of it." He carefully replaced the clipping in his wallet.

They shook hands in the shadow of the great cathedral, the white marble gleaming in the afternoon sunlight, planning a future visit. Johnny Joe turned to head back to his mother's for dinner as Michael watched, a ray of hope filling him.

Chapter Thirty-Three

Captain Boycott

December 1880

"Da," Michael asked Jeremiah as they were returning from market day in Mallow, "why didn't ye salute those folks as ye always do the neighbors?"

Jeremiah was amazed that this eleven-year-old was attentive enough to notice the omission. He hadn't acknowledged the Cunninghams who rode past in their cart on the way to town, nor would he. They were the family who had taken the neighboring Donlon farm.

Jeremiah had recently attended one of the meetings in Mallow, in the market square on the hill, where Parnell asked the multitude gathered, "What are ye to do with a tenant who bids for a farm from which his neighbor has been evicted?"

Above the scattered cries of "Kill him," Parnell answered, "A much better way, a more Christian and charitable way which will give the sinner an opportunity to repent, is what I propose. Ye must shun him. Shun him on the roadside, in the town, in the shops, at the marketplace and even in the church. Shun him so that in his isolation he may learn the moral revulsion he represents, so that he may feel, as the leper of old, the stigma of his crime."

How could he help young Michael to understand why he had joined in the shunning? How could he explain this method of punishing those who showed disregard for the suffering of those evicted? This was the same kind of shunning that had been so successful with Captain Boycott, whose name would go down in infamy, the detested land agent in County Mayo who was ultimately driven from Ireland, but not before his crops were saved after fifty volunteer Orangemen from Ulster came to help with his harvest, with seven thousand British military forces to protect them.

Jeremiah kept the trap and pony at a steady pace as he considered his own fortune. His family didn't need to worry about eviction or being behind in rent payments. Indeed, their own good fortune allowed them the luxury to worry for those with less. And Jeremiah wouldn't stand by in silence.

Jeremiah's land provided a sufficiency for Margaret and the children who worked hard, seeing to the cattle, making hay, feeding the chickens, gathering eggs, making butter, picking berries, sewing and weaving along with the fancy needlework of tatting. Jeremiah heard no whining from them and was sure that Margaret saw to that. At the female school Mary, Julia, Maggie and Lizzie were well occupied with reading, spelling, writing, arithmetic, grammar, geography and needlework. Tims, Michael and Jeremiah had taken many of the same subjects at the male school, substituting the study of animal husbandry for needlework. Tims had just recently finished school and was working full time on the land. Jeremiah was amazed at his ability with the cattle which easily exceeded Jeremiah's own.

He gazed over the gray horizon, as they passed a crossroad, and wondered how could he now explain to Michael what he himself sometimes had trouble reconciling? At least, Gladstone's return to office and his possible collaboration with Parnell gave him a flicker of hope.

"It's difficult to explain, Michael," he said, his eyes looking down at this sturdy boy, "but ye're a sharp enough lad to notice what yer da does and doesn't do. I can tell ye this; the neighbors I didn't salute with a regular greeting have done something considered very wrong. They've ignored the wishes of the people who believe in a civil and, mind ye, non-violent way of behaving. So we have decided to ignore them. It's a mighty trial for all of us."

"Are they the ones that took the Donlons' cabin, Da?" Michael said, his green eyes searching Jeremiah's face. "Mary's in class with a girl that no one talks to. Would that be the same family?"

Jeremiah sighed as he realized more fully how the troubled times affected all of the families, including the children.

He turned to his son, careful about how much to say, as he slowed the pony's trot. "Yes, Michael, it is the same family. The Cunninghams."

"Do they have another place to live, Da, if they don't live in Donlons' house? Would that be why they moved in there?" Michael said innocently.

Jeremiah reached a hand onto Michael's head for a moment. "Michael, I don't know that answer, but I can tell ye, they'll not find another place now. They've started on a path that will bring them an isolation that may drive them away. Hopefully, that will be the worst of it."

The most recent *Times* quoted a pillar of the British regime, General Charles George Gordon, who stated that the Irish peasantry during these times was "patient beyond belief. . . . Loyal, but at the same time broken-spirited and desperate, living on the verge of starvation in places we would not keep our cattle. . . . The Bulgarians, Anatolians, Chinese and Indians are better off than many of them are . . ."

The night before, Jeremiah had come from one of the mass demonstrations being held around the parish. The gatherings were usually orderly, despite the anger caused by the long years of injustice. The men were working to secure a reduction in rents, prevent any evictions they could and support those whose evictions they couldn't prevent. John Devoy from America largely financed the meetings, the speeches, and the official Land League Courts as part of the New Departure. Jeremiah held out hope that this approach would salve wounds that had festered for so long. He worked diligently, talking late into the night to those whom he could reach, in an effort to abate the underground violence—the threatening letters of physical harm to those who paid rents deemed by the Land League to be excessive; random gunshots into homes at night; bodily harm that included shots into thighs, pieces of ear removed and other physical torture to those who took holdings from those who had been evicted.

There was no Land League leadership support for any of the violence and yet it was difficult to stop. The perpetrators, many ex-Fenians, felt justified in their actions.

As he left the demonstration, he and Paddy Murphy talked of the hope for the cause. "It'll never go anywhere, Jer, without the support of the parish priests. They're the key to it." Jeremiah was in total agreement.

"Ye know, Paddy," he said as the two men walked to their horses, "there was help from Archbishop Croke of Cashel who delivered a sermon that spoke openly about the moral and just principles for all tenants' rights. I'd say he brought some of the needed clerical strength to this land reform movement."

"It's good news to hear that. I've heard that reductions of rents are running between ten and fifty per cent. Even a few evictions were prevented through physical intervention, though sad to say, not Eugene's."

Both men were aware of the recent *Times* description that saw the Land League as "a very distinct and potent government which is rapidly superseding the Imperial government . . ."

* * *

All in the townland suffered from the poor harvest and poor weather of recent days that rivaled the worst of the Famine of '47. Much-needed relief came from hundreds of private and religious agencies. Neighbor helped neighbor as best they could. Thankfully, the potato crop this past season had been good, but that wasn't enough. Now the struggle was for the rents. Jeremiah deliberated his next action. Never before could he have believed Joseph Bennett to be heartless, but what he saw at the Cronin eviction told him something else. He would bide his time, but he would not retreat.

* * *

Margaret missed Gran as she began the preparation for Christmas. She'd grown accustomed to Gran's counsel and her tales of days of old. During her declining years, Gran told stories to the girls that Margaret had never heard before. Gran had taken little Maggie under her wing like a protective mother hen, her death leaving Maggie with a sadness that bordered on melancholy. The twins with their antics and innocence had helped them weather the loss, each in their own way. Maggie prayed aloud each night for Gran who was "now in heaven with holy Mary Mother of God."

The preparation for the Christmas season usually began in earnest with the annual cleaning. Jeremiah, Tims and Michael had responsibility for cleaning and tidying the four outbuildings, including the hay barn, byre and chicken coop. The whitewashing of all the buildings including the inside and outside of the house also fell to them.

Meanwhile Margaret, Mary, Julia and Maggie were busy inside the house, cleaning everything in sight. All garments and washable linens were included in the frenzy, while tables and chairs were scrubbed with sand to smooth their surfaces. Pots, pans and delft didn't escape a thorough scouring, while the twins were at each sister's beck and call for fresh water, buckets and baskets to be carried.

The spiritual preparation for this holy day was seen to by Father Pope, who preached at Sunday Mass about Advent prayers to be added to each parishioner's daily rituals.

The children looked forward most to their part in helping, especially with the decorations. Mary, Julia and Maggie taught the twins to make the holly sprig cross, the central feature of the decorations, by tying two pieces of holly sprigs to two crossed pieces of wood. They also worked with loose holly, ivy and bay leaves, stringing them on pieces of linen to form patterns. The twins watched silently as Maggie created her first piece.

"Look now, Lizzie and Jer, at mine," Maggie exclaimed as she held up a tiny cross fashioned from the ivy and placed in the center of a red-colored paper. "It's the hope of the season, green for new life."

"Ah, our own Sister Margaret has spoken," Mary said to the

twins. Julia giggled. "Is there anything else we should know this Christmas season, dear sister of ours?"

"Just that if ye keep after me, calling me Sister Margaret, I'll tell the da not to let ye come to market for the festivities. I'm Maggie Buckley and ye, Molly or Mary or whatever ye want to be called this week, can just remember that." Lizzie and Jeremiah paid no mind to the chatter, freed now to make their own creations.

At the same time, Jeremiah came in from the fields with Tims and Michael in tow.

"We've prepared the pig for sharing. We'll be off to Paddy Murphy's with some and then over to Cronins with the rest. We've some *poitín* to take as well. Eugene deserves a drop of the good stuff. Is there anything you lovely girls would like to add?"

Since the eviction in June, the Cronins had been staying with a recently widowed woman by the name of Finnerty. Eugene had been a blessing to her and though there had sometimes been trouble for anyone giving shelter to those evicted, Mrs. Finnerty hadn't been approached by any of the gombeen men who were sent out to enforce the law. Eugene's work with Jeremiah had continued but with fewer hours per day to allow him time to help Mrs. Finnerty.

Maggie greeted Jeremiah with her ivy cross. "Da, will ye take this to the Cronins? It's a sign for them. The green is for hope and the red is about their suffering which is now to be over," she said, blue-gray eyes looking up at him.

Jeremiah bent down and gently took the little cross. "'Tis glad the Cronins will be of your handicraft and yer wishes, Maggie. Glad indeed." He stood and put it on the mantel, never dismissing the power of a child's good wishes.

Chapter Thirty-Four
Father John Joseph Riordan

August 1884

Mary pulled her light brown hair back and tied it with a blue ribbon to match her best and only dress, the blue one. She had washed and pressed it and polished her shoes. She was almost ready. She pinched her cheeks to give them a bit of color. She and Tims would venture off to the Lughnasa Festival Bonfire, up on the ridge in the Bogherra Mountains. They would take the pony and trap, with instructions to be back before midnight. Though Mary and Tims both invited her to go with them, Julia declined.

Mary had always dreamt of attending the Lughnasa bonfire, part of the festival of the Celtic god Lugh, that marked the time when corn was ripe and calves and lambs had been weaned. She would dance and dance until her head spun. She had talked after Mass with Nora Carroll, Dennis and Eileen's daughter. Mary knew that Tims was sweet on Nora, who had her father's thick, black curly hair and blue eyes. The two girls plotted and schemed to have Tims accompany Mary to the festival for she, because of custom, wouldn't attend alone. Nora was pleased.

Within the Church, there was growing condemnation of the Celtic rituals of the past. Many were seen as pagan, filled with sexual overtones, and all were closely monitored by the church. The bonfires had survived thus far. Jeremiah and Margaret, their childhoods steeped in these rituals, saw little harm in the children attending. They hoped it might be good for Mary, who would be in need of memories soon.

Mary would emigrate next spring. She had planned it for over a year, the decision finalized when Michael's letter arrived, telling of Father John Joseph's upcoming visit.

"It's time to let her go, Jer," Margaret said as they sat finishing their tea one fall afternoon, the harvest in, the day mild. "Ye must see that. She's all of a woman now and with no future here."

She reached over and put her hand on his as she continued.

"Ye know it yerself," she said plaintively. "Look around ye. What is there here for her? Tell me that. What image do ye see of her in five years, or ten years? She's almost twenty years old, Jer, and she's alive. Don't take her spirit."

Jeremiah stood and went to the hearth. Margaret ran her fingers through her hair, as she often did when she felt agitated.

She stood and walked toward him.

"I'm telling ye what I know of the child. She knows there's barely enough money for us. She hears your sighs when the rent is due. She sees yer distress when ye come home from the market day. She knows. And she's determined to find her fortune in America and send some of that fortune home to us. Let her have her dream. Let us have our good-bye."

Jeremiah turned to her, the reflection of the embers in his eyes. "I lost my first girl. I'll not lose another," he said, holding her gaze.

They were alone, Jerry, Lizzie, Maggie and Michael in school, Mary, Julia and Tims off doing chores.

Margaret looked into his eyes with fire in her own. Her voice broke as she cried out. "She was my first girl as well. I know the horror of it. Ye needn't tell me that. And I know the heartache I'm recommending now won't end when this Mary of ours leaves us. We'll have Julia and Maggie for whatever time we can keep them, and then little Lizzie, but now it is time for our Mary to go. She'll win her way and we'll have Father John to look out for her." She stood next to him at the hearth, trembling.

Jeremiah returned the kettle to the hook over the embers and stared. Margaret put her hand on his arm.

Her voice calm, she spoke again. "We have to let go, Jer. Would ye rather she sneak out in the night leaving no chance to wrap her in our arms one more time? Would ye rather that she sneak away without knowing yer tears of sorrow? Would ye rather lose her while she lives right here, all spirit and joy taken from her? Is that what ye want? For I'm telling ye that's what ye'll get."

He turned again to face her, his face twisted and full of fear. He took a step back and raged, "Ye're mad to think this child should be going off to America. Bloody mad. What have they in America but crime and confusion? Have ye not read Michael's accounts?" He crossed from her toward the door and spun about again. "There's worse poverty there than anything we've been put to. It's fine that Father John will be there to help but he can't be everywhere. What is this obsession with America?"

Margaret paused, her breathing shallow, her face and neck warm from her anger. She stopped pleading and sat down at the table, her blue eyes staring at Jeremiah. Her tears came silently. Seconds later, Jeremiah grabbed his cap and went out the door.

* * *

Father John Joseph Riordan had been stationed at St. Bernard's Parish in New York City when Cardinal McCloskey approved the notion of a Catholic mission at Castle Garden, to see to the welfare of the newly landed immigrants. Michael's letter, telling Margaret and Jeremiah of Father John's upcoming visit, extolled the virtues of the mission and of Father John:

> The Colonization Society felt that it was of utmost impor-
> tance that the Church should mount its guard upon the
> faith and virtue of the Catholic immigrants. After their
> meeting in Chicago a year ago May, they approved the
> mission and, of all the priests in New York, and there are a
> fair number, our own Johnny Joe was appointed. He'll be
> able to tell you more upon his visit. He is most eager to
> meet the children, about whom I've boasted tirelessly. He
> is quite pleased to have family to visit on his first trip to
> Ireland.
>
> He'll be speaking before the assembled bishops of
> Ireland at their annual meeting at Clonliffe College, where

I'm certain he'll share his three-fold message. I'm sure he'll tell ye of it. He's a tireless worker. Margaret, he looks so like Eugene. It's quite something indeed. God has blessed us.

Preparations for Father John's visit had gone on for weeks. Sweeping and cleaning the house indoors and out had preoccupied Margaret. Mary, who hoped to learn from Father John what to expect in America, was most anxious to make a good impression. Julia, who had turned sixteen this past March, said little about America or Mary's intention to go, but she was eager to meet the family priest about whom she'd heard so much.

It was as Mary and Julia pulled the bed linens from the clothes line and folded them that Julia finally talked a bit.

"Do ye think Father John talks like a Yank, Mary? He's never been to Ireland before now, ye know. Da says that Great-Uncle Eugene went over when he was just a young lad of eighteen and never came back.

"It's a shame Grandda didn't live to meet his nephew Johnny Joe. Gran said he would have been proud as can be to know his brother Eugene's son became a priest. It must have been hard when Johnny Joe left, wouldn't ye say, Mary? Especially without a proper good-bye. And they never saw him again. For some, leaving is like a death. Ye may never see one another again."

They folded the sheets, moving as if in a dance, the flowing cotton growing smaller each time they came together. Mary watched her younger sister whose sternness puzzled her. Tims was quite manly now and Maggie so often joyful. Michael could be counted on to be a jester, while Julia so often affected a serious air. Her dark hair and eyes reflected the soberness of her spirit.

"Would ye think about going to America yerself, Jules?" Mary asked as they folded the next sheet. "There's so much to do and it's not like here. They say there are lots of Irish men there already, men from Cork even. And there are wealthy Americans who think so highly of the Irish girls that there's quite a demand for us as domestics. Didn't our Eileen Murphy's letter say as much?"

She placed the folded sheet in the basket, watching for a reaction from Julia, before she continued. "Once I'm settled, I'll save the passage and send it. How would that be?"

Julia pulled the next sheet from the line. "And who do ye suppose will do the work when the ma and da get old? Ye can't be serious that Maggie would. She's barely able to take care of herself what with all her dreaming and praying. Mind ye, I think she's headed for a convent. And the twins are no prospect for help, sweet as they are."

Mary laughed as they folded the next sheet. "Ah, Jules, do ye think the da would allow Maggie to go to the convent? Why he's barely speaking to me since I've declared my intention to go to America. When I try to talk to him about it, he moves away from me. I'm half daft with him. I can't imagine him standing for his little Magpie going anywhere."

Mary pulled another from the line and said, "Ye know I'm going, don't ye, Jules? It'll be better for all of us. I've more than half the passage saved already. By spring, I should even have some extra from the embroidery I've done on Father Pope's surplice. Did I show ye how nice it's coming along?"

Before Julia could answer, a streak of lightning followed by a clap of thunder jolted them. They gathered the rest of the laundry from the line and ran inside. In just another day, Father John would be with them in Ahadallane.

* * *

"I see him," Maggie said from her front window. "He's coming down the lane with Father Pope now. I'd say he's quite handsome. He's not as tall as Father Pope and with his hat on him, I can't see his hair. But I'll bet it's a reddish brown like Ma says Uncle Mike's is.

"He's nodding now and Father Pope is saying something to him. I wonder if he's warning him about what a terrible lot we are. I wouldn't be surprised after Mary and Tims went off to the bonfire. Whatever must Father Pope think of us, celebratin' pagan festivals?"

"Hush now, Maggie," Margaret said sternly. "The bonfire is innocent, ye know that. And don't let yer da hear ye talk like that. He'll not stand for that kind of talk about pagan this or that and ye know it. And remember all of ye to call Johnny Joe by the title of Father. He's been consecrated and ye're to show respect. Michael, go on now and get yer da and Tims and find the twins. Tell them the Fathers are here now."

"Ma, are ye nervous to see him? Father John I mean? Yer own cousin? It's exciting now, isn't it?" Julia asked, far more exuberant than usual.

Mary set out the dishes for tea while her mother fussed with her dress and pushed at her hair.

"Ye look grand, Ma. He'll know ye're his da's niece. He'll be so glad to see ye," Maggie said.

Julia answered the door and extended a deep curtsy just as she'd seen demonstrated in a picture book. "Good afternoon, Reverend Fathers. It's an honor to invite ye in to our small but welcoming home."

Mary and Maggie stifled giggles as Margaret moved forward.

"Father Pope, it's good of ye to accompany our own kin to visit with us. We're pleased to welcome ye to our home. And Father Riordan, 'tis indeed a pleasure to meet the likes of ye. Come in, come in. We've just sent for Jeremiah and our two boys should be along with him presently. Our greeter is Julia and these two lasses are Mary and Maggie. Come in please, and be at comfort with us."

The two priests moved into the cabin and settled in chairs drawn up to the table. Father John did indeed look like what she remembered of Eugene. Margaret found herself staring at him.

"Can we offer ye some tea and bread, Fathers?" Mary said. "Our ma is known around the township for her brown bread."

"That would be lovely. Mary, is it? Yes, lovely," Father John replied as he turned to Margaret. "I can see why Father Michael misses you all so much. He talks about you all the time. He hasn't exaggerated your good looks, Margaret. He says I favor your father's side and I see that he's right. You're more like your mother with your red hair and blue eyes."

Julia and Mary worked at the sideboard, fixing the tray, listening to Father John speaking. "He sounds like a Yank," Julia whispered. Maggie sat spellbound in a chair across from the two priests.

Margaret moved to a chair next to Maggie. "Will ye be staying in Ireland very long, Father John? Michael wasn't clear in his letter or maybe he didn't know."

"I'll address the bishops' meeting next week and then I'll meet once again in Cashel with Most Reverend Dr. Croke. He has been particularly welcoming. It's been a beneficial trip already. I'd say I'll be here another two weeks."

Mary and Julia arrived with the tray. The plate of bread and jam trembled as Mary put it down. Margaret knew how eager Mary was for this visit. She was not wrong in her conviction that Mary should go.

Julia poured the tea and then withdrew to the background.

"We look forward to seeing ye in church this Sunday, Miss Julia?" Father Pope said as she moved toward the back wall. "I see yer name is down to lead the Rosary. And this week it'll be a special one for none other than yer own Father Riordan will be preaching at the Mass."

After a collective drawing of breath, the door opened. Jeremiah, Tims and Michael appeared with the twins in tow.

"Ah, ye're all just in time to hear the wonderful news," Margaret announced. "Father John will be preaching at Sunday Mass. It's blessed we are. Father John, this is my Jeremiah, Timothy and our Michael."

Maggie and Mary vacated the chairs, and Jeremiah and the others sat down and helped themselves to some tea; the extra cups were still on the tray.

"It's a warm welcome we extend to ye, Father John," Jeremiah said. "And to ye, Father Pope. It's glad we are of yer presence with us. Father John, we've been reading about yer time in Ireland. The newspapers have been generous in printing the story of yer mission. It's an honor to have ye here with us. From what Father Michael has written, ye've quite a mission there in America. And quite a bit of work to do."

Margaret held her breath. If Father John spoke of the dangers for newly arrived immigrants or the difficulties at the mission, she would not hear the end of the danger for Mary once Father John had gone.

"I was just telling Margaret and the girls," Father John said as he stood and motioned to Lizzie to take his chair, "that it's been a most productive time here in Ireland. Everyone has been so welcoming and gracious."

He moved over to the hearth as he continued. "I've been preaching at a Mass on each Sunday in different parishes where I've been able to extoll upon our progress. We have every reason to thank God, and the intercession of Our Lady of the Rosary, for any immigrant who lands at Castle Garden will be astonished and delighted at the blessed change that the Mission of Our Lady of the Rosary has brought about."

Margaret held her breath. Father John continued.
"No longer do friendless girls or forlorn families step straight from the emigrant ship among strangers and into the pitfalls of a sinful city. The comforts of their holy religion, and the friendship and counsel and protection of persons of their own faith and race, specially appointed by the Church for that purpose, greet them on their arrival."

Margaret said a silent *Deo Gratiás* while Jeremiah went to the cupboard and took out a bottle of Jameson Whiskey along with three glasses, and brought them to the table.

"I'd say yer presence calls for a celebration drink. To yer health and yer mission."

***

The visit extended into early evening. Mary listened with great attention to the way Father John pronounced his words. His "you" sounded like the female sheep name, not the customary "ye." She listened to his inflection and committed it to memory. It might help if she didn't sound so Irish.

The men talked of Ireland and America and of Michael. Though Father Pope had never met Father Michael, he had learned that Michael was now Chaplain at the Sisters of Charity of St. Elizabeth Motherhouse in Convent Station, New Jersey.

"It's strange how these things happen," Father Pope said. "Just last week I got a letter from my long-time friend Father McCartie telling me about the Silver Jubilee of the Sisters of Charity and mentioning in passing their new chaplain, a Father Michael Riordan."

He looked over at Margaret, who had joined them at the table.

"I knew ye to be a Riordan, Mrs. Buckley, and then within two days I received Bishop Croke's letter advising me that a relation from our parish, a Reverend John Joseph Riordan, would be visiting. It was my housekeeper, Mrs. Ryan, who put the pieces together for me. Without her help, I'd be quite lost in so many ways."

Jeremiah spoke as he poured another whiskey for Father Pope and Father John.

"Well, fancy that. Did he mention that Catherine Mehegan, who is the very well regarded Reverend Mother Mary Xavier, is a Cork girl? And I've heard that Father McCartie is to be the master of ceremonies at the celebration the end of September."

"I'm hoping to be in attendance, Jeremiah." Johnny Joe added, "I'll be certain to post a letter telling you about it."

Margaret listened as the men carried on and felt a tug in her heart. It was a good thing, this change for Michael. He was nearing an age when he was entitled to a bit less work. This chaplaincy at the Sisters of Charity Motherhouse could be just the ticket for keeping him in an active role that didn't have with it the rigor of parish life. He has the temperament for serving the women, she thought. Sure, didn't she and her ma provide a good training ground?

Chapter Thirty-Five

Fanny and Anna

August 1885

Jeremiah sipped the broth, letting the flavor of the lamb seep in, waiting for the healing he hoped it would bring. The turf fire hissed; shafts of soft yellow sunlight settled onto the table where he sat. The light was coming from what had become known as "Maggie's window."

This most recent bout of fatigue worried him. He didn't have the stamina he'd once had and he found himself, at fifty-nine years old, leaving Tims and Michael more and more of the work. Tims was certainly up to it. At age twenty-one, he had a strong constitution and when he put his mind to it, he could be quite disciplined. As oldest son, he was the rightful heir to this land. That was certain.

The year's harvest had been fair and Lughnasa, the traditional festival, continued to attract the young people. With Mary now gone, Tims went alone to meet up with Nora, Julia again declining the invitation to ride along.

"Why would I want to be going off into the night to see flames shooting up in the sky?" she'd said. "Sure don't I need my rest so I can tend to all the things ye're likely to forget?"

Jeremiah smiled. She had a tongue on her, that one did.

He missed Mary fiercely, savoring her letters as much as Michael's. Only her safe arrival and fortune in getting work within a fortnight eased his heart. Father John, good to his word, had watched out for her. And Mary had been as good as her word as well, sending money each month from her earnings as a domestic. She described the "all too grand house" in her letters.

> Da, do ye remember my first time at the Big House with ye when I was but eleven years old? It's the same feeling I

had when I first came to this house. There are chandeliers in all the downstairs rooms, even the hallways. And I'm only one of the servants. There's an upstairs maid as well. I'm assigned the downstairs for I'm lovely to look at, so said Mr. Stewart Browne, my employer. He's really quite decent.

Jeremiah took his bowl and spoon to the sideboard, moving slowly, his body sluggish even doing this simple act. Beyond this physical fatigue, Jeremiah felt an emotional weariness that left him with little or no interest in the affairs of the day, exhausted from years of trying to make the difference that so clearly needed to be made. He didn't know if he could keep trying. Leave it for younger men, he thought. Leave it for Tims and Michael.

**

Margaret came in from feeding the chickens to find Jeremiah standing by the sideboard.

"I'll tell ye, Margaret," he said, turning to her, his bowl still in hand, "these are different times. Too much water has gone over the dam for me to believe this most recent Ashbourne Act."

Margaret had become accustomed to his carrying on about this and that. What she wasn't prepared for was the paleness of his color or his inability to remember what he was about, which seemed more prevalent of late.

"Gladstone's proven to be sincere enough in all his dealings but putting Parnell in gaol was unnecessary. What was it he thought he'd prove? Did he think the Irish people would collapse, fold up, become silent? Thanks be to God for Parnell's sisters . . ."

"Do you propose to stand for the day with that bowl in yer hand? Is it alms yer seeking?" she said playfully, hoping he would see for himself what he was doing.

"Ah, yes, the bowl," he said as he put it down. "But I'm telling ye, Margaret, we can have this land if we want it. With what Mary is sending, we can buy this land. It's been our dream and yet I've a fear of attaining ownership that I never knew could take hold of me."

"Have ye taken the medicine from Doc Foley for today?" Margaret asked as she began to peel potatoes. "He says it'll bring ye back faster and stronger than ever. But ye have to follow his orders. That's the rub of it."

"Margaret," Jeremiah argued as he sat at the table, "I think he's making too much of it. A little exhaustion at my age is nothing to worry over. I'll be fit as a fiddle soon enough, medicine or no medicine. I just worry I'm putting too much on the boys. Our Jules is a help to ye I know, and so will Maggie be once she finishes her schooling next spring. Lizzie and Jer can carry on as well, I'd say."

"Ye're the one carrying on, Jer," Margaret said as she put two mugs on the table. "First, last and always about the land. Ye have longed since I've known ye to own this land. Ye've talked of nothing else and now yc're telling me of a fear." She put the teapot on the table. "Whatever of, Jer, whatever of?"

Jeremiah looked up at her with confusion in his eyes. "Now if I knew that, I'd be telling ye." He took a deep breath and gazed at the *Cork Examiner* on the table. "I guess it's the scoundrels I don't trust. They've set aside a five-million-pound fund and say I can take a loan from the government and pay it back over forty-eight years." He paused, then said with a laugh, "Do ye think I'm going live for another forty-eight years? And this four per cent rate they've fixed. Do ye know how much it would cost over those forty-eight years I'm supposed to live?"

He pulled a mug to him and reached for the sugar bowl. "And do ye think Mr. Bennett will sell at a decent price?" He put several teaspoons of sugar in his mug. "I've never said a word to him about the awful treatment of Eugene but he knows my feelings. I've not taken tea with him since that day."

Margaret joined him at the table and watched as he poured tea for both of them. She listened as he continued.

"Do ye imagine he'll be kind in his dealings? Paddy Riordan has been telling me that Mr. Bennett is not doing very well himself, physically and financially. If I were to go to see him, how do

I know what I'd be greeted with? I don't trust it, Mairéad, not for a minute."

They sat in silence, sipping the warmed tea, the cream softening its rich black flavor. After a time Margaret stood and went to the sideboard, filled the kettle with potato and hefted it to the hearth hook. She kept the peels in a separate pot, hoping Jeremiah would take them out to the pigs. He'd done very little of late and her worry went beyond the Land Purchase Act. She couldn't imagine life without this man, even if life with him was getting more and more complex.

"What's ailing Mr. Bennett, Jer, do ye know?" Margaret asked as she pushed loose strands of her still vibrant red hair in place. "Did Paddy say?" Margaret was eager to learn if she should send some of the lamb broth, a recipe from Gran that she'd followed for her own family that never failed to improve ailing health. She thought Jer's color a bit better already.

"He didn't say and I don't know. And if ye're thinking ye should send him some of yer healing broth, I'd say it'd be a fine idea, fine indeed. Once I'm up to it, it might be just the thing I need to make this trip."

* * *

Jeremiah felt what was becoming a familiar weariness as he walked out into the fields. As the sunlight darted in and out of the clouds, the beauty of the lush green and golds around him caused him to breathe in deeply. This land never ceased to fulfill him. As he approached the remnants of the neat rows of potato beds, he felt a satisfaction. The harvest had been a good one. There was no reason to believe the next one wouldn't be as well.

He slowed his pace now, sauntering up and down the rills, and found himself thinking about Parnell's imprisonment. Had three years already passed? Parnell's release was based upon the stipulation that the agrarian agitation be stopped. The Kilmainham Treaty, they called it. There was to be no more boycotting, no more rent strikes. Captain Midnight, the euphemism for the organized

agrarian crime, maiming cattle, setting fires and threatening landlords, often committed in the dark of night, was to be put to rest.

He stood on the crest of a small rise just beyond the front pasture and looked out over the hillside that gleamed in the afternoon's light. His da came to mind as he looked about the land. He
could see him in his collarless flannel shirt, his black suspenders
prominent as he bent to inspect the potatoes. The very thought of
him brought him some hope, knowing the da had seen similar
hard times. He wondered what the da would think of the turn of
events these days.

The peace that was hoped for with Parnell's release was shattered when a secret society, known as the Irish National Invincibles, smuggled surgical knives purchased in Bond Street in London
over to Dublin in the skirts of the seven months' pregnant wife of
Secretary Frank Byrne. The knives had been used on Lord
Frederick Cavendish and Thomas Henry Burke, an Irish civil servant, who were ambushed in Phoenix Park and hacked to death.
The public outcry had been vociferous, some implicating Parnell,
who offered to resign his chairmanship of the Irish party.
Gladstone was gracious in making clear that such a gesture was
unnecessary.

The persistent plague of violence tormented Jeremiah. Even
though Parnell was not involved in any way, the heart of the promised peace had been mortally weakened. He wondered about
Michael's American Fenians, and any of their solutions.

He sighed as he took in one last look at the hillside and turned
back toward home, his thoughts now on the coming Sunday night
gathering at the pub, which had become a ritual. The camaraderie
with others who cared as he did renewed him almost as much as
Margaret's broth.

* * *

He stood at the polished bar at Barry's, with Paddy Murphy, whose
solid frame was shorter than Jeremiah by half a foot. Within a few
minutes, Eugene Cronin and Dennis Carroll, pints in hand, joined

them. It was Sunday and Jeremiah felt lighter just being with these men.

"I'm here to say if it hadn't been for Parnell's sisters, Fanny and Anna, the whole of the movement might have failed forever," Paddy declared, his brown eyes scanning the room.

"Me Ellen says the same thing," Eugene added.

It was good that Eugene was there with them, Jeremiah thought, noting how sparse Eugene's toast-brown hair was becoming. His family was still with Mrs. Finnerty, Ellen not adjusting easily to being in someone else's cottage. It wasn't an easy time for any of them.

The men were referring to the Ladies Land League, an organization headquartered in Dublin, headed by Parnell's sisters, Fanny and Anna, which had sprung into action during Parnell's imprisonment. Many had been surprised by its efficient organization and its ability to raise money enough to help the more than sixteen thousand people who were evicted in 1881 along with another twenty-six thousand the following year.

"Leave it to women to get things done. That's what me Margaret said of them," Jeremiah said. "From what I've heard, besides building hundreds of huts for the evicted, they advocated the no-rent manifesto that Parnell and his colleagues were promulgating from their Kilmainham cells."

Dennis Carroll, his salt and pepper eyebrows raised, joined in. "I've heard it said that Parnell could barely keep up with those two."

"Aye, yer right there, Dennis," Paddy added as he pulled up a bar stool. "It's well known that Anna was more outspoken than Parnell would have liked. Didn't she announce, after the Phoenix Park murders, when all was to quiet down, that she would continue to organize the tenants regardless of what politicians like her brother might say?"

Eugene pondered for a moment, pulled a seat up next to Paddy and said, "Isn't it just like a woman to have her mind made up." He paused and added another tidbit. "All wasn't right about those two women. I've heard that on the head of all this unrest, Fanny took her own life."

"Aye, I heard about that, too. That mustn't have been easy on Anna," Paddy said. "Yet, imagine her, despite such a loss, still pushing on. She didn't take kindly to Parnell's disbanding the Ladies Land League." He paused and looked around at the other men, aware he had what might just be new information. "She's living in England now and they say she'll have nothing to do with her own brother."

The men stood in silence. The years of land wars, violence, political maneuvering, family feuds and dashed expectations had wearied them all, with not much hope on the horizon.

Jeremiah watched as Paddy ordered another round for them all, glad that Eugene wouldn't have to put what little money he had forth. While the talk of the Ladies Land League which had been such a force during Parnell's imprisonment continued, Jeremiah's mind drifted to Michael Davitt's original purpose for the Land League: first, to bring a reduction to the exorbitant rack-rents; second, to facilitate obtaining ownership of the soil by the occupiers.

With Parnell as President it had become a two-edged sword, asking farmers to withhold rents if the rates asked were too high, yet putting these very men at risk for eviction.

He nodded in appreciation as Paddy slid his stout down the bar to him. A violent underbelly of the League threatened those who paid any high rents with maiming and slaughtering of livestock. Incidences of such reprehensible violence were becoming far too common. Landlords became more and more desperate as they found themselves on the edge of bankruptcy. Word that shooting lessons had been organized for many of the gentry troubled Jeremiah. Yet he supposed, in their position, he too might try to defend himself. There were no easy answers.

He watched Eugene, glad that he seemed more himself again. There was a time, just after the eviction, he looked beaten, his face gray, his shoulders stooped. He knew that there were many more

Eugenes, men who had been torn from their homes with no recourse. At least the Land League offered one way to fight back.

He took a final swallow of his stout, preparing to leave for home. He felt bone-weary. He saluted his comrades and made his way to the door, aware of the many he knew who were paying their rents, despite the dictum of the League. Nothing was said to anyone of the silent agreement with Mr. Bennett which would remain unspoken.

Chapter Thirty-Six
Ballybawn

March 1886

The overgrown plantings surrounding the big house were the first thing that Jeremiah noticed. The ordinarily manicured appearance of the gardens and the bushes had been replaced by batches of weeds. The shrubs hadn't been clipped for weeks. He looked about for any evidence of attention, but found only further signs of neglect. The once pristine gazebo on the demesne showed peeling paint and a sizable branch from the nearby oak tree had pierced its roof like a sword.

Jeremiah, Michael and Tims stepped down from the cart.

"I'd say all is not right here, lads," Jeremiah said. "We best be cautious in our visit today. Mind ye, I haven't seen Mr. Bennett for over a year now. But there's something afoot. I needn't tell ye to mind yer manners."

Jeremiah led the way and his sons followed. He paused and stared as they approached the entrance where he'd been so graciously received in past years. He winced as he came closer, his dismay intensifying. His acquired status among the other tenant farmers as a quasi-representative had helped create a cordial and, for the most part, productive relationship with Mr. Bennett, often negotiating agreements during difficult harvest times. However, the breach made with Eugene's eviction was one Jeremiah doubted would ever mend.

The great tall oak doors and the brass knocker were weather stained. He wondered about Jonathan, who'd been the mainstay here. Jeremiah picked up the brass lion mouth replica and knocked on the door. The three waited. The silence was different. No sounds of scurrying feet or doors opening and closing signaling his arrival. Finally, the knob turned and the great door opened to reveal none other than Mr. Joseph Bennett.

"Why, Jeremiah, you've come at last," the landowner said. His face was more creased and the lines in it deeper than Jeremiah remembered, but he seemed genuine in his welcome, his voice warm and his brown eyes bright. "It's grand that you've brought your sons. Come into the parlor, please, and I'll be with you presently." His English accent was unmistakable, not altered in the least by the years he'd visited his land in Ireland.

Before Jeremiah could utter a word or introduce his sons, Mr. Bennett scurried away, Jeremiah noting his dark hair and trimmed mustache now showed a substantial amount of white, which was actually becoming. He wore a silk jacket with a cravat tied around his neck; his trousers were not creased and his shoes lacked their usual shine.

The boys and their father moved cautiously into the parlor where Jeremiah had once sat with Mary, recalling the cookies that delighted her so. Slits of light peeked through tears in the heavy damask drapes. Cinders of a past fire lay in the marble hearth. Jeremiah was startled to see some of the furniture missing—the fine mahogany sideboard he had so admired and the portrait of Mr. Bennett's mother. A small dark brown sofa and a matching side chair had replaced the elegant fuchsia-colored couch.

Mr. Bennett returned, carrying a large manila envelope and a few other papers. He looked harried. "I must admit to being a bit scattered today, Jeremiah. You see, I'm leaving Ireland," he said, his eyes distant, his mustache disguising his grimace. "By the end of the week, Ballybawn, this once cherished estate, will be on the auction block."

Jeremiah swallowed hard, surprised by the sadness he felt. He had come prepared to negotiate a settlement for his land, to be stern and compassionless. He'd even decided against bringing some of Gran's broth, not willing to forget it was Mr. Bennett who allowed the eviction of Eugene Cronin. Still, he would end on peaceful terms, showing his sons a way to keep their own good manners despite the ignorance of others.

Jeremiah cleared his throat. "Ye say ye're leaving Ireland, is it? How do you propose to dispose of yer lands?"

Mr. Bennett stood by the cold hearth, one hand on the mantel, the other clutching the papers.

"That's why I'm glad you're here, Jeremiah. And I'm glad your sons are with you as well." He looked at the two young men, one taller than Jeremiah by a hand. They were handsome boys, the younger of the two favoring Jeremiah's looks, reddish brown hair and serious eyes, the older red-haired boy a bit shorter and more flamboyant somehow. For now, both were attentive and silent.

He moved from the fireplace and motioned to Jeremiah to take a seat, and pulled a chair from the hearth closer to the sofa.

"I'm proposing, Jeremiah, to sell as much of the land as can be sold and at as reasonable a price as I can arrange. There's no way to keep Ballybawn solvent anymore, not with all the concessions we landlords are being asked to make these days."

Jeremiah avoided his gaze, amazed at what he was hearing. Lands that had been in English hands for over two centuries would now be available. A shiver ran through him.

As Mr. Bennett pulled out a folded paper from the manila envelope, Jeremiah noticed that despite Mr. Bennett's wrinkled trousers and weary look, he still had manicured nails and hands that showed no callus or physical stress of any kind. He handed the paper to Jeremiah.

"Here's a list of all the tenants. You know a great number of them. After you decide about your land, I'd like you to talk with the others. The Ashbourne Act will be of help to some, though I don't suppose you'll have much need of it."

Jeremiah looked over at his sons. Tims, his broad shoulders held back squarely and stubble of new whiskers on his chin, sat on the couch next to Michael. The boys glanced at each other.

All the way over in the cart, Jeremiah had been rehearsing aloud his speech to Mr. Bennett, preparing to pay a handsome price for the land which would finally be theirs for the keeping. As the cart jogged along the path up the ridge, he began, "Mark me words, lads, this land was rightfully ours before any of us were born. And it will be ours again, if I have anything to say of it." The more he spoke, the straighter he sat.

"'Tis with thanks to yer sister Mary and her new husband Paddy, a good Healy at that, we'll be making an offer that will be more than just. And with what we have now, there should be no need to borrow anything from the government." As they rode along, he stared silently for a moment and then added, "It mightn't hurt to set for ourselves a tidy payment that's less than the rent we've been paying for almost thirty years. We'll see what he does with our offer."

As if an afterthought, he said, "I can assure ye of one thing. The land will soon be Buckley land and that for as long as a Buckley is alive."

As they had waited for Jeremiah that morning, Tims had told Michael of his concern that the da was trusting the future of the land to them though neither of them had interest in taking it over, and neither of them had the nerve to mention it to him. The da had been crazy for the land but much of it wasn't as arable as it had been in the past. Last season's oats were half the normal yield.

Just before Jeremiah had come out to join them, Michael had said, "He's mad for the land, Tims. Ye can't be telling him there's a thing wrong with it."

Tims and Michael, now twenty-two and seventeen, were working the land more and more as Jeremiah's health continued to decline. They were good at their work but, unlike their father, it wasn't their passion.

Jeremiah unfolded the paper from Mr. Bennett. It was of fine quality, with an ink drawing of Ballybawn house at the top. The penmanship was meticulous. "The names here, Mr. Bennett, these are, for the most part, friends of mine. Yer aware of that, are ye?" he said as he looked at the paper, making certain Mr. Bennett knew what he was doing.

"I see here Tim Hanlon who leases much of his own land to others as well as the land he leases from ye. And I see Tim Reardon and Jeremiah Reardon, Daniel Delohery, as well as meself, along with the Graneys. Would ye be selling it all now?"

Mr. Bennett rose and walked to the window where he pulled the curtain away and gazed out. "I will sell the land to those able to offer the asked-for price. I am in no position to offer any charity, Jeremiah. You know I've come upon hard times myself."

A shaft of sunlight pierced the room. Jeremiah watched him closely, the visibly worn clothing and less than erect posture more evidence of the demise he was witnessing.

"Jonathan's death left me with little choice. He was in many ways the reason Ballybawn succeeded," he said, glancing up at the high Rococo designed ceiling, and the several ornate Italian paintings that remained.

"I must tell you that certain situations that have occurred over the past few years have aggrieved me greatly. Had I been here, take my word; things would have been executed differently. Yet, I can't fault anyone but myself."

He paused and fussed at the drape, pulling it back in place before he turned and spoke again. "I need to make it as crystal clear to each of my tenants as I can," he said as he paused and cleared his throat, "I've been generous to a fault and the time has come to take my leave."

Jeremiah stood and eyed Mr. Bennett, confused by the warmth he felt. Here Mr. Bennett was almost admitting to his absentee status as the problem for poor Eugene. And now he was leaving, selling it all. Before he could think of a response, Mr. Bennett spoke again.

"Jeremiah, about your land," he said, moving away from the window. "I've recently ridden over my holdings getting appraisals from the local solicitor. You hold a fine piece of property, though I'm not sure that the south hectares are as good for tillage as they once were."

Michael and Tims exchanged a glance.

"The trees have shaded much of it from being as fruitful as it once was. I'm prepared to sell it all to you. It would total all forty-six acres. I'll offer it at as fair a price, if not a bit more fair, than any I'm offering. You've been a decent man and your sons deserve to benefit from your labor. As for the others, you'll find offers for each of them in this envelope."

With that, Mr. Bennett moved toward Jeremiah and handed a large manila envelope and a smaller white one to him.

"I hope you'll represent me in a good light to the others," he said, looking into Jeremiah's eyes for the first time. The lines of his face were soft and his voice shaky. "Take note that the white envelope is for you. You'll also see that I'm asking that the transactions be handled by my solicitor. His address in Cork City is on the letter."

Jeremiah looked to his sons, wondering what it was they thought of all they were witnessing. Here he was as close as he had ever been to owning the land of his da and now of his sons. Yet he resisted opening his envelope. He turned to Mr. Bennett and with as much of a matter-of-fact tone as he could muster, said, "Well then, it's through yer solicitor ye'll know the results of it all. We'll be bidding ye a good day."

He moved across the room to Mr. Bennett and extended his hand, remembering Eugene as Mr. Bennett grasped his hand in return.

Tims and Michael stood and, following their father's lead, extended their hands to Mr. Bennett, who appeared visibly moved, his eyes moist, his stance unsteady as he shook their hands, clearing his throat more than once.

Jeremiah moved to the door. Mr. Bennett followed and reached for the knob. He turned it tentatively, then released it and turned to face the boys who stood behind Jeremiah.

He cleared his throat again and said, "You young men have been blessed with as fine a man as I've met in the hills of Donoughmore. I beg you remember that."

Tims and Michael nodded and looked down at the oriental carpet beneath their feet.

With that, Mr. Bennett opened wide the door and the three Buckleys descended the steps to the waiting pony and cart. Mr.

Bennett stood watching after them from the threshold, his silk jacket drooping from his shoulders. As they settled into place, Michael leaned over to Tims and whispered, "I'd say he's all right for an Englishman."

With a chuckle, they left Ballybawn.

Chapter Thirty-Seven

The Da

Spring 1886

Margaret stood at the doorway, her faded blue and white floral dress catching the soft breeze. She gazed out at the newly planted fields, the glimmers of green peeking through the soil. At one time, they might have given hope of a stable harvest, tempting her to trust the land, but betrayals of earlier days held her back.

The children had little notion how deeply the devastating hunger had affected Ireland. Nor should they, she thought, as she put the morning dishes away. Like all children, she supposed, they were inclined to take things for granted. There was a time when she had, but that was long ago. Now she knew that there was no guarantee of health or harvest. Both were gifts from God for which she offered daily thanks.

She began to make the dough for the scones, flouring the wooden board and mixing the flour and butter in the brown and beige crockery bowl. She was eager for Jeremiah's return from the Big House, glad he had taken both Tims and Michael so they could be witness to what would be a momentous time. She knew the power of the land in their lives and prayed that the boys would one day gain an appreciative respect for it.

As she kneaded the dough, she thought of the industry and forbearance of Tims, Michael and the other children which had helped to abate the worst effects of the Land War and recent harvest difficulties. While the older boys saw to the fields, the girls and the younger children washed, helped with chores and went with less without complaint. Early in their lives, they'd been taught that complaining only crippled morale and wouldn't be tolerated.

She shaped the dough onto the skillet, in readiness to be baked before the noonday meal. She was well aware that the political force brought about by the Land League was intimidating land-lords and tenants, the ongoing violence and fear pervading the countryside. She suspected that Tims, who had become secretive, out more and more in the evening, had been a part of the taunting and evening visits to landlords, and she feared he would be caught up in what had become a quasi-military state. She said nothing of it to Jeremiah, fearful of his over-reaction. She'd said nothing of it to Tims, remembering that the fervor of youth, like her own brother Michael's once had, burned fiercely.

She remembered the festive feeling they shared at supper the evening word came that Gladstone had been returned to power in 1880 for his second ministry. They were equally delighted with his Arrears Act of 1882 and his success in passing the Reform Act of 1884.

"Finally," she recalled saying to Jeremiah after the election of 1885, "all ye men who are owning or like us, renting, have voted in a parliamentary election. 'Tis finally a bigger Catholic electorate voting, not just the wealthier classes. Sure the cottiers and agricultural laborers are getting a voice and we can thank Mr. Gladstone for that."

Now as she placed the skillet on the sideboard, waiting for Jeremiah's return with the boys, Margaret recalled his excitement about the political maneuvering that went on.

"And sure, didn't Parnell help by putting his hope on the Tories instead of the Whigs?" Jeremiah had said, pacing the room as he so often did when he was agitated. "The Grand Old Man needed just such a push to make his move toward Home Rule." The *Cork Examiner* was full of the momentous news that Gladstone had brought a measure for Home Rule, the first hope of its kind in Ireland's history.

"But mark me words, Margaret," she recalled him saying, "first, last and always, it's the land that's the key."

* * *

As the morning closed onto the afternoon, Margaret clucked her tongue and turned on her heel away toward the doorway. Whatever was keeping them? They'd been gone since early morning and the sun was already high in the sky. There was so much to do and yet they hadn't returned. Easter, with all its chores, would be upon them in no time—whitewashing, scrubbing, meal preparation.

She minded the feeling of dread she had grown to associate with this time of year, the work demands overwhelming any joy she'd experienced of late. She wished she could return to the days of innocence and drink in the beauty of the customs that celebrated the end of Lent and the Resurrection as she had in earlier years when she and Jeremiah had gone to nearby hilltops to see the dance of the sun at dawn, enjoying the common belief that on Easter morning, as the sun rises, it dances, rejoicing in the Savior's resurrection.

Though she felt less spirited than in earlier years, she would still encourage the family to go to the "herring procession" to watch as a live herring, which had seen them through so many Lenten meals, was carried back to the water by the butchers, happy to have their customers back in line for meat. The gaiety and ceremony marked the beginning of a more hopeful season. It would be an occasion for the girls to parade about in their finery and perhaps a way for Margaret to lift her own spirits.

She knew that Lizzie, her smile so engaging, and Jerry who went everywhere with her, would carry on about the Easter eggs a bit, while Maggie and Julia would be far more interested in the Ahadallane crossroads competitive dance held on Easter Sunday evening, both with a good chance to win the prize. One thing about Julia was that she loved to dance and did it well.

Tradition held that a cake would be balanced on the churndash with flowers on top. Those assembled would watch the courting couple's dance, the girls shaking their flounces, the boys pounding the ground with their feet, until the best boy and girl dancer were selected to take down the cake with shouts of "you take the cake" echoing throughout the hillside.

Margaret sighed at such fond memories, the burdensome feeling of the mountain of chores that awaited her abated for a moment.

"Will there be a lamb this Easter, Ma?" Maggie asked as she burst in the door from the barn. "Julia and I were just wagering if it would be lamb or beef. We're starving for some meat now that Lent's almost past."

Lizzie and Jerry scampered in behind her, leaving the door open. Lizzie went back and shut it after Margaret motioned, then settled with Jerry in the old "castle corner," the blocks long ago replaced with books and puzzles.

"I wouldn't know what there'll be and if yer da and brothers don't get back soon, there'll be no accounting for anything I might propose to slaughter," she said, her cheeks flushed, her hands twisting her apron in knots.

"Do ye want me to go off and look for them, Ma?" Maggie asked, going toward the door. "I could take Tess and have a run at it."

"I don't need another pair of hands off and not coming back 'til any ol' time," Margaret retorted, smoothing her apron as she went to the sideboard. Then she asked sharply, "Where's Julia? Has she the butter churned?"

"She does, Ma. Are ye all right?" Maggie asked, sensing her mother's agitation.

Margaret turned and slowed her response, aware of the sensitive nature of Maggie. "I am, but I wish the boys and yer father were here by now. They're gone far too long." She moved toward the window and looked out.

"Ol' Mr. Bennett must be offering some fine tea," Maggie said, then darted out the door as quickly as she'd come in.

* * *

To Jeremiah, the ride back seemed to take triple the time. Fair weather soothed their travels, and Michael took the reins, an opportunity he didn't often get. He'd been more a scholar and though he carried his weight on the farm, his heart wasn't in it. When he wasn't at his chores, his nose was in a book.

"When we named ye for yer Uncle Michael," Jeremiah had said to him with pride, "we didn't think ye'd be a bookworm like him."

They passed through endless shades of spring green that colored the landscape that surrounded Ahadallane, the patchwork fields reflecting ownership and plantings. Dennis Carroll's farm across the ridge sat adjacent to Paddy Murphy's land. Paddy's Eileen had been faithful in her letter-writing for over ten years; Maggie and Julia still delighted in the almost monthly delivery.

Michael shook the reins and the pony moved a bit faster than Jeremiah might have liked, but he didn't say anything. He smiled. The boys were becoming men faster than he thought possible.

As they reached the ridge and began the slight decline into the townland, they heard a thud and felt the cart wobble, a rock almost toppling it. Michael kept his composure and hung on, urging the pony forward with the skill of a seasoned driver. Jeremiah sat back, breathless but proud. Michael had learned his lessons well.

"Ye might be all right there, Michael. That was a good save, wouldn't ye say, Tims?"

"I would, Da, I would," the older boy agreed, taking his father's lead. Michael sat up all the straighter in his seat, his chest expanded.

The recent bouts of breathlessness troubled Jeremiah. Over the last few weeks, he'd noticed it when he'd barely exerted himself. Here he was again trying to catch his breath and all he was doing was sitting. He tried to distract himself and looked out over the wide expanse of the hillside, blossoming trees and bushes all about them. The reality of Mr Bennett's offer was still seeping in. He was eager to peek in the envelope. There would be time enough when they got home.

Suddenly he felt a sharp pain in his chest and a numbness creeping up his left arm. He clutched at his upper arm and when he went to say something, found it difficult to speak. He cleared his throat and leaned in toward Michael. "Since ye're handling this little cart so smartly, turn us up toward Doc Foley's, would ye now?"

His voice was raspy and he wrapped his right fist tighter around his left arm. "I've a mind to ask him a question and now's as good a time as any."

"I can turn us that way, Da, and I will." Michael kept his eyes forward while Tims leaned over to look at the da.

"Are ye all right, Da? Ye look a bit pale. Do ye have any of yer medicine? Would it help ye?"

Jeremiah's discomfort grew as he tried to speak. He shifted in the seat and Tims reached behind Michael to touch Jeremiah's shoulder.

Jeremiah slouched deeper in the seat and managed to say, "Ah, I'm fine, now Tims, I'm fine. Let's just go on."

Michael looked at Tims and saw his forehead furrowed. He gave another shake to the reins and blessed himself. It would be another twenty minutes before they reached Doc Foley's. He held his breath, said a silent Hail Mary and prayed they'd make it.

Chapter Thirty-Eight

Home Again

Spring 1886

"The boys are here, Ma, and they're helping the da down from the cart," Julia called. The twins scampered to the window while Margaret rinsed her hands in the basin, dried them on her blue apron and rushed out the door past Julia. Her red hair was carefully pinned up to cover the thinness at the crown.

"I've been half-sick with worry, not knowing what had become of ye," she said as she ran toward them.

With Tims on one side and Michael on the other, Jeremiah moved toward her. The day that had favored some sunshine had given way to clouds. Jeremiah stopped as his gaze fell upon Margaret.

"I'm gonna be fine," he said, his voice cracking.

"Doc Foley will be here tonight," Michael said. "He says we should get the da to bed."

The trio moved toward the cabin. "I'm gonna be fine, Mairéad, fine," Jeremiah protested, seeing the lines of worry on her face. "I just need to rest."

He looked ashen and sounded exhausted. His green eyes were dull and his hands trembled as he walked. He looked seventy, not sixty.

Margaret followed them, wringing her hands, Julia and Maggie a step behind her.

"He's got dropsy, Ma," Michael called back to her. "Doc Foley's gone to Mallow for digitalis. He says it'll fix the da up like new."

Lizzie came toward Margaret, her rich red pigtails bobbing. "Is the da gonna die, Ma?" she asked, her voice bordering on hysteria. "Is that what's to happen? Mrs. Connolly had the dropsy and now she's gone."

Margaret spun on her heel, her eyes fierce. "Stop with such talk now or I'll give ye the back of me hand. Sure yer da's ill, but it doesn't mean he's to die. He's too stubborn for that. I'll have none of that talk."

Maggie and Julia exchanged glances and pulled Lizzie from Margaret, who rarely showed such anger.

Margaret followed the boys into the bedroom where they were helping Jeremiah onto the bed. The girls and young Jer stayed back. She bit her lip to keep from calling out when she saw how feebly he moved. Instead, she said, "Are ye in pain, Jer? I'll bring ye some of the Gran's soup. It'll make ye right as rain."

Before Jeremiah could answer, Tims said, "The da told Doc Foley the pain was in his chest and down his left arm but that it's stopped. Doc Foley said to get him to bed and elevate his feet and head. He's taken some of his medicine and it's helped."

Margaret pulled the quilted coverlet from the stand at the foot of the bed and placed it over Jeremiah. She moved to him, stroked his thinning speckled brown hair and kissed his brow. The children froze in place. An awkward silence filled the room: such acts of affection were seldom displayed in their home.

Tims broke the silence. "We need to take his shoes off. The doc says the swelling should go down once we elevate his legs."

"He should be propped up too, for the breathing, Tims. Remember?" Michael added.

Jeremiah spoke up now to all their relief.

"When yer through fussing over me, I'd like to sleep a bit, if ye don't mind. It's too early for the wake."

"Oh, Da, don't be talking like that," Julia said as she stood watching them, sounding like the eighteen-year-old woman she had become. "I'll get ye the pillow from the settle bed."

Lizzie and Maggie came to the doorway, furrowed brows, frightened eyes and pursed lips filling their faces. Margaret turned to them as she moved to the door, her blue eyes determined. "Yer da is a big strong man and nothing's gonna stop him for a long time. The two of ye can come help me fix the soup."

Julia, her dark hair pulled back tightly from her face, returned with the pillow, and while Tims lifted Jeremiah to prop his head up, Michael concocted a mound of blanket at the foot of the bed and lifted his feet onto it.

"Well, look at me now. I'll be bent in half in no time if ye keep propping me ends up. Go on with ye now and tell yer ma not to worry. I'm gonna stick around long enough to be a nuisance." Young Jeremiah, auburn-haired like his da, watched silently from the doorway, his heart pounding fast, hands thrust deep into his pockets, not knowing what to think.

***

"Michael, would ye have the da's envelope?" Tims, a strand of red hair falling across his forehead, asked as he came from the da's bedroom. "He's asking for it."

The dinner dishes had been cleared and the two girls were off tending to the animals, the twins off in the yard.

Michael got up from the rocking chair and put his book down. "I thought ye had it when we took him in to Doc Foley. The da was clutching it and ye took it from him so I could help him down from the cart."

"What's all this talk of an envelope? What envelope?" Margaret asked as she looked up from her needlework. "And keep yer voices down, will ye please?"

"It's from Mr. Bennett," Tims whispered as pushed his hair out of his eyes and moved closer. "It's the land settlement. The da was to give the letters to the tenants. Ballybawn is to be closed."

"Ballybawn closed, is it? My, oh my!" Margaret sighed and put down her needlework.

"Tims, do ye think the envelope is at Doc Foley's?" Michael asked softly as he stood by Tims.

"With all the confusion with the da, I imagine it could be," Tims said. Then he winked at Margaret as he continued. "I hope it didn't fall from the cart. There's no telling where it might be if it did. There was a madman driving us now, Ma, so the lanes weren't safe for man or beast."

Michael and Tims exchanged smiles.

Margaret smiled fleetingly and said, "Well, 'tis already half-seven. Do ye think ye can get there to find it or should it wait 'til morning?"

"I think I can go tonight, Ma," Tims said, his eyes gleaming. "I'll go there first and then stop by for a visit with Nora. 'Tis a good way to get out for a bit, if yer all right with that."

"Well mind ye," Margaret said as she rubbed her eyes and put down her sewing basket, "get home at a decent hour. We don't know what's to happen with yer da."

"Do ye think Doc Foley will even be back yet from Mallow?" Michael asked Tims as he moved to the door with him. "It was two o'clock before we even left him. It can be up to an hour and a half ride each way. And I wouldn't say the Doc is as fast as he might once have been."

"I'll take me chances there, little brother. I'll be off," Tims said as he grabbed his brown coat and wool cap and went out the door.

"Well, Ma, it goes to show ye," Michael said, as he came back to his chair. "Ye've two lads that can handle anything. It was a big day and we've at least brought the da home alive."

"Michael, stop that talk," Margaret said as she shivered and noticed his elbow poking through his plaid shirtsleeve.

"Of course the da came home alive. I've no doubt of it. 'Twas no easy thing for a lad like ye, not yet seventeen. But now, enough of yer smart talk, before ye find yer own self needing a doctor. Off with ye and take yer brother Jer with ye, to tend the cattle. 'Tis time he learned how to help. Yer sisters have done every chore except bringing them home. Doc Foley should be here by the time yer back. I'll be in with yer da."

Putting his book down, Michael stood and moved to Margaret's chair, bent and kissed her on the cheek, then vanished out the door, calling his brother's name.

***

Jeremiah had tasted some of the soup and sipped a bit of whiskey earlier. He'd fallen asleep and seemed to be resting when Margaret tiptoed in to check on him. His head, tilted awkwardly to the side, was sure to give him some stiffness in his neck. He looked better than when he'd come in. He wasn't as gray and overall he seemed less quivery. Margaret sat by the bed, content to see his chest rise and fall.

When he awakened, Maggie and Lizzie began waiting on him hand and foot. They fluffed his pillows, brought him tea and even offered to read to him. He told them the story of being with Mr. Bennett and the demise of Ballybawn. Over the years, Margaret and Jeremiah had visited Mr. Bennett often and had seen to it that the children each had turns going along so they would not be strangers to finery.

Julia joined them as Maggie asked, "Ye mean, we're to own the land, Da? Our very own?"

Before he could answer, Julia chimed in, "Don't be troubling the da with yer questions just yet, Maggie. There'll be plenty of time later on." She shooed the younger two girls out with a shake of her dark hair. "Now's time for the da to rest. Do ye need anything else, Da?"

"I wouldn't mind a melody on the squeeze box, if one of ye had a mind to play for me," Jeremiah replied.

"I'll gladly play for ye, Da," Maggie said quickly as she went toward the bedroom door. "I've a new tune I learned this past week from Mrs. Cogan. She has a memory for all the old songs and told me this one was surely a favorite. I'll fetch the accordion and be right back."

"Jules," Jeremiah asked, as he sat propped up by the pillow she'd fixed for him, "Can ye play the Jew's harp along with Maggie, now? It'll be good to hear the two of ye. That's a comfort for this 'ol man, I can tell ye that rightly. A true comfort."

He smiled at Margaret, who kept her place in the chair next to him. Margaret smiled back at Jeremiah as the three girls returned. Lizzie, her face serious, stood forward and as her two sisters accompanied, sang a popular Thomas Moore tune, "Believe Me if All Those Endearing Young Charms".

Margaret was pleased with their choice of a tune, and even though some believed that it told of love for a woman whose face had been scarred from smallpox, it was still a sweet tune. Maggie pumped the accordion bellows with practiced skill, while Julia handled the mouth harp delicately. Lizzie's lilting voice brought a smile from her parents.

Margaret felt her face relax, the tension easing from her brow. She was pleased that the girls understood the da needed peace, and that they had ceased their bickering for the time being.

Chapter Thirty-Nine
Easter

April 25, 1886

Easter Sunday dawned clear and bright and, according to legend, the sun had its dance. Margaret didn't mind missing the annual pilgrimage to witness it. She was on a more important pilgrimage, going to and from Jeremiah's bed, seeing to his comfort. The children would be on their own for Mass, since she not did not dare to leave Jeremiah alone for that length of time.

As promised, Doc Foley, his hair more silver recently, had brought the digitalis, and within a few days the swelling in Jeremiah's ankles had abated and his breathing become less labored.

As he put on his suit coat and snapped his black bag shut, he spoke to Margaret out of earshot of the children and Jeremiah. "There's no telling, Margaret. He could live longer than ye or me. He just has to take it easy. I've told him what I'm telling ye. He's not a young man anymore. His sons can carry on for him. It's time he took his rest."

Margaret stood a bit taller, aware of the uphill battle to be fought on this account. Doc Foley could attend to the body, but who would attend to the spirit of the man whose very being had always depended on his land, his precious land?

* * *

Almost a month had passed since Jeremiah first came home with the boys from Doc Foley's, and this morning as she looked into the bedroom, she found Jeremiah sitting on the side of the bed, his dark trousers and white shirt on, a brogue in one hand, the other already on his foot.

"Well, 'tis a fine one ye are," she said to him as she moved into the room. "Intending to be getting out of yer bed, are ye? Even after all Doc Foley's told us of yer need for rest?"

"Doc Foley isn't the one whose been cooped up for weeks like a hen," Jeremiah said as he fastened his brogue. "Besides, if the Lord can rise today, so can I."

Margaret held her breath as she watched him. He stood like a newborn calf, wobbling as he reached to the wall for support.

"'Tis a fine specimen of a man ye are, Jeremiah Buckley," she said, as she moved to him. They joined in a slow, gentle embrace. She felt his weight and his warmth.

"Shall we go to the table for some tea, is it?" she asked as she took his hand and moved to the doorway.

"We shall, indeed," he agreed as he straightened a bit and followed her lead.

The girls were out milking the cows, feeding the chickens and gathering the eggs. There would be an Easter feast today and if he didn't overdo it, Jeremiah would be the guest of honor. Tims had invited Nora and her parents to join them. Nora's da, Dennis, a cooper, had lived on a little piece of land given to him by his da. If things worked out as he hoped, Tims would be able to offer Nora a bit more.

"It isn't the best of times to be having company, Tims, but yer da won't hear differently," Margaret said to Tims when he had presented the idea. "He's as fond of Dennis and Eileen as ye are of Nora. Well, almost."

Margaret had prepared the goose for roasting earlier in the day. The potato, carrot and cabbage were ready for the pot.

As she helped settle Jeremiah at the table, she said sternly, "Mind me now, there'll be no talking of politics with Dennis, do ye hear me?"

She put the kettle on the hearth and put the mugs out as she continued.

"Dennis knows what can rile ye up and I've begged him not to put ye to it. Don't be baiting him on as ye might, now, or I'll put the two of ye out to pasture."

"Mairéad, don't be worrying yerself," Jeremiah said as he toyed with the sugar bowl. "From the little ye've let me read, I find Ireland's fight for the land is being won as we speak. Gladstone's been true to his word with his advances toward land ownership. And as for Home Rule, he's trying mightily to get it passed, if his own Liberal Party doesn't ruin things."

Home Rule was an issue Gladstone, in good conscience, had seized upon as just for Ireland. His Liberal Party was split in opinion on it, many refusing to support any reduction of British power over Ireland.

"Ye see what I mean, now. Ye say something like that about Liberal Party and the fight is on," Margaret said, her eyes flashing fiercely.

"If we don't talk of politics," Jeremiah retorted as he watched Margaret fix the tea, "what would ye have us talk of? What the missus was wearing or whose son was seen with whom? Or who said what to whom? I'd go daft with such talk and ye know it."

"Ye could talk of the new Gaelic Athletic Association," Margaret said as she straightened the tablecloth and rearranged the plates on the table. "It's a fine sign of the health of our spirit, despite our economy."

The GAA had recently been formed by Michael Cusak from County Clare to prevent Irish games from dying out. Cusak encouraged Irishmen to come out from their cabins and play distinctively Irish games with Irish rules that would improve their physical condition and morale as well as discourage anglicization and stimulate pride in place and nation. It had the endorsement of Archbishop Croke, Charles Stewart Parnell and Michael Davitt, and despite internal controversy, the GAA had quickly grown popular, with clubs forming in every parish in every county.

"Besides," she added, "Dennis and Eileen have promised after dinner to stay only for a song or two and see you settled back for an early rest. It's not only Doc Foley who knows what's to be done for the dropsy."

***

Eileen, Dennis and Nora arrived at three-thirty. Jeremiah had agreed to take a rest before their arrival while the girls finished the preparations for an afternoon that promised to be one of celebration. Margaret watched as Tims hovered about Nora, pleased that he had found someone with whom to share his affection, though she winced to think of the accompanying heartache. No marriage was without heartache, of that she was certain. She embraced the notion of "one and only moments" that filled her at times to overflowing, moments of joy beyond understanding. This is what she wished for her eldest son, should he marry Nora.

Nora was attractive, her black hair, green eyes and milk-white complexion as different as could be from the red-haired, blue-eyed or sandy-haired, hazel-eyed Buckley-Riordans. She could trace Nora's features to a combination of her father and mother, Dennis's six-foot frame, dark curly hair and green eyes a sharp contrast to the bird-like delicacy of Eileen's blue eyes and porcelain skin.

As Margaret watched Nora interact with the others, she saw beauty that emanated from within as well as without. Nora helped serve the meal with grace as she nodded to this one or that one and laughed easily in the patter of conversation. Her dark curls danced as she shook her head in agreement with Tims who waxed forth on the new GAA club that was forming in Ahadallane. He took his cues from his mother who remained determined to keep Jeremiah from conversation that would vex him.

As the goose was carved, accompanied by the obligatory oohs and aahs, and the vat of vegetables was slathered with butter, Dennis proposed a toast.

"*Sláinte*," he said in the familiar Gaelic as he held his glass of stout high. "To health for all within this place, a good laugh and a long sleep, the best cures in a doctor's book."

"Hear, hear," said Tims as he raised his glass and then downed the contents—yet another of Margaret's worries.

Talk turned to their children who had emigrated.

"Have ye word from Mary of late?" Eileen asked, looking at Jeremiah.

"Ah, we have a faithful daughter in that one, we do," Jeremiah interjected. "It's every hope I have that she'll find her way back to us. What do you hear of your girls?"

Dennis and Eileen's two other daughters were in Boston, employed as domestics.

Maggie didn't listen as the Carrolls spoke of their girls. Instead, she heard Jeremiah's voice, his broken heart slipping into his tone as he spoke of Mary and his hope for her return. They all knew better. Maggie cringed to think that she would cause him still more heartache with her plans, but she steeled herself with a promise to go despite that possibility.

She would be fifteen in June and would leave school as soon as she completed her examinations. She had excelled in reading, writing, spelling and needlework, producing some fine handwork she hoped would help pay for her passage. Arithmetic, grammar and geography had been successful subjects for her as well and she looked forward to beating Mary and Julia's scores.

The sound of her mother's voice brought Maggie's attention back to the conversation.

"After the meal, would ye like to hear a bit of our Mary's most recent letter? She tells of a fancy ball she helped serve. She's becoming quite adept at hobnobbing, I'd say," Margaret said proudly.

The conversation went on, Eileen and Dennis swapping tales of their children's adventures. Then, before Margaret could stop it, Jeremiah opened the door to the issue of the day.

"Will we see Gladstone's Home Rule bill pass now, do ye think, Dennis? With yer man Joseph Chamberlain gone and the new 'Unionist' Liberals on the charge, is there a prayer for the bloody thing with all their talk of Home Rule equals Rome Rule?" He sat with his back to the door, looking over this feast day celebration with family and friends. As the meal drew to an end, the twins along with Tims and Nora slipped out to the front yard, Julia and Maggie cleared the dishes and Margaret, Michael, Dennis and Eileen stayed at the table.

"Ah, Dennis," Margaret quickly interjected, "ye know there's so much pending these days, Jer can't possibly expect ye to know how to even respond, now can ye, Jer?" She dreaded the two men going on as they were known to do, pounding fists and calling names, proposing solutions to problems far beyond their reach.

"Ah, Margaret, ye needn't worry," Dennis replied. "I've known this man long enough to know he has the solution all squared away, so I'll save me breath for a pull on me pipe."

With that, Dennis winked at Michael, who was sitting on the edge of his seat, went to the hearth, heated a stick from an ember and held it to his pipe. Margaret sighed and beamed at Dennis who remained as fine a friend as any in the whole township.

"Not so fast there, me friend," Jeremiah cautioned. "If memory serves me right, ye've some answers of yer own. And I'd love to hear them and show ye the error of yer ways, but I think it would injure me Margaret's heart more than me own. So, with yer indulgence, I'll take the wisdom from yer fine toast this evening and go off for a long sleep as part of me cure. God willing, we'll have plenty of time to discuss the accursed politicians."

With that, Jeremiah stood, as did Michael. With a hand on Michael's shoulder, he moved to the bedroom, giving a wave good night.

Chapter Forty

The Envelopes

July 1886

Spring slowly turned to summer, the wild roses bursting forth, the green luster of the hillsides deepening and the days warming. As Jeremiah recuperated under Margaret's watchful eye, the girls continued to be attentive to his needs, often regaling him with music while Tims and Michael brought home stories from the pub and well-wishes from neighbors who hadn't yet visited. The season of Beltane followed on the heels of the unusually late Easter that year, and Jeremiah felt some of his vigor returning and began to make plans to deliver the letters from Mr. Bennett, a task he had thought much of as he was stuck in bed.

It had been four months since Jeremiah had met with Mr. Bennett and word had been about the parish of the upcoming closure of Ballybawn. Tims had indeed retrieved the missing Mr. Bennett envelope from Doc Foley the same evening it had gone missing. Margaret had kept it from Jeremiah, waiting for him to ask for it. Once he did, she put him off a bit longer, insisting he would be too agitated if things weren't right within. When he finally opened it, just after May Day, he found things were more than right. He smiled as he read Mr. Bennett's offer of the land at two-thirds its market value. He hoped the contents of the sealed envelopes for the nine others were as fair.

So it had come to this, Jeremiah thought as he dressed for the day, landlords unable to maintain their own high standard of living and still be fair to their tenants as the law now demanded. Even the wildly popular Parnell had almost lost his own Avondale through foreclosure, he recalled as he put on his brogues. He remembered the disappointment felt by those present, when in 1882, shortly after the Irish Invincibles were found responsible for the Phoenix Park murders and hanged that the Parnell Tribute was launched to help Parnell save Avondale.

The papal rescript that forbade any involvement was most certainly a result of direct English influence on the Vatican. Disdain for such involvement made the Parnell Tribute all the more popular, an indirect and Irish form of defiance.

Parnell was an odd duck of a sort, Jeremiah thought, somehow remaining ever popular. When Parnell had been invited to a great mass meeting in the Rotunda and was handed a check for thirty-seven thousand pounds, a gift from the people of Ireland, to help save Avondale and pay tribute to him for his public service, he pocketed the check without a word of thanks, maintaining the distant decorum for which he was known.

A simple nod of acknowledgment from Parnell at his receipt of the funds that had come from those with so little might have warmed the people, but there was none. Yet they still followed him. How different his experience of Mr. Bennett, whose warmth, though not expressed often, had been present throughout the years.

When Jeremiah appeared, dressed for his mission of envelope delivery, Margaret wouldn't hear of him going off on his own. It had been four months since he had first taken ill and she wasn't about to compromise his recovery with any of his foolishness. She stood facing him, her brow lined with distress. "Why can't the boys take ye, or for that matter, the girls?" she asked. "Ye'll not be risking anything happening to ye and no one with ye to help, do ye hear me?"

He had heard, and though he was a man who valued his independence, he acquiesced. He'd seen her concern and experienced her love in so many ways over these last weeks. He wasn't about to jeopardize what he knew mattered most in the remaining days of his life. He sat down to tea without an argument. They had waited this long, Lord know the tenants could wait a bit longer.

***

Julia had been the first to drive Jeremiah in the pony and trap, with her brothers and sister set to take turns driving their da 'til all eight envelopes were delivered. This first trip was to the Murphys', Eileen's family. Julia was eager to hear more of Eileen's time in America so she could report it to Maggie, who had recently begun her own plans for emigration.

Margaret was pleased that Julia was willing to take Jeremiah, especially at the beginning, for she knew Julia would chastise her father for any excessive exertions and refrain from granting any request he might make to go to the pub. She was also confident this first visit would tucker him out.

They struck out after mid-day and traveled through the green hills of summer, the trees full in their greenery and bird songs plentiful. Jeremiah, dressed in his work clothes, with a warm jacket against the coolness, reveled in the overcast day as he breathed in the scents of the season: the newly mown hay, the musky smell of tilled earth and the sweetness of the wild roses. He listened for his favorite mockingbird, glad for this time with Julia who had been a rock through his tumultuous illness.

He watched her as she drove them along, her posture straight as an arrow, her dark shawl pulled tightly around her shoulders. "I fancy yer glad to see the da back up and at 'em a bit, Jules, so ye can get on with planning yer own life, now. Would I have that right?"

Julia turned to Jeremiah, her dark eyes focused on him as if sizing up his ability to hear her.

"Da, it's glad I am yer gaining back yer strength, and as for planning my life, ye needn't worry for that." Julia gave a shake to the reins as she looked straight ahead, watching the little path ahead of her, the crows diving and the hares scurrying out of the way. "Father Pope has encouraged me in me calling. I'll be staying home with ye and Ma while Maggie goes off to seek her fortune in America." She paused, waiting for his reaction. She glanced at him out of the corner of her eye and blustered forward. "I imagine the twins will follow to America when they're old enough." With

a slight twist to keep the cart steady, she slowed the cart and turned
to the da. "Ye and I both know that Tims will be no good for ye if
there's ever a real crisis. And who knows what will become of
Michael." She didn't wait for a reply but turned her eyes again
ahead, the gray clouds pushing across the sky as if a storm were
passing through.

Jeremiah shuddered as he listened, the truth of it so raw. He
looked at the rapidly darkening sky, changing as fast as his world.
He took a minute before he responded.

"Then it's glad I'll be to have ye with us, Jules. Ye can sing to
me every night and dance those jigs I love to see ye do." He managed a smile as they turned up the laneway toward Murphys' cottage. "I imagine there'll be some lucky man who'll be asking for
yer hand, one fine day. The festival season has begun and there's
no telling what a young man's fancies will turn to."

Julia felt her cheeks flush, but made no response, They went
on in silence, droplets of rain now dampening the day. Jeremiah
wondered what would become of his children as their lives
unfolded. Would there be weddings and grandchildren? And
Maggie was off to seek her fortune, was she? This was the first he'd
heard of it, though he had suspected as much and hadn't wanted
to believe it. He pulled his jacket closer around him, fists tightened
as he thought of her with America in her sights. As ideas of how to
dissuade her came to him, he felt his breathing become shallow.
She'd been so taken with Mary's letters and he heard her chatter
constantly about Father John and what a fine priest he was, helping
the immigrant girls. At first he thought it was her religious fervor,
but that seemed to dissipate as she took to fancying the boys a bit.
Talk of her going into the convent diminished as well. He sighed
deeply and his thoughts turned to his two older sons. Both Tims
and Michael were good lads, young men actually. Maybe it was
time to have them take stronger hold of the reins than he'd
allowed. He'd have to see about that.

Julia pulled the pony up into the Murphys' yard, where the
garden abounded with clusters of orange and yellow chysanthe-

mums. She jumped down to come around and help Jeremiah, who didn't resist. Her vexation, he decided, would be worse than the humbling experience of her assistance.

Once inside, Paddy offered a welcome, studying Jeremiah's color and vitality. There'd been some weight loss but happily he determined that Jeremiah looked on the mend.

"To what do we owe this pleasure?" Paddy asked as he settled in a chair across from Jeremiah.

Julia stood nearby as Mary, Paddy's wife, cut the brown bread and arranged it on the serving plate.

Jeremiah beamed, his face expanding and the silver in his auburn hair shining. "Well, thanks to me Julia's fine assistance, I'm here to bring ye a letter I hope will be a pleasure," Jeremiah said as he placed the envelope on the table. "Mind ye, I haven't a notion of the specifics, but it's from yer man Mr. Bennett. Ye may have heard by now, he's selling Ballybawn."

"Aye," Paddy said. "There's been some talk at the pub, but mostly just rumor without much detail."

Julia placed a tray with brown bread and butter sandwiches, scones and jam, in the center of the table. Mary brought the teapot and mugs. Jeremiah watched as she poured him the first mug, the rich odor and dark color more pleasing to him than he'd expected. After she filled the other three mugs, she placed the teapot with its cozy on the tray. Jeremiah found himself with little appetite these days but as he sipped the strong black tea he reached for a scone, savoring the thought of it. The two women slipped into the two empty chairs on either side of the table, and Mary continued to serve the bread to the men. Julia took a piece for herself, delighting in the slathered butter on the savory bread.

"So 'tis official, is it?" Paddy asked, as he stroked his chin. "Ballybawn is to be sold? And these envelopes are the dispersal of the lands to the lot of us?" He shifted in his chair and asked, "Have ye yer own settlement papers as well?"

Jeremiah paused, eyes narrowed. Dennis Carroll had told him that there was talk afoot that he had received money from Mr.

Bennett for the help he'd given in keeping things peaceful over the years. While no actual money had exchanged hands, Mr. Bennett had treated him more than fairly and maybe more so than others.

During the recent Land War, when the landlords had been pressured to grant rent reductions and abatements, Mr. Bennett had refused to take Jeremiah's rent at all, saying it was "for the good of Ireland." Jeremiah suspected it was Mr. Bennett's way of thanking him for his work keeping the tenant farmers on good terms and timely in their payments. But his relationship with Mr. Bennett shouldn't be the concern of the others. He'd set them all straight on that account, starting with Paddy.

Mary interrupted the men to address Julia.

"Would ye like to see the quilt I'm working on?" Mary asked. "'Tis actually a pattern yer mother gave me. We can leave these men to their talk of the land."

Julia nodded to the men, picked up her mug and joined Mary. Jeremiah was just as glad to be able to talk openly with Paddy, away from Julia's monitoring ears and eyes. Now Jeremiah could be frank.

"Ye ask, Paddy, about my papers. And I can tell ye, all the envelopes have been sealed so I haven't any notion about the rest of ye," Jeremiah said as held his half-drunk mug of tea. "I can tell ye that I was more than satisfied with my offer, and I've accepted. I'll be taking my papers to the solicitor's office in Cork as soon as I've delivered all eight envelopes."

Paddy's eyes smiled as he sipped his tea; then he said, "Well, yer deserving of anything that comes yer way, Jer. Of that I'm certain." The two men sat silently for a long moment.

Their talk turned to the June 8th vote when only thirty votes took Home Rule down and Gladstone with it. The cry of "Home Rule equals Rome Rule" accompanied some of the worst fighting ever seen. Four hundred policemen at Victoria station could barely bring order.

Paddy looked squarely at Jeremiah and summarized, "A Parliament based in Dublin was too much for any of them to imagine or trust."

Their discussion excited Jeremiah. Margaret had kept him from so many of these details.

He was appalled as Paddy told of Catholics that had to be cautioned to stay inside, and innocent lives of both Protestants and Catholics already taken in what was to become the worst episode of violence in Ireland in the nineteenth century.

"But, Jer," Paddy said as he moved to the hearth and poked at the embers, "if ye think of it, there's still cause for hope."

Jeremiah turned to hear him. "We're witness to the first time in history that any British party has endorsed the principle of Irish nationalism. That's something to hang our hats on!"

Jeremiah smiled at the thought.

As they finished their tea, Jeremiah brought the conversation back around to the future.

"Paddy," he said, watching the embers turn a deeper red as Paddy sparked them with the bellows, "with the recent spate of poor harvests and falling prices there's talk of Dillon, O'Brien and other Irish Parliamentary Party leaders formulating a plan, a plan of campaign some have called it, by which farmers would refuse to pay rents and instead place the money in escrow to aid evicted tenants. Have ye heard about it?"

Paddy put the bellows down and picked up the tray from the sideboard. "Ye probably know more than I do, Jer. What I know is that the anti–Home Rule Conservatives in power now are talking of fairer laws for Ireland so they can show that Home Rule isn't necessary. 'Killing Home Rule with kindness,' is one slogan I've heard."

"Well, either way, kindness would be something to look forward to, wouldn't ye say?" Jeremiah said as he stood.

Paddy nodded as he put the tray on the table and reached for the envelope, his expression wary.

"That kindness might be contained in our very envelopes, Jer, by selling us the land at a fair price. I think I'll take a look now if ye don't mind."

Chapter Forty-One

Dynamite and More

Fall 1886

Michael smiled to himself as he gave communion to Mother Mary Xavier Mehegan, his new "boss," the foundress of the Sisters of Charity of St. Elizabeth. At age fifty-four, this new assignment suited him. The towering Motherhouse building on this two-hundred-acre property at Convent Station had been home to these Sisters for twenty-five years, with over seven hundred postulants admitted during that time. He learned that Mother Xavier was a no-nonsense woman, who had dismissed over one hundred seven postulants with documented reasons of "no spirit," "bad breath," "want of submission," "scrupulous" and "too worldly." With her obvious standards, Michael was curious how he had managed to pass muster and become their chaplain.

He strolled down the walkway toward the Academy of St. Elizabeth, founded at the same time as the Motherhouse was established, the first secondary school for girls ever established in New Jersey. Reverend Mother, he learned, had no ounce of arrogance about her, just a drive to serve. His first meeting with her had occurred in her well-appointed office on the first floor of the Motherhouse. It was a warm room, with lace curtains, a small framed painting of the Blessed Virgin, an impressive bronze crucifix, and Michael was surprised to see a portrait of Daniel O'Connell, a gift, he later learned, from a wealthy donor.

As they were served tea, in a style reminiscent of home for both of them, with the tea cozy wrapped about the pot and the plate of brown bread as well, the two found common ground quickly. They were both from County Cork. Her accent, as did his own, betrayed her county, Michael thought, and though there was little else of her person showing under all the black and white garb and regalia, he saw a lively set of blue eyes, a determined mouth and an austere gaze. She might be gray by now, Michael speculated, aware of the streaks in his own hair and noting a hint of white in her eyebrows.

After she thanked the Sister who had brought their tea, Mother Xavier had said, "So it's from County Cork ye hail, Father Riordan?" He sat in the chair opposite hers in front of the oak desk.

"'Tis indeed, Mother. And I understand it is yer home as well," Michael said, hopeful for a positive response.

"'Tis, Father,'tis," she offered with a grin. "I hail from Skibbereen, if ye know the place."

He had indeed. Some of the worst stories he'd heard regarding the hunger of '47 were from Skibbereen.

"I know the place a bit, though I've never traveled there," Michael confessed. "I meself am from Ahadallane in the parish of Donoughmore. Ye mayn't have heard of it for it's small and off in the hills, a sort of hidden treasure, if ye will. Have ye family left in Skibbereen, Mother?"

"Ah, that I do, Father," Mother Xavier replied, her face becoming more pensive. "Me father and mother, God rest them, are gone many years now."

She'd moved the plate of brown bread toward him as she continued.

"One of my sweetest memories was when me da lifted me, as just a wee child of maybe four or five, to see the great Daniel O'Connell," she said, glancing toward the portrait. "Ireland was blessed by O'Connell in many ways and I consider myself fortunate to have seen him."

Michael couldn't be more pleased to have a found such a soul mate.

She turned back to him as she spoke again, her face once again strong.

"My mother is recently died and of the ten of us, I have just two brothers remaining in Ireland. The rest are scattered around the globe, America, Australia and Canada. It's a burden, I'd say, to be separated from them. And ye?"

Michael sat forward, happy to tell of his relatives. "I've a sister still in Ahadallane who has seven wonderful children. One of them is here now in New York, the oldest daughter Mary," Michael said as he watched Mother Xavier stand. "I've also a cousin here ye may know of, Fr. John Joseph Riordan, recently named chaplain of the mission at Castle Garden."

Mother Xavier's eyes widened. He sensed she was not a woman easily impressed, but she seemed to be so now. "Indeed, I know of Father John Riordan," she said as she paused, turning toward Michael. "His work is becoming quite well known throughout this country and in Ireland." She put the cups on the tray, her eyes inquisitive. "He's your cousin, you say?"

Michael was pleased as he answered in the affirmative.
She smiled and said, "When ye see him next, extend my regards and tell him he's been in our intentions since we first learned of his work."

Michael sighed at the memory of those first encounters and picked up his pace as he came up the hill past the back side of the Academy amidst the golds and reds of autumn. He was pleased to have formed such a fine bond with Mother Xavier, helpful and even necessary to the task of seeing to the spiritual life of the young novices as well as the older professed Sisters as he said daily Mass, heard confessions and administered the sacrament of the sick, and held individual counseling sessions when requested.

As he returned to his quarters, a small house adjacent to the massive stone Motherhouse, Michael felt pleased. Here at Convent Station, he had time for reading and research, a lifelong love. His interest in the politics of the day, both here and in Ireland, provided adequate fodder for his free time. He paused at the little garden plot he'd inherited from his predecessor, not realizing until he dug his first spade full of dirt how much he had missed the land. There he found a sanctuary to which he often retreated.

His most current interest had been keeping up with the work of Clan na Gael without notice from the Sisters. The controversial group, founded by *New York Herald* scientific reporter Jerome Collins in June 1867, in response to the feuding within the Fenian Brotherhood, held Michael's attention, though his allegiance wavered.

As he fussed among the mums and dahlias, his mind wandered to the dynamite campaign being waged against England with explosives smuggled from America. Jeremiah O'Donovan Rossa, dubbed O'Dynamite, was using the newly discovered explosives as a way of getting British attention and promising retribution. The Queen was often mentioned as a target.

He knew that the Clan had a shortened romance with Parnell, who ostensibly supported a constitutional approach to liberty. Parnell's speech at Madison Square Garden, six years earlier, with a crowd of over five thousand, had been accompanied by much publicity. The *New York Herald* followed all of Parnell's sixty-two American speeches and so did Michael, especially when Parnell had addressed the House of Representatives.

As he read of the two approaches, Michael found himself beginning to believe that justice for Ireland could actually be achieved through constitutional means.

As he tugged on the spent blossoms of the mums, he remembered how much hope he'd put into John Devoy the day he'd met him at Sweeny's Hotel. Devoy's subsequent visit to him at his parish in Manhattan he'd not easily forget.

"I'm not a very religious man, Father," Devoy had said, his blue eyes drawing him in. "I'm in dangerous work, Father, but holy work, I believe, that I've been born to. I'm a baptized Catholic, Father, and I need to trust someone to listen and at times to give me guidance."

Michael had ultimately assented to becoming Devoy's confessor, warning that he would draw the line when he sensed the work was no longer holy.

After ten years, the departure from the holy occurred.

He still had the clipping from the *New York Herald* of an incident that had occurred in Salford, Manchester. Two men removed ventilating grids from an outer wall of the Infantry Barracks in Tatton Street and set up a crude bomb which exploded at 5:20 p.m., demolishing the garrison butcher's shed. Three were injured. The fourth, a workman's son, suffered for three days before he died.

His outrage led Michael to daily search the papers for Devoy's response, his disavowal of such violence. Instead he found Devoy's speech given in reaction to the newest Coercion Act. "For every Irishman murdered we will take in reprisal the life of a British minister. . . . For a wholesale massacre of the Irish people we will make England a smouldering ruin of ashes and blood." Not only did he find no remorse or apology to the child's family, but a vengeful promise to take more life.

His last meeting with Devoy, five years ago now, hadn't gone as he anticipated. He'd practiced what he would say when Devoy came to their regularly scheduled appointment. "I can't stand with ye if innocent children are to be a part of it." But when they actually met in Michael's Manhattan quarters, the small ante-room that was furnished with fresh flowers, two green brocade armchairs, a small matching couch and a table over which hung a hand-carved wooden crucifix, none of Michael's rehearsed words came forward. Instead he spoke breathlessly, trying to contain himself.

"There's nothing, nothing at all holy about a cause that kills children," Michael had said, his eyes burning into Devoy. "Ye can't think for a minute, John, that Our Lord would condone such activity." Michael saw Devoy's rounded shoulders, his hair speckled with gray. He seemed less elegant than when they had first met, his dark pants and coat worn and shiny.

When Devoy finally spoke, Michael listened in disbelief. "Father, ye've been a good friend and confidant for these ten years we've been meeting," Devoy said, his eyes fiery, emotion lacing his words. He took a deep breath as he continued. "And now I have to tell ye, Ireland's freedom won't be won without a fight. A fight that will take lives. As sure as I'm standing here, I can tell ye, the way to freedom won't be won without bloodshed." He stood silently, staring at Michael.

"And what of the child's death?" Michael growled. "Do you mean to tell me he's a hero for Ireland, an English child that never had a notion about the hatreds that have been going on for centuries? An English child who might one day grow up to be Prime Minister and settle this whole bloody mess? Ye can't tell me that the fight for freedom justifies that now, can ye?"

He turned from Devoy, his breathing shallow, his anger hard to contain. What other words could be said? When he turned back, he watched Devoy pick up his hat, nod and leave.

* * *

Michael stood and gathered up his spade and trowel, set them in the basket on the stoop and went into his rooms, tired now. As he made himself a pot of tea, sadness and tinges of old rage filled him. He spotted the afternoon mail and found a letter from Jeremiah which he tore open greedily, longing for the consolation of this long-time friend to soothe him.

It was as if Jeremiah had read his mind and knew just what to say.

"Mind ye, the poison of the anger will carry ye nowhere good. I hope ye've settled down on that score, Michael, and let the good sense of me da's words that have become me own, counsel ye. I'm seeing the end of me life and I know what I'm talking of. There's nothing good to come of the violence. As the da would say, mark me words."

Michael smiled and thought of his friend. In his response, which he began to pen immediately, he had been glad to assure Jeremiah that he indeed had "settled down on that score."

He was also glad to share the joy his garden plot was bringing him, reminding him of their early days, riding through the pastures of Ireland, tilling soil together and watching the earth swell with their labor as harvest season came. He glanced out the window at the rich autumn chrysanthemums, brilliant in the autumn sun.

More than ever, Michael found these things to be important. Beauty, and the time to enjoy it. He wished he could wrap the world up in his new understanding.

A knock on the door broke his reverie. He opened it to find Mother Xavier, looking quite fit, her stance solid and her gaze clear. She declined his invitation to come in. "I don't want to disturb you for long, Father, but I have here the July 24th issue of Ireland's *Freeman's Journal* that my brother sends on to me. Ye may have seen it yerself." As she handed Michael the paper, she continued. "This issue contains an article written by yer cousin, Father Riordan, during his recent trip to Ireland." Her round cheeks flushed with eagerness. "He tells the story of how the Mission of Our Lady of the Rosary began. It's a grand article in every way. I thought ye'd like to have it, if you don't already, Father."

Michael beamed. "I would, indeed, Mother. Thank ye," he said as he held the paper. "I've a brother-in-law who usually posts things of this nature to me but he's been under the weather these last months so I haven't heard of the article. Father John and I are expecting to have lunch soon so I can hear all about his trip. This will bring me a head start."

He turned and put the paper on the entryway table and turned back to this woman, who seemed to be aging as gracefully as he hoped he himself was. She seemed to be waiting for something more.

"Mother, when I visit next with Father Riordan, I'll see if I can't entice him to come of a Sunday and tell his story, if ye think it proper for the Sisters."

Mother Xavier smiled broadly. "Don't we all have relatives still coming to America with nothing but a dream and a notion of a promised land? It'd be grand indeed to have Father John visit with us. Grand indeed."

Chapter Forty-Two
Father Pope

August 1887

The spell of dry days worried them all. Donoughmore hadn't seen such a drought in more than a half a century. At least that's what the parishioners had told Father Pope.

If common sense defined a good pastor, then Father Patrick A. Pope had gained enough common sense in his forty years to become a fine one. His physical stature was average, so he didn't appear threatening in his height. His coal-black hair showed youth; his plain face was open and without guile. Initially, some considered him a bit young to have a parish of his own. The Bishop's assignment for him to be pastor was unexpected and was, so he was told, "a tribute to your administrative skills and ability with people." Father Lane had been well loved and respected. It would take a special man to follow him.

Patrick Pope learned quickly that the people of the parish had indeed loved Father Lane and would not forsake any of the rituals and practices he had established. When Father Pope suggested altering the starting time of the Sunday Benediction, there had been such an uproar he quickly acquiesced.

He had floated the idea after Mass one Sunday of moving Benediction from 5:00 p.m. to 4:00 p.m. to give more of an evening for families to be together. He first spoke to the Murphy sisters, two maiden women who lived down the hill from the church. They'd been faithful in their devotions and he was certain they'd have an opinion.

"Ye don't suppose we should change what's been working for us all these years, now do ye, Father?" said the elder sister, a robust women with gray eyebrows and a prominent mole on her lip. The younger sister quietly chimed in, her mousy brown hair matching her demeanor: "Father Lane set us up with just what we need and we're glad not to disrupt it. Don't ye agree, Father?"

Within the week, he'd received four more visits on the matter, word spreading that he was trying to disrupt things. Mrs. Healy was the last of them, her well-mended brown coat and matching hat firmly in place, her stance firm.

"There's word about the parish, Father, that you mean to change things. Might I warn you, Father, that's not a good idea. Too many of us count on our routines and have scheduled our days very carefully around our church times. I'm certain you don't want to disrupt that, now do you, Father?"

Mrs. Ryan had stayed on as housekeeper, her kindness and good will smoothing many a day. She remained steady in the aftermath of any turmoil he created, and helped sort it out.

"Mrs. Healy's coming to see ye, Father. She seemed a bit perturbed. Her family's been prominent in the parish for eons and she carries a sense of entitlement. Just being able to visit, and feel she's a part of the center of things, will quiet her."

Father Pope never did warm up to the Healys or their type. Mrs. Healy was an attractive woman but she had an air of superiority that annoyed him. Instead, he admired the success of the Healy sons who had become priests and were now in America: Reverend James Healy, Bishop of Portland, Maine; Reverend Patrick Healy, president of Georgetown University; and Reverend Alexander Sherwood Healy, professor at Troy Seminary who served as advisor at the 1870 Vatican Council and later became rector of the Cathedral in Boston.

While it was true that the Healys were important figures, he preferred the down-to-earth manner of other parishioners who boasted less of their family history and displayed some stamina and grace amidst adversity. He'd admired the hardscrabble small farmers and their heroic recovery from the effects of the great hunger.

Ahadallane had lost two hundred and thirty-two of its three hundred and eighty-one residents and thirty-two of its fifty-four houses had been vacated during those years. The neighboring townland of Pluckanes North was left with nine households from a former twenty-six and only seventy remained of the two hundred and three who had lived there. The people's resilience could only be admired.

Ironically, the Crimean War of 1853 fought by British troops occupying the Collins Barracks with seven hundred horses created a huge market for hay, oats and other agricultural products. Their presence dramatically increased the price of farm produce and helped the people come back unto their own. The local pubs and shops also benefited.

By the census of 1880 the village boasted two shoemakers, a blacksmith with a journeyman assistant, a gelder, three weavers, one buffer, three cattle dealers, and one nailer. Since his arrival thirteen years earlier, Father Pope had seen the people survive the bad weather, poor harvests and shocking prices for livestock that had marked the last three years.

But he'd seen nothing as bad as the current drought. The ground cracked beneath their feet, water levels of the Rivers Dripsey and Lee sank to scarcity levels, and the scorched fields withered in the harsh sun. The relentless rain that was so often cursed was now the object of prayer. At every Mass and devotion there was a special prayer asking for the heavens to open with God's blessing of sweet, life-giving rain. Faithful women came day after day to pray while men resorted to the safety of the pub, their own way of pleading with the forces of nature. Sunday Mass attendance declined. More than an economic depression had settled in. For the past five months, the spirit of the people grew as parched as the soil.

His role, Father Pope knew, was to support the faith that remained.

One of the faithful was Margaret Buckley, whose recent episodes with Jeremiah's health had added to her challenges. Her steadfastness to the sacraments, weekly devotions and the church upkeep appeared to be a comfort. Her attendance at the August 15th feast day of the Assumption did not surprise him. He was delighted to see that her two daughters, Julia and Maggie, had come along as well as the twins, Jeremiah and Elizabeth. He'd grown fond of these little ones, their handsome red hair and blue eyes shining with an innocence that was comforting to all who looked.

The Festival of Our Lady of the Harvest, traditionally a mid-summer Celtic celebration, eventually became a church holy day of obligation, the feast of the Assumption of the Blessed Virgin Mary and a welcome break in one of the year's busiest seasons. Pattern days, harmless local customs that were a carry-over from the old days of Patron Saint festivals, while sometimes more rowdy than the clergy supported, were often held at local shrines of the Virgin Mary and included prayers and rituals followed by dancing, song and storytelling.

After the Mass was over, Father Pope delighted in meeting with the parishioners. With the twins off in the church yard, Julia and Maggie greeted him warmly.

"Good day to ye, Father. A fine day for a feast of celebration indeed, isn't it?" Julia offered in her typically prim fashion, the blue of her skirt and blouse faded, her shoes worn but polished, her dark hair neatly pulled back with a matching blue ribbon. She and Maggie often dressed similarly. Today, Maggie wore a beige outfit, equally worn, her red hair piled high on her head, a few hairpins holding it in place.

"Ah, 'tis indeed there, Julia. It's grand to see ye two girls here with yer ma. I suppose yer keeping an eye on the twins for her, are ye? And the older boys are in the fields, are they, trying to scrape some life into the soil?'

Maggie and Julia exchanged glances. "No, Father," Maggie answered. "They're with the other lads at the pub. They take this as their own holy day of sorts. The da has told them of it from days gone by and they're certain to follow custom, as I am meself. Do ye know I've chosen this as my feast day, Father?" she asked, proud to be of age to follow the tradition of choosing a feast day for a birthday celebration. "I'll celebrate with a visit to Our Lady's shrine. Julia, Ma and the twins will accompany me for it looks to be me last time."

"Ye don't say, Maggie," Father Pope said with interest. He'd known of her plans for emigration and was keenly aware of the heartache that would accompany it. More and more the young ones were leaving and nothing could to be done to stop them. These last months had only exacerbated the problem. He watched as the two young women nodded to him and moved over to join another group of girls.

Margaret came toward him.

"I hope that Jeremiah is minding his recovery," Father Pope said as he extended a hand in welcome. She looked tired, her face drawn, her blue eyes watery. "It's a worry ye have keeping a man with such a robust spirit from not overdoing it."

"'Tis, Father," Margaret replied as she took his hand. "Me brother, Father Michael, could usually talk sense into him. I'm hoping for a letter from him soon to help calm him," she said. "He's counted on his letters for these twenty years since Michael's been in America. He pores over them as if they were the gospel, keeping up on all the American politics and happenings in these troubling times."

Troubling times they were indeed, Father Pope thought. Two harvest seasons ago, at the height of the land war, Mary Landry, a woman parishioner, had her clothes torn off by an enraged mob for living in the cottage of an evicted farmer. At his own Christmas Mass, he'd been astonished to witness another man boycotted for taking the farm of an evicted family. When he turned to face the congregation, he found all the parishioners had moved to the side opposite from where the fellow named Lynch was sitting, head bowed. When Father Pope bowed and turned back to the altar, the parishioners began to hoot and groan. He listened and hesitated but decided to go on with the words of the Mass. When a silence finally ensued, he turned again to find the man had left the church.

Father Pope struggled with such behavior and was ambivalent about speaking out. Like so many of his colleagues, he believed it his responsibility to stand for what was right. The people of Ireland deserved to own their own land. It was time for the Protestant Ascendancy to come to an end. If this shunning was the path to their goal, then so be it.

Patrick Pope had been ordained while Cardinal Cullen was still in power. He had watched with caution the political maneuvering that took place after Cullen's death almost ten years ago. The church had become increasingly political. County Tipperary was a center of Land League agitation and many priests were encouraged by Thomas Croke, Archbishop of Cashel, to be agitators. Croke was noted for delivering nationalist diatribes and handing out parliamentary seats as if they were parishes.

In addition to land agitation, the Irish bishops had expressed openly their disappointment at the defeat of Home Rule.

Father Pope had hoped to be given a parish in Cork City, just 25 kilometers east-southeast of this rural parish, where there would be more activity and more robust life. He feared being sent to the rural outreaches where there was little but farming to consume one's life. Yet in these dozen years at Donoughmore, he found that the true heart of Ireland was within the hillsides and among the small farmers who had so much at stake in their country.

He'd grown to appreciate the rich history of Donoughmore Parish which comprised thirty-two town lands. Remnants of ringed forts regarded as dwelling places for fairies and spirits had been preserved. The fact that the parish also included three monastic settlements and three saints—St. Lachteen, St. Trian and St. Finian—had intrigued him. The preservation in 622 A.D. of St. Lachteen's arm had given the parish a place on the map. The saint's hand had been credited with many cures. He hoped, on a future Dublin trip, to view it at the National Museum when time permitted.

"Might I have a word with ye, Father, in private?" Margaret said as she fidgeted with her pocketbook and twisted her handkerchief in her hands. "The girls will visit with the young folk and I have need of yer counsel if ye can spare a moment or two."

"Of course, Margaret, of course," Father Pope said with a warm smile. "I'll be but a minute."

He spoke briefly to two others waiting to see him, then turned to Margaret and gestured that she go with him. As they walked down the pathway to the rectory, he asked, "Has Jeremiah given any thought to this newest Plan of Campaign, do ye know, Margaret?"

Margaret wondered at the question. The Plan of Campaign that called on tenants to unilaterally demand lower rents or withhold payment altogether, though controversial, had received formal approval from Parnell. It was common knowledge that Archbishops Thomas Croke of Cashel and Archbishop William Walsh of Dublin supported the plan even though it was considered, by some, a direct assault on the principle of private property. Margaret had never underestimated the power of the church.

"Ah, Father, he's chomping at the bit to find out all the details he can. I've been keeping him from anything that would be agitating but he has a way of finding out things."

Margaret followed Father Pope into the same small parlor where, more than twenty-five years ago, Father Lane had given her relief from the banshee. She was comforted, as she often was, to note that the crucifix and the holy water font were in place.

As she settled herself in one of the two chairs at the table, she thought of that time after the loss of Baby Julia when she wondered if she would ever have children. Now she had seven more. With Mary in America and Maggie getting ready to go, she was determined to keep the rest healthy.

Father Pope said, "Margaret, I might suggest to ye, that keeping Jeremiah from this news will ultimately vex him worse than knowing about it. I'd say he's up to the news of the day now, and truthfully there's much he should know about."

He gestured to the teapot and Margaret declined with a shake of her head.

"Will ye be meeting with the Papal envoy, Father?" she asked, delaying her real purpose for asking to have a word with him. "I hear he's to be in Cork in November."

Father Pope was impressed with Margaret's knowledge of this upcoming visit.

"I will indeed, Margaret," he said. "And from what the other priests have told me, Father Ignatius Persico hopes to learn things first-hand. I'll tell ye, he's already learning first-hand that there's strong Catholic support for Parnell. And he's found out by now that getting land into the hands of peasant proprietors is a continuing aim that won't be side-tracked. Archbishops Croke and Walsh are seeing to that." He felt himself stirred as spoke.

"Do ye think Rome is in favor of it at all, Father?" Margaret said as she leaned toward him. "I mean the Irish becoming independent? And of the Plan of Campaign?"

She'd had enough discussion with Jeremiah to recognize the complexity of the issues, yet she wondered if men didn't make them more difficult than necessary. "The English surely have a different opinion for his Holiness to sort out. I know Jer's all for our freedom. He and me brother, Father Michael, have been for years."

Father Pope was surprised at the astuteness of the conversation. Many of the women of the parish were not literate nor did they follow the events of the day, but then if one were married to Jeremiah, he supposed that politics was as important as morning tea.

"There's much afoot these days, Margaret, and there's no telling where it will end. Whether yer for Parnell or against him, he's a force to be reckoned with. And the quest for Home Rule won't go away in our lifetimes, I'd say."

They both knew that the anti-Parnellites were impatient with the constitutional approach to reform and often sought more radical means to a solution, with violence often a trademark.

"Well now, Margaret," Father Pope said as he ran his hand through his dark hair and adjusted his eyeglasses, "I don't suppose 'tis politics ye came to talk with me about. What is it ye want to talk of this day?"

Margaret rested her pocketbook against the leg of the chair and held her handkerchief tight around her hand and began to twist it.

"Father, in a way, ye've answered me question. I'm after worrying about how much to burden Jer with these days." She paused and found herself choking up but went on. "I'm troubled beyond meself about our Tims. I hate to even say it out loud but I think he's in trouble with the drink. And I'm not sure Jer sees it. Or if he does, he looks past it. He hasn't said of word of it to me."

Margaret sighed and felt some comfort just to have the words out of her. She was grateful that she found it so easy to talk with Father Pope, who leaned forward as she spoke and carefully listened.

She told him of his blotchy skin, runny eyes and inability to get up some mornings. "And somehow, Father, I fear Jeremiah can't see it."

"Yer a wise woman, Margaret. Yer Jer is a strong man and I'd say he's up to hearing yer worries. He has a good sense of handling things. Too many young men like your Tims are struggling. We'll pray and act. I'll have a talk one day with him as well."

"I feel relieved already, Father," Margaret said, her face relaxed, the lines in her brow now dissolved.

"Sometimes we're too close to see things as they are. And if, as ye say, Jer is up to hearing of the troubles of Ireland, he's certainly up to hearing the troubles of his son."

Father Pope smiled at Margaret and stood. As she stood, she reached out for his hand and held it firmly in hers.

"Thanks be to God, for ye, Father Pope."

She dipped her hand in the holy water font, blessed herself and went off to find the children. Just as when she had left the same room so many years before with Father Lane, she felt relief. Today, she felt, would be a celebration day after all.

Chapter Forty-Three

The Letter from Michael

January 1888

Margaret pulled her hair back and stared out over the pasture. A light dusting of snow covered the hillside. She was glad the Christmas season was over. The preparations had seemed particularly overwhelming this year with Jeremiah unable to assist, and with little or no help from Tims. Julia and Maggie had been grand even though thoughts of America had distracted Maggie. Michael had continued his steady ways, but still there had been much to do.

They had skipped whitewashing inside the cabin, for Margaret thought it would disturb Jeremiah's rest. Just remembering how she had to cajole Tims to help Michael with whitewashing the outbuildings made her tired. She hoped that Michael wouldn't grow any more resentful than he already was at the inequity of labor. He had worked tirelessly, yet he managed to keep a pleasant attitude and actually brought a bit of levity to the table. His brilliant hazel eyes danced when he spoke and he had a charming manner of winking as he delivered a punch line.

She'd still not found the right time to talk with Jeremiah about Tims. She was held back when she thought of her own father and how she'd never once heard her mother mention the drink. She only witnessed the silent treatment that she gave him and later the forgiveness for his stumbling or belligerent behavior. She thought at times that she should adopt such an attitude but her seething anger kept her from it. Tims had heard her wrath more than once, and it was coming time for his da to take charge.

The state of affairs in the country didn't help any. Jeremiah read whatever newspapers Margaret provided him, and followed the speeches and political maneuverings of the day.

A great chasm between Rome and Ireland was growing.

While the Pope presented a copy of Raphael's representation of Poetry to Queen Victoria for her Golden Jubilee in June, the Irish bishops talked of holy war. The Plan of Campaign was gaining ground; the Irish clergy was solidly behind Parnell. Rome was not pleased. The Irish clergy followed the papal envoy's November visit with a mix of hope and apprehension, but ultimately the visit did little to quiet things.

Parnell's coolness made him a formidable force on the floor of the House. Michael Davitt, whose early liaison with Parnell helped bring about a successful conclusion of the Land War, worried about Parnell's total control of the party but found little support for his concern. The cult of "Parnellites" was firmly embedded in the Irish culture.

Margaret and Jeremiah had both followed the newspaper stories that were more frequently telling of attempts on Queen Victoria's life. The dynamitards, as those espousing dynamite as a way to independence were called, were in place and keeping the Queen in hers.

Jeremiah longed to know more and had finally received Margaret's blessing to meet up at the pub weekly with the band of men whose friendship he treasured. "Not a blackguard among them," he'd said of them.

The bitter wind of this January day didn't deter him from his regular visit and as entered the pub, smelled the turf fire and felt its warmth he was glad he'd persisted. Paddy Murphy, Dennis Carroll and Eugene Cronin were waiting for him when he arrived, with a pint in place for him at their table by the hearth.

After a few salutes from others around the room, the four men resumed where they'd left off, as if a day hadn't passed. They each looked a bit older, Jeremiah thought. Dennis was grayer now and appeared to have gained a few pounds. Paddy's dark hair had become a bit thinner and he detected a bit of gray, though his brown eyes were as bright as ever. Eugene was the worse for the wear of his difficult times; his once brown hair was now silver and had receded to the middle of his head. His gray eyes lacked the luster they once had, but he was here and that was all that mattered.

"A salute to ye, Jeremiah," Dennis proposed. The men joined together in drinking to Jeremiah's continued health. Paddy was the first to offer a nugget to digest.

"Well men, yer man Jenkinson has supposedly worked for the Home Office in Dublin with a network of his own agents. He's said to be an insider of sorts. He's working to sway Lord Salisbury toward Home Rule and is in close communication with Gladstone."

Paddy was always the one with connections and somehow knew the stories within the stories. They listened as he continued.

"Some say he has secret alliances within Parliament. Yer man James Munro, Inspector-General of Police, rightly accused him of extra-legal activity."

Jeremiah took a long drink and waited. This latest information was certain to be of interest. The American Clan na Gael, with its resources of both money and men, was seen as far more powerful than any other organization. If any ties were found to Parnell, it would discredit him and be the end of him.

"The Yanks might well support Parnell but there's a mighty cost," Eugene said.

Jeremiah worried for the integrity of Parnell.

"The dynamite campaign has been a continuing worry and threats on Queen Victoria's life are more than idle," Dennis continued. "Did ye see the letters they say Parnell wrote that were published this week in *The Times*? They've tried to tie him to the Phoenix Park Murders."

"They're a forgery, I'll guarantee," said Paddy. "The whole place is full of spies anyhow."

It was difficult to unearth the truth though they were each certain something was amok.

Paddy spoke again, sharing his insider information.

"There's a bit of a row with yer man John Devoy and Clan na Gael, as well. An in-house trial of their deposed leader Alexander

Sullivan has been started in Buffalo, New York. Devoy is asking them to address charges of illegal use of funds."

Jeremiah thought of his old friend and wondered what Michael knew of this inner division and what, if anything, of Devoy these days. He'd spoken highly of him over the years but recently had said little. Disheartening as all the news was, Jeremiah felt a new resilience just knowing what was happening. He also knew the land could soon be his. He looked forward to Michael's next letter.

***

Convent Station December 1887
    My dearest sister and brother-in-law,
     It is with a heavy heart I write to tell you of the death of our dearest cousin, Reverend John Joseph Riordan whom the Lord has called back for His own. His illness was the result of his service and devotion to the Mission of Our Lady of the Rosary. None can fault him for his self-lessness, for he was the epitome of such . . .

Margaret put down the letter and stared out at the fields, her eyes filled with tears. She took out the attached newspaper clipping, trying to make real this unbelievable news:

    In the prime of his manhood, but peacefully as a child going to sleep, The Rev. Father Riordan, for so long pastor of the mission at Castle Garden, passed away at St. Vincent's Hospital yesterday morning. He was conscious almost up to the moment of his death, which occurred at ten minutes past ten o'clock. By the side of the reclining invalid chair in which he died — for his asthma would not allow him to lie down — stood his aged mother, Mrs. Margaret Riordan of 301 West Forty-Second Street, early on Thursday morning. All through the morning hours she watched his face and noted his difficult breathing . . .

She turned again to Michael's letter, wishing he could be with them now.

I was called to Johnny Joe's bedside and arrived just after he breathed his last. I was invited to bless him, and did with these words: "May the angels and archangels, especially Archangel Michael, guide you to eternity. In the name of the Father and of the Son and of the Holy Ghost."

Margaret imagined the scene and the heartache that was Michael's as he blessed the man who was only thirty-six years old. She turned back to the obituary to find answers.

Father Riordan caught a severe cold on December 4th while coming home from Staten Island, where he had gone to attend the requiem mass in memory of Rev. Father Lewis, who before his death particularly requested that Father Riordan be present at this memorial. Dr. McNamera, Father Riordan's physician, then urged him to stay indoors and not expose himself, but the duties of the mission were so important that Father Riordan insisted on going to the Garden to attend to part of them. Bronchitis ensued and this was aggravated by asthma. He had also suffered from heart trouble.

The list of those in attendance at Father John's bedside was impressive: Rev. Father Hurley, a lifelong friend, and Dr. L.J. McNamera who attended him from the beginning of his illness. Dr. Moore, the house surgeon, came in just before the last. Drs. McCreery and O'Rourke had also been in constant attendance. Father O'Kelly, of Our Lady of Counsel on East Ninetieth Street, an old classmate, came in along with his cousin, Fr. Michael Riordan of Convent Station, New Jersey, just after his friend had died.

The funeral, Michael wrote, had been a grand send-off for a grand young man, one far too young to be called to his maker.

Archbishop Corrigan had presided, and the New York clergy were out in force. Nuns and priests clustered throughout the assembled. Michael told of the huge numbers in attendance, and of those he met afterwards who couldn't keep from giving testimony about the kindness of Father John.

"He gave me ten dollars and steered me clear from the charlatans waiting at the docks."

"He said the rosary with me for the safe passage of my children who were to follow me once I sent the passage money. They're all here now and safe, thanks be to God and to Father Riordan.'

"The good father found me work within a fortnight and I've been employed ever since. He wouldn't take any money from me but told me to pass on the favor to someone else."

Margaret smiled to think of Father John's kindness to the new immigrants, remembering how his enthusiasm was so evident to them on his visit.

Michael's letter finished with a special note to Maggie. While Margaret dreaded telling the others of Father John's death, most of all she worried about how to tell Maggie. She left the letter and its accompanying obituary on the table and went in to be with Jeremiah.

∗

Maggie saw the opened letter on the table when she came in from her chores. Recognizing Father Michael's handwriting she eagerly began to read. Within a few lines she began to shake. She bit her lip as it began to quiver. She fought back tears as she read.

In his eulogy, Archbishop Corrigan told of Father John's most recent trip to Ireland. He also mentioned the joy with which he spoke of his visit with cousins in County Cork. His love of Ireland made his work all the more meaningful.

The tears flowed as she continued:

Please assure your youngest daughter Maggie that one of the things Father John said to me in our last lunch together was how he looked forward to her arrival. Though the future of the Mission is as yet undetermined, it is my intention, God willing, to be on hand to see her to safety upon her arrival.

Maggie felt a gush of tears and a sob she could hold back no more. She ran from the cabin and went off beyond the pasture fence and up into the hills, blinded now by the flood of tears. She wept openly and loudly, not caring who could hear.

How could Father John be gone? He was to meet her at Castle Garden. He was to take her to his Mission and help her get settled. Mary had written to tell her about the plans that she and Father John had made for her May arrival. She had dreamt of the ship pulling into the harbor, just like the scenes described in the letters from Mary and Eileen Murphy. She had imagined seeing Father John's kind face as she finally walked down the gangway. She had just written to Father John at Christmastime, telling him of her hopes and dreams, and of her gratitude for his work. She even thanked him in advance for the help he would be in securing employment. He couldn't be gone. Father John was so young. Why couldn't Father Michael be taken? He was older and from the picture she'd seen, not nearly as handsome.

She sank into the hillside and threw herself across the heather.

Chapter Forty-Four

The Bloody Drink

February 1888

The time had finally arrived. Jeremiah had been patient and here at last was the Land Act of 1887, the extension of the Ashbourne Act that increased the opportunities for farmers to buy land. Money could be borrowed at reasonable rates and paid back in amounts that were less than the outrageous rents had been.

Jeremiah had watched many in his townland take advantage, and now he would. He went off on Tess to find Michael and Tims, who would be off in the upper fields by now, to share his intention. In the two years since he'd started with the dropsy, he'd learned to pace himself. He found a ride into the hills quite invigorating. He still didn't work a full day but when he was out and about feeding the chickens or helping to shear the lambs, he found a returning vigor that gave him some hope.

The day was overcast yet he treasured the sheen that covered the valley. He prized these hills, tucked in beneath the Boggeragh Mountains between the Blackwater and Lee valleys. He remembered the rides with Michael when they were young, their youth leading them hither and yon for the adventure of it. Over the years, they'd explored miles and miles of the townland and never tired of it. Whatever the weather, there was something new to see. He watched the circling hawks and listened to the calls of the majestic red-winged blackbirds as they screamed by. The fields of oats were just beginning to show their color and the neat rows of potato filled him with bittersweet recollections.

He'd had to reconcile so much in his life amidst the blessings that had been his. He never thought he'd recover from the losses that, in his early years, seemed constant. He still thought often of his mother, and sister, and Baby Julia, but no longer felt hopeless.

He didn't pray much in a formal way but he did have faith. He believed in something beyond himself and felt a reverence for it that went beyond words. Such magnificent order could not be explained.

The Church had been a part of his life since his boyhood. He remembered Father Lane and his kindness. Rome could learn much from such priests, he thought. Father Pope had agreed with him when he shared this latest insight at their last encounter.

"Yer right, Jer, as usual," Father Pope had said as they sat in the parlor. "All this fuss from Rome about the Plan of Campaign shouldn't be. Those men aren't here in our hillsides to see the struggles and witness the truths. They should trust the priests. We're here for the people; we're here with the people."

Father Pope had told Jeremiah of Archbishop Walsh's visit with Pope Leo XIII in February.

"The Pope grilled him again and again about our situation here. Father Walsh told him that Ireland only wanted the same kind of autonomy that the German kingdoms enjoyed in the German empire."

The Pope agreed with a Bavarian-style autonomy but didn't agree with what he heard about the war being waged against the landlords. Hope of support from Rome vanished within several months of Walsh's visit, when a papal rescript condemned the Plan of Campaign.

The uproar caused by the rescript was unprecedented. The bishops felt angry and miffed, while the politicians favoring Parnell were outraged. Archbishop Croke, disturbed as he was by the decree, knew it had to be promulgated. It was a moment of crisis for the Irish Church.

Jeremiah wondered what would happen. The Irish MPs weren't about to let Rome dictate to them, of that he was certain.

He rode closer to the back pasture where he thought Tims and Michael were. There was no trace of them. As he turned to go north, he spotted Michael above on the ridge. He saluted and rode toward him.

"Da, whatever are ye up to? Is everything all right with ye?"

"Ah, 'tis, me Michael, 'tis. I was after finding ye and yer brother for a bit of a talk. Is he about with ye?"

"Ah, Da, Tims wasn't feeling so well today. We're only after fence mending since the crops are in, so I told him he needn't come along. He's asleep in the barn, I think."

"The barn, is it now. I see. Is he all right? I mean, not really sick now, is he?"

"Da, it's a bit of the drink, I'd say. He'll be fine come tomorrow. But Da, look here, what I've found. Up here on the ridge."

Jeremiah rode next to Michael and looked at the irregular mound down in the bramble.

"I've just dug it up, Da. I've laid it alongside there. Can ye see it?"

Jeremiah rode closer.

Michael looked at his father. "It looks to be an ol' pike, like the ones they used in '67. It must have been left behind, do ye think?"

Jeremiah dismounted and knelt next to the pike, its blade dulled but its purpose clear. It was old and rusted, but it was a pike indeed. He looked up at his son Michael, whose thrill upon his discovery brought to mind another Michael.

"It must have been left behind, lad, it must have been."

The two parted ways as Michael went off to tend to more fencing. Jeremiah rode back slowly, remembering and wondering.

***

"What of the bloody drink?" Margaret said to Jeremiah as he fussed with the fire. "Is that what ye want for our son—our first baby boy who thrilled us beyond our imaginings? Is that what ye want? Ye can see for yerself—he's leaving us, his ambition gone, his eyes red and runny. To clap the climax, last night not even coming home, sleeping God knows where. Ye can close yer eyes if ye like but at some point ye need to admit it. We're losing him, Jer. We're losing him like we lost our Mary, but this time it's not to America, it's to the drink."

The children had all gone off for the evening, Maggie, Julia and the twins to visit with cousins, Tims and Michael to a *seisiún* at the pub. Jeremiah and Margaret were alone. He watched as Margaret wiped her hands on her worn apron, picked up the dishes from the table, and put them in the sideboard.

She was right. He had closed his eyes to it.

Tims was going down into the shadows. One day he seemed fine and the next he was gone, slacking off on his chores, giving excuses and mumbling incoherently when questioned. Jeremiah had made his own excuse for Tims' loss of weight, putting it off to extra work he was doing because Jeremiah could no longer do his own chores. Tims and Michael had filled in with the harvest and doubled up on the myriad of chores that needed daily attention.

When Jeremiah finally did allow himself to look, he saw his once handsome son's face had become sunken, cheekbones protruding, eyes ringed in red, fair skin blotchy with red patches. He was often late to breakfast, if he came at all.

Jeremiah tried to recall when it started. Initially, his work didn't seem to suffer. He excused the times Tims had taken a day off, or stayed in bed later in the morning. Michael had filled in cheerfully enough. He didn't notice the frequency for he was busy blaming himself for the hardship the boys were enduring at his expense. He'd been blinded to what was in front of him.

"*Thon Mon Adieul*," Margaret muttered in Irish, "your soul to the devil," a sure sign she was vexed beyond reason and then went out the door. He could say nothing. He couldn't imagine why his firstborn son, handsome and talented, gifted in his husbandry skills and, from what he had seen, even successful in his relationship skills, had begun to slip into the inky reaches of the drink. The damned drink that had claimed so many. The drink that had made Margaret's da less than the man he could have been.

At his birth, Tims had favored Margaret with his red hair and blue eyes. As he grew, they saw the resemblance to Margaret's father, Tims' sturdy frame several inches shorter than Jeremiah's six feet. Jeremiah feared the resemblance didn't end with physical stature.

In days past, he had watched Tims at the pub, his boisterous behavior less than becoming. He'll learn, he had thought. Nora had distanced herself from Tims during these episodes. Now he hoped she could influence him for the better.

He closed his eyes and, though not a praying man, offered up his own vulnerability to a creator he wasn't sure existed. After a time, a deep sigh caused his shoulders to shudder.

With a sudden resolve, he went out the door, whistled for Tess, mounted the gracious chestnut mare and rode with deliberateness, hoping he was not too late. Margaret and Doc Foley's warnings rang in his ears: "If you overdo it, ye can kill yerself." He had no intention of this being a death-defying act but rather a life-giving one.

Chapter Forty-Five

Tims

Late February 1888

Michael was the first to see the da as he entered the pub. He looked quickly toward Tims, who was slumped alone in the corner, his eyes closed. He watched as his da strode down alongside the length of the mahogany bar toward Tims, nodding to this one and that, pushing past young men who hadn't been shaving for more than a year. The da didn't see him or, if he had, he'd looked past his second son and pulled up a chair next to his first. He leaned in and talked low. Michael set his beer down and wished he could hear. He saw Tims rouse a bit and then lean back again. Then, with alarming alacrity, the da grabbed hold of Tims by the collar and stood him up. Men standing nearby moved back as Jeremiah dragged Tims down the length of the room, through the pub and toward the door. As he pulled open the door, his eyes met Michael's and he nodded. Michael watched as his father and brother went out the door into the black night. He silently followed, cloaked by darkness.

* * *

Margaret cringed as they came in, Jeremiah's face flush, his breathing heavy, Tims staggering, barely able to keep his balance.

"Here's our baby boy, Margaret. Our firstborn son," he said breathlessly. "Would ye have a cup of tea for him or shall I put him off to his bed? He mightn't be very good company for us tonight, now would ye, Tims? But all that will change, lad, all that will change."

Tims, his brown work clothes hanging off of him, his red hair disheveled, swayed and almost fell, but Jeremiah grabbed hold and led him to his bed.

When he returned, Jeremiah pulled his jacket off and slumped in a chair. His breathing was shallow, his cheeks still flushed. He looked up at Margaret, standing by the sideboard.

"Ye've been right before and yer right again," Jeremiah admitted. "I'll not let this lad slip from us. If it's the last thing I do, I'll see to Tims."

Margaret put the kettle over the flame and readied a pot of tea. The girls and the twins would be back soon and Michael should be coming along from the pub. She wondered what Michael had seen at the pub, and if there'd been a ruckus; Jeremiah was stirred up enough without reliving whatever happened. She would wait to find out.

A knock at the door startled them both. Jeremiah rose to answer it.

"Why, Nora, 'tis good ye could come after all. Come in, come in. Warm yerself by the turf fire and share a bit of tea with us, won't ye?"

Nora moved in, her dark eyes soft and curious. Jeremiah took her green shawl and placed it on the peg next to the other coats. Nora found a place at the table and slid gracefully onto the chair.

"We're glad indeed to see the likes of ye, Nora," Jeremiah said openly. "It's been a long while. Margaret and I have just put our Tims to rest for a bit. While he sleeps, perhaps we can talk of what we might do for him, if ye get my meaning." He brought the teapot to the table and continued. "Michael and the others may be along shortly as well. We'll make a fine evening of it, for there's much to discuss." Jeremiah was pleased that Tims and Nora were still seeing each other though he knew how easily a relationship could be ruined by the drink.

Margaret brought a plate of sandwiches and scones to the table. Nora stood to help with the dishes and Jeremiah sat back, a look of contentment spreading across his face.

* * *

Tims woke late the next morning and found his way to the table. The cabin appeared to be empty. The teapot was cold. He found a bit of bread under a cloth napkin, took the warm kettle from the hearth, added a bit of its hot water to the teapot, then slathered the last piece of the brown bread with gooseberry jam and ate hungrily. He remembered the da bringing him home last night as if in a dream. He didn't recall much more except his da's heavy breathing as he tugged and pulled him off the horse when they arrived. He couldn't for the life of him imagine what led the da to come after him. Why now, after all these months? Didn't he know that he was a grown man of twenty-four years? Didn't the da know that he would be off on his own but for fear of the da's health? He felt trapped. He was the oldest and that was what he was to do. Carry on the farm. The da would expect it.

Jeremiah came in a few minutes later, his color better than Tims had seen it in months, his eyes lively.

"Ah, Tims, ye've chosen to join us for another day of living, have ye? It's glad I am to see ye," Jeremiah said as he pulled up a chair. "We've much to discuss this day, much indeed. I see ye've had yer tea and bread that yer mother left for ye. She's gone off to Cork City for the day with Maggie, Julia, Lizzie and Jer. They've big plans, today, getting Maggie ready. Michael's off doing the work of three men. So it's jest ye and me that are home for a spell."

He stood, put the kettle back on the fire, and went to the sideboard to get his tea mug.

"Michael will be back from the fields by noontime," Jeremiah said, his back to Tims. "He's tending to the fences on the back forty acres. The mending didn't hold like we'd hoped."

Tims shifted in his chair. The da was more talkative than he'd ever remembered. Usually he grunted a greeting and went about his business. Now, all of a sudden, he was jabbering like a magpie.

Jeremiah moved to the hearth and stoked the peat, white ashes leaping as the flames rekindled. With his back still to Tims, he asked, "Do ye remember anything at all from last night, Tims?"

The crackling of the peat filled the silence. Jeremiah waited.

Then he spoke again.

"I wouldn't think ye would remember. Ye were pretty far gone when I came upon ye. It was a wonder ye were able to walk at all once we got home. We can thank yer brother for getting ye up on Tess. Yer too big fer me to lift anymore."

The da took the iron kettle from the fire, and poured the hot water into the teapot on the sideboard, careful not to spill any. After returning the kettle to the hook on the hearth, he brought the porcelain teapot to the table and slowly poured the tea into his mug. Tims sat back in his chair cautiously.

"Yer smart to move back from me, boy-o," Jeremiah said, "for had I the strength, I might try to beat some sense into ye. I've clenched me fist more than once when I think of what yer doing to yerself and to this family."

He put the teapot down on the table and took a seat.

Jeremiah continued in a more even tone, a softness coming through. "I'll be straight with ye, Tims. In many ways, ye're a talented lad, but ye've no skill with the drink. It's not for ye. Some men can handle it, but I can tell ye, the drink is handling ye. And that can't go on. I won't allow it."

Jeremiah pushed the teapot toward Tims. "It's not very strong, but it's hot now."

Tims shook his head, his matted red hair falling over his forehead, his blue eyes ringed with red, his handsome face drawn. It was the first response of any kind he'd given since his da came into the room.

"Tims, we met last night, all of us. Yer mother, Michael, Julia, Maggie, Lizzie, Jer and Nora to discuss yer future."

Tims sat forward when Nora's name was mentioned.

"That's right, boy-o, Nora was with us. I invited her to come before I collected ye from the pub. She told us everything. I might say yer a bit of an eejit but I imagine ye can say that for yerself."

The sound of circling crows filled the silence as Jeremiah paused to let the words sink in. Tims, his plaid shirt drooping on his shoulders, stared straight ahead.

"The thirst is a shameless disease, Tims. Ye best face it now. It'll bring ye to no good and that wouldn't be fair to any of us now, would it?" Jeremiah sipped his tea, watching Tims' eyes before he spoke again.

"Nora told us of yer proposal and her response. She sees it too, Tims. She's a good woman and yer a lucky man for she'll still have ye, if ye swear off the drink."

Tims squirmed in his chair. Jeremiah continued. "I can't think of a finer woman than that, save yer mother who's put up with the likes of me these almost thirty years."

Tims looked away from his father and slumped back, his head hung down. He felt his face flush, his throat tighten. Tears burned at the back of his eyes. He thought of them all sitting around talking of him. He thought of Nora, her porcelain skin and dark hair. He felt embarrassed to think of her but grateful at the same time. Did she care that much? Was the da right?

"Tims, I've given ye much to think about. And there's one more thing to add," Jeremiah said as he stood by his chair. "Mind ye, I've given this much thought. Yer me oldest son and I'd like nothing better than to have ye carry on the land. Nothing better at all."

He turned away from Tims, feeling his eyes moisten, surprised at the emotion pushing up within him. He was about to tell his eldest son that he'd have to choose between the drink and the land. He couldn't have both.

Tims sat up straight in his chair and turned to face his father. "Da, ye needn't say it. I'm not fit for the land and I know it. I've known it for longer than I've said it. That's what Nora knows, too, but she wouldn't tell ye. I begged her not to. The land is everything to ye, Da. Everything that has any meaning. It's not to me, Da," he said, shifting his weight in the chair, his eyes focused and gleaming. Jeremiah turned from him, looking out the window. Tims continued, "I can do it, but it's not what I want. It's never been what I wanted. Ask Michael. He might be good for it. It's not for me, Da. That's all I can tell ye and I'm sorry for saying it, sorry indeed."

With that, Tims stood up, put his half-drunk mug of tea on the sideboard and walked out of the cabin.

Chapter Forty-Six

The Holy Well

March 1888

"Come with me, Jules. There's something I want to show ye."

Maggie was several yards away, calling to her older sister, who was in the brambles, her bucket of berries overflowing. Both girls wore their long dark skirts with white blouses and scarves tied around their long tresses of hair. Julia's skirt was a conservative dark plaid pattern, and Maggie's as lively as she was, with swirling flowers abounding.

"Is it far now, Maggie? I'm dog-tired and not up to any of yer shenanigans."

Maggie and Julia had been berry-picking since early afternoon. The hazy sun brought with it a surprising heat and an accompanying fatigue.

"I think it's just over the ridge. Ma first showed it to me when I was just little. I've come back whenever we're out this way. It's getting overgrown but I'm sure I can find it. Come on with me. It may do ye some good."

Julia trudged up to join Maggie, both of them finding a safe tree limb onto which they nestled their buckets of blackberries. The plump and firm little round fruits were at their peak, the red giving way to the shiny black color that signaled rich flavor. It was the anticipated prize of the blackberry-filled scones and cakes that kept them from eating more of them now.

"I want to show ye this, Jules, so ye can have yer own place to come after I'm gone to America," Maggie said as she skipped over clumps of grasses and rocks. "It might not be easy for ye with the da and who knows what's to become of Tims. Ye can come to this special place to remember our good times. Ye can forget the bad times, if ye would, please."

The three years that separated Maggie from her older sister sometimes felt like thirty. Julia kept a demeanor and distance that didn't invite intimacy. Maggie's school chums had nicknamed her Julia Rulia, for she was forever making sure each rule was followed. "That's not the way it's to be done," she said whenever the occasion allowed for it. Maggie transgressed on more than one occasion, inviting Julia's acerbic tongue.

"Little Miss Mix Up, would ye mind taking yer things off the bed now? It's time to make it up, not that it ever crosses yer mind to do it. I thank ye kindly to keep yer mess to yerself."

For the most part, Maggie hadn't minded. Julia reminded her of Gran before the stroke had softened her. Maggie had always been closer to Mary, who was the oldest and had good sense without being bossy. The twins had been the recipient of more of Julia's rigor but hadn't been too harmed by it, Maggie thought. They had each other.

"Ye can count on Julia to get things done," the da had said more than once when Maggie was late to supper, bringing in bunches of wild roses rather than finishing butter churning or collecting eggs.

Mary had continued to send money from America to the da every month, with often an enclosure for Maggie and Julia, sometimes a holy card, other times a coin. Maggie kept everything Mary had sent in a special box tied with twine. Between the money that Mary had sent and the money that Maggie had made with her needlepoint work, she had finally saved her passage fare. She hoped for a position like Mary's, close to a safe boarding house.

The conversation with the da about leaving had yet to occur. He knew she was going and Mary had said as much in her most recent letter:

Tell Maggie that Father Michael said he'd come with me when the ship arrives. He knows the new priest who's to be assigned to the Mission and he's making plans now for her.

Maggie and Julia crested a modest hill and as they looked down the lush green valley, Maggie stood still and said, "Jules, I'll miss ye, ye know. I'll have Mary in America but I won't have ye to remind me how to act and what I should do to be polite. Ye've been a good big sister to me."

"Ah go on with ye. Ye never minded me anyhow."

"Just the same, I wish ye were the one going. Ye deserve some adventure."

Maggie was ready to hear the same refrain Julia gave each time Mary offered passage money.

"Just who do you think will look after the da and the Ma?" Julia said righteously. "Ye know we can't count on our Tims, and Michael has his hands full just keeping the fields producing. The twins are fourteen all right but they may as well be four; they don't seem to have a lick of sense between them yet."

She moved down the knoll ahead of Maggie, who was nibbling from a cluster of gooseberry bushes she had discovered.

Jules pulled her skirt up as she stepped over a rock pile. She turned back and called, "Besides, I'm not sure America is all it's cracked up to be. Even Mary's letters are less enthusiastic than they used to be. I'll wait for ye to send me some of the fancy stockings they have over there. That's enough of America for me, thank ye."

Mary's letters had changed. She spoke more often of her work as if it was drudgery and stories about her days off were less exciting. She mentioned Mr. Browne, her employer, less often, but she did speak regularly of Father Michael.

Father Michael and I met again at the park by the swans where he and Father John and I used to meet. It's a comfort to be by water. The beauty of the place thrills me each time I go there. We walk and talk of this and that and always of Father John.

There's not much to say about my work. It's become routine, fetching this or that for the missus and serving the tea every afternoon at four o'clock on the dot. They're nice enough people, but I feel a bit like a Dresden doll. Especially when they say how quaint my brogue is. Ye'd think I wasn't one of the thousand Irish in New York the way they carry on.

Speaking of carrying on, Uncle Michael speaks highly of Parnell. He's become quite silent about the Fenians but he's quite taken with what he thinks is a great push for freedom that Parnell can gain for Ireland. He quoted him to me just this past Sunday. "No man has a right to fix the boundary of the march of a nation." I suppose he's right. Though in America, I don't worry much for Ireland. It seems so many Irish are in America now. I've met several from County Cork and one man even knows where Ahadallane is. Fancy that. I don't feel like such a greenhorn after all.

They crossed over a cow path and climbed a low stone wall and then crossed into a newly plowed field.

Julia took giant steps to catch up with Maggie, who had practically skipped ahead. She called after Maggie, her tone scolding, "Margaret Agnes Buckley, this little adventure better be worth it. I've no mind to be traipsing all over kingdom come to see some magical, mystical place of yers. Mind ye, the only reason I came is because ye said Ma showed it to ye first."

Maggie reached up and pulled her head scarf tighter as Julia caught up. She grimaced at her older sister. "Don't I know, Miss Julia, that it's Ma ye'd listen to before any of us." She paused and watched Julia come across the field toward her. "Well, Ma did show me this place and it's something ye'll be glad for knowing about. It's from ancient times. It's to a place like this ye can come and renew your spirit. And ye can believe it or not, but this place can heal ye."

The two continued across the field and entered into a copse of woods to the north. They passed some bramble and lichen-encrusted stones, relics of an old structure now gone. Then Maggie took Julia's hand and climbed up a low circular mound where there were tall grasses and low tree branches of a hawthorne covering it. She pulled Julia's hand and they both crouched down to see the sky reflected in a round pool of water bounded by fieldstone, no more than two feet in diameter, with a smaller one formed just below.

"Is it these puddles in a rock ye've brought me to, Maggie? Is that what yer about?" Julia's eyes were wide, her tone filled more with surprise than disgust.

Maggie sighed and looked at Julia intently. "My dear sister, this is no puddle yer kneeling by. This is St. Lachteen's Holy Well. It's from prehistoric times. There's lots of holy wells all about Ireland and this is ours."

"Maggie, do ye mean St. Lachteen, the saint with the preserved hand? This is his well?" Julia's facial expression was curious.

"I do mean that, Jules. In ancient times, Ma says, the people used to walk about in a pattern, around the holy well and the sacred tree."

Maggie turned about her and exclaimed, "Look, Jules, it's the hawthorne. Ma says they're a special tree in Ireland. She says they'd say a prayer after they walked and then drink the water for wisdom and luck."

"Well, ye won't find me walking around like a dolt and kneeling to drink from a puddle. I've more sense than that now and besides, I don't believe in luck. Ye get what ye work for and trust the good Lord will see to ye. I don't believe yer holy well can bring wisdom or luck."

Julia pulled up her skirt and stepped up onto the other side of the water.

Maggie sighed audibly. "It's certain I am, dear Jules, that ye can only be helped by these waters. I'll say a prayer that ye find happiness here in Ireland. For me, I'll pray that I find me way in America and meet a great strong Irishman and that we'll have a great large brood of children all who will call ye Auntie Julia."

Julia laughed, as she heard her younger sister talk of a family, the notion of her being a nun having diminished when talk of

America began. "Be gone with ye, Maggie Buckley. Auntie Julia, indeed."

Maggie walked purposefully around the small stone basin that formed the fresh-water well and then circled the hawthorne tree before kneeling reverently next to the pools. The light blue of the sky and wispy gray clouds moved about as she looked down at the two pools of water, each reflecting different colors of the sky. She silently blessed herself as Julia looked on.

"May the healing power and wisdom of St. Lachteen go with me to America and may I always remember this place and my big sister Julia. Amen." She cupped both hands, dipped them into the water, raised them to her lips, smiled and drank, savoring the sweet water. After a few minutes she scampered to her feet. As she turned to leave, she was surprised to see Julia bending silently over the well, scooping water and drinking it. Maggie watched as Julia blessed herself. The scowl she ordinarily wore was gone and was replaced by a beautiful countenance—one Maggie had never seen. Julia's eyes had a light in them that sparkled as if she saw something. Maggie wasn't certain, but she thought Julia was talking to someone. . .

Chapter Forty-Seven

Mary's Visit

April 1888

So Maggie would be coming along to America next month, Michael thought as he waved his farewell to Mary, whose visit to Convent Station had been like a tonic to his spirit. She had looked so grown-up in her azure blue dress, her shiny black shoes laced up like a true Victorian lady and her chestnut brown hair piled high and joined with fancy combs. The matching bonnet so prim and tidy, with her beige shawl draped loosely over her shoulders, certainly added an air of elegance. Her coloring favored the Buckleys. He smiled. Such captivating green eyes; they gave one little room to wander. So winsome and bright she was; it had been a delightful visit.

Her letter announcing the visit was most welcome. Michael hadn't been to the city since Johnny Joe's funeral over three months ago. He had written Mary hoping to arrange a meeting for the spring, glad she took the initiative to venture out to Convent Station, New Jersey, where he'd lived almost four years already. How the time had flown. He'd remembered his ma warning him, "When yer young, time seems to linger like a soaring eagle, but when ye get to be my age, time is more like a raptor. It dives onward, looking neither forward or behind."

She was right, he thought.

Young Mary, since their meeting at Central Park with Johnny Joe over a year ago, was now quite a young woman. As she sat with him after the tea and brown bread had been served, she chatted about Maggie's arrival and what she'd heard from home. She was confident that Jeremiah was recovering satisfactorily. Michael was delighted with the talk and delighted when she finally told her own good news. She was to be married to a young man named

Patrick Healy. She beamed, looking so like a woman in love, as she told of her future plans.

He felt a tug in his chest, the familiar pain that he knew would abate in time. He sat back. She could do worse, he thought. The Healys from Donoughmore had been prominent enough. They were a good clan, though there could be a slacker in the best of clans. Well, he needn't worry for that. Soon enough, she'd have her little sister to add her opinion.

Michael had never met Maggie. Tims and Mary were just babies when he'd left in '67; Maggie had been born in '71. "She's sixteen," Mary had told him, "and she'll be with us in America for her seventeenth birthday in June. We'll be able to celebrate it with her." From what Jeremiah had written, Maggie wasn't a bit like Mary or Julia. "She's quite the good listener with a serious heart and ever a light manner. She's a lover of nature and all things living. It just feels good to be around her," Jeremiah had written.

Michael had heard that Maggie might have had aspirations to become a nun, but little had been said of it since talk of her emigration started. He wondered if that had ended and why.

He would plan, along with Mary, on meeting the ship. There should be no trouble arranging the time. She was to arrive on the Inman line's *City of Chester* on the fourteenth of May. She would probably be leaving Ireland just after the first of May, and if the ship stopped in Liverpool first, as so many of them did, the passage to America would take ten days.

Michael recalled that it had been almost a year earlier on the 11th of June that the *City of Chester* carried three men from New York to Liverpool with a different mission: a deadly dynamite agenda, set to arrive in time for the Queen's Jubilee on the 21st of June. The appearance of General F.F. Millen on his doorstop the last February had drawn him into something he dreaded to think of to this day.

General F.F. Millen, a well-known Fenian that Michael had learned about through John Devoy, apologized for not contacting him before arriving. Michael was intrigued. Surely Devoy hadn't sent him. Michael sized the man up as he led him to the parlor. Millen's stature was not what Michael had expected. He'd imagined a larger man. The dark bearded face fit him, Michael thought, holding the view that men with facial hair were hiding something. He knew F.F. Millen had secrets, but he was not prepared for the depth of them nor the agitated state of the man, whose twitching face and anxious breathing troubled Michael.

Millen revealed his hope that Michael would hear his confession. He pleaded his case by telling Michael that John Devoy had at one time told him of Michael's sympathy for the cause. Michael drew a deep breath. It was evident the man was disturbed by something. His name had been associated with the Jubilee Plot and reported widely. While the plot had been successfully squelched, the three bombers identified, Millen had been named as the instigator of the plot along with Jeremiah O'Donovan Rossa, though no formal charges ever substantiated the link. Why now would he seek out Michael? Anxiety? Remorse?

Only after Michael gave the proviso that he might not be able to grant him absolution, did he agree to hear his confession.

It was then Michael learned why the man was so greatly distraught. His revelation caused Michael to think long and hard about whether or not to bring the Church's power of absolution to this curious man.

Michael had read in *The New York Herald*, a paper that employed Millen, that he was the head of the "Jubilee dynamite gang," which Millen had denied at every opportunity. As Michael listened carefully to Millen's words, noting the man's breathing which became more and more shallow, he felt twinges of anger building up in his own belly. Millen sobbed as he confessed his sin. He was, he said between sobs, and had been for a number of years, a British spy.

Michael was horrified. A British spy, sobbing in his parlor? Asking for absolution? Michael was aware of the presence of such men, despicable in their lack of integrity, but he'd never been face to face with one. Millen sputtered that he'd done it for the money, paid by Lord Salisbury himself to make up the Jubilee Plot as a means of discrediting Parnell, hoping to link him to a group that espoused terrorism.

The sobbing Millen told of his dismissal by the Crown, and his final payment accompanied by a threat that he keep silent about all that he knew or he could fear now for his own life, his service to the Crown putting him in jeopardy.

Michael remembered sitting in silence for a time with the sniveling Millen, before speaking.

"General," Michael began, "your deeds and your reasons for them are your own affair. Your lack of remorse and attempts to justify your actions lead me to tell you, I cannot on behalf of Holy Mother Church absolve your sins." Michael saw a frightened Millen looking up at him. He felt a brief flicker of compassion and added,

"It's evident, sir, that you are in great distress. Could I arrange for some tea for you before you leave?"

Millen staggered to his feet, his eyes red, his cheeks damp. The twitching persisted as he stammered, "No thank you, Father. I only thought that maybe you could help." He moved to the door which Michael opened for him. No more words were spoken between them. As Michael watched him walk down the pathway, he realized that the seal of confession prevented him from sharing this damning information with anyone. It was a day he wished he'd never answered the door.

* * *

He watched now as Mary readied herself to leave. Their visit had been a tonic to him. As she pulled on her shawl and fixed her bonnet, she promised to send along a note with the details of Maggie's ship's arrival. He hoped it would be mid-morning. By then he'd have said his Mass and still have a bit of time to rest before the journey to the city. He hadn't let on about his health concerns to anyone in Ireland. In fact, Reverend Mother was the only one who knew of his condition and only because of the doctor visits that started when he'd fainted after Mass on the feast of St. Brigid. Ironic, he thought. His mother had had her stroke on that very feast day.

Mother Xavier was willing to keep his confidence. She even told the Sisters that their prayers for his complete recovery had been successful. He wasn't certain how long he had. The doctor had been direct. "This kind of lung disease can take a long time before it knocks you out entirely. If you take the medicine, follow my orders and keep those nuns praying for you, another Christmas could be yours. Don't overdo it. Listen to yer body, Father. It'll tell ye what's right."

He hadn't told such detail to Mother Xavier. Not yet. He was glad Mary had no hint of his weakened state and that she didn't notice his woefully neglected garden.

He stood gazing out the door, seeing Mary wave as she left for the train. Just then, Mother Xavier came in view. He waved her in to tell her of his visit and the news of Maggie's coming.

"She'll be here in less than a month, now," Michael had told her excitedly. "Can ye imagine having two nieces, me own blood, in America. 'Tis more than I ever dreamt of."

Mother Xavier smiled at his radiance, glad to see him looking more lively, her concerns growing daily.

"They're lucky young ones to have such an uncle, if I might be so forward. It's a good Cork man ye are, Father Michael Riordan."

He'd noted that since he'd taken Mother into his confidence, she'd been more complimentary and even shared some of her own heartaches, her task as Superior being a burdensome one.

As Michael led Mother Xavier into the parlor and indicated a chair for her, he asked, "How's the newest crop of postulants shaping up, Mother? Will they be ready to take their vows in June?"

Mother Xavier answered with her characteristic optimism, the strong reality that tempered all her work and was perhaps the reason for her successes. "Ah, most of them will, Father. Sister Margaret Michael, our Novice Mistress, assures me they've come a long way from the giddy high school girls who arrived last September. But when I watch them fidget about as they walk, whether on the grounds, in the refectory or, God forbid, in chapel, I have to close me eyes. Maybe I'm too old for this generation, Father. They've gone beyond my comprehension in many of their ways, what with their interest in the latest fashion in hemlines. They even wanted to modify the length of the veil. I put my foot down, you can be sure."

Michael *was* sure. There was no equivocating with Mother Mary Xavier. The Mehegan clan must have been a mighty one for they spawned a true warrior in this fine woman. She stood her ground for justice, he'd learned over the years.

"Father Michael, I've been meaning to ask you about John Devoy. Ye say ye knew him in person, didn't ye?" She accepted the cookie from the plate he offered, her discerning gray eyes searching Michael's face. "Have ye seen his writings and his book? He hasn't let up for a minute for the cause, would ye say?"

Michael took a cookie himself and tiptoed into the discussion, careful not to slip into any little rabbit holes waiting for him. He would guard John Devoy's confessional secrets, as he would honor any who sought asylum in the confessional, even General Millen. Though he couldn't always give absolution, he was bound always to keep the confidence.

"Ah, now Mother, I'd have seen the Devoy book. Indeed I have a copy and I'd say it's a grand history of the land leagues in both Ireland and America. It's still a struggle we're in, I'd say."

Michael didn't say that he had followed Devoy as closely as Devoy was now following Alexander Sullivan, the head of Clan na Gael and a man with whom Devoy was on a collision course, as another chapter of history was about to be written. Since Michael had parted ways with Devoy over seven years ago, the only word he'd received was a signed copy of his book, *The Land of Eire*, with the inscription: "For Father Michael Riordan, in gratitude for all ye've given me. John Devoy." He'd read it from cover to cover and had been pleased with the tone of reason and the hope that it held for a constitutional means to freedom. He wasn't so naïve as to think that their talk had changed the course of John's path but he hoped he had at least given him pause.

He knew that since the publication of his book, Devoy had gone on to start a Manhattan-based newspaper, *The Irish Nation*, in 1881 after he stepped down from Clan leadership. M i c h a e l was pleased that Devoy kept from supporting Rossa's Skirmishing Fund, which was used for dynamite activity. He wondered if it was true that Parnell had taken the Fenian oath as some had claimed? Was there a direct link between the Land League and the Clan na Gael? Michael remained curious.

Reverend Mother reached for a napkin, wiped her lips and stood. "Father, at some point, will ye tell me what ye know of the Jubilee Plot? When that gentleman, General Millen I believe, was here to see ye a few months ago, I wondered about it."

Michael felt a pain stab his chest. She couldn't possibly know anything, could she? She moved toward the door and then turned. "I'm brought to mind the phrase 'Speak truth to power,' the Quaker charge. Ye know, Father, it's the only way, now isn't it?" She turned the handle and looked back at Michael. "Truth is ancient . . . love endures and overcomes; hatred destroys."

She opened the door and faced him as she continued, the words tumbling from her, her voice strong.

"Some see it the other way, but I'll tell ye, if there's a truth at all, it's that there'll be no freedom with bloodshed. It's not the way."

She turned to the door and stepped out into the mild day, the newly budding dogwood tree branches waving in the breeze. She looked older, her frame a bit more bent, yet her vigor was evident.

"They can rationalize it all they want, Father, but you and I know it'll not bring a lasting peace, the peace that comes from within, where ye can sleep at night without visions of the men ye killed crawling into yer bed with ye. Ah, but yer tired now, Father. Let's save this discussion for a special chat over tea, shall we?"

Michael was startled and relieved to end the discussion here. As curious as he was to know what Reverend Mother knew and didn't know, the promise of a rest was all that interested him at the moment. He managed a smile and waved Mother Mary Xavier on her way. Indeed, the Jubilee Plot was a conversation for another day.

Chapter Forty-Eight

The Leaving

April 30,1888

Maggie pulled her blue cotton shawl about her, feeling the coolness of the evening creep in. She stepped around the dung and negotiated her way up the cow path toward home. She'd come out into the fields after dinner for a last look, filling herself with the images that she hoped would last her a lifetime. She tried to memorize them all: the stone fence that the boys and her father had built that meandered down the slope; the copse of woods that separated the fields; the low-hanging boughs of the hawthorns that fairly swept the meadow below; the dozen or so sheep that dotted the green patchwork-quilt fields beyond. It all looked miniature to her. She scooped up the Queen Anne's lace, twisted it between her fingers and watched the wispy pattern of white specks dance about.

She hurried her steps a bit as the sun began to set over the far ridge. Even though she knew her way in the dark, she also knew she might not be alone if she dallied. This was May Eve, the time when the fairies might be about, and it wouldn't do to be taken by them as she was preparing to leave for America. Her mother had taught each of the children to be aware of the Other World. "Mind ye pay attention, for there are things that can't be explained any other way. Be respectful, do no evil and ye'll fare well. Ye won't learn these lessons in school, so mind me on this."

It was true that some of the teachers made light of the Other World, putting it off to superstition and the old ways. But most of Maggie's school chums were as observant as she was, aware that something lurked beyond that needed to be honored. Especially around the full moon or a night such as this, May Eve, when there was likely to be more mischief. She'd heard her brother Michael scoff openly, but she'd also noticed his caution when he was out in the dark of night. He often took a lantern with him just to go to the barn. Julia Rulia was silent on the topic, which gave her to believe all the more.

* * *

Maggie found the da alone in the cabin. Tims, as usual, was nowhere to be seen. The rest of the family—Michael, Julia, young Jer and Lizzie—had gone with their ma to visit Cousin Julia. She'd invited them all but Maggie had declined, feeling the pressure of these last days. She wanted to stay home with Da, who declined most evening invitations.

She watched him now as he poked at the turf, sparking the fire to flame. His once thick auburn hair was now flecked with silver and becoming sparse, the crinkles around his hazel eyes more intense. He moved more slowly and deliberately, minding his step wherever he walked.

She knew she'd miss him desperately. For all that angered her about him—his silences, his dogmatic pronouncements, his roaring discourses about the politics of the day, his blind obsession with the land—all this took a backseat to the heart of the man that tugged at her own heart. He had a way of getting you to forgive him that infuriated her. A sheepish, little-boy grin would appear on his face as he looked at ye with his hazel eyes. When she was vexed with him, it was all she could do to resist. She'd seen him turn Ma as soft, even Jules. That was saying something.

She'd miss Ma so much she daren't think about it. She looked about the room, memorizing details and finding things she'd never noticed before. The stone shelf above the hearth with the oil lamp. The picture of Parnell. How long had that picture of Parnell been there, she wondered. The wooden cabinet filled with mugs and dishes on the bottom shelf, the special meat platter with the for-get-me-nots pattern sitting proudly on the top shelf. She and Julia had saved up to give it to Ma one Christmas. She moved to her window, so named when she was just a child. She gazed out and saw that Jules and Michael had pulled the trap into the yard to ready it for the upcoming trip to Queenstown.

How she would miss those two. For all Jules bothered her, she adored this sister whose gruffness was just a cover for a kindness few got to see. Jules had given her an envelope with a letter she wasn't to open 'til she was aboard the ship. She knew it would have money in it, for that was how Jules was with her—generous. And that spoke volumes, for Jules was one who counted every penny over and over and wouldn't hesitate to accuse whomever she was transacting with that they may have cheated her.

"I know ye believe ye've counted correctly, Mr. Sweeney," she'd say to the storekeeper, "but I believe if ye count again, ye'll find ye owe me an extra shilling." Mortified and wondering why people tolerated Julia, Maggie would move away. Mr. Sweeney inevitably would prove to her that he hadn't made an error. She would sigh deeply and say, "I shouldn't imagine there was an error this time. It's the other times that have alerted me to check on it."

Michael, dear Michael, was another one to miss. He'd carry on nobly, she imagined, keeping his good humor and filling in the days with some of his nonsense. She hoped he'd find a girl and some day have children of his own to whom he could pass on his good humor. He read enough for all of them and had a singing voice that sometimes brought tears to her eyes. She'd miss that too. She'd miss the music. She'd become quite polished on her mother's button accordion. Though she could also play the Jew's harp and had planned to take it with her, it was the accordion music that held her. She knew she'd always be able to dance a jig and a reel, for music filled her head even when there was none playing.

She hoped the twins would follow her to America as they had talked of. They only had two years of school to finish and surely she and Mary could send their fare in due time. They needed something to work toward and she needed to know they'd be with her in America, if things worked out that way. It gave her courage to go ahead and plan the way for them.

Tims. She hadn't seen hide nor hair of him in days. According to Michael, he'd broken up with Nora. When he did make an occasional appearance, he was silent. He was nearly twenty-five years old but looked much older; the gray color of his skin and sunken face added years. Maggie vowed to continue her prayers for him.

She moved back to the table where the da had finally settled with a teapot and two mugs. She drew up a chair and reached for the mug. The da picked up the teapot and started to pour. Save for the crackle of the newly ignited turf, silence filled the room. They sat together for a moment. Then the da spoke:

"So girl-o, you're leaving us, are ye? Off to Americay along with yer sister Mary and yer Uncle Michael? Off to find yer fortune? Is that it now?"

She treasured yet dreaded this time alone with the da.

"It's America I'm off to, Da, not Americay! I'm bound and determined to speak proper English so I'll fit in and there's no harm in starting right now."

"Well pardon me, Miss Proper English. I'm just a poor farmer without much schooling. So I'll cease now before I offend yer sensibilities again."

"Oh, Da, don't be like that. I hate this. Ye know I do." Her eyes were moist as she continued. "I hate that I'm leaving and I hate that I can't stay. I hate that there's no life here for me. And ye know that our Mary longs for someone from our family to come over. Don't be hard now or I'll burst into a bucket of tears and drown meself." She sat back in her chair, her arms folded across her chest, her matching everyday outfit, a black skirt and white blouse, looking worn.

"Well, before ye do that," Jeremiah said, his eyes crinkled into a smile, "ye might consider the expense a funeral might cost me. We've hardly enough for a dinner."

Maggie unfolded her arms and spoke with laughing exasperation. "See what I mean, Da? Ye're impossible. I still know I'm gonna miss ye like mad. And ye know what I'll miss the most, the very most?"

Jeremiah took a pull on his pipe and waited. She studied him before she spoke. His eyes were distant, his face drawn, his pose relaxed. He was looking right past her and out her window. Can he see something? she wondered. Did he know about the Others? She knew better than to ask.

"I'll miss dancing for ye, Da. I'll miss yer tapping toes as ye mark the time and yer knee slapping. I've promised meself that every time I dance, I'll think of ye. And I'll teach me children 'with a heel and a toe' like ye taught me." She smiled at him, looking directly into his eyes.

Jeremiah nodded. "Mind that ye do that, lass, mind that you do." Then he put down his pipe, stood, went around the table, bowed and extended his hands.

She stood and took his hands, and as if in one of the greatest castles in Ireland, dressed in the finest silks, accompanied by the best string quartets and courted by a king, Maggie moved with her father to the imagined music, their hands joined, their eyes meeting. Without saying it, they both knew she wouldn't be returning to Ireland, that this dance together was their last.

**

"'March will search, April will try, and May will tell whether you'll live or die,'" Julia chanted as Maggie awoke. "Isn't it grand that no one we know got sick or injured last night, it being May Eve and all? It's time to gather the herbs now, Mags. I'll be packing ye a whole set of them for yer trip. Do ye believe yer leaving tomorrow? I wish it weren't so soon. May is just the perfect month in Ireland, what with the 'All-May' butter, the healing herbs and the promise of better weather. Do ye think some girl has seen Michael's image coming to her when she looks in a well, like the myth says? Cousin Julia says he's a good catch. And I'd say so too, wouldn't ye, Mags?"

Maggie listened to Jules, knowing that she was excited and scared all at once, just as she was herself. Tonight would be the going-away party. Father Pope was to come as well as the cousins, the Cronins, the Murphys, and even Nora and her parents. They would sing the old songs, some filled with laughter and others that spoke of sorrow and pain and loss and heartache. She loved them all, knew them all by heart and would carry them with her.

And tomorrow she would be gone, bound for America! She was glad for Mary and Uncle Michael, glad to have relatives to greet her. She steeled herself when she thought of all she would miss and she wondered how it was that she was actually leaving. One day she was a child, looking out her window and waving to Gran. The next day, she was watching Tims drag through the yard, looking like a mangy dog. She understood so much more than she dared say aloud.

Jules left to gather the herbs while Maggie folded her last bits of clothing to put in the trunk. She'd saved out her light blue confirmation dress to wear to the party tonight and on the ship, the *City of Chester*. She'd heard it was a fine vessel and very seaworthy. She had no fears of it sinking. There'd been great advances in the steamships of late and she felt fortunate to have gained passage.

She pulled together her small brown valise, a sturdy cloth bag in which she would put her most prized possessions: a black wooden rosary, the envelope from Julia, the Jew's harp, a black and white school notebook of her songs and poems, a pencil, a white handkerchief that Gran had embroidered with tiny strawberries and blackberries around the border, a snail shell from the garden, an old button from the da's trousers, a hand-carved whistle from Michael and a smooth marble stone from Tims. She would save room for the food Julia was threatening to prepare. She was happy to receive the bounty, for from what she'd heard, the ship had no guarantees of good or even plentiful food.

She laid out her dress and as she turned, saw Ma watching her.

"Ye mightn't think I'd let ye go without a word or two of me own, now would ye?"

She came in and inspected the valise and the contents of the small trunk that lay open at the foot of the bed.

"Ye've accumulated a lot for a young one. And ye'll have to deal with one more thing, I'm afraid. For besides me armsful of love, I'll be asking ye to take this off me hands."

With this, Margaret went out and returned with the button accordion, which she placed on the bed next to the trunk.

Maggie gasped.

"Oh, Ma. Ye can't mean I'm to take yer accordion?"
Her face lit alternately with horror and delight. She loved the accordion, not only for its music, but because it was Ma's. She knew the story of Da giving it to her on her fortieth birthday and how treasured it was to her. Maggie had learned to play it when she sat by her mother, watching her fingers dance over the white and black buttons. It was a bond between them that she cherished, Ma often giving it over to her to play in the midst of a *seisiún*.

"Ma, I can't take yer accordion. What'll ye play? Where will the music come from when I'm gone?"

With this question, Margaret wrapped Maggie in her arms and with tears falling down her cheeks, said, "That's the question I've been asking meself since I knew ye were to go to America. Where will the music come from? And I don't know the answer, but I guarantee I'll find it."

Margaret pulled her away, held her by the shoulders, and looked her in the eye. The steel-gray eyes that looked back amazed her. This child seemed so wise. Dear Lord, how she would miss her.

"And ye'll find yer own music and ye know I'll be singing right along with ye, for ye'll have me old accordion that ye've been playing since ye were a wee one. So ye see, it's been yers all along. I was just keeping it for ye 'til now."

Chapter Forty-Nine

Imagining Jeremiah

Tuesday, May 2, 1888

Jeremiah found the dawn eerie and oddly comforting, a white-gold sky, as if in a pre-Raphaelite painting. Michael and Julia were readying the horse and trap for the trip to Queenstown. Jer and Lizzie were helping Maggie with her last-minute remembrances— a piece of turf, some knitting needles, a booklet they had made for her. The ship would sail the next morning at seven. She and Julia and Michael would stay in a small inn by the quay arranged for by Father Pope, whose kindness and connections had been a great gift to the entire congregation. He was careful in his promises, but always delivered the offered support without fanfare but rather with a certain pleasure that bespoke his sincerity. The thanks he received often came in handy. Margaret would make an extra batch of brown bread for him and Jeremiah would send up some bacon and ham when next they could afford it.

Jeremiah stayed in the cabin, watching the hustle and bustle from Maggie's window. No one ate any breakfast to speak of, though Margaret had made a good batch of porridge and even some griddlecakes. He'd see to it they were saved for later in the day.

Father Pope had stopped earlier this morning with an envelope for Maggie that he asked her to open on board ship. She tucked it into her cloth valise and smiled. "Ye'll not be forgotten by this young Irish lass, Father Pope. I've me rosary ready for the ship and ye'll be among the first for whom I'll say one."

She's a grand one for showing appreciation, Jeremiah thought.

Tims had made an appearance this morning and even helped hitch the horse to the trap, checking the wheels and straps for any weak links or frayed buckles. He looked half-way decent as he poked about in the yard. It was hard to imagine there was so much wrong with him. Hard to imagine. Jeremiah had seen him sitting with Nora at the party, hopeful that Tims was realizing what he stood to lose and what he stood to gain.

Jeremiah had imagined a lot these past days. He'd remembered his own childhood, the bright flashes of trips with the da, the days of O'Connell, and then the darkness that came with the hunger. It seemed so long ago, yet it was never far from mind.

He watched Margaret as she moved in and out, around and about, helping to ready things. He remembered her as Michael's little sister and then as the young girl with whom he fell hopelessly in love. He remembered his foray into rebellion with Michael as they rode for Ballingary, their youth making them fierce warriors for the cause. And he remembered his wedding day, the birth and the death of their first child. And the struggles that came with the land, the droughts and the rainy seasons. He felt a tug at his heart as he remembered Michael, whose presence had been like a perpetual turf fire, lending light and warmth when it was most needed.

As his children had grown, so had Ireland. Since the days of An Gorta Mor, there had emerged a new sense of dignity and presence. It had been slow but it had been steady. Gladstone, Isaac Butt, even Cardinal Cullen and especially priests like Father Lane created a landscape of dignity for the people of Ireland. Daniel O'Connell, William Smith O'Brien, Thomas Meagher, and John Devoy with whom Michael was enamored for a time. They were all heroes for Ireland. Eugene Cronin, Paddy Murphy, Dennis Carroll. All of them, living and making life better for one another. These were the Irish heroes. Even Mr. Bennett who was caught at a time in history when right and wrong were blurred by the need for money, punts and cents replacing dignity and sense.

Jeremiah considered himself blessed to live in these times, unable to imagine any other time or any other place he'd rather have been. His final purchase of the land had been his private victory. He made no fanfare of his trip to put in the paperwork.

Ashamed maybe to be saddling Michael and whoever else would inherit his forty-six acres with payments that might last another forty years. But proud. Proud to be a landowner, an Irish farmer and a Buckley. He had imagined this life since he had first heard the da tell of the English and the Protestant Ascendancy, first heard the stories of injustice that accompanied the Penal Laws. He savored the sweetness of a victory achieved by the pen, and not the pike.

It remained to be seen what Parnell could provide for Ireland. The talk wasn't good. But then, talk was just that—talk. Jeremiah had learned to sift and sort it. He roared less and listened more. Maybe he had learned it from his da.

He watched as Father Pope rode off, Margaret and the children waving after him. Then he felt his heart pound in his chest as he saw Michael, grown now to over six feet tall, lift Maggie into the trap seat. Jeremiah had said his good-bye and had no intention of going out there. But still, the pain was real. As the twins climbed up to hug Maggie, he watched Margaret step back and wrap her arms around herself, as if holding herself together, or maybe imagining that she was holding this precious daughter for one more hug.

As the trio moved forward, he watched Tims wave from atop the fence. So there was something left in Tims after all. Jeremiah felt a calm come into him to have this little ray of hope. Then he saw Maggie, almost pitched over backwards in the trap, waving with all her might, as if she could summon the breeze to carry her back for one more hug, for one more good-bye. Michael and Julia sat on either side of her, the trunk securely fastened behind. Jeremiah had heard some of the carrying-on that went into the wee hours until the party had finally disbanded. He hadn't slept well, nor had Margaret. The music rang in his head long after the fiddling stopped. He saw Maggie dancing her last dance for him and he bravely fought from bawling in front of them all. He never imagined he'd have to say good-bye to two of his daughters. As a boy, he never imagined there was a place called America that could draw his children from him. He remembered Eliza and Baby Julia. Losses that were part of the rhythm of life. He didn't understand this American loss. Michael's departure in '67 had been the first of them. Since then America had claimed handfuls from nearly every family he'd known. He'd heard of Queenstown, renamed for the Queen when she visited in '47. It was Cobh to him as a child and Michael had stubbornly refused to call it anything but Cobh.

"I'll be off in the morning to Cobh, Jer. Off to do the Lord's work. Remember me, if ye would, as I will remember ye as one of the finest men I've ever had the blessing to know."

He'd been naïve when Michael had left, certain he would see him again, certain they would once more share a pint and solve the problems of Ireland as the sky darkened with the work of the day accomplished. Then when Mary left, he'd believed again. Believed that because transportation was getting better and faster, Mary would be back and forth to Ireland, back home. Father John might bring her on one of his trips.

Now Father John was gone and Maggie was too. Gone to America. He memorized her in his heart. Then he reached into his pocket and retrieved the telegram that he had intercepted just two days ago.

Dear Mr. and Mrs. Buckley,
It is with deep sorrow, I write to inform you of the death on the evening of April 28th of Reverend Michael Riordan. His death was not unexpected though the doctor had hoped he would live into the next season. Last rites were administered by his friend, Father Patrick Sweeney, and he was attended by the doctor up to the last. At his request, his body will be returned to Ireland for burial after a funeral service is held here at Convent Station on Monday, May 10th. We share a great loss.
Yours in Christ,
Reverend Mother Mary Xavier Mehegan
    (nee Skibbereen, County Cork)
Sister of Charity of St. Elizabeth Motherhouse
Convent Station, New Jersey

Jeremiah carefully folded the paper and slipped it back into his pocket. There had been enough grief for this day. They would learn soon enough of Michael's death. Soon enough.

For now, they would continue to work the land and tend the stove. For that is what they did.

Epilogue

Maggie stood on the gangway of the *City of Chester*, the ship that had brought her to her dream. She surveyed the people below, awed at the variety of dress and color. She couldn't say why exactly, but the blueness of the sky was different from any she'd ever seen, the breeze softer on her face. The mass of people below seemed to move as one. How would she ever spot Father Michael, let alone her big sister Mary, who now called herself Molly? Would Mary's husband Paddy Healy come with her or would he be at his work on the docks? She was full of questions and felt her stomach churning. She took a deep breath, gathered her blue skirts about her, pulled the black shawl tightly around her shoulders and gripped her brown leather valise. She pulled her small steamer trunk behind her, remembering tales of "greenhorns" who'd been robbed of their possessions before they ever met up with their people. She edged her way down the gangway following the throngs of people ahead of her. She stopped to retrieve a shawl that had fallen from the shoulders of the woman in front of her. Kind eyes received it.

Irish accents of all kinds filled her ears, many difficult to understand. She saw the small family with whom she spent much time aboard the ship. They hugged relatives that had come for them. They would travel on to Buffalo together, they had told her. Maggie waited, looking at the faces and small gatherings of people breaking off from the crowd, but still she saw no one for her.

Smells of food wafted up from stands where fires burned brightly, cooking sausages perfuming the air. She was reminded of her hunger. Now off the gangway, her tiny stature didn't allow any advantage as she struggled to look over and around people to find Mary and Father Michael. She did see a priest but he was much older than Father Michael and he was alone. Surely Mary would be here. She saw several people bend and kiss the ground as they made their way off the ship. It had been a tumultuous passage, the seas unforgiving for the sick and dying, a challenge for the healthiest. She shared their sentiments of gratitude for a safe landing, for arrival here in what she hoped would be her own promised land. Except that she didn't dare let her valise and trunk down for even a minute, she'd kiss the ground she stood on as well.

She worked her way toward a fence along the edge of the crowd where she wouldn't be shoved so much. If she could be patient and wait a bit for more of the others to leave, they would find her. The hand clutching the valise began to stiffen. A parting gift from Cousin Margaret who seemed so pleased to give it to her young "namesake," the valise was the perfect size to stow her ma's accordion, which was now quite heavy.

She had felt exhilarated and had nearly skipped across the upper deck as New York City came into view, the skyscrapers taller than she had ever imagined, huge steamer ships lined up along the docks with multi-colored paper streamers running down gangways that welcomed people. But her excitement began to diminish the longer she waited and was replaced with a fear that she might never find them. Her stomach knotted and her shoulders tightened, her hands balling into fists as she clutched her bag and pulled her trunk along. She thought of Father John, her American cousin who had founded Our Lady of the Rosary Mission for young girls like herself in need of guidance and succor upon arrival. She remembered finding the letter that told of his death; her tears felt endless. As more fears crept in, she shook her head to clear it. Surely Mary and Father Michael would find her. Didn't thousands come to this grand country and reunite with their loved ones? She needn't worry. Despite the reassuring thoughts, her heart was pounding and she began to perspire.

She straightened herself and told herself a new story. Was she not a child of great love and fortune? Hadn't her own father released her to this new adventure, glad she could be company for Mary and find hope for her own life? Hadn't Father Pope back in

Ahadallane reminded her to keep the faith despite odds against it? And couldn't she feel her ma's arms wrapped about her as she held her one final time and told her, "God Bless and God speed"?

Soon the crowd began to thin. She moved from her spot against the fence toward the gate, careful not to stray too far from the ship which had been her home these last eight days. She watched hordes of men, women and children file out the gate once the uniformed inspectors checked their belongings and their documents. Maggie followed, suddenly realizing that neither Mary nor Father Michael were probably allowed within the secured area. As she walked she felt a new confidence and prayed with all her might that her new life might find her worthy.

It was the 10th of May, 1888, her first sea voyage. In a little more than a month, Maggie Buckley would be seventeen years old.

* * *

"There ye are," a familiar voice rang out. "I've been looking everywhere for ye." Maggie knew that voice, but had not heard it in over three years. She spun round to see Mary, her older sister who was exactly as tall as she, whom she'd hardly have recognized, for she was such a lady now. Her brown hair was cut short and framed her face. Her beige wool shawl was patterned and soft. A gush of water fell from Maggie's eyes as she dropped her valise, put down her trunk and reached out for Mary. The two girls wrapped themselves in each other's arms, sobs interrupted with gales of laughter. They'd never felt this close at home. But they were not home anymore. This was America.

"Paddy couldn't get away from the docks but ye'll see him tonight." Mary exploded with chatter as she picked up the brown valise and indicated that Maggie should follow. "We've a surprise that's sure to please you. Let's go this way now. You'll have to clear a few more checkout points." The two sisters chattered, Maggie pulling her trunk and Mary holding the valise as they made their way through the lines, the questions, the checkpoints, and out into the streets of New York City.

Maggie's head spun round as she looked up at the skyscrapers, and around her at people with faces different than any she'd ever seen, heard languages she didn't understand and saw foods cooking she'd never imagined. The store windows were another matter, but her sister took her arm and pulled her through the streets. She breathed in, and followed Mary's lead. Maggie was finally in America.

* * *

Soon enough, Maggie would learn of Father Michael's death, of Mary's pregnancy with her first child, and within a fortnight she would meet John Donegan, a man from Kenagh, Ireland, older than she by five years, whose handsome face had deep hazel eyes that seemed to look right through her. And before long, she would marry him, live with his sister Annie and her husband Hugh Galena at 235 West Thirty-Seventh Street. Her first child, Hugh Michael, would be born on November 19, 1890, and be baptized at the Church of the Holy Innocents at 128 West Thirty-Seventh Street.

In less than two years their second child, Jerome, would be born in July in a small upstate town called West Bloomfield, south of Rochester where they had traveled, escaping the crowded streets, poor sanitation and fetid air that filled the bustling metropolis.

John would begin farming, a trade he'd learned as a child in County Longford where his family moved from farm to farm finding work. His small town of Kenagh held fond memories, with its stone church and handsome Memorial Clock-Tower erected by the tenants of the town in honor of their landlord, Honorable Laurence Harman King-Harman.

He and Maggie were fortunate in their experience with landlords who used their power, for the most part, for the good of the people.

Over the next twenty years, as their family would grow from two to four boys and ultimately to twelve children, Maggie and John moved to the nearby town of Lima, a place that would become as much a home to them as Ahadallane and Kenagh had been to their parents.

Fifteen grandchildren from Maggie and John's union survive today, all with memories and stories of survival and love. One of them wrote this book.

* * *

But that is all to come, and not yet known to the young girl with golden-red hair shuffling through the New York city streets on an early May day in 1888, her heart thumping as she follows her sister, her blue eyes wide to the future, her heart tied to the past.

References

Asbury, Herbert. (1927) *The Gangs of New York*. Alfred A. Knopf. New York.

Bartoletti, Susan Campbell. (2001) *Black Potatoes*. Houghton Mifflin Company. Boston.

Black, Jeremy. (1996) *A History of the British Isles*. Palgrave McMillan. New York.

Brown, George W. (1942) *Building the Canadian Nation, Vol. II*. J.M. Dent and Sons, Canada

Campbell, Christy. (2002) *Fenian Fire*. Harper Collins Publishers. London.

Comerford, R.V. (2003) *Ireland*. Hodder Arnold. London

Connell, K.H. (1996) *Irish Peasant Society*. Irish Academic Press. Dublin.

Cullen, L.M. (1968) *Life in Ireland*. B.T. Batsford Ltd. London.

Danaher, Kevin. (1972) *The Year in Ireland*. Mercier Press. Cork.

Dooley, Terence. (2007) *The Big Houses and Landed Estates of Ireland: A Research Guide*. Four Courts Press, Ltd. Dublin.

Foster, R.F. (1988). *Modern Ireland*. Penguin Group. London.

Golway, Terry. (2000) *For the Cause of Liberty*. Touchstone. New York.

Golway, Terry. (1998) *Irish Rebel*. St. Martin's Press. New York.

Healy, Elizabeth (2001) *In Search of Ireland's Holy Wells*. Wolfhound Press. Dublin

Hooper, Glenn, & Litvack, Leon. (2000) *Ireland in the Nineteenth Century*. Four Courts Press. Dublin.

Hoppen, K. Theodore. (1989) *Ireland Since 1800: Conflict and Conformity.* Longman House. London.

Jackson, T.A. (1947). *Ireland Her Own.* Cobbett Press. London.

Jenkins, Roy. (1997) *Gladstone.* Random House. New York.

Johnson, Paul. (1980) *Ireland.* Academy Chicago Publishers. Illinois.

Kee, Robert. (1972) *The Green Flag.* Vol. I. Penguin Group. London.

Kee, Robert. (1972) *The Green Flag.* Vol. II. Penguin Group. London.

Larkin, Emmet. (1987) *The Consolidation of the Roman Catholic Church in Ireland,* 1860-1870. Gill and Macmillan Ltd. Dublin.

Laxton, Edward. (1996) *The Famine Ships.* Henry Holt and Company, Inc. New York.

McEniry, Sr. Blanche Marie. *Woman of Decision.* Imprimatur: Thomas A. Boland, Bishop of Paterson, New Jersey.

Miller, Kerby. (1985) *Emigrants and Exiles.* Oxford University Press. New York.

Moody, T.W., & Martin, F.X. (2001) *The Course of Irish History.* Robert Rhinehart Publishers, Maryland.

Morris, Charles R. (1997) *American Catholic.* Vintage Books, New York.

Murphy, James H. (2003) *Ireland: A Social, Cultural and Literary History,* 1791-1891. Four Courts Press. Dublin.

Nie, Michael. (2004) *The Eternal Paddy.* University of Wisconsin Press, Wisconsin.

O'Connell, Anne. (2001) *Take Care of the Immigrant Girls: The Migration Process of Late Nineteenth Century Irish Women.* Eire-Ireland, Irish American Cultural Institute. Winter 2001-1002.

O'Laughlin, Michael C. (1999). *The Families of County Cork, Ireland.* Irish Genealogical Foundation. Missouri.

Tanner, Marcus. (2001) *Ireland's Holy Wars.* Yale University Press. New Haven.

Walker, Mabel Gregory. (1969) *The Fenian Movement.* Ralph Myles Publisher, Inc. Colorado Springs

Woodham-Smith, Cecil. (1962) *The Great Hunger.* Old Town Books. New York